MAKE
ME
EVEN

MAKE ME EVEN

A COMING OF AGE NOVEL

JERROLD FINE

OPEN ROAD ROAD
INTEGRATED MEDIA
NEW YORK

Copyright © 2018 by Jerrold Fine

ISBN: 978-1-5040-8060-6

This edition published in 2022 by Open Road Integrated Media, Inc.
180 Maiden Lane
New York, NY 10038
www.openroadmedia.com

To Sally,
Truly One of a Kind

MAKE
ME
EVEN

I've never really told anyone my story. Probably no one would believe me, anyway. I'm a little embarrassed with the success thing—all the good fortune makes me feel uncomfortable. When I look back at the unlikely chain of events that got me here, I can understand why someone might think I'm exaggerating, that I'm really full of it. But it's all true.

R. S.

GROWING UP IN THE "CITY OF SEVEN HILLS"

FRIDAY NIGHTS. MY FATHER DID HIS BEST TO HAVE DINNER alone with me once a week. Usually, it was a Friday dinner at his club near the hospital. He felt comfortable there, at his usual table surrounded by men who knew him well and who would only nod greetings and then leave him to his solitary thoughts. Ever since I was a little boy, I could sense how others felt about him. I knew that he was well respected as a doctor who made a difference in his patients' lives. He loved being a doctor, and I was a very proud son. His other true love was his family, and that consisted of only one living person—me. My mother died when I was a young boy, a tragedy my dad and I shared but rarely talked about. It was an open wound that refused to heal.

Those dinners were important to both of us. Sometimes they were lighthearted, full of funny anecdotes about things that happened to us. Sometimes we just recalled good memories. And sometimes, like this evening, he was sullen or serious, making him feel surprisingly distant to me. The highlight reel of tonight's dinner was delivered to me in a soft monotone accompanied by forced eye contact. Tonight Dad would be all business: How was his son going to reach his full potential? I silently thought, *what the hell is that?*

My junior year in high school was approaching, and the doctor had decided it was time for his son to get serious about his future. There would be no sidetracking him. I could often control our evenings together with a quirky vignette, an interesting current event, or, if all else failed, I would lean forward and in my most sincere tone ask about one of his most challenging recent cases. In fact, no matter the topic, if you got his interest, if you could redirect him to medicine, philosophy, controversial people of note, or even baseball, his responses would be totally engaging. His wide-ranging mind, coupled with his myriad interests, was a wonder to observe. And, when he wanted to, Dad could really tell a good story—he could spin a yarn like Will Rogers. Unfortunately for me, tonight he was focused as a laser beam.

"Dad, I'm only sixteen. I'm not sure about anything, but I'll be fine."

"Rogers, you only have one chance in life. You must be aware of that. I want you to be happy, but I also want you to have self-respect. They go hand in hand. To achieve this you must try harder. Most everything comes too easily for you. In school you excel in subjects you care about while only putting out minimal effort. And if you don't care, or if you manufacture an excuse like you 'don't respect your teacher' or 'who needs Latin anyway,' your grades suffer. I want you to promise me you'll really try hard this year. That you'll really stretch yourself. Will you do that?"

It was decision time. I knew if I placed my hands on his, gave him a sincere look, and committed to delivering excellence, he'd buy in. But I don't like lying, especially to him. After looking around for a waiter to interrupt this conversation and failing to find one, I leaned back, desperately calculating my alternatives. Unfortunately I couldn't think of a good one. I guessed it was time to accept the inevitable, to cut the bullshit and get serious. In truth this kind of reality has never been my strong suit. I would prefer to concentrate on what interests me and fluff off the rest.

What followed was a deep breath, a firm handshake, and, yes, a commitment to follow through and put forth the effort to excel. As the honorable doctor would say, "It's time for me to alter my priorities." Less poker, more studying. Reduced social life, more reading and research. And I even agreed to help out at his office on Saturdays. Yikes, I caved in! As I saw it that evening, my life was about to change forever.

I was too stunned to sulk on our drive home, and I also knew it would represent the kind of immaturity the doctor detested. Of course, Dad was right. Everything he was doing was guided by a desire to help his son improve himself. My self-confidence was so overwhelming that I was sure I could get top grades, slam the College Boards, and be accepted at a college that would make him proud. As sure as I was of that, I'll admit that I wasn't so sure of my ability to strive to succeed in areas that didn't interest me. I loved studying US history—all of it from day one to the present. I pictured myself as a character living through the growth and plot twists of America's past. Math came easily to me, but even if it was difficult, I enjoyed it simply because there was always a right or wrong answer. And reading. What's better than living with and learning from a fabulously well-written book?

But to achieve the kind of class rank that would please my father required excellence beyond history, math, and English. I would rather sit in a dentist's chair than in a Latin class. Where is the challenge in memorizing vocabulary and verb tenses? What a waste of time, I thought. I could perform if I could just stay awake the full hour of class. And then there was science. Here I can't concoct a valid excuse. It's just that for some unexplainable reason, I never cared enough to put forth the required effort. So there it is. The gauntlet had been thrown down. Would I pick it up? I'd have to find the motivation to succeed from within. *Look around*, I thought. *There's no one here to help you.*

For almost as long as I can remember, I've known I was on my own. I had no choice but to grow up fast. For the first years after my mother's death, I refused to accept the reality that I would never see her again. When I sat in the kitchen, supposedly hunkered down in study mode, I longed for her voice, her warmth, and most of all, for her presence. My father was supportive, but, in truth, most of the time he was dealing with patients in his office or at the hospital. So there I would sit with my books spread out on the kitchen table, alone and waiting for my dad to return, dreaming of what it would be like to smell dinner simmering on the stove while gabbing with my mother as she prepared a meal for her family.

After the short drive home, we adjourned to Dad's study to prepare for our traditional post–Friday dinner gambleathon. It was his idea, and we had been at it for years. I liked it because it was just the two of us. I also relished the chance to prove to us both that I could compete. The event was—what else could it be?—a one-on-one poker bake-off. We each had our own gambler's identity. He chose to be "Fast Doc" and I was "the Kid." Dad took his jacket off, loosened his tie, and prepared for the game. I poured him two fingers of scotch with no ice, in a wineglass, just the way he preferred it. The chips were properly allocated and the cards shuffled.

The rules of the gambleathon were simple. Each combatant received $100 in chips—twenty-five white dollar chips, nine blue five-dollar chips, and three red ten-dollar chips. Each ante was a dollar, and the game was dealer's choice. The maximum bet was five dollars, but on the last card you could bet up to the pot. The dealer alternated after each hand. The match lasted one hour unless both sides agreed to play longer. Whoever owned the most chips at the end was the winner. No real money exchanged hands. Gloating was permitted. Poor sportsmanship was discouraged.

The doctor was partial to five-card draw, guts to open. Sometimes he would deal five-card stud, one down, four up. I preferred seven-card stud, two down, four up, and then one more down. But my favorite game was two down followed by four up, low card down wild, last card up-or-down optionable for a three- to five-dollar penalty. I believed this was an advantage for me because of my self-perceived bluffing skills. Dad thought the enhancement of wild cards wasn't professional, but I reasoned we were playing poker and not performing open-heart surgery.

As the hour moved on, I kept pulling the better cards and my winnings were piling up nicely. Dad was usually talkative during these games, full of energy and wit, and I could feel his warmth engulf me. We would laugh together and tease each other and sometimes he would reach across the table and scruff my hair or hold me by my chin and smile while looking directly at me. This night, though, he seemed remote.

"Is something wrong? Is there some news you need to share with me?" I asked.

"No. It's not that. It's just that I'm concerned about you and it's distracting me. I love you so much. You are my only link to here and now, to reality. I feel like you have entered a place I don't understand. I have always believed that hard work ends with accomplishment. You have seemingly unlimited talent, but you don't care to see where it can take you. I guess I'm worrying that you will regret this later on."

We looked intently at each other. I was acutely aware that he had never before directly criticized me or flat out told me I was disappointing him. I didn't know how to react. What I did say was that he should have confidence in me, have faith, and I'd probably surprise him. What I didn't say was how much this conversation unnerved me. Then I briskly shuffled the cards and dealt out seven-card stud, low hole wild, five-dollar penalty for an up card. But Dad's speech had thrown me off, and I lost my concentration. I made a classic mistake because I got emotional and let my arrogance best me. Rather than being patient, I overplayed a hand, bluffing that I had matching wild cards. I paid for this arrogance by taking my last card up. Dad didn't cave. The doctor bested me with a flush, two clubs up and three down, and he won the gambleathon. The night that started so promisingly for me ended on a down note. We shared a quick hug and went to bed.

The weeks and months of my junior year raced by in a blur. I grew taller, unsuccessfully chased a few skirts, played some baseball, aced the college boards, and performed well in school. I even forced myself to be engaged in chemistry. This all resulted in a reasonable amount of satisfaction and an honors grade. In truth, all of my grades went according to plan except Latin. I think I tried, but I couldn't muster the energy to catch up. I never said I was perfect. The highlights of the year (in no particular order) were Dad's robust hug and congratulations on my academic performance, a couple of gutsy plays on the baseball field, a near score with the ultrahot Beverly Cummings, and then a sexual experience that I might decide to describe later on. Also, my poker winnings kept mounting from a variety of games.

In late spring I had my first meeting with the school college counselor. Mr. Hibbett was tall, gaunt, and slightly bent over, as if he wanted to scratch an itch below his knee. He had a habit of taking his glasses off and cleaning them with his tie while looking upward as if hoping for divine intervention. In school it was generally believed that he was a good man, quite professional. The only knock on Mr. Hibbett was that he worked harder for the exceptional students than the overall student body. I was unsure about how he would view my performance. I was warned that he expected consistency and effort from the school's better students. I decided to be modest, project sincerity, and, above all else, reach out for his help.

Our conference lasted a mere fifteen minutes. The good cop praised my GPA and my standardized-test scores. He told me that certain teachers gave me ultrahigh recommendations. He knew all about my father and the expectations that I was Ivy material. Then the bad cop appeared. What about last year's "spotty" performance, and could I explain, I quote, "How could someone of your caliber fail so miserably in Latin? It was downright disrespectful. Why should top colleges take a risk on someone who can't motivate himself to care?"

While he was lecturing me, I had a strong desire to challenge him to a poker contest for his positive support, but I remained quiet. I maintained my composure, recognizing that I had just learned a new life lesson: in the real world, excuses won't help carry you to the Promised Land. I left the meeting realizing the need for another angle to achieve my goal. I didn't tell my father about this conference, rather, that evening I asked if he could help me get a summer job at Prescott & Prescott, a well-respected local stock brokerage and investment banking firm. I knew that Julian Prescott was a good friend and patient of my dad's. I figured that if I was successful at poker, I probably would enjoy and excel at the biggest gambling casino of them all. The thought of taking this step excited me. Also, serious summer employment highlighted by a strong endorsement by a man like Julian Prescott had to enhance my college applications. At least I hoped so.

As the school season cruised to the finish line, our baseball team was locked in a second-place tie with our archrival. Like most of the guys on our team, I would have run through a stone wall to help us win. On nights before games, I would even consider praying. I weighed the odds of my prayers being a significant contribution to a victory but backed off, because as a nonbeliever I worried about cosmic backlash. I loved baseball and above all else wished that I was a better player. My fielding skills were decent. I could hit for average but not for power. I was constantly analyzing my swing, which looked good in the mirror, but when I made contact, all I could produce was a crisp single or an occasional weak double. I did have a live arm and pretty good control. Coach taught me to throw a slow, big breaking curve that I used for a changeup. Putting it all together, I wasn't good enough to be a starting pitcher, but I was effective enough to relieve for an inning or two.

Dad was an avid baseball fan. When we went to games together, he always bought a scorecard and kept precise records for every at bat and play. He counted pitches, balls, and strikes and kept track of every detail imaginable. He taught me to appreciate the slow pace of the game. He equated baseball to ballet. Little details excited him. His favorite plays were the rarely executed squeeze bunt and watching the drama of a runner on first trying to go to third on a single to right field.

Dad insisted on sitting behind home plate. Pure fastball pitchers didn't impress him. "They're only hurlers," he would say. He saved his respect for a successful pitcher who never really had an explosive fastball or, better yet, one whose dominant fastball had faded with age and who, through sheer determination, had taught himself to master a new arsenal to confound hitters. "These are the pitchers you could learn from, Rogers," he would prod me. "You're smart enough to do it. You just have to devote yourself!"

I did learn quite a lot sitting with Dad at those games, watching the better pitchers work over hitters and at times make them look silly. I went home and practiced and improved, but the truth was I couldn't throw hard enough, make the ball move enough, or keep hitters off balance enough to become a starter on our team. So in the biggest game of the year, I was relegated to right field and seventh in the batting order. I didn't embarrass myself in the field. I went one for four at bat, a soft liner over third. I ran hard on every play, hustled in the field, and cheered with heartfelt feelings for my teammates. But no matter how hard I tried, I could not produce the hit or the fielding play to actually influence the outcome of the game. We lost, five to three. After the game I sat on our bench with the other stunned players, mute and dispirited. I would remember this loss for years to come.

In between the last days of classes and final exams, Dad had arranged for me to meet Julian Prescott, whose office was in the most important building in the city. His firm occupied three entire floors. He had a massive corner office with sweeping views of the Ohio River and the neighboring state of Kentucky. His secretary greeted me with ramrod posture and a kisser that made me think she was related to the farmer's wife in *American Gothic*.

"You must be Dr. Stout's son," she said.

"Yes, thank you," I managed. "I have an appointment with Mr. Prescott."

"Well, of course you do. I'll see if he's available."

Julian Prescott rose from his chair, extended his hand, and told me that it was a pleasure to meet me. He must have been hired by central casting. Medium build with hazel eyes and wavy silver hair. Discreetly suntanned, fashionable black brogues, a pin-striped dark-gray suit, and a blue polka-dot tie. And his fabulous smile. I could instantly imagine a wealthy family entrusting him with its fortune or to provide corporate services for the family company.

I was, of course, nervous meeting Mr. Prescott. Dad rarely had good words for any lawyer or businessman. He viewed them as pariahs only interested in money and power. He actually did like Julian Prescott; otherwise he would never have recommended me to his tutelage. I had prepared for this meeting by going to the library and reading whatever I could on him and his firm. I wanted to be serious, certainly not flip, and excited about a chance to learn. I would do whatever they wanted me to that summer.

We sat in leather chairs around an oval table sparsely decorated with business magazines and a few choice pieces of fine crystal. His secretary served us chilled water sans ice, placing the glasses on coasters that I noticed were emblazoned with the Williams College crest. Both Mr. Prescott and his office were so perfectly dressed that I wished I had remembered to shine my shoes that morning. Determined to follow Dad's advice, I sat tall and looked J. P. straight in the eye.

In soft tones gushing sincerity, he took charge. After a few highly complimentary words about Dad, he began, "I was quite surprised when your father called requesting this meeting. I'm sure you know he is no champion of the business world. I always assumed that his only child was destined for a career in medicine. My guess is that still would be his preference. So tell me why you are so interested in a summer internship at P&P. Really, Rogers, would this just be a summer filler, or do you have a genuine interest?"

I had decided in advance to be warm and courteous, but not to openly kiss his ass. "First of all," I said, "thank you so very much for your time and even considering my request. My father has always spoken highly of you and your firm. My dad is a man of science. He is special at what he does, and I am very proud to be his son. I, on the other hand, want to chart my own course. I love numbers and I excel at math. More than almost anything, I enjoy putting that talent to work in practical ways. It's true I don't know a lot about stocks and bonds and investing, but I am a very thirsty young man."

I quietly admired his style. Like the British aristocracy, he probably never sweat, much less perspired. We talked back and forth for a few more minutes as he was taking my measure. I wanted to tell him that I did have a talent, that I was a damn good gambler. I had promised myself absolutely not to voice that interest/skill, even though I sensed he would understand why it could become relevant to my future.

"Thank you for coming down to see me," he said. "I would like you to meet with Andrew Stevens, head of our corporate finance department."

I was secretly hoping to bag the internship with just this one meeting, but I should have known better. "Thank you, Mr. Prescott," I said. Then I couldn't resist adding, "I appreciate that you met with me because of your relationship with my father, but if you give me the chance, I promise you that you won't regret it."

He answered with a quizzical look. "We'll give you a call after you meet with Andrew."

I was escorted down a hall in which the walls were decorated with portraits of partners past and present and into a small but elegant conference room. Andrew Stevens was seated at a table, simultaneously adjusting his suspenders and spinning a pen between his fingers. As he barked orders into a phone, he motioned me to sit. I immediately felt ill at ease. He seemed distracted as he asked about my background and qualifications. I wondered why he wasn't asking the obvious follow-on questions. Just as I thought he was only a pompous jerk, he changed tack and rapidly fired question after question, wanting to know why I was being interviewed and if I was willing to work long hours doing mundane chores. He didn't seem to care about my grades or college boards, but rather homed in on my ability to take orders and deal with pressure.

He then abruptly stood, shook my hand as if the interview was over, yet turned and asked me a final question: "Do you really want to be very rich?"

Surprised, all I could say was that I would do whatever was asked of me with my best effort. Then I added, "I don't know what it's like to be rich, but I do know what it's like to win."

When I got the call from P&P that an internship was mine, I was ecstatic. I couldn't wait to tell Dad and give him a hug. He obviously was pleased, but couldn't help asking me if this was something that I truly wanted. The implication was clear—*is medicine out?* I wasn't even old enough to vote and here Dad was wondering if I was already planning my future. One thing, though, that's really great about Dad was when he realized that he'd made a mistake, he readily admitted it. He shouldn't have thrown the doctor dart, and he knew it. "Son, I'm happy for you. I really am. If this is what you want, then make the most of it. Go make us millionaires," and he smiled. If he were on my baseball team, I would have slapped him a high five. Instead I hugged him again and whispered to myself how lucky I was to have this guy as my father.

With my junior year essentially over, I prepared for summer. Dad was busy with a heart conference in Baltimore at Johns Hopkins. He looked forward to this because he had fond memories of his medical school days there. He trusted me to be on my own with his usual speech: "You're on your honor. Remember that." Even though I wanted to fling, I still found it difficult to disappoint him.

Once again I was about to live solo for an extended period of time. I was used to shopping for groceries, maintaining my corner of the house, preparing my own meals, and eating alone. But I couldn't get accustomed to a house where nothing else existed except Dad's collection of cactus plants. Our house was so quiet, I sometimes thought I lived in an annex to the city's main library or the downtown morgue. My savior was the RCA television sitting in the corner of our small living room. When Dad was away, I turned it on the moment I entered the house and left it playing until I went to bed. TV was my constant companion during meals, while studying, phoning friends, or just chilling out. I wasn't choosy. I'd watch whatever was available, whether it was sports, news, comedies, or dramas. I just needed to hear voices and see people performing on the screen.

I was anxious to begin my internship at Prescott & Prescott. I could barely sleep the week before I was due to begin. Though I certainly have lazy tendencies, I was energized by the chance to learn about financial markets. I wondered if the stock market was just a giant gambling orgy or if fundamentals and research actually mattered. I was eager to find out for myself.

I had been told to arrive at P&P at 8:00 a.m. on Monday, July 1, and to wear a business suit. I drove up Reading Road to Robert Hall to buy a couple of summer suits, because the price was right and you could get two pairs of pants for the price of one. I was careful to be ultraconservative. Then I headed downtown to Shillito's for dark dress socks and a few blue button-down shirts. I planned on borrowing Dad's ties. It felt good using my poker winnings for a purpose. The summer's heat and humidity in the Ohio Valley is brutal, and the downtown crowds only exacerbate the situation. I'm not a shopper and I've never been accused of being a sharp dresser, but I did feel that I at least would now look like I fit in at P&P. My little adventure left me limp and in need of a reward, so I cruised two blocks east to Stanley's Deli for a cold Vernor's ginger ale and a bag of pretzels.

My first day at Prescott & Prescott essentially was an orientation requirement. A pleasant woman from human resources shepherded me around the offices and introduced me to everyone I would need to know. I met a compliance officer who read me the firm's rules and ethics policies, the head librarian who lectured me that every piece of paper has a designated home, and a variety of folks in the corporate finance group, each of whom I assumed would treat me like a plebe. I was taken on an office grand tour: top floor was for executives and corporate finance; middle floor for research analysts, brokers, and traders; and bottom floor for back office, etc. I was even shown which bathroom I was supposed to use. I was assigned a desk in the middle of a large room, a phone, and a Quotron. The next day would be all business.

Andrew Stevens had claimed me as his slave for the summer. He sat in the corner office surrounded by his team. To enter the holy shrine of his inner sanctum, one first had to get by Ms. Schiller, his Prussian secretary. She was a very large woman who never smiled and whose mission was to protect Andrew Stevens's privacy at all costs. My guess was that the entire office feared her, and with real justification. I believed she disliked me from my first day. Each morning I was told what to do by one of the associates. My tasks usually involved accessing material from the library or punching out row upon row of numerical calculations. The math was quite simple—normally ratios showing margins or rates of return or three- to five- to ten-year percentage growth rates. The job wasn't difficult, but it was time-consuming and tedious and had to be done error-free.

While I was grateful for my opportunity at P&P, after a few weeks I was already finding my chores too repetitious. The associates and partners were all so involved in their work that I didn't feel I could approach them and offer to do more than just errands in the library or performing as if I were a math drone. Each day I came in cheerful and bursting with energy. I hoped someone would sense my enthusiasm and need me for a new project. Andrew Stevens was clearly a dedicated professional, incredibly busy but organized and seemingly always in control. He would nod good morning, sometimes tell me what he wanted from me that day, and on rare occasions thank me for being punctual and accurate. Never more than that.

Around twelve o'clock, I would break for lunch downstairs at the office cafeteria. For the first week or so I sat alone, ate rather quickly, and went back upstairs to my desk. Everything was to change once I started sharing lunch with Ronnie Davis. R. D., as he called himself, was a trader working under local legend Jimbo Burns. Ronnie had grown up downtown in the distressed neighborhood known by locals as Over-the-Rhine, which, since the late 1800s, had been a home away from home for German immigrants. In more recent years, the area had become rough ground, but Ronnie was a tough kid who knew how to survive, and he was a hell of an athlete. In a city where you were revered if you starred in sports—defined as basketball, football, or baseball—R. D. was that rare basketball player who could both handle the ball and shoot the lights out. The city newspapers anointed him a sure hit in high school. When local Xavier University awarded him a full ride, he excelled in college until he tore his Achilles tendon during his junior year. He never fully recovered, but never quit trying.

It was Jimbo Burns who came to the rescue. He was also a Xavier graduate and an outright basketball junkie. He hired Ronnie straight out of college and taught him about stock trading. They became an inseparable duo. Jimbo ran P&P's trading department, and R. D. made sure his wishes were carried out. Ronnie knew about loyalty, having learned the hard way in his home neighborhood, and he respected Jimbo's experience and talent. Jimbo needed someone who would protect his backside and felt sure he had chosen the right guy.

I only asked to join Ronnie's table because I was tired of eating alone. I had seen him in the cafeteria, always sitting in the same seat. It took a few lunches for a modest relationship to develop because we both were tentative with strangers. When he asked what I was doing at P&P and I told him I was an intern assigned to Andrew Stevens, he frowned.

"Oh, so you're one of those rich kids they take in here for a summer."

"Not exactly," I said, defending myself.

"Well, why else would they bring you in?"

"Hey, I live alone with my father near the hospital. You know where that is. He's a hardworking but underpaid doctor who probably spends half his time treating people for free. The firm gave me the chance, and I grabbed it."

I might have sounded too pissed off, but I didn't appreciate his tone. Ronnie nodded and then surprised me by volunteering a quick sketch of his own background and job at the firm. I nodded back, and we reached across the table and shook hands. His hand was so large and beefy and his fingers so thick and coarse that I thought I was shaking hands with a professional boxer. Apparently we were destined to become friends.

As the summer progressed lazily, I settled into a routine. Weekdays I worked in numbing boredom for whoever in corporate finance needed me to run numbers or fetch material from the library. I appreciated my opportunity but knew that I had already ceased to grow. I lunched with Ronnie at noon and we gabbed about sports, our lives out of the office, and whatever. He wasn't interested in what I was doing at P&P, but I was very interested in learning about markets. He talked in generalities, but never about what he and Jimbo were currently active in. I was like a sponge, trying to absorb more and more. Friday nights I had dinner with Dad and, if we had time, cleared the table for our gambleathon. I wouldn't miss those evenings for the world. Saturdays I played ball for a very average American Legion team put together by my high school coach. The weeks went by too quickly, but I was in good spirits most of the time.

In late July Dad suggested we head to the ballpark to watch Hoyt Wilhelm spin his magic against our beloved Cincinnati Reds. In the twilight of his professional years, and almost fifty years old when he moved over to the National League to pitch for the Atlanta Braves, he was still a winner. Dad felt we had to see him once before he retired. After all, Wilhelm had come as close as anyone to perfecting the nastiest of all pitches—the knuckleball. For this experience we definitely wanted to sit behind home plate to see the ball dance. What made the knuckleball so different was that the pitcher did not wrap his fingers around the ball, but rather bent his fingers so that the ball was held in place by a few knuckles at delivery. Another approach was to dig one's fingernails into the ball and push outward at the release point. Thrown properly, the knuckleball fluttered up to the plate and then would dive abruptly downward. Even the best professional hitters despised facing a master knuckleballer.

It was Wilhelm's first visit to Cincinnati, and the fans were abuzz with anticipation. Before the new stadium was built down by the river, Dad would wax eloquently on the special landscape of Crosley Field. The old home stadium of the Reds was small by major league standards, seating fewer than thirty thousand, thus befitting the small-market reality of our City of Seven Hills. The outfield bleachers—affectionately known as the sundeck in the daytime and moon deck in the evening—were only in right field, which negated a typical stadium's symmetry. And then there was the outfield itself. Unique to Crosley Field, as the outfield approached the distant wall, there was a grass terrace to warn a fielder that the wall was nearby. Visiting players would regularly trip on the terrace as they retreated to catch a long fly ball. Naturally, local fans relished the idiosyncrasies of Crosley, while guests probably snickered at its quirks. It wasn't surprising that Dad felt the new Riverfront ballpark lacked the special charm that Crosley had delivered to its fans.

We had good seats that day, directly behind Atlanta's catcher. Unfortunately for the Reds, Wilhelm was in good form and all business. Dad and I were amazed at the movement of his pitches. They would seemingly float up to the plate, an appetizing gift to power hitters, and then suddenly dive out of the strike zone. These pitches confounded and frustrated the Reds players. The harder they tried, the worse they did. Wilhelm did have control issues, but his walks were overshadowed by his strikeouts. He lasted seven innings before tiring. A relief pitcher closed out the game for Atlanta's four-to-one victory. We enjoyed ourselves immensely even though our guys lost. When the game was over, Dad and I looked at each other, sharing the same thought: *Rogers has got to learn how to throw that pitch!*

James "Jimbo" Burns was Prescott & Prescott's primary trading contact with the city's financial institutions. Over the years he had developed close personal relationships with fellow traders at the local banks, insurance companies, and investment advisers. His talent was his effervescent personality, coupled with an ability to make people like and trust him. When Jimbo decided that a potential client should be courted, he doggedly set out in pursuit with service, entertainment, and personal attention that swamped the competition. The New York and Chicago trading communities couldn't afford to focus on the regional markets. Jimbo worked hard to develop his franchise for P&P and was rewarded by Julian Prescott himself for his success. A few years after being named head of stock execution, Jimbo convinced the firm's management to allocate a modest slice of capital for his group to trade on a discretionary basis. In other words, he carved out a pot of chips to play with for his enjoyment and profit.

Jimbo was one of those people whose individual features didn't seem to originate from the same Irish assembly line. He was blessed with bright, almost kinetic blue eyes, thick, curly brown hair turning prematurely gray, and a round pink face that was capable of flashing a Hollywood smile. Unfortunately, this mug sat atop a squat body that didn't provide for any normal form, such as a waist. Jimbo was overflowing with energy, and when he talked directly to you, his confidence and excitable personality were electric. He probably could have sold used cars as easily as stocks.

In early August Ronnie invited me down to the trading department to show me around. I had no preconceived idea of what to expect. As I walked down the staircase, I heard the action before I saw it. *Wow*, I thought, *I'm entering a gambling wonderland!* Coats off, sleeves rolled up, chatter all around. I tried to put on my unflappable face as I searched out R. D. Ronnie introduced me to Jimbo, who swung his chair around and blurted out, "So you're Dr. Charlie Stout's son."

For the record, no one called Dad Charlie and for certain never, ever Chuck or Chuckie. I'll admit I was intimidated and a bit speechless that day, but thankfully R. D. bailed me out. We all made small talk for a while, Ronnie ushered me around on the ten-cent tour, and I left to go back upstairs. To my surprise Ronnie called after the market closed. Apparently that very afternoon Jimbo had executed the firm's biggest trade of the year. A celebration was in order, and I was invited. I couldn't possibly have known what was coming in the next few hours.

I was to meet Jimbo's crew in the bar downstairs around six o'clock. This gave J. B. time to attend a partners' meeting and Ronnie time for his gym workout. I arrived a bit late, so as not to seem too anxious to join the group. It was obvious that the group was being treated as regulars and that Jimbo was in charge. They sat at a large circular table in a corner that I later learned was christened Burnsville. I was introduced to Jimbo's team, a closely knit group he chose and trained who were absolutely loyal to him. They were six youngish guys who were more alike than not. All were local public school athletes who made an attractive first impression, were effusively personable, and who certainly liked to party.

Ronnie had prepped me about what to expect and to try not to be too self-conscious or else I would clearly be viewed as an outsider. When Jimbo made the introductions, I shook hands with everyone, congratulated them on *the trade*, and then was handed a Bud poured from an enormous pitcher. I felt more relaxed after Jimbo told his team that I was his new good-luck charm and that after meeting me for only a few minutes, he had successfully orchestrated the firm's most profitable trade of the year. Being the wise guy I am, I have been called various names, but surely never one denoting good luck.

As the drinking continued, the stories got more exaggerated. For someone thought by others to be excessively overconfident, in truth, I am awkward with people I don't know well. I faced another issue because I was a lousy drinker, and even with my minor-league drinking friends I was usually the first to either throw up or pass out. Therefore I sipped my beer, smiled, but added very little to the celebration.

I was encouraged when Jimbo slammed the table with an open hand, rose, and led the caravan across the street to a local steak joint. Most of the group checked out to have dinner at home, so our party shrank down to Jimbo, Ronnie, me, and a convertible bond trader named Bobbie V. We were treated to a warm welcome by the owner, who threw his arm around J. B. and seated us at a prime table. Jimbo addressed the waiter by name as if he was a longtime friend and ordered steaks, home fries, and (believe it or not) spinach for the table. When he moved into the red wine, I knew for sure to nurse my glass and hope no one would notice.

I was famished and already feeling the booze when the food was served. Stuffing myself with a heavy meal probably saved me from gross embarrassment. Even while drinking more and more red wine, Jimbo calmed down and was engaged with the table. I saw that Ronnie let J. B. take the lead and only chimed in when he was asked a question or was needed to embellish a vignette. Ronnie sat composed, projecting a quiet dignity. For some reason I felt that this group wasn't really his element, and that he was here specifically to support Jimbo and to protect me. I didn't know Ronnie that well yet, but I was drawn to him and wanted to get to know him better.

Throughout dinner Bobbie V was quiet, smiling as if he were a happy piece of furniture fortunate to be included. After Jimbo settled the bill and Bobbie V headed home, our host somehow got his second—or was it his third?—wind. The next stage of the evening was about to begin.

Ronnie was driving, I was riding shotgun, and J. B. was lounging in the back seat instructing us to head south. I had never even crossed the Newport Bridge before. My father was emphatic about the dangers of Newport, Kentucky—"A wide-open city where you can get into a lot of trouble. I don't want you even near there!" I knew I would have to keep this escapade a secret.

We crossed the muddy Ohio, headed straight past two traffic lights, took a sharp right, and parked the car in a lot next to a place called Rory's Tavern. I had no idea where we were and surely didn't want to drink any more, but I was at my host's mercy. I looked over at Ronnie and he gave me the "don't worry" sign. We left our coats and ties locked in the trunk and entered the tavern. The room was quiet and dark with a few scattered tables by the left wall near the window and a long wooden bar on the right. The room smelled like athletic socks after a summer's double-header. The place was mostly empty, with only a handful of men seated at the bar. They were bent over their drinks and seemed aged and beaten down by their lives. No one looked up at us. I wondered why we were celebrating in this grungy downtrodden bar in Kentucky. It didn't fit with my image of James Burns.

Then we walked down a long hall, lighted only by ceiling bulbs. Jimbo knocked firmly on the gray metal door at the end of the hall. I heard a sliding sound, and an opening appeared. Two dark, bloodshot eyes stared out at us, the door was unlatched, and we stepped into a small, noisy gambling casino. Ronnie looked over at me and laughed as J. B. led us inside.

Newport's reputation as a sin city was well-known in the valley. While there were no billboards advertising bourbon, sex, and blackjack, you didn't need a road map to find your way to their doorstep. I would not have had the courage to go to a place like Rory's on my own. I harbored a deep fear of the unknown and of most situations in which I felt the environment was beyond my control. But as I looked around the room, I thought that, yes, Rory's might seem unsavory, but it sure was high on local color. When I heard the chatter and sounds of poker chips clinking on the tables, I couldn't help but secretly pinch myself. Clearly the time had arrived for me to grasp this life adventure and see where it would take me.

Jimbo roared into the room and quickly sat in as the sixth man at a poker table. Ronnie motioned for me to join him at a neighboring blackjack site. I only had about fifteen dollars in my back pocket, so I decided instead to walk the room for a while and ponder my next move. Also I didn't want Ronnie to know that I was taught by Dad to believe that blackjack was essentially only a game of luck, that it overemphasized the quality of cards you are dealt and didn't require the skill of reading your opponent and making him read you. I didn't want him to think I was a snob. I spent the next hour or so studying the poker players. I wanted to know who was timid and who was overly aggressive, who played the percentages and who played pure chance, and if there were players whose outward emotions told a tale of truth. Before I checked in with J. B., I signaled Ronnie with a thumbs-up or -down and was happy for him when he smiled and held up a victory sign.

A house employee dealt at each table, skimming the pot as a fee for the privilege of playing at Rory's. My general observation was that the dealers were pros but the players ranged from very good to half-drunk beginner. I positioned myself discreetly at Jimbo's table to watch the trading maestro at work. He seemed to be treading water, his winnings offset by stubbornly staying too long in games where he had a losing hand. I thought maybe he was drinking too much and permitting frustration to creep into his decision making. Suddenly he rose from the table for a toilet break. Then he shocked me, handing me some of his chips and telling me to hold his seat and play for him. I shot him a baffled look, but he just slapped me on the back and walked off. I looked over at Ronnie, but he was concentrating on his own cards.

While I tried to look calm as I replaced J. B. at the table, my internal motor was operating at warp speed. I folded my hands tightly to prevent them from shaking, but I couldn't stop my right leg from thumping under the table. I can't seem to control that annoying habit when I'm anxious. Even so, when the dealer gave me the "are you ready" look, I nodded and then did a quick scan around the table. To be honest, I wasn't ready. I needed to play a few hands to compose myself and mentally prepare to play the game I so loved. I kept waiting for the dealer or another player to question my age, but no one seemed to mind that a teenager was sitting at the table. After about ten minutes, I was down a bit, but I felt I was starting to find my rhythm. At the same time, I was coping with the difficulty of playing poker when my fear of failure exceeded my hope of winning. To reverse that phenomenon, I needed a couple of positive hands in the bank.

Fortunately I did avoid big losses. I remembered that nothing is worse in poker than having the second-best hand when you are compelled to stay in to the end—only to be bested. And then, as if directed by some otherworldly spirit, the tide turned and I really started to win. As my chips piled up, I leaned back in my chair, looked around, and became aware that Jimbo was standing behind me, nodding approval and encouraging me to stay on and play for him.

Shortly thereafter the big hand of the evening was dealt. The house game was an unusual version of stud—six cards, two down and the next four up—so I had to recalibrate the definition of a winning hand from the Ohio version of seven-card stud poker. As the hand was being played, the betting was surprisingly vigorous, with four of the six combatants remaining in the game. My concentration was on full alert as I studied each bet carefully and made sure I was counting and remembering every card. The dynamics of the game changed after the sixth card was dealt. The other players folded when the big winner of the table paired his king and significantly raised his bet. I had counted two kings already discarded, so I figured the best Mr. Big had was a full house with his two down cards matching either his ten or his six. I tried to control my breathing and facial expression. I knew I had a winning hand with two down queens matching one queen showing and a pair of threes.

Holding back my excitement, I reminded myself queens over threes bests tens over kings. Before I could bring myself to push my remaining chips into the middle of the table, I squeezed my hands into tight fists in isometric desperation. I was absolutely scared shitless. I called Mr. Big's bet and turned over my lovely ladies. The first sound I heard was a loud "Holy Christ!" from my Irishman banker standing behind me.

I didn't realize I had sweated through my shirt until I stood up from the table. Jimbo grinned as I dumped my winnings into his greedy hands. Ronnie joined us, content with his twenty-one profits. As soon as we were outside, J. B. spun me around and questioned, "How did you know he didn't have three kings?"

"I was counting the cards," I replied.

"You were counting kings or all the cards in the deck?"

"When I play for money, I count them all," I said.

"So when the guy in the striped shirt was still in the hand with two eights showing, you knew he didn't have two more underneath?"

"Yes, because the tall guy in the Levi's coat sitting across from me drew one of the remaining eights on the fourth card before he folded."

Jimbo narrowed his eyes and studied me with such intensity that I felt my face flush red, then, looking at Ronnie, he said with a loud laugh, "Hey, R. D., this kid's okay!"

My heart was still pounding as we headed back toward the Newport Bridge. I thought that the evening's celebration was over, but I was wrong. Ronnie bypassed the bridge entrance, eased the car onto a quiet, dark road parallel to the river, and then made a sharp left and parked midblock in front of a grouping of midcentury two-story houses. When I asked who lived here, Jimbo grinned, said, "My friend Lilly," and motioned Ronnie and me to follow. Lilly herself answered the doorbell with a flourish, decked out in a powder-blue jumpsuit crowned by a huge head of brightly dyed red hair. She invited us into an ornate sitting room that suffered from an overdose of sweet-smelling perfume. She seemed to recognize Jimbo but not Ronnie. I might have been sheltered and naive, but I had a strong sense that Lilly was not just J. B.'s friend or distant relative. Everything became clear when she called for the girls in the adjacent room. Jimbo surveyed the five nymphs then chose a bubbly cheerleader type and headed upstairs with a "see you guys in a half hour" wink.

I needed some fresh air and time to think. Standing outside alone, my brain and desire in conflict, I had trouble controlling the rush of thoughts I was experiencing. My first thought was of my father and his moral compass. Would he be disappointed in me or would he understand and agree that Newport was just part of my growing up? We actually never had the "father-son-into-manhood" talk, but I knew him so well that his first question would be about the well-being of the girl. I tried to focus on why she would be doing this. Was she being forced into some kind of sexual slavery, or was this just business as usual to her? If I went upstairs, would she have contempt for me? As I vacillated and questioned myself, weighting the heavy issues of morality, desire, and the important if-not-now-then-when, one of the girls came out, took my hand, and led me back inside.

Once the decision was conveniently made for me, my brain turned off and my pecker took over. She said her name was Shani even though a silver *R* dangled from her necklace. She was short and well built with thick brown hair worn long in a ponytail. Her angular face was offset by a seductive, natural smile. I didn't dare look into her eyes. She was wearing a short pink robe and white plush slippers. Shani walked me over to the stairs, and as we climbed I looked up and gasped. She turned and grinned, knowing full well that I was salivating over her perfectly constructed bare

ass. "There's more to come," she whispered, guiding me down the hallway. "Lilly says your friends are treating you to a celebration. Happy
whatever," she said in a soft voice as we entered the room that I was sure
I would never forget.

I had not given much thought to how, where, or with whom I would
lose my virginity, but I increasingly knew I wanted it to happen and soon.
I fantasized about sex with everyone from Dad's nurses to virtually every
decent-looking girl in school. I would peek down blouses, admire tight
sweaters, and discreetly position myself to view the crossing of legs
housed in short skirts. My dreams ranged from perverse to erotic but
oddly never involved love. I had been in like with a few girls in recent
years but never in love.

Shani closed the door and the blinds and turned to face me. I couldn't
help from mumbling aloud, "So this is really going to happen, isn't it?"
The room was small with low ceilings, the only lighting being a tall lamp
in the corner crowned with an absurd red tasseled shade. The bed was
covered by a faded navy-blue sheet that I hoped wouldn't transmit some
awful rash. In the far right corner was a toilet and pedestal sink. Shani
was in charge, and I followed her directions like an obedient puppy. I
undressed and dropped my clothes on a worn sofa thinking that this was
the first time I'd stood naked in front of a girl. Rather than being aroused
by that fact, I literally could feel my penis shrink. I was too embarrassed
to stand tall, but I did resist the natural impulse to cover up.

I studied the room as best I could because I wanted to remember every
detail. When Shani motioned me to join her at the sink, my analytical
side took over and I thought, *why?* Like a trained nurse, she took "my
guy"—her term—in her hand and slowly washed me in warm water. That
did it! I'd messed around with my share of girls but never had one of
them been willing to even touch "my guy." I went to full husky immediately.

"Let me guess," she said. "This is your first time." When I didn't answer, she simply smiled and walked me over to the bed and removed her
robe. She stood there, hands on her hips with no hesitation, not at all
self-conscious but rather posing as a confident, sexy young woman.

I sat on the edge of the bed ready to inhale and devour her, but she was
in control, knowing that I would likely explode in about thirty seconds

flat if given the chance. Jimbo had paid double to make sure his young friend was going to fly first-class, so Shani used her considerable skills to slow me down. She sat on my lap and pulled my head to her breasts. She smelled of sweetness and tasted even better. "Take your time," she purred. She laid me on my back and sucked on me until I couldn't wait, but she then abruptly stopped and flicked her index finger at the top of my dick with such force that it stopped me cold. "Easy, make it last," she said while her small hands worked their magic. As I lay on my back breathing heavily and looking up at her, she climbed on top and put my hands on her rear and started to move and do things with muscles that I didn't know existed. The rest was a blur, except no matter how long it lasted, I wanted more.

After we finished I wasn't sure my legs could carry me back over to the sink. Shani was still naked when she washed and dried me carefully as if "my guy" was a newborn. I wanted to hug her and say that after tonight I would never be the same. For some reason I wanted to thank her and say something warm and personal, but I couldn't find the words. We both dressed in silence, and I said a weak goodbye and went downstairs. Ronnie was leaning on the car when I came outside.

"Did you finish already?" I asked.

"I didn't play," he said.

"Why not? Is something wrong—too much to drink, are you sick?"

"It's just not something I do unless I'm with a girl I really care for."

"You're serious?"

"Yes. If I'm going to confess on Sunday, I don't want to explain that it was with a hooker."

"I didn't know you were so religious."

"Well, now you do."

Jimbo's raucous approach ended what was becoming a tricky conversation. He almost skipped up to the car, wearing a broad smile, laughing while jabbing his index finger in my chest and asking me if we were even now.

P&P's star trader was snoring loudly before we crossed the river. As Ronnie drove, I closed my eyes, pretending to be asleep, but I was still alert. I was thinking about Shani. Why would someone not much older than me sell her body and dignity for a few dollars an hour to whoever walked through Lilly's front door? How could her situation already be that hopeless? I shuddered when I wondered what Shani must have been thinking about me as I was with her, panting like an animal.

It was late when I got home, so I exercised my very well-practiced stealth entrance. I washed off the scents of the evening and stood dripping water in front of the mirror. I looked the same—not older, not wiser, but I knew for certain that something was different. I was too tired to analyze it, but I couldn't help and look down at the exhausted "my guy." He was shrunken and red and in need of rest.

Ronnie called late the next morning. I was organizing some numbers for A. S. while at the same time still in a state of reverie. My head hurt, my balls tingled, but the memory of the queens over threes and the experience with Shani was still crystal clear.

"How're you feeling, big boy?" he chuckled.

"Great and lousy at the same time."

"Sorry, but I can't do lunch today."

"No problem. I don't have an appetite, anyway."

"So, you've told me you may stink at basketball, but you're the man in baseball. I need you to prove it on Sunday afternoon. Are you free?"

"Sorry, I'm lunching with the president."

"Seriously, I need you to fill in for a game at Xavier at two o'clock. The guys from my old basketball team have been challenged by the young bucks. We have to round up a few more players. You okay for some outfield and a little pitching?"

Even though I knew I'd be nervous playing with R. D. and his pals, I couldn't let him down, and I was available, so I gave in.

"Sure, where and when?"

"Meet me in the parking lot by the field house at one forty-five. Get a good night's sleep. I'll be counting on you."

"Will it help if I cross myself before I hit?"

"Don't be a wiseass on that subject," he reminded me.

I realized I'd probably gone too far with the religious humor, so I thanked him for thinking of me and hung up.

Xavier was only fifteen minutes from my house, and once I exited Victory Parkway, the school's historic stone buildings emerged atop a small hill. Amid old trees and well-kept greens sat the impressive Bellarmine Chapel, the centerpiece of the campus. I arrived early and rested against my car, waiting for Ronnie. The sun was high at midday and the humidity was already suffocating. Having grown up here, I was used to the summer's wet heat, and while it affected my endurance, it did keep me loose and limber for sports. It all felt quiet and peaceful—a few students wandering about, a priest attired formally in a cassock sitting on a bench reading, the sounds of competition on a soccer field. Standing there I tried to suppress my one experience with a nun or priest. I couldn't prevent the memory from flashing into my mind . . .

Dad had shipped me off to a sleepaway camp in Indiana. I was ten years old, and this would be the first time I was alone in a foreign land. All went well until I contracted pleurisy in the second week. The camp was in a rural area with only a nurse on the premises, so I was sent to the closest hospital, which happened to be affiliated with the Catholic Church. The on-duty doctor and nurses were caring and sympathetic for the sick little boy far from home. I quickly improved and was anxious to leave to swim and play with my new friends. On the evening before I was to be discharged, an elderly nun entered my room with a large pan of water and a sponge. She insisted on "cleaning me up." It was all so foreign to ten-year-old me—naked in front of a nun, whose wrinkly old hands sponged me everywhere. There I was, alone in a room with a crucifix and an old woman in a habit. Now, thinking back, I grinned to myself, comparing the wash job from Shani to that of the nun nurse.

Ronnie's arrival put an end to my daydreaming. When he hopped out of the car and introduced me to his friends, I felt like a puny teenager. I was still a high school kid, tall but skinny. They were all in their midtwenties, former Division I athletes. A couple of them had already acquired beer bellies, but the others maintained impressive physiques. R. D. was wearing his old X shorts and a tight gray T-shirt that didn't attempt to hide his hours in the gym. He was revved up and clearly in a good mood.

"Hey, you ready to go?" he asked me.

"I'll do my best," I answered meekly. "Your friends are huge!"

"Settle down, Jolly man, we're just here to have fun." But then he added, "Still, I'm here to win."

The field was beautiful, with manicured grass offsetting a groomed dirt infield. The outfield fences seemed to be about a mile away. Painted benches in Xavier's blue and gray were on either side of home plate. A new scoreboard in left field was, thankfully, turned off for today. As we warmed up on the sidelines, the younger versions of the crew showed up, and the razzing and friendly insults began. I surprised myself by feeling loose and upbeat. I would hide in right field, maybe get a scratch single, and hopefully not have to pitch to these monsters. My baseball ego was fragile, and I didn't need the humiliation of watching someone smash my fastball over the center-field fence.

Ronnie claimed home field for his team on the slim basis that they had been the ones challenged. Amid the back-and-forth banter, it was agreed that the game would be seven innings, and balls and strikes would be called by the catchers on the honor system. Just observing the way these guys ran, caught, and threw a ball made it immediately clear to me that they were real athletes. Some were surely out of shape, but it didn't matter, for they moved with effortless grace. All the teasing, shouting, clapping, and cussing made it easier for an underage outsider to feel comfortable. R. D. was in the middle of it all, boisterous and in his element. Watching him with his college friends, relaxed and smiling, made me wonder why he wanted to spend time with me.

Jogging out to right field, I put the psychological session with myself to rest. All I had to do was look at the beef on the opposing team to know that I'd better be prepared for some action. My fielding skills were soon put to a test when the moose batting third hit a towering fly ball in my direction. After initially misjudging the clout, I ended up making an easy catch look harder than it should have been. Back on the sideline, my teammates gave me a lot of crap. I also was teased for my performance at the plate; the good news was no strikeouts, the bad news was I could only produce a couple of lazy grounders to second base.

In the fifth inning we broke a three-three tie with two additional runs, including a solid double in the gap by Ronnie. He slapped hands with his teammates and, with an intensity that I had never seen at P&P, stared me in the eyes and said, "Let's see what you got, Jolly R. We need two innings from you." Then he slammed the ball in my mitt. Almost instantly I became a nervous wreck. My body emitted the classic fear signals—dry mouth and nausea. Between Little League, Babe Ruth, high school, and American Legion, I'd been pitching for seven years, so I knew the signs. I also knew my athletic limitations.

As I warmed up, searching for positives, I silently begged the baseball gods for new arrows in my quiver. I knew I couldn't throw hard enough to blow a fastball past them. They were too big and strong and athletic. My only hope, a quickly conceived strategy, would be to tease them with my fastball and make them hit my curve. If I threw some junk at them, slow breaking balls that tantalized their egos, maybe they would overswing or chase pitches off the plate.

The big question was did I have the nerve to introduce my newest pitch, the one I had been diligently practicing in my backyard. John Jones was a neighborhood pal who lived down the street. He was the third baseman on my AL team whose skills were the opposite of mine—he was slow and clumsy in the field, but he could hit with real power. Jonesy volunteered to catch the dreaded knuckleball before practice and sometimes in our backyard. He was a good guy who kept encouraging me to work on my mechanics. I initially tried the classic method of gripping the ball with my knuckles, but my hand wasn't big or strong enough to control the pitch or make it do anything but float up to the plate like a fat baked potato. When I switched to the fingertip release, I made real progress. I grew my fingernails longer and toughened the ends of my fingers by striking them against our brick fireplace. By digging my fingernails into the ball, I now had the ability to push the ball out of my hand at the same time I was throwing it to the hitter. I wasn't sure why, but this action reduced the ball's rotation and for some reason allowed mysterious air currents to create turbulence and make the ball drop. I felt I was gaining some control over the pitch, but I knew I was still a long way from perfection. In fact, sometimes it would break sharply into the dirt and often it didn't even break at all. So I rarely threw the pitch in an AL game, simply because I had no idea where it was going.

My strategy was working well in the sixth inning until two hitters crushed doubles, producing a run. We maintained our one-run lead on a nice running catch in center field and a nifty curve that I slipped by the remaining hitter. After we wasted two hits that didn't create a safety run, a few of our guys came over to where I was hiding and slapped me on the back and butt for encouragement.

Ronnie saved his sermon until I was already on the mound. "You'll be fine. You're not pulling for a royal flush. Remember, you've got a team behind you!" Then he grinned and winked at me.

The last three outs were a glorious adventure. The first came when the hitter anxiously reached for a fastball that was clearly way off the plate and popped it to the second baseman. The second hitter demolished a slow curve foul, and when I threw him a better one, he did it again. I didn't dare serve up a third and throwing my whatever fastball for a strike was out of the question, so I steeled myself and delivered my first knuckleball of the game. It danced magically up to the plate, and as the batter swung, the ball broke sharply downward, causing him to whiff for strike three.

"What the hell was that?" yelled my shortstop, Mr. Ronald Davis. I was on such a high that I came right back at the next hitter with nothing but knuckleballs. After a called strike and two wild pitches in the dirt, the batter hit an off-balance grounder back to me. When I flipped it to first, the game was over. At that moment I felt taller, faster, and happier than anyone on the field. I didn't give a damn about school, P&P, or even sex. I did wish that Dad had been here to witness his son's knuckleball adventure. I couldn't wait to get home to tell him all about it.

Just as my What a Summer! was winding down, Julian's assistant called and asked me to stop by one afternoon. I knew my father would be pleased by this gracious gesture. I was hoping that the corporate finance department conveyed satisfaction with my efforts and that I could use J. P. as a reference for college. As I came through the door, his secretary waved me toward his kingdom with her usual disdain. Mr. Prescott looked positively regal in a blue double-breasted blazer highlighted by an embroidered gold crest from one of his many clubs. He apologized in advance, telling me that he was expecting a call, so, if I didn't mind, he would move straight ahead.

"Did you enjoy the internship and P&P?" "Did you find the summer suitably productive?" (Whatever that meant.) "You'll be pleased to know that I've heard you did a fine job."

And then he smoothly and elegantly changed course to remind me on how much I would disappoint my father if I did not choose a career in medicine.

"You have the talent, Rogers, and I'm sure it's in the Stout gene pool." He concluded the sermon with some irrelevant small talk and waited for me to respond.

For sure I was surprised by the real meaning of our little chat. However, playing poker had taught me the advantage of keeping my emotions in check and to reveal only a placid exterior. After all, I wanted his recommendation, so I hid my disappointment and thanked him profusely for helping me. I then assured him that my focus was on my senior year in high school and that I had no thoughts yet on a future career. I wanted to think of something light or funny to say in conclusion, but I couldn't, so I thanked him again and wished him a good end to his summer.

On the way back to my desk, I decided that I had just learned another life lesson: just because a man has a fancy name or title, fancy clothes and manners, and was apparently well respected, doesn't mean that he is less cunning and out for himself than the average snake. This insight made me think about what a jerk I was to prejudge my immediate boss, Andrew Stevens. He wasn't the elitist golden boy who, I'd assumed, had inherited his lofty position at P&P. Yes, he was short on warmth and made only feeble attempts at normal social graces. But he was focused and believed hard work led to performance, which in turn would lead him to the gates of financial heaven. The more I had observed Mr. Stevens over the summer, the more I came to realize that he was a classic American success story. Born to a middle-class family in Chicago, he'd earned a scholarship to Northwestern. After graduating cum laude, he worked for two years at McKinsey and then moved on to an Ivy League business school. He married his college girlfriend, a schoolteacher from Iowa, and returned to Chicago to work at Northern Trust. With a little bit of good fortune, an officer at the bank introduced him to Julian Prescott, who then convinced him to move by offering him a senior position at P&P. It didn't take Andrew too long to vault over those with seniority to become partner in charge of corporate finance. He accomplished all this while not seeming to care if he was liked, but he did demand to be respected. I filed all this history in my memory bank along with the thought that maybe I should ask his advice in the future.

I would be back in school in a few days, so I popped downstairs to thank Ronnie and Jimbo for accepting me into their clan for the summer. A serious Jimbo asked of my future plans, college, etc., and when I said I had no idea, he lobbied for staying local and attending Xavier. He questioned why I would want to go anywhere else. Before I could respond, Ronnie pulled me aside and, placing both his paws heavily on my shoulders, said he expected me to stay in touch. I told him of course I would and then added how much I valued his friendship and that I hoped it would continue in the future. As I walked back upstairs, the emotions of the moment surprisingly caught up with me. R. D. was already a college graduate with a few years of work experience. We were raised in altogether different circumstances and were from very different family backgrounds. Yet in a few short weeks, I felt as close to him as if I had known him for years. Growing up so alone, having to share my father with his patients, I had learned to protect myself. I buried my emotions, hid my deepest private thoughts, and deflected most personal questions with sarcasm or witticisms. The thing about Ronnie was that I trusted him, I respected his quiet strength of character, and I believed he honestly wished me well. Back at my desk, I learned that Mr. Stevens was away on vacation, so I wrote him a note thanking him for putting up with me, saying I hoped I didn't embarrass myself, and that I very much enjoyed my experience at P&P.

I wanted my senior year to be a success. I probably wasn't more mature after that summer, but I was at least more experienced. From hanging out with Ronnie and his friends, to functioning like a grunt at P&P, to the very real pressures at Rory's, to the time I spent upstairs at Lilly's, I felt different. I knew I needed to continue to grow and not approach school with my usual attitude of "let's get it over with." I vowed to be determined and reach out and stretch myself.

That was the plan, but as with all my plans that require effort, I could always find an avenue of excuses. The real problem was that I had become incredibly seduced by the stock market. I started reading the *Wall Street Journal* and any business magazine I could find at the school library. I would wonder what was happening on the trading floor at ol' P&P. I would bet with myself on how the market would react to news I read or heard on the radio. The fact that my batting average in this game stunk did not deter me. I started following the price action of local companies and would then wonder why they went up or down. I would daydream about this in class, which of course did not please my teachers. I found myself having to apologize to them far too often. Fortunately, alone in my room with no distractions, I managed to concentrate and produce good work. My grades were fine, but my teachers' subjective evaluations were bound to be questionable. I'd always been honest when evaluating myself, yet when I now looked in the mirror, I wasn't too critical. I didn't see the lazy, cocky Rogers. What I thought I saw was a hungry Rogers who needed to focus if he expected to fulfill his goals.

One October day I was surprised when a package arrived from P&P. In it was a short note from Andrew Stevens, a deck of cards, and brochures about the University of Pennsylvania and a place called the Wharton School of Business. The note said that he regretted not being in the office to tell me I did a creditable job, and that he wished me well. Interestingly, he didn't mention the reason for including the cards. (What did he know? Did he really possess a sense of humor?) In any case, he had taken the liberty of requesting and then sending on the package of Penn and Wharton material, because he thought they presented an opportunity I should explore. That night I sat on my bed and read about the university and its famed business school. As I read on, my heart rate jumped.

When I called Stevens's secretary the next morning, hoping for a few minutes of her boss's day, she acted as if she had forgotten my name. After I ran through the gauntlet of questions she used to shield him from unwanted claims on his time, I finally secured a meeting on the following Friday afternoon after the market's close. I needed to talk openly to someone I respected about my college options. I couldn't think of anyone better than Andrew Stevens.

As I entered his office on the appointed day, he loosened his tie, eased into his favorite chair, and lazily crossed his legs. "I'm honored that our resident poker guru wants to meet," he began sarcastically. He seemed to enjoy the fact that I appeared tentative. He smiled then added, "That was meant to be a compliment. I like gambling, too. My game is bridge." Before I could tell him why I'd wanted to meet, he asked, "Why do you think you excel at poker?" I wasn't sure where this was heading, if he was joking or serious, when he added, "Really, I'm interested."

"Were you ever much of a poker player, sir?" I asked, in response.

"I played a bit in college," he answered. "Never for big stakes. I always felt you had a better chance to win with bridge if you were the superior player. Less luck involved."

I told him that I'd never played bridge, that I grew up playing poker for fun with my dad and then it just kept going from there.

Mr. Stevens came back with, "The word in the trading room is that you're really a young stud with balls of steel."

I was surprised to hear him talk this way, but it did create a relaxed atmosphere, so I continued.

"I love poker and love playing for money."

"Why is that?"

"Because it changes poker from a game with no consequences to a contest with very real consequences. You have to play the game right, and you have to manage your money. Maybe it's something like the stock market—your guys downstairs call it risk management. Fancy phrase, right?"

"Wait a minute. With stocks you can tilt the odds in your favor with research. You can't research a poker hand," he continued.

"Sure you can, by counting the cards and studying the betting patterns of the other players. Also, you don't have to rely on research by some analyst you don't even know. You get to rely on yourself. I like that better."

"You actually think your poker skills can outperform a seasoned money manager in stocks or bonds?" he questioned.

"All I meant to say was I would want to be the captain of my own money. I'd rather make my own mistakes."

"You're a real pistol, Rogers." A. S. laughed out loud. "So get back to answering my question—why are you good at poker?"

"When I look in the mirror, I know I'm only a teenager, but I've been playing poker against my dad since I was a little guy. He's a student of the game, and as with everything else, he was tough on me. I started playing for money a few years ago, and I've been developing my own style ever since."

I knew I was being tested, but I wasn't afraid now because we were playing the game on my home field. So I decided to continue with my theory on how best to hone one's poker skills.

"I don't want to sound like an egomaniac, but I believe to excel at poker you need a variety of skills, and you'd better be good at all of them. The easy part is learning the game like it's a science project. Study the odds. Know what the chances are for a flush, full house, etc., based on the cards still outstanding. You must be able to count all the cards and remember where they are on the table. Learn the science of the game and know what cards have been played, when they were played, and by whom. Really, this part isn't rocket science, it's just fundamental knowledge plus concentration.

"Next comes the artistic part. You must know who you are playing against. What are their tendencies, such as do they ever bluff, do they only bet a strong hand, do they keep feeding the pot hanging around hoping for great cards, and do they play differently if they're up or down a lot, etc. Then there is an intangible that I believe is necessary to be a consistent winner. This might sound like voodoo, but some people have a talent for reading what others are thinking. I wouldn't be surprised if you were thinking right now this skill is required when negotiating a corporate finance deal. You would be trying to read the buyer or seller on the other side of the table to determine if you should raise or lower a bid or offer. Am I warm? Anyway, if you can get in there—I mean, surmise or sense what an opponent is thinking or feeling—it sure will be helpful. Should I go on, sir?"

"Please do. I'm enjoying myself," A. S. said.

"Next comes the hardest part. You absolutely must know yourself! I've got plenty of room for improvement here, I'm sorry to say. I want to win so badly that I sometimes let my emotions overtake my brain. I've learned that you need patience; you need to know when to strike and when to quit. I'll share with you my little secret. I decide before the game begins just how much I'm willing to lose. I keep that money in a separate pocket and promise myself I won't go beyond that limit. I've been in games where I'm out in only fifteen or twenty minutes. Believe me, I'm upset, but I stand up and leave. I may be mad all the way home, but by the time I'm in bed, I'm okay. Not good, but okay, because I know I maintained my discipline. On the other hand, if I'm ahead, I return my own money to its home pocket and then press on with my winnings to see how lovely the evening can become. Because I can be a real pig, I do need to learn when enough is enough. I'm not very good at that yet."

I thought for a second about continuing on but decided I had said enough. I also decided I had nothing to gain by arguing his point on bridge versus poker.

Now A. S. interrupted the flow. "So you are telling me that you're a maestro because you possess all of these skills. You still haven't told me why you seem to win a lot."

I was ready for him and answered, "Studying the game, counting cards, and all that was never an issue for me. What I had to learn was to manage myself. To stay focused. To be in control under pressure. To know the difference between my brain and my stomach and when to trust either or both of them."

"And luck?"

"I have to believe it evens out for most everyone."

"How about the voodoo crap?"

"I don't know how to say this without sounding like an ass but, for whatever are the reasons, there are times I just feel it, I just know I'm right. I've tried to figure out why, but I don't have an answer. Maybe it's just informed intuition. My father thinks it's because I try to read people and predict their actions as a self-defense mechanism. I don't know about that—I'm not a psychiatrist. What I do know is that I observe and listen to people and situations very carefully and have learned to trust my judgment since I was very young. It's part of growing up so alone." Then I added, "Pardon me for that personal note. Oh, and by the way, I don't always win. I often lose. I'm just trying to win more and more often than I lose."

Andrew Stevens was staring at me intently. Had I been babbling far too long? Did I sound like a know-it-all jerk? Just as I concluded that I had been trying too hard to impress, he leaned back and began to massage his chin.

"This feeling thing," he said. "I guess it's difficult to explain, but I get what you're saying. It's not something I experience on a regular basis, but I can remember a few times when an inspired idea came to me seemingly from outer space. Maybe we should research a way to bottle it. We'd make millions!" he concluded with a loud laugh. He took a sip of water and continued, "Let's move on. Before we talk about schools and your future and all that, tell me if the internship was worthwhile. I've never had a high schooler in my department for the summer."

"Yes, sir, it was," I answered. "I hope I did a satisfactory job."

"You were fine. I assume it became tedious, but we could not, for instance, permit an intern to attend confidential meetings, even if you just sat there and listened. I hope you understand that you would need to be an employee here first. I wasn't being hard-ass—it's just that those are rules."

"Sir, I'm not complaining. Believe me, I appreciated the learning experience this summer."

"All right, one last question. Julian tells me he thinks you want to follow in your father's footsteps. He also believes that is your father's wish. Your dad has a very special reputation. I don't think I'm overstating it when I say that in this city, he is viewed as a respected man of science. I know that is Julian's view. Being a doctor is a noble profession. If medicine is your long-term goal, just say so. My feelings won't be hurt, and don't worry, I'll still give you my personal thoughts."

I took a deep breath and answered, "Thanks, Mr. Stevens. I guess you can tell that there's a lot of pressure on me. I think it's unfair. I'm only seventeen. I've never even had a job other than helping out at my father's office. I've never been east to New York, or even west of Chicago. My only adult influence is my dad. He's the best. He really is the best, and I do know where he wants to direct me. That's not hard to figure out. But I want to explore other interests and I really do want to hear your ideas." And then I said something that at that very moment I really believed—"I feel that you will understand my situation and where I am coming from. I feel I can trust you."

A. S.'s secretary interrupted by announcing his wife on his private line wanting to know when he would be home. He flashed me the "hold on" sign and reached for the phone. "Hello, babe, what's up? Right. Tell her I'll be home for dinner and promise her a good story tonight." He smiled. "The little one owns me." *Good for you, Coach*, I thought. *It's nice to see you are a warm, regular guy with your family.* He then leaned forward in his chair and said, "How can I help?"

It's amazing how a single incident, confrontation, encounter, or even gesture can influence me to alter an opinion of someone. I guess I was just that immature and unworldly. When Andrew Stevens first interviewed me back in May, I'd thought he was haughty and egotistical. By the end of August, after observing his work habits, the firm but polite way he treated people, his analytical, even temperament, and especially now listening to him talk to his wife about his daughter, even if just for a minute, I thought he was the kind of person I should listen to. I knew I needed to talk openly to someone besides my father to help me make decisions on my future, and A. S. was going to be that guy. So I feebly inquired, "How do I decide where to apply to college? There are so many opportunities out there, so many choices, so much to consider. I also have to think of my father and how wonderful he has been to me. I don't want to hurt his feelings. I know I'm young, but I know where I want to get to, I just don't know how to get there."

He calmly looked at me and with a trace of benevolence said, "Slow down, Rogers. Deep breaths help. We'll talk this out and weigh all the pros and cons. In the business world, we call it T accounting: assets or positives on one side, liabilities or negatives on the other. Remember that in all probability there is no one perfect college for you, and if there were, there is no guarantee that you'll be accepted. Also, we live in a big country, with all sorts of wonderful schools for you to investigate. Let me ask you some questions and we'll take it one step at a time."

I sat on the edge of my chair, totally engaged, alert, waiting to respond to a series of questions that were about to be fired at me. Andrew Stevens rubbed his hands together, as if preparing for a physical task in cold weather, and pointed his index finger at my chest to indicate an emphatic "LET'S GO!" What followed was a Q&A version of a Ping-Pong match. A. S. would serve up questions in rapid succession, as if fired from a Gatling gun, and I would react by answering them as best I could. The clouds of uncertainty began to lift as his questions helped me to narrow my focus down to a handful of schools.

It soon became apparent that I preferred to be in a major eastern city environment at a school big enough so that I could be private, yet small enough that I wouldn't feel like it was too impersonal. When A. S. inquired about my interest in sports, social life, and fraternities, I confided that I hadn't thought about those questions. I told him of my love for baseball but that I probably wouldn't be good enough to play at the college level. I added that I wasn't a huge sports fan, but I was passionate about the Reds and did actively follow the National League. It felt awkward telling him that I was a loner and liked it that way and that I couldn't imagine joining anything like a fraternity. I emphasized that all I needed to be content was a couple of friends and a girl here and there. I wanted A. S. to believe that I was truly open-minded, that I was ready to spread my wings and tackle the challenge of competing at one of the great eastern colleges.

The questions kept coming. Did weather matter? Was reputation and what other people thought of a school important to me? And then came the big one—leaving home and my dad. I didn't respond initially. I had to gather myself to answer the question I'd dreaded most of all. I looked my questioner squarely in the eye and said, "It's not going to be easy. I think you know that there are just the two of us. We're very close, and I would be lying if I acted like I wouldn't really miss him. He preaches Johns Hopkins to me day and night. It's in Baltimore, and that's plenty far away."

A. S. took another sip of water, and then his voice took on a new timbre. Looking me directly in the eyes, he said, "A short while ago you said you knew where you wanted to get to. I think those were your exact words. What did you mean by that?"

"I don't want to feel walled in. Whenever I feel trapped, I get anxious. I want to be free and independent. I can't put it any better than that."

"You've just raised the threshold quite a bit."

"I know I'll have to earn it. My dad did and so did you."

Andrew Stevens sat back in his chair with his hands behind his head. As he stared off into space, he lowered his voice and said that he felt a little like he was looking into a mirror in Chicago twenty-five years ago.

For the next ten to fifteen minutes, we talked about education, its importance and what might be good for me. I told him how much I loved American history and that I was a voracious reader. I admitted my inability to
motivate myself in courses that didn't interest me or if I didn't respect the
teacher. When I told him my math scores, he actually let out a "Wow."
His advice was clear and straightforward: undergraduate college is a special opportunity, a once-in-a-lifetime chance to taste every dish in the
cafeteria. Don't limit yourself. Try everything and don't back off if a particular subject is difficult. Also, embrace cultural knowledge. If you are
fortunate enough to attend an elite school in a great city, reach out to
learn the basics of art, music, and theater. Lastly, he brought up the subject of what he called "practical success."

"Rogers, if you want to be free and independent, you have to be realistic. That kind of freedom requires financial accomplishment. I doubt you
can achieve that playing poker in Kentucky."

He gave me the opening I was hoping for, and that's when I asked him
about Penn and the Wharton School. He confirmed my assumption that
he went there for graduate school. He said he didn't particularly enjoy
those two years, but he credited the school with preparing him for "the
real world." It was "academically rigorous, hugely competitive, and beloved by recruiters." He'd sent me the brochures because he thought it
was a unique school, the only A-plus business program offered as an undergraduate major within an Ivy League or similar university. We talked
awhile about the school, Ben Franklin, and the pros and cons of Philadelphia, then his telephone rang. We both knew who was calling. He promised his wife he'd be home in thirty minutes. As I stood to thank him
profusely for his time and advice, he rose, shook my hand, and assured
me, "It will all work out fine, you'll see." It felt good to be treated so well
by him. I borrowed a phone from a secretary's desk and called Dad to
confirm dinner at seven. It was time for us to have *the conversation*.

It was a short ride from downtown to Dad's office near the hospital. As
usual he wasn't ready to leave, so I spent my time flirting with the nurses.
I had been forewarned by the good doctor to never, ever get involved with

the women in white, but there were a few who were absolutely too tantalizing. I made a valiant effort to remain discreet, but I was a pushover for long legs in white stockings. And how about the bending over for files or test kits on the bottom shelves? I was sure they sensed my lustful interest, but fortunately they knew better than to respond, and I was resigned to just smiles and small talk.

Dad finally approached down the hall and all frivolity ceased. We said our goodbyes and I chauffeured us to Claudia's, his favorite neighborhood bistro. He looked more tired than usual, excused himself, closed his eyes, and dozed briefly on the way. Whenever he did this, I worried about his health. It was a classic role reversal, a young son feeling responsible for an older parent. Dad, of course, would be angry if he knew of my fears. Even though he never exercised, enjoyed food and scotch, and worked long, grueling hours, he portrayed himself as being indestructible. In the washroom at Claudia's, he splashed his face with cold water, straightened his tie, buttoned his sports coat, clapped his hands together, and declared he was ready.

Dad ordered his Dewar's with no ice and a ginger ale for me. We both craved the house specialty—steak au poivre with pommes frites. We split a homemade roll—no butter allowed—and settled in for our special meal together.

We hadn't seen much of each other that week, so we spent some time catching up. Dad was researching a paper on congestive heart failure for a medical journal and apologized for being preoccupied. I had no excuse other than schoolwork and a very pathetic social life.

I was determined to take the initiative tonight, to be respectful but also to be bold when our agenda progressed toward college choices. My goal was to introduce the idea of Penn-Wharton as one of a package of eastern schools to which I'd like to apply. We could discuss other alternatives, pros and cons, his thoughts and mine, but the subject I had to avoid was Johns Hopkins (i.e., medical career) pitted against a potential career that primarily involved material gain (i.e., business). If I let him take the moral high ground, I knew his passion would overshadow any argument I could offer. His views were deeply held, and even though I couldn't disagree with him about the merits of serving society as a doctor, practicing medicine wasn't how I thought I would want to spend my life.

I've often wondered why aberrant thoughts race through my brain, normally at inappropriate times or places. Teachers often accused me of daydreaming when, in fact, I was working hard to solve a problem or thinking through a complicated premise. So here I was tonight, dining with my dad, my favorite person, and preparing to make important decisions about my future, when dissecting frogs in ninth-grade biology class overtook my consciousness. I had hated the procedure: a dead frog submerged in nasty formaldehyde, splayed and pinned on a wooden board as if being drawn and quartered for a vile medieval punishment, and then sliced open, all to teach an awkward fourteen-year-old—what?

So I was thinking over dinner, if I found this simple lab test so utterly repugnant, how could I possibly want to attend medical school and deal with real physical issues affecting real human beings? Dad's questioning pierced my concentration and demanded my attention.

"Tell me more about your summer at Prescott & Prescott. I enjoy hearing the details, especially what it's like doing research in a Wall Street environment."

"Dad, it was wonderful. Thank you."

"Did you learn a lot about the stock market?"

"No, I was interning in corporate finance, where I spent most of my time calculating series after series of numbers."

"That sounds tedious to me."

"It was, but I did enjoy being in that atmosphere. I think there may be an opportunity for me to intern next year as an assistant to a security analyst. That would really be interesting, even though I would still primarily be pushing numbers around."

And then Dad changed the course of the conversation. "I understand you had a heart-to-heart with Julian Prescott."

"Am I allowed to be honest?" I asked.

"I expect you to be," he answered, as I knew he would.

"All I did was listen while he talked. He told me I would disappoint you if I didn't become, to use his words, 'a man of science.' Dad, I'm sorry, but I can't relate to him. I think he's a bag of hot air. But I did have a good discussion with the man I worked for who was the head of the department. I liked him a lot."

It was time to tell him, I could feel it. I had rehearsed my speech in the car and thought it was pretty good. Yet when it came to actually telling him something that I knew he wouldn't approve of, I balked. I sat wondering what it would be like to have brothers and sisters to share private thoughts with, who could help me perform in moments like this. At times I'll admit my envy of friends with large families, but my relationship with my father was so deep, so full of pure friendship and love, that maybe it would have been diluted if I had to share him. Thinking of all this and looking into his eyes, the emotion of the moment made me alter my confident tone.

"Dad, last year you asked me to work harder and play less. We both know I'm not perfect, but I did try, and I think it's fair to say that I mostly succeeded. I'm being told by Mr. Hibbett, the school's counselor, that I have a good chance of being accepted at colleges most everywhere. I have to ask you two important questions: Can we afford this and do you mind if I go east for four long years?"

Dr. Charles Stout leaned forward, gently took my hands, massaged them slowly with his thumbs, and then firmly kissed my forehead. I swear I'll never forget it. He leaned in even closer to me, so close we almost touched, and said, "I'm so proud to be your father. I only wish your mother were here to witness your growth and development. If you want to head off to Philadelphia, do it. I'm sure you'll impress them and excel at whatever you choose to do. We're not rich, but I've saved money for this, and we'll manage."

I don't like crying—I think it is a soppy sign of weakness—but I couldn't hold back a few tears. For all these years, whenever I thought Dad was going to disappoint or let me down, he surprised me instead with his intelligence and generosity of spirit. And how did he know of Penn-Wharton in good ol' Philly? Better not ask, I decided. And yes, I also wished she were here. I suppressed that thought as best I could. It was my usual defense when faced with the reality of her not being present to share life's experiences.

I spent the next few weekends preparing college applications. Then on one boring Saturday morning, Ronnie Davis called to invite me to play in a friendly poker game at an old teammate's house. It was a nice gesture, but while I always enjoyed being with him and we did need to get current on each other, I was so focused on my college stuff that at first I waffled. When he added dinner at Grammer's, just the two of us, I caved in.

Ronnie had grown up near the restaurant, which was also only a few short blocks from Findlay's food market, another Over-the-Rhine institution. I can still dig deep into my memory bank and vaguely recall my mother leading little me through the market stalls, carefully choosing fresh produce and breads, commenting on the wonderful smells. My father also knew the OTR well and frequently regaled me with stories of this special neighborhood before it deteriorated into a deep inner-city decline. He highlighted the architecture, the Art Academy and Music Hall of the 1800s, the food and the glorious local beer. He reminisced that before he graduated to scotch, he was a Moerlein man. I remember him explaining to me the significance of a "cultural pocket" and how the Over-the-Rhine was such a distinctly ethnic German example of this social phenomenon. I, of course, had no idea of what he was talking about. I asked a few questions to show I was interested, which proved to be a big mistake, for then he proceeded to lecture me on the sociological history of the city. This was typical Dad, sharing with me his thoughts on history, social issues, and current events or suggesting I read articles or books well before I could understand their meaning or significance. Only later did I appreciate how much this influence was a positive force in my life. Dad also possessed a marvelous sense of timing. Just when I was about to shout "enough," he would change topics and relate a colorful story.

One of my favorites was the time he saw Otto the Prussian Giant wrestle Strangler Lewis in a cavernous old hall down at OTR. He was particularly gleeful as he described Lewis's famed viselike headlock, where he pressed on an opponent's neck with such force that the normal blood flow was restricted and the man either passed out or conceded the match. When the Giant could no longer manage the pain of Strangler's grip, his face florid red as he was about to be put to sleep, he slammed his fist into the mat, signifying defeat. I never tired of these wonderful stories and would beg Dad for more and more details. I was thinking about my father's description and tall tales of the OTR as I drove up Walnut Street to Grammer's Restaurant.

Grammer's looked and smelled right: the old wood bar and tiled floors, the leaded-glass windows and scenic rural murals as a backdrop for the scents and sounds of people enjoying beer, brats, spaetzle, and schnitzel. This place felt so authentic, I imagined I was in Bavaria and should have been wearing lederhosen and some silly mountaineer's hat. Then Ronnie sauntered in, waved to the bartender, and offered me his usual hand slap. He was in a good mood, obviously comfortable and relaxed, seemingly unburdened by the market's current machinations. I felt myself moving into a similar state, which for me was all too unusual. He ordered a pitcher of Hofbräu München lager and pretzels with a side of hot mustard for the table. Just then I noticed a picture of him in his high school basketball uniform on the wall behind the bar.

"Who is that tall skinny kid on the wall with a wiseass smirk on his face?" I asked.

Ronnie laughed. "He's the kid who just scored twenty-five points versus Purcell in the city championships!"

"Oh, I thought he was playing against the Sisters on the Mount."

"You know, you really are a sacrilegious son of a bitch."

"Hey, thanks for the compliment."

Once again I marveled at how R. D. had become such a good friend in such a short time, especially considering our different upbringings and personalities. I felt at ease with him, that I could tell him most anything. I hoped he felt somewhat the same.

After Ronnie briefed me on P&P, Jimbo, and a few personal vignettes, I told him about my decision to try for Penn-Wharton. He knew of the school's reputation, of course, and said he thought it would be good for me to reach high. But then his quizzical expression unnerved me when I told him that I had been following the stock market and the progress of certain companies.

"Rogers, listen carefully to me. It's not a game down there. You're not going to learn how to beat the market from some book. It's not like a math problem, where there is a definite answer. And you can talk to all the Andrew Stevenses you want, but guess what—all they will do is confuse you, because they will give you ultra-sophisticated mumbo jumbo. But they don't have any crystal balls. And here's an issue that you in particular are really going to find hard to swallow. All the economists and finance professors at all the hotshot schools don't have a clue, either. That's right: Dr. Brilliant from Harvard or Stanford or Wharton can lecture a good game, but you would probably be appalled if you saw their own investment performance. Are you ready for the ugly truth? To win in the stock market is freaking difficult. You can study all you want, you can work crazy long hours, you can have a superhigh IQ, you can have connections up the wazoo, and still you'll probably fail and feel like a sap."

I interrupted, "Well, someone wins. Why and how do they do it?"

"I don't know," he answered.

"Come on. Tell me what you think," I pressed on.

"Once you've been working at it for a while and you get to the point where you understand the fundamentals of the business, then all you are is in the starter's block. From there it's anyone's guess. There are some people who have the gift. You just can't predict who they are, why it works for them, and when the gift will turn on them and bite them in the ass. I'm not even sure if they know why they have it. Did they earn it or do they just have some special sense of when and how to act? I'll tell you one thing, though—you can't buy it in a store."

"Does Jimbo have the gift?"

"Sometimes," Ronnie answered. I thought about asking more questions but decided I would probe some other time.

I looked at Ronnie, and all I could do was shake my head and say, "Wow. Thanks for the eye-opener. Maybe I should become a zookeeper." He studied his watch and motioned we should finish our sauerbraten because the game was to start soon.

R. D.'s friend Dylan lived on the ground floor of a two family house in Mt. Adams. It was a small, early-twentieth-century wood-frame home absent architectural taste but blessed with a dynamite view of downtown Cincinnati and the Ohio River. It was more than halfway up one of the highest hills in the city, so the vistas were uninterrupted. I recognized some of the group and was introduced to the others. It was to be a friendly game, modest betting with no sandbagging. I was uncomfortable from the start. It didn't feel like the summer baseball game, when we were all on the same team. Tonight we were competing against each other, and the scorecard read *money*. I decided to play ultra-conservatively, make a little or lose a little, have a few laughs and go home early. These guys weren't my friends; I was just a guest in their game. They were seven or eight years older than me and had been working for a couple of years. I hadn't even gone to college yet and was only there because of Ronnie. I hoped they didn't resent me too much.

I was handling the situation reasonably well until Dylan began singling me out with "kiddo" and "high school hotshot" references.

I looked over at Ronnie for support, but he only shrugged and whispered, "Forget it." The karma was all wrong, and I knew it. Actually, it was worse than I thought, because I started to lose. At first I was bleeding from antes with hands I had to fold after only one or two cards, but then I really hemorrhaged from two second-best hands I felt had to be played out to the finish line. I feigned a toilet break and stood outside for a while, took a few deep breaths, and admired the view before returning to the game.

The very next hand was one I would not forget. My losses were approaching my self-imposed limit as Dylan dealt a fateful round of seven-card stud. As the hand played out, there were just three of us left. While Dylan prepared to deal the last card, I studied the board to make sure that I, at last, had a winning hand. Across from me sat a definite loser, so I turned my attention to Dylan. Based on my card counting, the only way he could win would be if he had four of a kind, three of a kind facedown that matched a face-up card. It would have to be an eight or a ten, because at least two of the other cards he showed had already been played. An eight was folded earlier by a player sitting on my right, so I could only lose if he had all the remaining tens. I liked that the odds were clearly in my favor, so I bet the max. We bet again after the final card was dealt. When we turned our cards over, Dylan smugly declared, "Read 'em and weep, High School Harry," pointing to his three eights down in addition to the one showing.

I was stunned. "Four eights, that's impossible." Everyone looked at me when I pointed at Sean across the table and said, "He folded an eight on the fifth card."

Dylan stood and screamed at me, "What are you saying?" Ronnie jumped in before the situation got out of control. He grabbed me by the sweater and pulled me outside.

"What the hell is wrong with you? I never thought you would be a whiner or poor loser! And do you realize you are accusing him of cheating?"

"Ronnie, you've seen my memory at work. That eight had already been played. Unless he's Houdini and mastered a reappearing card trick, then he cheated."

"Can you prove it?"

"All I care is that you believe me."

"I want to. I know Dylan can be a prick. But I've never seen him cheat. How can I be sure?"

I turned and started to walk to my car. I don't think I ever was more angry.

"Stop, dammit! Don't let him know he hurt you. Never let your opponent know you are injured or bested."

"Ronnie, this isn't basketball."

"No, that's true, but it is a life lesson. Isn't that one of your favorite phrases?"

By now I was so mad that I had forgotten how much older and more physical these guys were than me. I needed Ronnie to once again prove his friendship and transport me back to some level of sanity. "Rogers," he said, "go in the house, thank everyone for the evening, and bid farewell. If you need to get more pissed off, hit your car with that wooden head of yours."

I knew his advice was the right course. It's not like me to lose control of my emotions, so before I went back in the house, I forced myself to close my eyes for a brief meditation, then pressed my hands hard against each other and practiced a few more isometric exercises to help me return to near normal. I'd read in one of Dad's medical journals that this was helpful. The game was already well into another hand when I apologized for my outburst, thanked them for inviting me, and then excused myself to go home. Still, I just could not leave without Dylan knowing that I was on to him. For some reason I wasn't afraid, so I pointed to my eyes and then at him and mouthed, "I know."

Ronnie walked me to my car, promising me, "I'll take it from here."

"You believe me, don't you, R. D.?" I asked him one more time.

All he said was "We're on the same team."

I was too upset to drive off right away, so I walked to the top of the hill, sat on a bench, and wondered what had just happened. It was a cool November evening, but my blood was boiling and I could feel the perspiration under my shirt and sweater. I found it hard to accept the fact that a nitwit like Dylan could pull this caper off on me. I vowed to learn from tonight's mishap, but at the same time, promised myself to not forget "Read 'em and weep."

Dammit, I shouldn't have come here in the first place. I'd known I wasn't one of them and that I was on foreign turf. I could play ball and share laughs with these guys, but always knowing that we had little in common. Ronnie Davis was different from his friends, and he proved it when he stood beside me in this fiasco. Maybe this night proved that I wasn't as street smart as I thought I was, and that I was young and inexperienced and still had a lot to learn. I had to accept that. If I looked in a mirror and carefully examined myself, I would have concluded that I had to climb the stairs first before I could get to the top floor.

I took this life lesson with me from the top of Mt. Adams and returned to my car. At the bottom of the east side of the great hill, my car mysteriously turned south on Columbia Parkway, headed downtown, and I decided to cross the Newport Bridge to Kentucky. By the time I parked at Lilly's, I was so ready that I had to rearrange myself to avoid the embarrassment of a teenage bulge. Lilly greeted me with "Jimbo's protégé returns!" I couldn't hide my immature blush and had trouble containing myself as I asked for Shani.

"Sorry to disappoint you, but Shani went back to Tennessee with her daughter."

"What?" I gasped.

"Yes, she has a two-year-old. Cute little thing, but she got in the way of business."

"What's she going to do? How is she going to support her child?"

"That's why she went home. Her mother will help with the girl while Shani goes back to work as a waitress."

As if on command a tall, skinny, albino-like woman approached. Before I could complain about Shani's absence, she was walking me upstairs. I was so distressed I forgot to look up her nightgown. In the room, without even a single word spoken, she removed her clothes and motioned for me to undress. She stood by the sink studying her fingernails. I had lost my hard-on downstairs and was embarrassed as I dropped my underpants.

"Come on over here so I can wash you up," she said with an exaggerated drawl. Standing next to her pale whiteness, I noticed scars on her back and shoulders. Even though I was less than a foot away from a naked woman I wasn't aroused. I suddenly asked myself what I was doing here. I didn't belong at Dylan's, and I didn't belong in this room with this woman, either. I knew I had to leave right away. I reached into my wallet and dropped some money on the bed. I told her that this should be enough, that it was twice Lilly's charge. She walked over to the bed, grabbed the money, and pushed me out the door.

I lowered all the car windows to make sure I stayed awake on the ride home. I felt pissed off and ashamed of myself and hoped the cool air would cleanse me from the night's poker and Lilly escapades. Then I turned on the city's favorite disc jockey, Bugs Scruggs, the man with the plugs, to blast some rock 'n' roll. By the time I got home, I was through with Dylan and my botched stopover at Lilly's. I didn't expect to see either in my future. I made sure to take a long, hot shower before going to bed.

With the holiday season only a few weeks away, Dad was especially busy. I'd seen him like this before, when he was wrapped up in a special case, immersed professionally and sometimes emotionally as well. It seemed he was hardly at home. When I asked if he wanted to tell me anything, all he would say was that he was dealing with an extremely complicated, puzzling issue and wasn't sure of his diagnosis. I could read the frustration on his face yet knew for sure he wouldn't quit. When he did have some time for me, he tried to be upbeat and engaged, but I could tell he was preoccupied and that his brain was working overtime. This was when I respected him the most, as a man totally dedicated to helping another human being.

Left alone with free time to spare, I became more of a newspaper junkie, in a valiant attempt to follow the financial markets in general and the stocks of a few local companies. I loved it. At Ronnie's suggestion I started keeping a paper portfolio. He said this would make me honest with myself. I quickly discovered how challenging this was for someone who was essentially self-taught. I made countless mistakes that I compared to swinging at bad pitches out of the strike zone. But I would dust myself off and step back in the batter's box and try again. As I tallied up my paper portfolio each weekend, it became obvious that I had a lot to learn. What a pain in the butt it was to accept the fact that numbers don't lie! They were there on the paper in front of me, as naked as a stripper.

R. D. was right when he said it's too easy to believe you would have done this or that to improve a position's profit or limit a loss. "It's like jerking yourself off," he would say, "but if you actually do keep a journal and post every buy or sell—the price, quantity, and date—then there's no place for fantasy. It's like looking closely in the mirror." So, like a kid learning to ride a bicycle, I fell all too many times. But I did gradually improve. I wasn't nearly ready to ride on a busy street or down a steep hill, and while I continued to take my share of spills, I gradually improved and fell less often. I was glad my education was taking place on paper—my savings account couldn't afford the losses. Fortunately I was a realist, readily accepting the fact that my knowledge of the world of stocks and bonds was in its mere infancy. I made a mental note to thank Ronnie for his ideas, because I knew if I'd suffered all my errors and losses with real money, I probably would have cut and run at some point along the way.

I grew up without celebrating Christmas, or Chanukah or, for that matter, any religious holiday. We didn't talk too much about religion around our house. Dad never characterized himself as part of any group other than what he called the Society of Scientists. As for me, I knew better what I wasn't than what I supposedly was. Arguing with friends, all of whom practiced some kind of religion, I would assume Dad's position even if I didn't totally understand it.

A couple of days before the twenty-fifth, Dad reminded me that I was to join him on Christmas Day for our usual visit to the children's ward at the hospital. I never figured out how this became a family tradition, but I knew that Dad took this occasion very seriously. The majority of the basement floor of the hospital was reserved for children with precarious medical conditions. Most of their parents would stop by on holidays but at some point returned home to celebrate with the rest of their family. Dad didn't want these kids to feel rejected. We would spend the afternoon going from room to room bringing small presents to those who received none and hopefully some cheer to those who were resting in a dreary room all alone. This was absolutely the most difficult day of the year for me. If you want to see how shitty, how utterly unfair life can be, all you have to do is walk through a hospital ward full of children suffering from life-threatening diseases and look at their shrunken faces, the outline of their skulls, hairless from chemotherapy, and into their dark, sad eyes as they sat in wheelchairs or lay in bed connected to countless tubes. Yet in most cases, when you sat and talked to them or handed them a wrapped gift of a book or colored pencils or a simple game, they would actually show a grateful smile. Their bravery always amazed me.

We went together or sometimes alone to the children's rooms until the nurses on duty asked us to leave. Dad asked me not to cry or show sadness. He said it would only be self-serving and not beneficial to the kids. That was a tall order to follow. When I entered a room to gather up Dad, I saw him leaning over a young girl, maybe six or seven years old, gently rubbing her forehead and cheeks and softly singing to her. It was a moment of such genuine compassion that I felt I had to join in. It was all too familiar. Why should anyone have to suffer like this?

As I bent down next to Dad, he looked at me and smiled. I knew he was thinking of my mother.

No restaurants were open in the city on Christmas, but Dad reminded us about the kosher place he knew up in Roselawn. Gabe's Place was little more than a deli except for the few tables in the rear. We both were drained after our hospital visit. Gabe's pot roast with potato latkes was the perfect antidote. We ate quietly, lost in our own thoughts. When our plates were cleared, Dad ordered his tea and asked me about my plans for New Year's Eve. I told him a large group was going to my friend Joe Morrow's house.

"Do you have a date?" Dad asked.

"I don't have one. There'll be plenty of single guys and girls there."

"Don't you have any girlfriends?" he continued.

"I have friends but no one special. Okay?"

"Rogers, why don't you have a girlfriend?" he persisted in a soft voice.

I laughed. "I'm too good-looking. I think they're intimidated."

"Seriously, you should have a date for New Year's."

"Thanks for worrying about me, but really, I'll have a good time anyway."

Dad sipped his tea, seemingly lost in thought, and then as if he had a sudden brilliant idea, sat up straight and suggested, "What about Charlotte Marks?"

"Lottie Marks. Dr. Marks's daughter? Dad, she has hated me ever since she was ten when I locked her in your office supply room and turned off the light."

"I'm glad I forgot about that. I hope Larry Marks has."

"Is she still short and pudgy with braces?" I asked with mock innocence. He stared ahead and reminded me not judge people by their looks. I waited for one of his favorite homilies: *you can't tell a book by its cover!* But he went on.

"She was in the office a few weeks ago, and I promise you she has changed. You'll be surprised."

"Why, is she even shorter and heavier?" I couldn't resist teasing him every once in a while.

"Son, I have an idea—why don't you just offer her a ride to the party? That way if I'm right you'll have a sweet date, and if I'm wrong you won't be committed. That would also please Dr. Marks. Remember he's a partner in my office. What do you think?"

I gave him a noncommittal shrug, my preferred way of not answering a question. Back home I turned my attention to Charlotte Marks. She was well-known in school for being outer-edge sarcastic, sassy, and plenty smart. She was decidedly the wrong girl to debate in the classroom. Contrary to what I said when joshing with Dad, I knew that Charlotte was attractive and blessed with a figure worthy of admiration. I sat in my room wondering why we always seemed to find ways to avoid each other. In fact, I couldn't think of any concrete reasons why we weren't friends. So I decided to make Dad happy since all I would be promising was my chauffeur services.

When I called her the next afternoon, she said yes, she was going to the party at Joe's, yes, she'd appreciate a ride, and then she emphatically added, "But don't consider this a date!" I immediately liked her spunk.

As soon as Charlotte got in the car on New Year's Eve, she leaped into action. "So whose idea was this?" The contest had started earlier than I expected. She sat there like a tightly wired ninja. Confident. Determined. She exuded energy. She wore no makeup or jewelry. Her shoes reminded me of a policeman's on his beat. She was dressed all in black, with her thick brown hair twisted and somehow pulled up on top of her head. I normally enjoyed verbal jousting and felt I could hold my own with most anyone, but decided nevertheless to try to defuse the evening's hostility. I took the high road and told her that I didn't want to go to a New Year's party alone and assumed she didn't, either. And then I swallowed hard and apologized for my juvenile stunt seven years ago. "You were a real dick," she reminded me but then changed her tune and added, "Anyway, thanks for the regrets. Let's try to have a fun New Year's." I was suddenly rather pleased that we were going together.

The party was as noisy and chaotic as any typical teenage blast. I spent much of the evening with Charlotte. She wasn't like the other girls I knew at school. She wasn't obsessed with clothes and didn't seem to care what others thought of her. I liked the fact that she looked directly at whomever she was talking to, seemingly oblivious to the crowd and chatter around her. She wasn't aloof, but she wasn't touchy-feely, either. I noticed she made no attempt to flirt with the other guys floating about.

What I really liked about Charlotte was her first-class wit. During the party she came right up to me, close enough that I could see the flicker in her gray eyes, and said that I deserved the Distinguished Service Cross for having the balls to call her. To piss her off, I responded, "Thanks, Lottie."

She laughed out loud as she poked her index finger into my shoulder and said, "Once, that's pretty good. Twice, and I'll start calling you Jollyboy, like the nurses did in the office when you were a little snot."

Later in the evening, I saw Richie Turner ask her to dance to a Jackie Wilson number. I thought for sure she would blow him off. Instead she transformed into a rocker with great rhythm, shaking every limb of her body. She was in her own world by the third song, jumping and grinding with moves both sexy and acrobatic. She knew I was watching and later, apparently to one of her favorite songs, said, "Let's see what you've got," and reached for my hand. I was a lousy dancer with oversize feet and the skill of a water buffalo, but I refused to reveal my shy side. I did my best, but the futility was obvious. She didn't seem to care how inept I was. As she gyrated and shook her body parts, Charlotte leaned closer to me and screeched, "You gotta love the Isley Brothers!"

When most of the couples drifted off to the dark corners of the room, I found myself sitting alone with Charlotte sharing small talk. Our fathers worked in the same office, we went to the same school, yet we hardly knew each other. She seemed determined to analyze me as she took the initiative. "My father told me last night that you are virtually brilliant. Is that true?"

I joked, "What does virtually mean?"

She told me, "Please don't be a smart-ass tonight. You know that's your reputation."

"What, being virtually brilliant or being a smart-ass?"

"Both," she said emphatically.

"I'm not so good talking about myself. How about you? Do you have lots of friends you share innermost thoughts with? Girls you gossip with every night about what happened that day at school or in the back seat of a car on Saturday night? I hardly know you, but my bet is you think you're different from the other girls we both know, that you want to chart your own path and you want to get there on your own terms. Am I getting warm? And all this bold self-confidence you so proudly project. Is it bravado or is it the real deal?"

"Whew," she said, "I didn't expect to be in therapy tonight." She didn't answer my questions. Instead she confessed that she usually hated New Year's parties but was having a swell time this evening.

I moved on. "What I detest about New Year's is the false frivolity. That you're supposed to get drunk and be loud and crazy and kiss everyone just because it's December 31. I'll be rowdy when I choose to, not because of some arbitrary date. And I don't like kissing or being kissed by just anyone, only a girl I really feel close to. I don't want to throw the double standard out on the table, but if I were you, I would be repulsed by the slobbering kisses of these guys here tonight."

Charlotte turned to face me. She was resting her chin on folded hands. She didn't say a word. We seemed to be taking the measure of each other. I was thinking that we were both surprised that there could be a spark here. Friendship? More? My best guess was that neither one of us was prone to hasty decisions. The mood was jolted as a few of the guys started to loudly count down to midnight. I panicked with indecision. *Do I or don't I?* She made it easy by saying straight out, "I don't kiss anyone on New Year's except my dad." I then enjoyed watching her avoid the sex-starved masses. An hour or so later, the party was winding down. We said goodbyes to our friends, and I drove her home.

I walked her up the driveway to her house. We decided it was a better New Year's than most and agreed to get together some way or another after exams in January. She opened the front door and turned to face me. Her hair was windblown from the walk and her cheeks were flushed from dancing. I froze. I hesitated. I had no plan. Charlotte saved me when she asked, "Aren't you going to kiss me goodnight?" I told her I was afraid she might bite my lips off.

We both laughed and then I kissed her.

With exams and college applications behind me, it was time to refill my tank. It had been a pressure-packed couple of months that I found surprisingly exhilarating. The challenges made me feel like I was competing in a tight baseball game. I was too close to the end of the ninth to screw up, so I uncharacteristically concentrated and put forth some genuine effort. For a guy who usually operated on cruise control, this was quite a change. Now that the ordeal was over, I was ready for a diversion, and sure enough, it came by way of a call from Charlotte.

"Hey, hot shot. Are you as burned-out as I am? I'm calling to throw an idea on the table. I know it's not light fare, but I love Fellini, and his new movie is playing at the Guild. You want to join Rachel Lewis and me Saturday for the nine o'clock? We could grab some food at my house first, say sevenish."

My reply could have been classified as a gimme putt, but I threw it back at her just for laughs anyway when I innocently inquired, "Is this a real date?"

Ever quick with a response she answered, "Why don't you think of it as a platonic ménage à trois."

Dad gave me the "I told you so" look when I told him about my plans for Saturday evening. Over the years I never thought that he understood how funny he could be with his facial expressions, especially when he was proven right after I had disagreed with him or surprised him for some reason or another. I made sure to tell him that Charlotte and I were possibly becoming friends, nothing more than friends. He cocked his head to the side and smirked when he said, "Sure, Rogers, I understand completely."

I arrived at Charlotte's just as her parents were leaving for a dinner party. Even though they lived only ten minutes from us, I had never been inside their house. She lived in an old, established neighborhood in a solid brick and stucco house decorated for comfort. I was waved into the kitchen, where my dateniks were pretending to cook. I barely knew Rachel other than as someone I would occasionally see in our school hallways. I had heard that she aspired to be an artist, so I wasn't particularly surprised to see her dressed as if she were headed to a seedy gallery on the Left Bank.

Charlotte was in high spirits. As she moved about the kitchen while dividing Chinese food from containers onto plates, she somehow maintained conversations with both Rachel and me with occasional interruptions so she could sing backup to a favorite Platters song on the radio. She generated such energy just being herself that I thought the room felt brighter. As Rachel was setting the kitchen table and Charlotte was serving up our Chinese dinner, I asked if there was anything I could do to help. Charlotte said, "Sure. While we're playing homemaker, you can help with the mood. The movie we're seeing is set in the 1930s in Italy. Why not tell us about the socioeconomic and geopolitical state of Italy prior to World War II? Also, it would be helpful if you educated us on the significant similarities and differences between Fascist Italy and Nazi Germany."

"Would you like me to lecture in Italian or English?" I asked.

"How about Swahili?" She laughed and then, "Seriously, let's eat our Midwest version of Chinese and vamoose over to the Guild."

I held things up with "I'm not leaving until we walk down the hallway over there and hear an explanation of those pictures of you two guys growing up together."

"Not a chance," they said in unison.

"Come on. I promise I won't laugh too hard. If we were at my house, I'd show you what a great-looking little devil I was."

"I've heard from Charlotte you were a little shit growing up," Rachel volunteered.

"That's because she had an unfulfilled crush on me."

"Okay," said Charlotte. "Enough of the small talk. I'm making an executive decision here. First we finish dinner. Then we clear and clean up. Then we do a quick stroll down the hall. Then we move our cans out of here so we can see the movie. Rogers can tease us about the pictures all he wants on the way to the Guild."

In the car, after dinner and seeing the montage of them growing up together, I had wanted to be entertainingly witty. But the truth was that the pictures showcased two really spunky girls who were clearly best friends and who cared for each other over the years. So instead I felt warmth for them both. When I let my guard down and shared that thought as we walked toward the theater, Charlotte took my hand. I felt a warm rush that headed straight for my chest.

Rachel added, "Hey, Char, he's not so bad after all."

The movie was about to begin as Charlotte announced that there would be no talking during the film. When I looked over at her, she added, "That's the way it should be in an art cinema!"

I felt awkward walking both girls to Charlotte's door after the movie. Fortunately, Dr. Marks was downstairs pretending to look for a misplaced book. Good old Charlotte quipped, "Oh, Daddy, it was so nice of you to wait up to make sure your little girl got home safely." Mrs. Marks made her preplanned entrance, then suggested we sit and chat about the movie for a few minutes. The transparency of all this made Charlotte and Rachel actually giggle.

Charlotte briefed them on the movie's plot while Rachel added her thoughts on what Fellini was trying to accomplish and why the film was genuinely "Felliniesque." Dr. Marks turned to me and asked if I enjoyed the movie. I said I appreciated Fellini as an artist. His films were original, in many ways groundbreaking, and while I found all the fantasy and bizarre imagery interesting, his subject matter didn't always resonate with me. Suddenly I felt four sets of eyes studying me. I knew I shouldn't overdo my answer, but I needed to continue to respond. I tiptoed forward cautiously.

"Like everyone I also like being entertained, but my preference is a movie that I will remember for its content. I want to learn something, to be challenged or emotionally moved."

Charlotte interrupted, asking me to give an example. So I went on.

"A few years ago I saw *The Garden of the Finzi-Continis* with my dad. It was a powerful story of the downfall of a wealthy, aristocratic Jewish family in Italy. They were decadent and self-centered and seemingly oblivious to the dangers of Fascist anti-Semitism. They thought their social position would protect them but, like all the others, they were deported to concentration camps. The depiction of war, prejudice, and devastation of a proud country was utterly raw. You couldn't help but be affected by this film."

"Is he always like this?" Rachel asked.

"Well, are you?" dear Charlotte inquired.

"I'm sorry if I went too far. It's just that when I think about that movie, I can't help wondering what I would have done in such a circumstance."

When Charlotte pointed to her wristwatch, I got the message. On the way to the front door, she told me I was in rare form, then squeezed my arm and flashed me a smile that accompanied me all the way home.

There wasn't any plan, we never even talked about it, but we started calling each other in the evenings just to chat. We'd talk about school, future goals, friends, family, books, and assorted gibberish. It occurred to me that before these phone calls, I had not opened up or had serious conversations with anyone other than my dad. The closest I came was the few times I talked in earnest with Andrew Stevens and on occasion for real with Ronnie Davis. I had found it simpler to keep my opinions and beliefs private, and I never felt the need to talk about myself nor be analyzed by someone else. But I was different with Charlotte. She was an unusual combination of both a good listener and someone who spoke with her own voice. She would concentrate intently, mull over her thoughts, and then deliver an inevitably insightful response. She could be instinctive or analytical, depending on the question or her mood, and she could also be outrageously funny. Moreover, and most specially for me, when you talked with Charlotte, you always felt that she cared.

One of my father's golden rules was to listen first. He would tell me, his young baseball player, to study the hitter and the game situation before even beginning my windup, well before deciding what pitch to throw and to what location. Another favorite of his, on poker, was to study an opponent's tendencies and the cards already dealt, and analyze the betting patterns before pushing even one extra chip into the middle of a poker table.

These were some of the listening lessons Dad preached. He believed his gift as a doctor was his ability to diagnose a difficult medical problem. He took pride in what he called this "intellectual aspect" of medicine. He wanted me to learn that random questions rarely have much value. Questions should follow answers within a controlled game plan and should build one upon another. Also he would emphasize "Don't rush!" and to remember you are managing an organic process. In his world questions and their answers were also the key to ordering tests and procedures to reveal the cause of a particular disease. To Dad that was the listening before the concluding. "Accurate listening helps your next questions guide you down the path to answers," he would lecture. When I talked with Charlotte, I marveled that somehow she must have read his book. As for me, I long ago had decided that most challenging diagnoses were more art than science. Science could be learned; I wasn't so sure you could teach someone to play the art game.

Our evening telephone chats were not all serious or full of penetrating questions and thoughtful answers. There was plenty of silly talk: *Did you see her strutting about in that ridiculous outfit? What the hell was the class thinking today? I can't believe he/she actually said that to Principal Johnson, can you?* I never knew one evening to the next what we would be talking about or where it would lead. I liked that. I also enjoyed the friendly put-downs and laser-like teasing. We each were good at it, we both knew that, yet we quietly established guidelines without ever talking about them. Charlotte could compliment me, tease me, agree with me, or disagree with me all in the same sentence. "Rogers! Great idea! What, are you nuts? I love it! I hate it!"

I found it easier to share thoughts with Charlotte on the phone, when I wasn't distracted by the way she would look at me. I had never met anyone who could convey such a range of emotions by just the magic of her eyes. When we talked I would lie on my bed tossing a baseball up in the air. The game was to see how close I could get to the ceiling without making contact. If Charlotte knew what I was doing, she would have teased the hell out of me. "You really are still a little boy, aren't you," she might say. We could start the evening with small-talk BS: *How was your day? Anything unusual happen? What's on your docket?* etc., etc. Then we'd head anywhere. It was absolutely unpredictable. After a few weeks of feeling each other out, our conversations morphed into *our futures.*

In time I learned that Charlotte wasn't just a fastball cruising down the middle of the plate. Besides the sarcastic, sassy, smart attributes she wore on her sleeve like a badge of honor, she was passionate about virtually every aspect of her life. She loved her parents, her friends, growing up where and when she did, but she also said she was ready for a move. I wasn't surprised when she told me her class rank (cum laude) and her dream about going to New York to attend Columbia University. I knew the first night I was with her that she was big-time smart. Her response to the usual question of "What do you want to be?" was a huge hee-haw but then a firm "I want to make a difference!" She felt it was time for her to grow, to reach out and take new risks. She wasn't sure where she was headed but confidently believed that she would achieve her goals. It wasn't hubris—it was pure Charlotte. When she talked like that, I was ready to push my remaining chips forward. I just had this feeling about her. I couldn't help thinking that she was a winner.

"Okay, Lone Ranger," Charlotte joked one night, "what about you? I know it's not easy for you to speculate on all the imponderables, but come on now and try."

"Only Tonto knows all of my secrets," I continued with her Lone Ranger theme. "He knows my real identity, where I hide the silver bullets, and where I applied to college. He's advising me to attend the Wharton School at Penn, head to Wall Street and make millions before I'm thirty, then take time off to reflect on my future. If I succeed, and he assures me I will, he thinks I should then be a force of good to battle all the evil in the world we live in."

That earned an enthusiastic "Wow" from Charlotte. She then asked for Tonto's telephone number so she could follow Kemosabe's progress when he was in Philadelphia. I told her Tonto's number was unlisted but she could communicate with him via smoke signals. "Great," she said, "I earned a Girl Scout honor badge in smoke signaling."

I then turned serious when I explained to her why my situation was actually quite complicated. If all went well, I would be turning my back on Johns Hopkins to attend a school to help prepare me for financial combat. In all probability Charles Stout's son would never become a doctor. I would be leaving him to an empty house, where his only child would be an eleven-hour drive away. His response would be to further bury himself in his work while encouraging me to go where I wanted to go to challenge myself and to take advantage of the opportunities at Penn. But I would know that I hurt him. No matter what he said or how he said it, I would know.

After what felt like an awkward pause, Charlotte's tone changed. I appreciated the supportive message she delivered.

"I'm optimistic this will all work out well for you. Your father will understand. Don't forget he raised his son to think for himself. He'll respect that you thought out this decision very carefully."

When our acceptance letters arrived in early April, we were afraid to call each other. Naturally Charlotte was the courageous one to break the ice. "I'm so excited I wet my pants. How about you, are you dry or wet?"

Even under these circumstances, I tried the light touch. "I've been wearing a diaper these days, so I'm not sure. Wait a second and I'll check . . .Okay, I'm in."

Charlotte couldn't be totally serious, either. "Just think, only twelve years from now you'll be rich and famous and I'll be a struggling do-gooder."

"As long as you're not married to an insurance salesman and living in a split-level in Dayton, you'll be fine," I teased.

"How many kids will I have?" she asked.

"Too many."

"You're a shitty fortune teller!" was her quick response.

It was a good time to ask about Rachel.

"Her parents are really narrow-minded. They told her to draw a circle around our city with a compass limiting her to two hours from home.

You know she wants to be an artist, so her choices were few. The good news is she was accepted at Antioch. They are known as the liberal outpost of the Midwest. Perfect for our dear Rachel. I can't wait for her parents to visit her on campus. They'll have a heart attack."

"That's great. Tell her congrats from me."

"Rogers, have you told your father yet?"

Actually, I had not, but I should have known that Dad would shine when I told him the news. He never once mentioned Johns Hopkins or that I had turned down Yale, his other preference for me. Dad might have been a modern version of a Renaissance man, but no one ever accused him of being a comic. Yet for days after my decision was made, he would walk around the house as if he were Milton Berle or Jackie Gleason. He couldn't stop teasing me: What's in a cheesesteak, anyway? or Why is the Liberty Bell cracked? He would laugh at his own jokes while he pointed at me—"An Ivy Leaguer, my son's going to be the next Bernard Baruch." His favorite gibe was asking me to invent something over the weekend: "Why not, Ben Franklin did!"

I had never seen Dad act like this. I was happy and relieved that he wasn't upset or disappointed, but the detective in me wondered what the hell was happening. To my surprise the new Dad kept on humming. Almost every night he would break into his jokester act. He wore my defenses down so I decided to laugh with him, stop worrying, and enjoy this comedian who happened to be my father.

At one of our Friday dinners in May, Dad told me he would not be able to go with me to that Sunday's Reds game against the New York Mets. I knew the meeting at the hospital had to be mucho important, because this would probably be the last time we could see the great Willie Mays play before he retired. Dad thought he was the absolute best, most complete baseball player he ever saw. Willie hit for both power and average, could run the bases like a gazelle, and was a dynamic fielding phenom. When he was a younger player, his love for the game was painted all over his face, dominated by an infectious smile that went ear to ear. What Dad remembered most about Willie was a play he made against the Reds when he was still starring for the San Francisco Giants. It occurred in 1962, the year they won the pennant. The play wasn't in the newspapers, but Dad swore he witnessed it. There was a man on third and one out. A towering fly was hit to dead center. Rather than just catching it at the base of Crosley's infamous terrace, Mays ran uphill to the wall, turned, and raced back down the terrace. He caught the ball on the run and then threw a perfect strike all the way in the air (a "clothesline," according to Dad) to the catcher. The base runner was out before he even began to slide.

After dinner that night, Dad handed me two prime tickets for the game. "Keep a scorecard," he told me and, "Please remember every little detail about Willie. I really don't like missing this one." When we returned home, I called Ronnie. He jumped at the invitation. Everyone who loved baseball appreciated the talent of Willie Mays and the excitement he generated by the way he played the game. Ronnie was no exception.

What could be better than a baseball game on a sunny spring afternoon? The Big Red Machine against Mays and gang set up an enticing contest. The game was a sellout and the stadium was rocking. We decided to get to the park early to watch the warm-ups and see Willie hack around with his teammates. We were seated in a high-rent district halfway between third base and home plate. Between munching peanuts and commenting on the players, Ronnie and I caught up with each other. He told me he won ten bucks off Jimbo when I accepted Penn over Yale and resisted the pressure from Dad about Johns Hopkins. "I hope you know what you're doing," he said and then added, "Promise me you won't become a typical Ivy League asshole." I described the Wharton program to him and why I thought it would be good for me. I shrugged off the Ivy League comment.

"Hey, I get it," Ronnie said. "Everyone knows their reputation. I'm sure you'll get a first-class education, but I can't help worrying about you."

"Why?" I asked, turning in my seat to face him.

"You've never been away from home, you're a big fish in a little pond here, and where you're headed is the kind of place that can change you into a know-it-all."

"There's nothing wrong with wanting to grow. Trust me, R. D., I know where I'm from and what I know and don't know. I'm going to be on a mission in college—I'm going to be a giant sponge, and when I graduate I'm going to sprint, not walk, to the finish line."

"What's at the finish line?"

"Independence!" I immediately answered.

Then R. D. interjected, "Before you run off to the East Coast, let me repeat a lesson I learned the hard way."

"I'm all ears, great one."

"All the stuff you're going to learn in Ivy Land matters in the long term, but it can get you into deep doo-doo if you don't listen to the markets. They have a way of speaking. You have to live it, breathe it in, understand the rhythms, feel the pulse and what it's trying to say to you. Most of the time you'll just go along for the ride. Sometimes, though, you have to make a statement: Are you going to fold your cards and go home, or do you think a change is coming and that you have to prepare for it?"

"It's a tough game," I agreed.

"You have no idea how tough it is!"

I protested a bit. "Are you saying that studying finance and accounting and all the rest is a waste of time? That it's all crap?"

"No. I've seen a few guys use it right, but I've seen most of the MBA types have their balls chopped off. They think they know more than the market. That they're smarter than the market. Guess what? No one is."

"Maybe I should junk this Wharton thing and become a poet or a philosopher."

"Sure. That'll make you rich real fast," R. D. quipped.

Our attention reverted back to baseball as the Reds took the field to a raucous ovation. Like all real baseball fans, Ronnie and I immediately became absorbed in the game. With one out the second batter hit a line-drive single over third and Willie Mays sauntered up to the plate. I got excited just watching him rub dirt into his hands, dig in, and take a few lazy practice swings. He was at the end of his career but still looked to me like a Greek god. A respectful Midwest crowd cheered. Willie flashed his signature smile. He took a ball, then a strike, and on the next pitch unleashed his famed compact swing, yet it only resulted in a lazy, long fly out to center field. Mets outfielder Rusty Staub smashed a wicked line drive to right, but the next hitter struck out to end the inning.

During the game Ronnie and I talked on and off about our families, his life at P&P, the upcoming basketball season at Xavier, and how my dad would manage with me away at school. Ronnie beamed when he bragged about his twin sisters. "They're really beautiful, talented, and smart, too. I'm paying for them to go to private school. I want the best for them. They were in our family's rear window when I was at Xavier, so they deserve their chance now." Honestly, for a moment I thought he was going to tear up, but macho Ronnie just closed his eyes for a second, smiled to himself, and moved on. It didn't surprise me that R. D. wanted to do his best to help his younger sisters. He had a special way of doing the right thing.

Between the fifth and sixth innings, I introduced Charlotte into the conversation.

"You're not joking, are you?" Ronnie asked.

"I still can't believe it ever happened. I was minding my own business, doing Dad a favor, and shazam, this bundle of energy and intelligence and sheer joy burst into my life. The craziest part is that when I look into her eyes, I get so dizzy I'm afraid I'll fall down."

"You're really in trouble here."

"I guess I am, but it's only been for a very short time, so we'll see."

"What have you told her?"

"So far we're just friends. I swear, nothing more."

"Look at the calendar, buddy boy. You're going far away in a just a few months."

"You've had girlfriends before. Plenty of them. I haven't. Any advice?"

"Be careful. For her and for you."

The last third of the game got interesting. Mays hit a hard grounder with glasses on that found its way between short and third. Then big Rusty Staub hit a homer deep into the bleachers. It was one of the longest hits I'd ever seen. The hometown crowd gasped. The good news was that the Red Machine got oiled up in the eighth, and we scored five runs thanks to extra base hits by Morgan and Bench and then a go-ahead blast by Perez. When the Mets went down quietly in the ninth, the game was over. It was a pretty good game, except I would have liked to see Mays contribute a little more. I knew that when I got home, Dad would grill me for details like a detective from the city's finest. How did Mays look in the field? Does he still have that great arm? When he ran did his hat ever fall off like it has done so many times? Did he look old at the plate? He'd expect me to be an accurate reporter. He'd want the facts, but he'd also want the color.

As the stadium slowly emptied, I asked Ronnie how he was faring at P&P. With school winding down, I had been spending even more time at the library in a vain attempt to grasp what was going on in the world of stock markets. Times were awful, but how awful were they? I knew that in January, wage and price controls were relaxed. They had artificially suppressed inflation, so when the plug was removed from the bottle, the cost of all kinds of goods and services soared. Even amateurs like me understood that. Ronnie likened it to shaking a Coca-Cola bottle with the cap still on—when the cap is removed, all hell breaks loose. In the financial world, this meant both stocks and bonds got trashed.

R. D. said it was really quite simple: inflation increases, interest rates follow, which means bonds plunge. When higher rates are baked into equity valuations and investors start worrying about the effects on the economy, then stocks say, "Look out below." R. D. mused that this game had been played too many times before. "Read up on 1969 to 1970. Pretty damn similar. It's like night following day." In other words, he said, the trading department at P&P was at war with twin bear markets. I was trying to learn about trading and markets, but I was a mere neophyte. Also I knew very little about economics. I listened carefully to Ronnie's explanation and secretly hoped that my years at college would deliver me to the mountaintop. *So much to learn*, I thought. When I asked Ronnie what his strategy was, he said, "Survive!"

I considered what Ronnie had just told me for a while then asked, "If you believe this will continue, why not bet against the market like you can when you bet against the dice in craps? Is that possible in the stock market?"

Ronnie pointed his finger into my chest and almost shouted, "Go to the head of the class! It's called going short, and I've been trying to get Jimbo to do it for months. He's afraid to go short."

"What does 'going short' mean?" I questioned. "I've never heard that term before."

"It's a technique you use to bet a stock will fall," R. D. educated me. "Think of it as the reverse of a normal trade. Instead of buying first and selling later, you sell first and buy later. You win when the stock declines and you buy back your position at a lower price. You lose if the stock rises and you have to pay a higher price."

"How do you sell something you don't already own?"

"You borrow the stock from a broker before you sell it," Ronnie answered.

I was dumbstruck. "You can do that?" I asked. "You can sell a stock that you borrowed?"

"It's not as unusual as you may think," Ronnie continued. "Professionals sell short to hedge their bets in difficult market environments. When it works it's a savior. When it fails it can be extremely painful!"

It was time to leave. I made a mental note to study up on this shorting concept. Then I planned to go back to Ronnie to test myself. The funny thing about Ronnie was he didn't realize that he actually was one hell of a teacher.

In early June school was essentially over. Most of the seniors were already committed to colleges and focused more on summer than final exams. I was firmly in that club. But I did care about our baseball team. Our best offensive weapons had graduated, so if we were to win some games, we'd be forced to play scrappy ball—aggressive base running, strategic bunting, solid defense, and hopefully superior pitching. I had moved up into the second starter's role. Coach wished I "threw the pea with more heat," as he so eloquently phrased it, but he liked my control, that I pitched with a variety of speeds, and that my new knuckleball had become effective. But when the knuckler for some reason just wouldn't break or when it took on a life of its own and went bonkers, then I was in serious trouble. We were having a reasonably good season. I was having a swell time, but our team was in only third place.

In the middle of a week, the stock market experienced a violent downward flush. To show support I called Ronnie after the close. He was clearly pissed off because Jimbo still refused to sell short and it was hurting the department's performance. He said that if this were to continue, he'd probably like to run over to Rory's on Saturday night to blow off some steam. Would I join him? We agreed to talk again that Friday afternoon.

When Charlotte called on Thursday night, she was in a feisty mood. "Yo, Jolly R, are you as impatient as yours truly for summer to arrive?" Charlotte and Rachel wanted to experience a "summer of purpose," so they had signed up to join a work project building a school in rural southern Kentucky. They would be living in tents and doing manual labor seven days a week. The conditions would be rough, but according to Charlotte, "I can't wait to get on with this. Finally I'm doing something important!" The fact was I knew I would be lonely with her gone the entire summer.

"By the way," Charlotte said, "you've never told me your plans for this summer."

I knew my idea for the summer would bore her, or worse, that she would lose respect for me. So, as usual, I resorted to weak humor.

"I haven't decided yet. I plan to either compose an opera or else write a five-hundred-page novel."

"Hey. Come clean with me. What are you going to be doing besides missing me terribly every second of every day?"

"Well, I promised my dad I'd earn some money to help with college. I'll get some sort of a job, play some ball, and be thinking of you guys squatting behind a bush to relieve yourselves while I sip a beer in the sun and watch the Reds win the pennant."

"I'm sorry about the job for dollars thing. I really am."

"Please. I mean this. Don't ever feel sorry for me!"

An hour later Charlotte called again to tell me that she didn't like our earlier talk.

"That wasn't us," she said.

"I know. Don't worry about it," I told her.

"I want to do something different on Saturday night. Let's shake it up, just you and me, and have some fun. Nothing intellectual. Nothing too serious. Just some good old-fashioned fun."

When I told her it sounded swell but I had already committed to Ronnie, she surprised me. "That could be a blast. Why don't I go along? Deal me in. Besides, I'm good at blackjack and I'm super good luck."

Now another surprise. R. D. said he had wanted to meet Charlotte anyway and agreed to watch over her at the twenty-one table while I played poker. We would leave Rory's early and finish up at a beer garden Ronnie knew where we could talk and listen to music. It all sounded too good. I can't help it—I always worry when there are no clouds in the sky.

I made sure to tell R. D. and Charlotte about each other. Naturally they both belittled me for worrying about the evening. Charlotte opened with, "So you're the master of the universe that Rogers always talks about."

Ronnie shot back, "He warned me that you're special because you're the first girl who knew what a knuckleball was."

"Does he ever get that pitch over the plate?"

"Only if someone bets him five bucks that he can't do it."

"I've heard a lot about Rory's. And I'm anxious to see for myself and to break the bank."

Finally Ronnie came back with, "Rogers, I can already see what you mean." Charlotte, bless her, turned and flashed me that special smile she saves for when she is really happy.

Ronnie took charge of his two eager cohorts and ushered us into Rory's. Charlotte hugged my arm, leaned in to me, and whispered, "I feel like I'm in a movie and all these characters are actors. I've never been at a place like this. I'm tingling all over with excitement. Thank you for believing that I'd be fine here with you and Ronnie."

R. D. walked her around the floor and positioned her at the least grubby table. I found an opening for myself and prepared to play poker.

It was going to be one of those nights when I was on fire. I was pulling good cards, pressing when the odds were favorable, bluffing now and then to be unpredictable, and reading the table accurately. The other players were rather obvious, except for a cagey older woman wearing an absurd "I Love Niagara Falls" sweatshirt. I couldn't figure out why, but she kept winking at me.

Two players down on my right sat a pathetic case. He was a young factory worker still wearing the work shirt with his name, Everett, sewed onto his chest pocket. He was drinking heavily, J. T. S. Brown, sweating profusely and complaining that he was being dealt bad cards. He kept refusing to drop out of hands where he had no chance of winning. I found it difficult to sympathize with his predicament until I saw that he was cashing his weekly paycheck to play and that he was wearing a wedding band. As each hand was being dealt, he would look skyward, close his eyes, and inaudibly mumble some phrase. He was going to be the table's big loser.

I felt Ronnie and Charlotte standing behind me. Ronnie leaned over my shoulder and said we should leave soon. I nodded and then Charlotte quietly mouthed, "Holy shit, you're winning a fortune." I would only know later that it would soon be time for another life lesson.

I was dealt a clear, no doubt winning hand, and everyone at the table dropped out but Everett, who refused to fold. I tried eye contact to convince him to quit, but to no avail. Then to my shock, he tried to bluff me out. I couldn't help myself when I said, "You don't want to do that. Listen to me."

He took a huge pull on his bourbon and pushed his chips forward. Everyone there knew he was an irrational drunken idiot. When he lost I heard him plead to the heavenly Big Guy for forgiveness and then beg, "Make me even and I'll never gamble again."

I pocketed my winnings and stood to leave. Between the tables and the door, Charlotte spun me around. She was crying. "You can't take his money. He's a desperate person who needs help." I'd never seen her cry before. Her face was already red and swollen. Her eyes were intense and fierce and shined almost too brightly.

I looked over to Ronnie for support but got none. He didn't say a word. I had always believed that a bet was sacred and refusal to honor it was the same as cheating. Nevertheless I searched out Everett and pressed the money into his hand. I told him that his prayer was being answered and I hoped he would keep his word to never gamble again. I said it even though I knew he would be back at Rory's in the near future.

At the beer garden, R. D. and Charlotte were getting along well and talking it up. She was drinking iced tea while we were working cold steins. I was quietly pensive. I needed to make sense of the incident at Rory's. When the music ended, Ronnie said he had to get up early to take his sisters to church and said his goodbyes. "You guys are a good couple. I wasn't sure anyone could put up with this guy," he said to Charlotte. She smiled at him.

"He's okay in small doses."

In the car on the way home, Charlotte scooted next to me and pulled my arm around her. She rested her head on my shoulder. I was so comfortable that I wanted to drive to Cleveland and back. "Is that what we are—a couple?" she asked. I didn't want to answer that question. It was way too loaded with dynamite.

"Whatever we are, let's not ruin it with words" was all I could say.

The closer my departure date for Philadelphia got, the more nervous I became. Had I made a grand mistake applying to Penn in the first place? Should I have stayed closer to home, comfortable near my cozy cocoon and the city I knew so well? I even obsessed over simple issues: Where would I do my laundry, buy toothpaste, or cash checks? Most importantly I worried about how I would deal with being separated from my father for months at a time.

With only days remaining before I was due to board the train east, I pulled myself together and prepared to leave. I made sure to say proper goodbyes to the people who mattered most to me. I wrote Andrew Stevens, thanking him for the summer internship and his helpful advice. I also told him how much I appreciated his volunteering to write a letter of recommendation to the Wharton School at Penn. After leaving the letter on his desk, I headed downstairs to the trading department, where I felt like I was entering a mortuary. Most of the traders were reading the *Enquirer* sports section or gazing out the window at the river. It was so quiet that it appeared as if the market had already closed for the day. I guess tough markets have a way of taking the air out of a room.

Ronnie stepped out and slapped me on the back. There was so much I wanted to say to him that I had held in over the months, but before I could, Ronnie heard Jimbo calling for him and so motioned that he had to return to the battle.

"I want you to know . . ." I started to say, but he interrupted me.

"I'll see you at Grammer's over the holidays. If you haven't fumbled the ball with Charlotte, bring her along." He gave me a thumbs-up and, like the professional fighter he had become, turned to reenter the ring.

Charlotte wanted to meet at her favorite place in the city. I drove up the steep hill past the conservatory and entered Eden Park. She was sitting on a bench studying a barge working its way down the river. When she saw me coming, she stood and unleashed her hair, resulting in a spectacular chestnut-brown waterfall. I forced myself to breathe deeply. Neither one of us wanted to speculate on the future. There was no need for that. We believed in each other and knew that the future would be challenging, but exciting also. Before I could say anything she was in my arms. Her lips were soft and passionate, delivering a message straight from her heart.

I knew Dad so well that I was sure he would not want us to say anything to each other that resembled a goodbye. A few nights before D-Day, he calmly broached the subject. "You're ready, aren't you?" I nodded yes. "Let me see your hand." He held my right hand, turned it over palm down, and studied the scar that held a special meaning for us both.

When I was a little guy, my favorite baseball player was Vada Pinson. At first I was enamored with his name but, after watching him through his long career with the Reds, I learned to appreciate his speed and defensive prowess while playing center field. One Saturday afternoon he fouled off a pitch that landed in an aisle not far from where Dad and I were sitting. I jumped out of my seat and dived for the ball. A minor melee ensued. I was lying facedown protecting the ball when someone buried a cigar in my right hand. I screamed out but wouldn't let go of the ball. Dad rushed me to the burn unit at the hospital, with me still squeezing my prize.

He gently ran his fingers over the faded purple circle, pondering its significance, then looked up at me. "I should have known then," he said. I was taller than him now, so with some effort he reached up and kissed my forehead and repeated, "You'll be swell. You really are ready."

The day before the long trip to Philadelphia, I found myself standing alone in my father's bedroom. I wanted to take a last look at the pictures on his bureau and nightstand. I knew it would sadden me, but I felt the need to include my mother in my thoughts. When she and Dad eloped, he was a resident at the hospital, while she was working on a graduate degree in education. In the early pictures he stood erect, projecting optimism and confidence; she was a natural, serene and joyful, smiling as if at peace with her world. All that would change when she was attacked by a rare blood disease. My father had helped save countless patients, yet the one he cared for most died as he sat by her side, holding her hand. Her young son was but six years old.

I could barely remember my mom, so I counted on these pictures to tell me her story. How do you mourn a mother that you didn't really know? I pressed the photograph of her that I liked best against my chest. She was sitting on my father's lap, both arms around his neck. They sat forehead against forehead, smiling at each other. A baby rested in a bassinet next to them. The family was together.

APPRENTICING FOR THE BIG GAME

IT WAS HOT AND HUMID EVEN FOR PHILADELPHIA WHEN I arrived in early September for my senior year. My apartment was only a few blocks off campus on the second floor of a charming but run-down walk-up. After living in Penn's ancient dorms the last three years, I was eager for a change. The building was overrun with Penn students due to its modest room rates. Today I appreciated the antique air-conditioning unit clanking away but still doing its job. I chose this particular hovel because the one-room all-purpose living room–bedroom–study had high ceilings and abundant natural light and was only a five-minute walk to the library, classrooms, and, most importantly, the area's only authentic delicatessen.

I had not put much effort into decorating "Le Chateau," yet, in the end, it was quite comfortable. The centerpiece of my furniture ensemble was a beaten-up oversize brown leather recliner. It was surely tasteless but nevertheless amazingly welcoming. It probably occupied a quarter of the entire room. I expected my eastern friends to single it out as a testament to my midwestern roots, but I was proud of my seventy-five-dollar purchase from a secondhand dealer up on Market Street. I might be overstating my negotiating prowess, but I was convinced I had outdueled the old buzzard. The landlord lent me two large, funky bookcases that were oddly carved with pudgy cupids armed with bows and arrows. My other books, notebooks, and various accessories rested on a card table I had found in the basement. The bathroom was dark and cramped, but everything worked, so that was good enough for me. I was pleased with my new surroundings and felt ready for this year's games to begin.

Even though it was my fourth year at Penn, I had decided to arrive a few days early. I enjoyed wandering the halls of Dietrich, peering into vacant classrooms or sitting alone in grand auditoriums where professors lectured their eager flocks. I was like a visiting baseball player checking out a field to sense its atmosphere and peculiarities. I closed my eyes and remembered past classroom debates, usually civil but sometimes wonderfully raucous.

Every Whartonite knew that job recruiters emphasized class rank, so it wasn't surprising that the student body was exceptionally, and often ruthlessly, competitive. I had enjoyed the competition and refused to get rattled when challenged by a classmate or even a professor. Most of the better students could read the assigned materials and regurgitate the answers with little effort. The fun came when one of the school's finest went on the offensive. These were the types who were attracted to the smell of blood in the water. To me their frenzy was predictable and quite entertaining. My usual approach was to tantalize them with tasty bait, encouraging their confidence. Only when I was sure that I had them securely hooked did I launch a pointed counterattack. I really relished these moments. I viewed these encounters as a form of mental jujitsu, because I would use their aggression against them to win my point.

I could never claim to have a strong visual sense, nevertheless, as I strolled Penn's campus, I felt the overwhelming history of the place. I had visited my home city's art museum only once on a sixth-grade school day trip. To the best of my knowledge, my father had never purchased a painting or piece of sculpture. The only thing that hung on our walls were family photographs, a mirror here or there, and an antique clock my mother had inherited. It was my job to keep it wound and in perfect working order. I had virtually no space to hang anything in my apartment here other than a poster of the Reds championship team. It's embarrassing to say that I still had not visited the Rodin or the Philadelphia Museum of Art located downtown just ten minutes away. I had only had a mere three years to make the trip! But ambling along Locust and Spruce Streets and weaving the campus back and forth from Thirty-Third to Thirty-Eighth Streets was an undeniable treat. There were so many impressive buildings that held the campus together, and each one had an old-world character and individual architectural presence.

I knew myself well enough to know that when school began and the pressure cooker warmed up, my visual appreciation of the environment would rapidly diminish. I would forget admiring the dormitories first built all the way back in Ben Franklin's era, stately College Hall, the absolutely magnificent Furness Library, and even the dignified Penn Art Museum. I was on another mission. I would be all business, and that meant sucking out all the nectar that this education could offer me.

In the late afternoon's stifling heat, I heard a madman's cussing down the hall. He sounded extremely pissed off by the moving-in nightmare. I couldn't help but tune in to his choice of words and the way he strung them together. "Cocksucking, motherfucking, ball-breaking, nipple-pinching son of a bitch!" This guy's way with obscenity was clearly fresh and different. I had to meet him.

His door was wide open. I knocked and introduced myself, saying, "My grandmother wondered if you were an aspiring poet or just a recently released lunatic?"

He looked up at me and responded, "Are you offering help or just here for comic relief?" I still warmly remember that first meeting with Jacob Steiner, my soon-to-be great friend.

Over the course of the next few weeks I pieced together Jacob's story. He had grown up on the Upper West Side of Manhattan, a lazy walk from Lincoln Center. Both his parents were musicians who taught at the Juilliard School. His father was a pianist, his mother a violinist and a member of a well-respected string quartet. Their talent apparently bypassed Jacob and he grew up knowing he disappointed them. He tried to impress his parents with classroom excellence but could sense that high-performance classical music was their only measure of achievement. He competed in long-distance running events as an outlet from the pressure he felt at home. He loved to run, because he could turn his hyperactive brain off and let his body take over. He said he didn't feel anything when running other than a pure form of release. When he accepted an academic scholarship at New York University, his parents finally relented. He said he believed his relationship with them was improving with time. As I listened to his saga, I became even more impressed with my own father's ability to understand and encourage his son even if I chose a life path so different from his dream of creating another Dr. Stout.

Jacob had graduated from NYU with honors in economics and dived headfirst into the master's program at Wharton. He had worked every summer at a variety of jobs, saving most of his earnings and helping his parents fund his advanced degree. In one more year, armed with a Wharton degree in management, Jacob expected to begin his climb to the very top of a major American corporation.

I helped Jacob unload his ageless station wagon and resettle his apartment. He had sublet it for the summer, so his so-called furniture was already in place. He said he would unpack his clothes later if I would help carry in his records and stereo components. Like an idiot I agreed, not realizing that his guy was a music freak. By the time we trekked in virtually every opera ever recorded, copies of his mother's string quartet sessions, the complete compositions of Gustav Mahler, and, believe it or not, his personal collection of gospel music, I had sweated through my shirt and was exhausted. As I sat on the floor panting, Jacob proceeded to smile and then point at me. "You never should have come down the hall." He was short and wiry with dark hair and dark brown eyes. Everything about him sent off sparks of intensity. When he bellowed out a laugh, I couldn't resist wanting to get to know him better.

Jacob had no problem talking about himself or the issues he faced at home. He knew where he came from and was brutally analytical when weighing the pluses and minuses of the hand he was dealt. He felt on track with his game plan and was highly confident that he would reach the finish line. While I prided myself on being a good listener, I didn't like talking about either myself or my family. I could tell he sensed this, and I was grateful when he didn't press me for details. I was reminded of a day, while walking in Sharon Woods back home, when I'd come close to telling Charlotte everything I held so dear. But even with her I couldn't help but pull back. Bless her, she understood how hard it was for me. She had taken my hand in hers and just kept walking along.

After a quick shower, we were headed down South Street in Jacob's Ford wagon. He insisted on treating me to dinner after all the heavy lifting was finally over. He knew his way around South Philly and claimed to be an expert on Italian restaurants. A few blocks off the main drag, we parked in front of a place called Tony and Carmela's. We bypassed the sidewalk tables where couples were sipping wine and sharing intimacies. Jacob wanted to sit in the air-conditioned Naples room. There were no restaurants like this in my hometown. Wood floors, candles burning in old wine bottles, garish chandeliers, and framed prints of the important churches of Naples gave T&C's its form of local color.

Jacob was a carbo fan. "I burn like a furnace from nervous energy and long-distance running. I need to refuel constantly."

I said, "Where I come from, Italian food only means spaghetti and meatballs. I had never heard of fettuccini or manicotti before I came east to school."

Jacob followed up, "I always carbed up before a race in high school. Now I do it before a big test or even an important interview."

"Don't laugh, but before baseball games I always ate peanut butter and grape jelly sandwiches on rye bread. It actually got to the point where I believed in their powers," I confessed.

"Holy shit! PB&J. I'm going to have to be the one who orders here."

Jacob flashed a smile at our elderly waitress, whose name, Rosey, was pinned to her uniform. He ordered in a miserable Italian accent that made her frown. "Well, I tried," he said.

It was only when our waitress placed the focaccia and olive oil on our table that I noticed the business cards stuck under the glass tabletop. "Look at these," I almost shouted.

Jacob added, "Great idea, don't you think?"

"Maybe we should introduce Wharton's marketing professors to this concept of advertising," I suggested. And then we started, inspired by the cards.

"Let's get a buzz at Sal's hair salon and barbershop."

"I think I'll get my toilet repaired at Vito's and Assoc. Plumbing Specialists."

"Joe Racci Exterminator. Down here in Little Italy, what the hell does that mean?"

His appreciation of sick humor was as warped as mine. We went on and on for ten minutes, laughing uncontrollably, until Jacob won the first-place prize with "Oh my God, catch this one. South Street Crematorium and Family Funeral Home. Call Big Al."

Later, after polishing off five thousand calories each, we took turns describing the paths we'd traveled so far and where we wanted to be the following year after school. I wasn't used to this kind of conversation, but it all flowed easily with Jacob. He felt he was ready to build something important right now, and that this last year at Wharton was only a formality. I wanted to understand why he was so exceptionally confident. His answer was simple: "I just am. I don't want to study other people's successes anymore. I want to start yesterday to build a Jacob Steiner success."

Everything about Jacob was so urgent that I was tempted to think of him as one of those religious fanatics you see standing on a street corner preaching about talking directly to God.

My goals were no less ambitious, but I had no desire to build anything, nor did I want to manage a throng of employees, as was implicit in Jacob's career goals. I knew I would have little patience for committees or for regularly scheduled meetings. I had decided that one of the benefits of the financial world was the anonymity of buyers and sellers in public markets. It wasn't like poker, in which you were directly confronting your opponent for the spoils of the game. Here there was no face-to-face contact. No verbal interchange. Just buyers' and sellers' orders meeting at a neutral venue to trade positions. I liked the idea of this impersonal code of commerce.

I believed I had learned a lot since my summer at Prescott & Prescott a few years ago. I regularly read the newspapers and periodicals, followed the markets closely, faithfully maintained my paper journal, and slowly, slowly graduated to trading a few stocks with a broker who was a close friend of Ronnie Davis at P&P. I had yet to figure out if I was investing or gambling, but either way it sure was exhilarating.

The Sunday before Penn would open for business, I put on comfortable shoes and planned a day's walk. I thought I was a history buff, but for my three years at school, my world was limited to West Philadelphia between Pine and Chestnut and the blocks within Thirtieth and Fortieth Streets. It was time for me to visit downtown Philly and its historic landmarks. I bought a tourist map from a street vendor for a dollar, hopped on a bus, and headed east to experience the city by beginning on Front Street at the Delaware River. Then, after paying homage to the Liberty Bell and a few well-known Founding Fathers' homes, I just wandered about, lingering here and there absorbing the atmosphere, until I came upon an old cemetery.

I've always liked cemeteries, because they tell provocative stories without revealing definitive answers. For a brief while, I sat on a bench and let my imagination take over. Then I gobbled a slice of pizza on the run and, following the advice of Andrew Stevens, found myself many blocks away from Independence Square, climbing the stairs to the Philadelphia Museum of Art. I have a poor sense of direction, so it didn't take me long to get lost in the Early American Paintings wing. It didn't work for me. I must be a boor, because staring at portraits of sullen old men with preposterous beards and women wrapped in kerchiefs whose expressions denoted gas pains just didn't impress me. I tried hitching up with a guided tour by hovering around the edges of a group of serious art lovers, but that didn't prove interesting to me, either. So, after a quick look at a few of the museum's most famous paintings, I called it a day and headed back to home base. So much for being a tourist.

So there I was, beginning my last college year with a new place to live and a new friend living just down the hallway. Three short years earlier, I had arrived in Philadelphia fresh-faced, naive, but ready for the challenge ahead of me. I missed everything I cherished about home during the first few weeks of my freshman year. I missed the hills, local haunts, even the box scores of the Reds' games. And for sure the feeling of being so very comfortable in an environment I had known all of my life. I had never been away from my father for an extended period of time. I kept a picture of us on my nightstand, the one where he was hugging me on my tenth birthday. I vividly remember him announcing to the world that I was now a double digit. He looked proud and I was smiling. And then there was Charlotte. What had we become? Where were we headed? Would it all work out as she had envisioned? "Rogers, don't overanalyze everything. We're both like eagles in flight. When we're supposed to land, we will."

During the first two years at Penn, I was required to take 40 percent of my classes in the liberal arts program in the college. Fortunately I wasn't forced to study Latin or organic chemistry, so I enjoyed most of the classes and, therefore, performed well. The core Wharton curriculum represented the remaining 60 percent of my course load. Whether I was taking courses on economics, finance, statistics, or management, it all seemed to me as if I was studying a subject I already knew. At times I felt as if I was

floating down a river in an inner tube on a beautiful day, propelled by a
gentle current. I heard my fellow students grumble and complain. I kept
to myself and I kept quiet. This didn't gain me any friends, but I wasn't
there to star in a popularity contest.

Recalling the urging of Andrew Stevens, I focused considerable attention on understanding the concepts and rules of accounting, which were
taught during my freshman year. He assured me that I would need these
skills in the future if I selected a career in corporate finance or investments. Dogmatic accounting wasn't really interesting to me. I couldn't
get excited by just allocating expenses or differentiating between assets
and liabilities or building models for income, balance sheet, or cash flow
statements. But I was challenged and fascinated by the tricks one could
play with these statements. I particularly liked playing accounting detective—as, for example, what was included in goodwill, deferred expenses,
amortizations, and depreciation. And then there were the tales that footnotes could reveal—as in off-balance-sheet assets and liabilities, contingent exposures, and dilution, just to name a few. What did all this mean
and how was it being used or abused? Now this did capture my attention.
I was beginning to comprehend why good ol' Andrew Stevens stressed
that a solid foundation in accounting was necessary to succeed in the Wall
Street game. I had no desire to be an accountant, but I did want to grasp
the craft.

In my sophomore year, I was mesmerized by a sociology course I had
selected only by chance. The professor, Dr. Whittles by name, was sort of
an outlaw who created a syllabus meant to encourage debate and debunk
preconceptions. He was a character of the first order. He always seemed
to be a few minutes late for class, arriving with a flourish, as if he had
been lost. He'd sit at his desk and slowly look around the room, making
sure to establish eye contact with each student. His first words usually
were "Okay, my friends, let's tussle." He then would ask the class if there
were any questions we needed to deal with before we forged onward. He
didn't recite prepared lectures, nor did he read from published articles or
books. He didn't even carry a briefcase. He would glance down at scribbled notes he had handwritten on a yellow legal pad and then state a
premise or introduce a theory or just ask the class a question. For the next
ninety minutes, we would offer opinions, argue, ask questions, and listen

to him provoke the group. He would suggest that the class might want to read certain articles or journals or books. He rarely offered his own view, even when the controversy rose to a fever pitch. His goal was to make his flock think for themselves.

Each week was different. Sometimes he would pick up where we left off the week before. He would say he wasn't satisfied. On those occasions he would seek to peel the onion back more and more, stopping only when nerves were so raw that the classroom became unruly. Sometimes he would jump shift to an entirely new subject, then reverse course and relate those issues to prior discussions we'd had. But he could just as easily let past classes fade, never to be revisited. He was so totally unpredictable that some students were baffled, left wondering what we were supposed to be learning. I, on the other hand, couldn't wait for his class to begin each week. I devoured everything he suggested we read and surprised myself by being an outspoken, active voice in his classroom.

In the student course book, Dr. Whittles had described his class as "Discussions and study of the individual's relationship to the group, and the group's relationship to the individual." How wide-open was that? I needed another liberal arts credit, so I had signed up. I figured that if I didn't like the first class session, I could transfer to another. But I was hooked after hearing his introductory comments. He made fun of his name by promising us he would "whittle away," he would "shape and reshape," he would "fashion and refashion," and gradually he would "chip away" at our collective conventional beliefs. How would the good professor accomplish that? He wanted us to read as much as possible and would be suggesting various materials over the course of the year. He also would be judging us on our classroom participation. "Don't worry, my faithfuls," he said, "I will know who's with us and who isn't."

It took most of us some time to get into the flow of his class. There was little doubt that we were dealing with a complex mind. He could be distant at times, even aloof, but minutes later he would be concerned that his students were lost or off track. "Come on now. Think this through. Is that really the way 'they' would act? Maybe 'they' would react the opposite. No? Yes?" I was impressed that even though he was always stirring up the pot, he also was encouraging and respectful of his students. By the time I was officially hooked on Dr. Whittles, I knew I would be prepared for his classes and throw him my very best pitches. His class turned out to be the highlight of my sophomore year.

One Friday afternoon before Christmas break, I climbed the stairs to the top floor of College Hall. Whittles's office door was ajar, so I knocked and peeked in simultaneously. Surrounded by open books, he was bent over his desk writing. His office was cluttered with books and papers piled on the floor and on top of every available filing cabinet. The overhead lights were turned off and the windows were wide-open, because he believed natural light was easier on the eyes and fresh air helped to sustain life. I didn't have an appointment.

"Mr. Stout, are you lost?" Professor Whittle inquired.

"Probably, sir," I said. "I usually am. It's one of my most endearing qualities."

"Well, it's good to see you. Is there something you need to talk to me about?"

"Sir, I'm not an apple polisher or a you-know-what kisser, but the more I sit in your classroom and observe the dynamics at work, I keep thinking there is more to the course you are teaching than the individual to the group and vice versa."

"Really? I'm all ears."

I continued, "I've played poker for years. I started playing against my father, then with high school friends, and then graduated to playing against real people for real money in gambling halls in Kentucky. I learned that counting cards and playing percentages is for beginners. To differentiate yourself from the pack requires a keen sense of psychology. You need to have the ability to reasonably predict human behavior."

"Where are we headed, Mr. Stout?"

"Reading your suggested material and listening to the back-and-forth in class makes me want to know more about how pressure from a group can affect an individual's decision making."

"How will that improve your poker playing?"

"It won't, because poker is essentially a one-on-one game. I want to transmit the skills one needs to succeed in poker to investing in the financial markets."

"I'm listening."

"My theory is that studying markets at an academic level, even at a prestigious university, is analogous to learning to play poker by reading books on the subject. I'm not discounting the value of that approach, but it just isn't enough. It's only the science. The art part is in predicting when and how an individual will react. I wonder if understanding how group thinking influences an individual's actions is a helpful addition to the predictive process."

"You've thought this up all by your lonesome self?"

"I never said my little brain was normal."

"What can I do to help?" he said in an encouraging tone.

"I was hoping you would suggest some relevant reading materials that could help me explore this theory of mine. I'll have some spare time over the holidays to dig in."

A few days later, I stopped by the professor's office to pick up my holiday reading. The maestro was once again bent over, concentrating on his writing.

"Excuse me, sir. I just came by to pick up the reading you suggested."

"Mr. Stout, join me for a minute. I'm in need of a break."

His offer surprised me. As I sat down, I couldn't help but feel my pulse quicken and my nerves rattle a bit.

"My crystal ball tells me that you are a Wharton student about to major in finance."

"Is your crystal ball always accurate?" I said.

"Only when it already knows the answer," he laughed.

"Yes, sir, that is my current game plan."

"Would you share with me why you are so ready to commit to a career path? You're obviously a bright, inquisitive young man. Why not give yourself more time to explore the universe?"

I had an answer ready. "I hope this doesn't sound egotistical, but in my mind I'm only dedicating myself to the financial markets long enough to achieve independence."

"Explain, please."

"I don't want my life choices to be determined by monetary needs. To achieve that goal, I'll have to first earn my way to financial security. I'm hoping that success on Wall Street will take me there."

"Why Wall Street?"

I answered, "I believe Wall Street is a real meritocracy. If I prove to be talented and excel, then I should be compensated accordingly. No one will care what I look like, where I come from, how old I am, or about any of my personal beliefs. In today's world that's rather unique. I like that."

The professor interjected, "There have to be other opportunities that consider similar criteria."

"Maybe, but whatever skills I may have seem to be suited for the Wall Street jungle."

"So you really thought this out and you appear to be determined. All right, let's say you succeed and you're only thirty-five or forty years old. Then what?"

"It won't surprise you if I say that I truly don't know. What I probably would do is take a long, cold shower, close my eyes, and say thank you."

Professor Whittles ended the conversation. "If you'd like to stop by in the spring, we could continue our little chat," he said as he returned to his writing.

I hitched a ride home for the holidays with a senior who wanted company on the long drive. Once we exited the Pennsylvania Turnpike and eased our way into West Virginia, the weather turned ugly. We climbed high, bypassing Wheeling, and then kept going through a series of depressing coal mining towns, on slippery roads covered with a thin layer of icy snow. Over the border in Lancaster, Ohio, we briefly stopped to fortify ourselves with greasy cheeseburgers and coffee. The weather report indicated more snow on the way, so we plowed on through the night and entered the homeland just before dawn.

I slipped a note under Dad's door informing him that his beloved son was safely home and that I'd meet him in the kitchen for breakfast. I made the coffee, rested my weary head on the nearby table, and dozed off. I was awakened by a man wearing slippers and an ancient terry-cloth bathrobe who immediately wanted to know *everything* about my last few months at school. Then he gave me a warm hug and, as usual, messed up my unruly hair. He flashed an ear-to-ear smile and asked, "How's my favorite son?" I was exhausted and he was expected for an early-morning consultation at the hospital, so we talked only briefly, hugged again, and went to our rooms. Then he dressed and headed off to his office and I climbed in bed.

I slept soundly until early afternoon, showered, and ate a peanut butter and jelly on rye. It was sure good to be home, and even better because Dad had stopped at Karl's and bought my favorite—a German rye with thick, salted crust. I wolfed down a second sandwich with a glass of iced tea and thought out my options. With Charlotte not due back for another day and Ronnie having told me on the phone that he was so busy he couldn't even leave his desk to hit the head, I got in my car and let it drive me on a homecoming tour. I cruised by my old school and walked the empty halls. I couldn't resist visiting the library and sneaking into the history stacks, where, in my sophomore year, I first experienced the utter bliss of touching a girl's breasts. In truth the anticipation was better than the five-second feel. It was cold and windy outside, but I still jogged the baseball field, full of memories of both joy and disappointment.

I drove up and down my favorite hills, along the now almost clean Ohio River, dodged the downtown traffic, and ended up, but where else, at Eden Park. I wrapped a scarf tightly around my neck, buttoned up my coat, and sat on the bench where I had said goodbye to Charlotte before we both headed off to college. Now we both were enjoying and doing well at school. We wrote each other weekly letters meant to be descriptive and entertaining. Mine were informative yet often serious and most probably pontificating. Hers were more as if we were lying on a blanket staring at the stars talking together and she was telling me an intimate story. I couldn't wait to grab hold of her, to spin her around while cheek to cheek so that her glorious wild mane flowed around us both.

I had scheduled a late-afternoon meeting with John Sawyer, the broker who R. D. thought should handle my account. He was a classmate of Ronnie's at Xavier and now a stockbroker at Prescott & Prescott. R. D. chose him for me because he would follow instructions and never, "even on the rack," tell anyone about my account or the trades I was making. John revered Ronnie because of his storied athletic career and important position in the firm's trading department. My account would definitely be modest, but he promised to treat it as if he was dealing with J. Paul Getty.

A few days before I left for my freshman year, I had opened a margin account at P&P with Sawyer and, after consulting with R. D., deposited half of all my poker winnings. It was such a significant move for me that I can still remember the day I signed all the papers. It was on a Wednesday, the first week of September 1973. I waited patiently for a sweet pitch.

It didn't take too long. I called Ronnie after war broke out between Israel and a coalition of Arab states in early October. We agreed that this was yet another negative for the market. So with interest rates rising, the economy apparently looking fragile, and the potential of some kind of energy crisis upon us, we decided to explore shorting a few market-sensitive stocks. It felt like a pitch might be coming right down the middle of the plate. I took a few deep breaths and began to bet against the market. It must have been beginner's luck, because I started to really profit as the market swooned about 10 percent. Then, on October 19, a number of oil-exporting Middle Eastern nations announced they were cutting off oil shipments to the US. I sensed a further opportunity and, like the shark that I was becoming, I pressed my bet, invested the rest of my savings, and shorted more and more. John Sawyer must have thought I was the second coming of Jesse Livermore, because I stayed short with most of my positions until I was about to return to school the following September. By then the market had dropped about 30 percent and my basket of shorts had declined even more.

The markets had delivered a punishing blow to investors both large and small, yet a majority of indicators still pointed to more pain ahead. Pundits, who only a year ago were advocating aggressive investing, were now predicting a continuation of the "death spiral." I had been arguing with myself for weeks over whether I should cash in my chips by covering my shorts. Ronnie was reluctant to offer an opinion: "The tape has cancer, Rogers. I don't know when it will bottom. No one does. I'm just trading 'em here." When I initially went short, both my brain and stomach were in sync. That was why I felt confident during this short-selling escapade. But as I was preparing to return to school for my sophomore year, my gambler's instinct took over. I had made a grand amount of money. Much more than I expected or deserved. While it was true that I had no fundamental reason to believe the market was at a bottom, there also weren't any new inputs that would have made me incrementally negative. In retrospect my gut decision to leave the party was simple. I vividly remembered prior mistakes I had made playing poker when I wasn't disciplined enough to walk away from the table. I had made enough. It was time to get in my car and drive home.

After the dust settled and all my positions were covered, Ronnie and I got drunk together at Grammer's. He had pushed Jimbo to do some shorting also and was due a sweet bonus. We went from giddy to ecstatic to silly as the evening wore on. We weren't sure if we had been lucky or smart. As we were leaving, I promised Ronnie I would follow his advice and sit on my hands for a while.

After all this had happened, it was obvious that my broker was trying to impress me when he suggested we meet at a conference room at P&P that he had reserved. I knew it would be well appointed with dark wood paneling and rich carpets. There would be elegantly framed prints of English rural scenes and discreet lighting. He would offer me a choice of sparkling or still water as we sat at a table more appropriate for a board meeting of a Fortune 500 company. Instead I asked him to meet me downstairs at a quiet table in a restaurant near the office. I patiently gave him the requisite ten minutes to kiss my fanny as he praised my timely market call and superb stock selection. His well-rehearsed speechifying continued painfully as he reminded me that almost all stock market investors "got destroyed in this correction." The meeting had almost ended when he asked me three questions: "How did you do it? How did you see it coming? It took a lot of guts. How did you sleep at night with all that pressure?"

If John Sawyer hadn't been recommended to me by Ronnie Davis, I would have ended our little talk before he even posed the third question. But it would be hard to find a broker who would follow orders from a nineteen-year-old neophyte and not blab about his trading to every living human being in town. I knew I could rely on R. D. to better clarify what P&P would call our broker/client relationship. Sawyer was an okay guy, I just felt awkward as the beneficiary of his oozing charm. He could be my trusted broker. He didn't have to be a trusted friend.

After I had covered my short position in early September, the market continued to decline until it ultimately bottomed a month later, down an additional 10 to 15 percent. Sawyer reminded me that I had been in all cash since I covered my shorts. I had learned the hard way to control my emotions at Rory's, so I refused to let the oink in me surface even though virtually every day I couldn't help but mentally calculate how much money I had left on the table. Sawyer asked me when I was planning on shorting the "bullshit year-end rally" we were experiencing. I didn't tell him that I had been talking with Ronnie about reversing course and betting on a market upturn.

The market had been going south for almost two years and the negativity was monumental. The average stock had dropped well more than 50 percent, and even some pristine stocks like Coca-Cola had fallen 70 percent. I read somewhere that stocks were yielding more than bonds. Did that make sense, I wondered? I had been out of the market for three months and was itching to return. I wasn't sure if it was my brain or my gut talking to me. Ronnie thought I might be too early. He advised, "Don't be a wise guy, Rogers. You don't have to be cute." I remembered the many impetuous mistakes I made learning to play poker and that oftentimes the hardest thing to do was to do nothing. I wondered if that theory also applied to financial markets. Complicating my decision making was that I knew I didn't have the knowledge or the resources to select individual stocks for a rally. Ronnie instead suggested a basket of mutual funds, because "those yahoos are always 100 percent invested, so you're bound to participate if you're right and the market turns around."

"What if I'm wrong and I want to sell?" I asked.

"Don't worry, you can redeem your shares with only one day's notice," he answered. With all this going through my head, I thanked Sawyer for the coffee and headed home. I needed to do some serious, dispassionate thinking.

I met Dad at his club for dinner. He was in a feisty mood and even insisted on introducing his "Ivy League son" to everyone but the busboys. "This must be my new, outgoing social father," I teased. "Are you planning to run for club president?"

It seemed as if it had been a very long time since we had enjoyed a quiet dinner together. We both knew that these times were important and we had to make sure to share them whenever possible. Dad said he had let himself get drawn into a major budgetary issue by the chief of staff of the hospital. He bemoaned this waste of his time but felt he had to stand up for the interests of his department. When I asked him a question or two, he immediately changed course. "Don't concern yourself with that nonsense. Let's hear about you and school." I assured him all was well on the Philadelphia front, but he needed details.

I wanted to avoid the perfunctory business school interrogation scenario, so I told Dad about my interest in Dr. Whittles's class and the course I was taking on great American authors of the twentieth century. He dove headfirst into the dynamics of the individual and the group. He wanted to know everything about Whittles, including his background and where he could access the books and articles he had written. He asked to see a list of the required reading for the course. He saved his most penetrating questions for my description of how Dr. Whittles conducted the class itself.

"You're telling me that there is no required reading. That there are apparently no tests, no papers, no prepared presentations demanded of the class. How can he grade you?"

"He constantly mentions suggested readings," I answered. "They may be articles, journals, published lectures, or books. He commands your attention in class and has a remarkable way of encouraging his students to speak up."

"Is that all?" Dad pressured me.

"Dad, you have to sit in his class to appreciate how stimulating the conversations are. He's always questioning the class. He makes you defend any premise or position that you state. He calls it stirring the pot! I leave his class mentally exhausted."

"Do you agree with his conclusions?"

"He doesn't definitively state his own position. He wants us to search out our own answers."

"But in the end he has to give each student a grade."

"We all worry about that. He says to trust him, he will know what we deserve."

"I'd like to meet this man," Dad finally said.

As we were finishing dinner, I could tell Dad was tiring. It was hard for me to accept that with each year he would get older. He didn't like talking about his age or the inevitability of his having to pace himself and work fewer hours. He was proud and defiant and almost stern with me if I ever questioned his aura of invincibility. As we drove home, I wondered if even he knew how much I relied on his support and inner strength.

Later on, I was reading in bed when Charlotte called.

"I'll give you three guesses who just got home tonight, and the first two don't count."

"Let me think for a second. My first guess is Lady Dracula. My second is Madame Defarge. My third is the ravishingly beautiful, remarkably brilliant, and prodigiously talented . . . oh, what's her name—I can't seem to remember."

"Wow. Once a wiseass always a wiseass!"

"So you finally made it back. When can I see you?"

"Where else but Sugar n' Spice? How about breakfast tomorrow at eight? I need a fix of their famous french toast."

"Sounds good."

"I'm expecting a welcome like I just returned from coming down the Amazon River."

The next morning I drove north on Reading Road in record time, hung a left just before Huber's gas station, and parked in the lot behind the restaurant. Charlotte was standing next to her car in a heavy cardigan sweater and wrapped in a plaid scarf. When she saw me, she started to run in place while clapping her hands as if urging me to hurry over to her. I had this primeval urge to consume her. We hugged and kissed as if we hadn't seen each other for years. When we entered Sugar n' Spice, the waitresses smiled at us. "My husband's just back from a space mission," Charlotte explained. We sat down and ordered french toast for two.

Sugar n' Spice was a local institution situated at the bottom of a hill flooded with small, early-twentieth-century houses and on a busy north-south road. It was open all day, serving both loyal hilltop families and the traffic going to and from the city. Xavier University was only ten minutes away. Charlotte loved breakfast and favored Sugar n' Spice because it was "a genuine food- and service-first joint." She was just as happy sitting on a counter stool joshing with a waitress as sharing a booth covered in a hideous imitation red leather. After she ordered a breakfast fit for a lumberjack, she would fiddle with the jukebox and sacrifice a dime to hear the Drifters or the Shirelles sing their hits. She was in heaven.

"There's so much to talk about," she said. "You first."

It didn't take me too long to recap life since September. I told her I attended classes, studied, camped out in the library, ate in local dives, went to an occasional movie, played poker with aloof rich preppies, followed the stock market, and thought about my dad and ached for her. I told her about Dr. Whittles and how much I enjoyed the challenge of his class. She interrupted me with an enthusiastic "That's my guy!" She was taking a similar English course so we compared views on Faulkner and Hemingway. She didn't want to argue, so we agreed to disagree on the latter. "What about your Wharton courses?" she asked. I told her I had to plow through a rigid core curriculum that I found quite tedious—marketing, insurance, management—before I could dig into the stuff that really interested me. "How do you do so well when you don't like the subject matter?" she inquired.

"Because I have to. It's as simple as that," I answered.

Charlotte flashed an earnest look. "Since when did you become so determined?"

Then it was her turn. She lived with three other girls in a high-rise on the edge of campus. It was cold and impersonal but convenient. She was taking a broad array of classes and working hard. "I think I'm doing well," she said. "My adviser told me I'm actually on track for some type of honors. This place is supercompetitive; I hope I don't burn out." She was impressed by her teachers and the diversity and caliber of the student body. I wasn't surprised when she told me that she liked a lot of her classmates but was really friendly with only a few. "My closest buddy is my roommate Ruth. She's a hearty soul from Minnesota. Smart, energetic, inquisitive, and fun, too. I think you would like her—she knows a lot about baseball."

"How about life in New York?" I asked. "Is that an advantage or not? Has it played out the way you hoped it would?"

"I'm at least a half hour from the museums and theaters. The art galleries and the younger scene is even farther downtown. I can't afford the nifty bars and restaurants. I don't care about the stores, and they're ridiculously expensive."

"That's all disappointing," I agreed.

"It's extremely frustrating. Everything is so close yet so far away. It's like having a huge bowl of your favorite Graeter's ice cream on a table just inches beyond your reach."

"If it were their butter pecan, I'd go nuts," I offered.

Charlotte and I knew we were destined to be intermittently separated for almost four years. Before leaving for college, we had sealed a pact to avoid probing questions on each other's personal lives while we were away at school. We both knew that could only be destructive.

"Are you still happy that you went to Columbia?"

She rallied: "Of course I am, Grandpa. I just wish that New York played a bigger role in my life there." She looked at her watch and then proceeded to paint me into a tight corner. "Will you come with me? My grandma Rose is deteriorating, and I need to visit her. She's at Hilltop House in Pleasant Ridge. It'll be a half hour at most. I promise." I wanted to spend more time with Charlotte, so I succumbed.

I was willing to bet even money that most everyone I knew had an aunt or grandmother named Rose. Charlotte had a special relationship with her Rose. She had lived at Hilltop House for the last year or so. It had been a nursing home in an old mansion in Walnut Hills but had now been reincarnated as an assisted-living facility farther north of the city. I followed Charlotte as she drove out Montgomery Road to the new Hilltop. From earlier visits she knew the nurses' names and the directions to the dementia wing.

"How's Rose doing, Anna?" she asked the nurse at the reception desk.

"About the same, in and out," came the answer. I followed Charlotte down the hallways like a well-trained dog. I had virtually no experience with dementia and wasn't looking forward to this visit.

"Just be yourself," Charlotte said. "Speak slowly when you talk to her and be willing to do whatever she asks."

I hadn't expected yet another life lesson when I left home to meet Charlotte for breakfast. But after witnessing Grandma Rose's dignity in the face of her slow decline, I understood why so much effort was being focused on conquering this cruel disease. I felt absolutely helpless. Charlotte was brave and cried only afterward on the way to her car. What stayed with me was when Grandma Rose challenged me to a few hands of blackjack. She handed me the cards and giggled, "I've heard you're a gambler. I was too in my day." She looked over at Charlotte. "Don't tell your mother or I'll get in trouble." She was 100 percent coherent while we played. She knew the rules and played a good game, taking cards with sixteen or lower unless I showed a weak card and staying pat with seventeen or over. When she won a hand, she laughed and reminded me, "I told you I was good." Five minutes later she didn't even know her granddaughter's name.

In the parking lot, holding Charlotte, I whispered, "You are a warrior."

The next day, John Sawyer called to tell me that Ronnie was going to be playing basketball with some old Xavier teammates in an exhibition game to benefit a local charity. Charlotte jumped at my offer to join us to watch the game. "I'm in," she said enthusiastically and then asked if Rachel could come along.

I couldn't avoid Sawyer, who had arrived early and saved some midcourt seats. He salivated when he met Rachel, who was sporting her new "I'm an Antioch artist" look. She wore a black knit top that was two sizes too small, leaving little to the imagination. With her black hair pulled back tightly in a bun and her lips painted dark red, she was one sexy artist.

We stood and gave R. D. a raucous welcome when he was introduced. He returned our cheers with an embarrassed grin and a weak wave. The game started with Ronnie's team looking lethargic and disorganized. "What's wrong with them?" Charlotte asked. "They look old and slow."

For the rest of the half, Ronnie passed to his teammates and tried to encourage them to hustle. Charlotte was getting more and more agitated. The fact that she knew virtually nothing about basketball didn't stop her from alternating between cheering and criticism. Whenever Ronnie made a basket or stole the ball, she would poke me in the side and squeal, "Here we go!" At halftime Ronnie's team was down by ten points.

Sawyer was content to flirt with Rachel, who appeared to be enjoying the attention. I leaned over and whispered to Charlotte, "What an odd couple they would make—a securities salesman and an underground artist. What do you think?"

"I think Ronnie better get off his rear and start scoring some baskets to win this game," she said while slugging me not too gently on the shoulder.

The second half was all vintage Ronnie Davis. He was everything I had read about in the *Enquirer*. He was fluid, moving effortlessly past defenders and scoring at will. When they double-teamed him, he would either pass to an open man or abruptly stop and swish a jump shot. His entire attitude had changed. Even during time-outs he looked serious, almost menacing. With one minute left in the game and a twelve-point lead, Ronnie finally loosened up and smiled to the crowd that awarded him a standing ovation. Sawyer leaned over. "Can you believe that guy?"

From the peanut gallery came a response from Charlotte—"I knew it all along. Good ol' Ronnie."

As Charlotte wrapped herself in her winter coat preparing to leave, I kissed her on the cheek and told her, "You never told me you were such a basketball authority!"

I was to meet Ronnie after the game and his coronation. He suggested I wait for him in the chapel because I might find inspiration there. "Do you think it could help me time the market?" I asked.

"Only if you swear celibacy," he laughed. I told the comedian I'd meet him outside the locker room.

Waiting for R. D. in the hallway, I reflected on an encounter I had had a day or so earlier. On a whim I had stopped in a Merrill Lynch office boasting a seating area for customers to watch the market as it streamed across a large viewing screen. I sat in a comfortable chair surrounded by men older than my father, who were "studying the tape" and simultaneously chatting with anyone who would listen. They looked at me as if I were either lost or deranged. The audience was divided between the loners and small clusters of men who seemed to know each other. I overheard them claim that "the tape was talking," just as the traders at P&P would cry out to each other. It might have been talking to them, but it sure as hell wasn't communicating with me. I noticed that a few of those sitting alone were taking notes and calling their brokers to place orders. You could read the tension in their faces and in their body language. I wanted to know what was influencing their decision making. Could it actually just be the ticker tape? How could they consistently win at this game by just watching numbers fly by on a screen? I imagined them sitting in the same chairs day after day, believing that they were professional investors when they probably were just chronic gamblers who were unfortunately destined to lose.

After a couple of hours, I gathered my stuff together to leave when the man I had secretly nicknamed Leader of the Pack walked over and sat next to me. He was a kindly looking grandfather type, dressed in an old tweed sport coat and a gray sleeveless sweater. He wore a starched white shirt buttoned all the way to the top. He leaned over to talk to me as if our conversation was going to be intimate.

"My name is Saul Stone, but everyone here just calls me Saul," he began. "I haven't seen you here before. Are you a player or just curious?"

"I'm a college student fascinated by the market," I whispered.

"Have you ever bought a stock?"

"Every once in a while."

"Let me give you good advice from someone who's seen it all. I was working for a New York firm during the Big One. This downer is only a sell-off versus what I saw in '29 and the early '30s. You don't see people jumping out of windows, do you? This is only a pimple on a horse's ass. You understand? See all these old codgers in this room? They all want me to hold their hands, to help them get through this mess. You want to know why? Because I'm a survivor."

"I appreciate your kindness to me, a total stranger," I said, attempting to camouflage my sarcasm. But then my curiosity took over, "So what's your view here? Should we buy, sell, or hold what we already own? I'm all ears."

"I'll tell you what. Why don't you join me and my guys for some corned beef at Izzy's? You'll learn more than at that college of yours."

"That would be an honor, sir," I replied.

By most measures the stock market had bottomed in early October. It rallied thereafter, but December 1974 was still a harsh month fraught with crosscurrents that were difficult to analyze. It was on one of those tricky days that my new friend Saul Stone led his followers like a Pied Piper down the block to Izzy's. Waitresses were on duty from eleven to two on weekdays, so our group of seven crowded around a circular table and ordered the house specialty—corned beef, pastrami, and coleslaw on rye. "Don't forget the pickles and mustard!" someone called out. When one fellow broke with the crowd and ordered turkey, he got roundly booed. Most of them drank seltzer. They glared at me when I asked for a root beer. After a few minutes of small talk, they turned in unison for advice from the leader.

"Saul, what do we do here? I looked between my legs this morning and couldn't find my balls," one of the guys stated.

As if conveying an act of benevolence, Saul smiled, nodded, and the sermon from the mount began.

"Okay, gents. Yes, we're still in a bear market. I told you all to sell out this past summer. So we were a little late. Don't worry. We'll make back our losses by shorting this market. This recent rally is a joke. I'm selling 'em right now, right here."

"But Saul, the market's already down a ton. What if you're wrong and we go up from here?" one of the group meekly asked.

Saul lectured him, "You didn't want to sell out this summer. Remember? But you listened to me and it saved your bony ass. I'm telling you, this country is going down the toilet and stocks will follow."

A short, frail-looking man with a neatly trimmed beard said he was afraid to short. "There's no limit to your loss if you're wrong, Saul," he implored.

"Why would they rally from here, Ben?" Saul said confidently. "Interest rates are high, the economy's for shit, oil's going to the moon because of those Arab pricks, and the president is a schmuck."

As the sandwiches reached the table, it was clear that the leader of the pack was on a roll and capable of intimidating his cronies. But the more Saul bullied the group with his smug exaggerated confidence, and the more I witnessed their blind submission, the more I wanted to load up on stocks. *Remember Dr. Whittles's class*, I thought. *Remember how group thinking under stressful conditions can influence an otherwise independent individual to follow along.* Saul wasn't telling the group anything that hadn't been worked over and over by the press for months. Was it already discounted by the market? Would the situation appear better or worse in the next few months? Those were the questions I was pondering when one of the crew asked Saul, "Who's your new friend?" as he pointed to me.

Before I left Izzy's, I explained to the gang of six that I was a college kid wanting to learn about the financial markets. I was a neophyte who really appreciated their insights and help. They invited me to return to learn even more. No one asked my opinion on the market. The truth was that I had been thinking virtually every day about a possible market turn since I had covered my short position. The more I considered the magnitude of the two-year bear market and the depressed investor sentiment, the more I felt there was a good chance of, at least, a reflex rally. The major stumbling block was the economic backdrop, which was murky at best. If one were reading the *Wall Street Journal* they probably would want to move into a bomb shelter. I was so obsessed with psyching out the market's volatility that I had been calling R. D. twice a day for his opinion. Ronnie's feeling was that we might be close to a turn, but he wouldn't chance it yet. "You don't have to, Rogers. Be patient. Keep it in your pants."

Back at the gym, my reflective mood was over. I stood and applauded Ronnie Davis as he lumbered down the hall. He said every muscle in his body was asking why he pushed them so hard. He figured he would ache for a week. I told him that he was superb and basically won the game single-handed. Then I shared Charlotte's analysis with him: "Why does he pass so often? He should just take the ball down the court and shoot. They can't stop him!"

He laughed. "She's a pistol. That one is surely one of a kind."

Ronnie needed a beer, so we went to a Xavier hangout where we could talk quietly at a table in the back. That was when I told him about Saul and his followers at Merrill Lynch. I didn't want to jump to any conclusion, but I thought it might be a significant sign.

"That doesn't surprise me, but what does it prove?" he challenged.

"I understand that it's a big leap, but I'd bet you that those guys are typical of the majority of today's investors. They've lost a lot of money. They're crapping in their pants. I'm hearing this fear everywhere, especially in the papers and in the TV news. I can't read the ticker tape like you, but I can feel this. I'm thinking the market is oversold."

He said, "I agree that the bad news is out there. Tell me, what's going to change it?"

"I don't know. But what if the market just starts to go up? Couldn't that behavior convince people that the black clouds are lifting? If that were to happen, it could feed on itself and just keep going up. People will then be desperate to recoup their losses," I speculated.

"Let me guess then. Fear becomes greed?"

"Not initially, but it could be one hell of a rally that I won't want to miss."

"You've got the disease real bad, don't you?" R. D. sounded critical.

"This is a big decision for me. I know my account is small, but I've built it from scratch. All the hours I've worked. All my good fortune at gambling. And with your help, I scored during the sell-off. I watch over every dollar like it's the last drop of water in the desert. But to reach my goal, I have to take risk. This may not be the fattest pitch I've ever seen, but I think it's probably hittable."

"What about corporate earnings and interest rates and all that good stuff? And why now? You could have said the same things you're saying now months ago and gotten murdered!"

I cut to the chase. "Ronnie, what do you think, should I start buying?"

"I'm not there yet. I've covered our shorts but haven't gone long yet."

I finished with, "Tell me I can count on Sawyer if I start to buy and then head off to Philadelphia."

By the time I got home, my nervous system was out of whack and my heart was pounding. For the first time in my life I actually had built up a tidy pile of investable chips, maybe not enough to impress Saul Stone, but enough to permit me to sit at the table and play a few hands. I started feeling like a two-headed monster. I was afraid of losing, but I was also afraid of missing out on an opportunity. My rational side respected the fundamental uncertainties, while my emotional side sensed a potential rally. It was time for yet another life lesson. It was time to look in the mirror and muster the courage to rely on myself. It would be a lonely decision, but I made it. The next morning I called Sawyer and started to buy.

Dad couldn't resist needling me as he watched his son don a coat and tie for a New Year's dinner with Charlotte. "Is that the way a proper Ivy League gentleman dresses for dinner? Do you want me to help pick out a tie? You're not wearing cologne, are you?" He was sitting on a chair in my bedroom with his legs crossed and his hands clasped behind his head, thoroughly enjoying himself. I missed these lighthearted times when he was relaxed and not preoccupied with the pressures of his practice.

"Where are you going for dinner with the girl who is only a friend?" he asked.

"The Golden Lamb in Lebanon."

"Seems like you're trying to impress your 'only a friend.'"

"I just thought it would be different."

"Different and almost an hour drive from here!" I acknowledged that I had no comeback for this retort, so I said goodbye and went on my way.

The Golden Lamb had a rich history. Built in 1815, it was the oldest hotel-inn in Ohio and claimed to have been visited by Presidents John Quincy Adams, Ulysses S. Grant, and William Howard Taft, as well as Charles Dickens and Mark Twain. It was located on an old highway between Cincinnati and Columbus and well-known as an upscale restaurant and for its authentic colonial atmosphere. I had actually read about it in an obscure American history book. I had reserved a table in a quiet room next to the inn's charming tavern.

Charlotte grilled me like an experienced district attorney most of the way up to Lebanon. She hadn't heard of the inn and wanted to know its history and about the famous people who had dined or lodged there. "What a wonderful surprise."

She smiled. Her great brown mane was pinned up and secured by a bizarre serpentine silver comb. She wore no makeup except for a subtle touch of lipstick. Her only jewelry was an antique moonstone ring given to her by Grandma Rose, and delicate dangling pearl earrings. I had never before seen her dressed like a seductress in a James Bond movie. When I looked at her walking to my car in a slinky navy-blue dress, I felt faint. Ever since puberty I was an oversexed degenerate who couldn't resist mentally undressing any attractive female within sight.

Charlotte looked ravishing tonight, but I successfully buried my carnal thoughts and instead blurted out, "Wow, you look stunning!"

Her gray eyes sparkled. "You've never said anything like that to me before."

When the waiter arrived, Charlotte didn't hesitate. "It's our anniversary. I'll have a glass of champagne, please." I'd never had champagne but was convinced to join her anyway. It was typical Charlotte, urging me to try something new. "Come on, you'll learn to love it." One of the traits I liked best about her was the lady's immense appetite for life and the way she approached most everything with enthusiasm and a positive attitude. I watched as she sat alert to everything around her. She was studying the other guests and the room's colonial decorations: worn area carpets on wide-planked pine floors, faded chintz wall coverings and vintage paintings of village greens. She liked the way the tables were strategically placed to ensure private conversations. Charlotte whispered "perfect" when the waiter lit the two small candles on our table. She scanned the room again and concluded that "this place is the real deal. It's authentic. It even smells right. Mucho thanks for this New Year's treat."

I was enjoying everything about the evening. We had so little time alone that we both were anxious to make every precious opportunity count. The formality of the restaurant seemed to encourage us to share our more private sides. But no matter what we were discussing, I couldn't help feeling that she was a magnet pulling me deeper and deeper into her vortex. She had recently taken to holding my hands, drawing me closer to her, and staring directly into my eyes when she spoke or asked a question that mattered to her. The fact was that I couldn't deal with the intensity of those eyes that looked as if they belonged to a member of the feline family. They could sparkle when she laughed, darken when she was sad, or flash a brilliant light when she was serious or inquisitive.

The waiter brought warm corn bread with our appetizers. I was so wired that I could have demolished the entire bread basket. Charlotte closed her eyes when she sampled her shrimp cocktail. The impressive presentation of the house specialty, rack of lamb, silenced us when it arrived. Charlotte was most definitely an eater; she didn't nibble at her food like a small bird, rather she consumed with a flourish every morsel on her plate. We agreed that the food was even better than advertised. As we sat back sipping our champagne and sighing with contentment, Charlotte pointed to an elderly couple across the room smiling at each other and toasting with their wineglasses. "Aren't they wonderful? Still in love after fifty years. It can happen, you know."

We bypassed dessert even though the waiter raved about the restaurant's berry cobbler. Charlotte ordered mint tea, folded her hands, then leaned forward and continued.

"Rogers, it's a huge gift to be in love. It's also a blessing to love what you're doing day in and day out."

I had been fantasizing about getting a room upstairs. It didn't have to involve sex. I would have been happy just to lie next to her and feel her falling asleep on my shoulder.

"Wait a second," I said, back from my daydream. "What makes you think I disagree?"

"It's just that everything seems to come so easily for you. You win at cards, you win at school. You know where you want to go and what you want to become. Do you realize how fortunate you are?"

"Haven't you ever heard that it's a long way from cup to lip?"

"Listen, kiddo. I don't know how or when, but you're going to achieve your goals."

I shot back an objection. "Just for the record, my journey hasn't been without potholes."

"But you're focused now, and that brain of yours will take you to wherever you want to go. My problem is that there are so many valid causes and problems in the world I would like to have an impact on that my head is spinning. I need to be passionate about what I am doing and I want to achieve something of value, but I'm having trouble concentrating. I don't know which road to travel."

"Would it help if we talk about the issues that concern you the most, the ones that keep you up at night?"

She thought for a moment. "How much time do we have?"

"You've got my full attention. Let it fly!"

It was the first time I had heard Charlotte confused. Having seen her reaction to the fate of the drunken gambler at Rory's and to the deterioration of Grandma Rose at Hilltop House, I wasn't surprised that she would be sympathetic to any and all of the world's injustices. I listened carefully and asked a few questions I hoped would keep her on target. She said she wanted to be "a giver, definitely not a taker" and was weighing a commitment to social causes or political change, and, like me, she also felt pressure from her father to consider a career in medicine. "There are too many ways for me to go. There's pros and cons to every alternative I can think of." She needed to vent. By the time she had finished her second cup of tea, she was back. "Sorry, but I had to get that out of my system. I'll work this out, it's just going to be tougher than I thought."

On the way to the car, she suddenly stopped and hugged me with all her might.

"What am I going to do? I think I'm falling in love."

"What? By now you must know I'm a borderline lunatic."

"Hey! I'm getting serious here."

"Is it the champagne?"

"I said I'm getting serious."

We had planned to attend a party with old high school friends, but dinner ran overtime so we drove to Charlotte's instead. On the way back, Charlotte was napping with her head resting against me when I suddenly felt a deep ache and longing for the only other woman ever to talk to me of love. My memory sharpened, and as the clouds lifted, my mother was gently rubbing my back and neck while singing softly to me. It was past my bedtime, and I was having trouble sleeping. She whispered, "All is well with us. As long as we are together, there's nothing to fear. We are in a safe place." Her lips were so close to my ear that I could feel her breath. I closed my eyes and prepared to sleep, knowing that she understood me. She told me she loved me and kissed me goodnight. Then I looked at Charlotte right next to me. I couldn't help thinking that they would have been a very special pair.

Charlotte's parents had gone to bed early. "Boy, are they bons vivants," said their devoted daughter. It was approaching the magic hour when she took my hand. Before I knew it, we were slow dancing to her favorite '50s music. Neither of us spoke. I could feel every inch of her as she melted into me. "Well, it's been one heck of a New Year's," she whispered into my neck. The whole experience had overwhelmed me. I closed my eyes and vowed to whoever might be listening that I would not fuck this one up.

Back in Philadelphia during a cold and dreary January, I was expecting school as usual during my second semester. The only change in my course load was a required finance class entitled Money and Banking. Ol' Andrew Stevens had told me that I would find this subject matter challenging but I should "dig in and develop a good grasp of this stuff. You'll need to understand how the Federal Reserve system works, what factors influence interest rate movements, and the tough part—all about international money flows." At that time I had no idea what he was talking about.

I entered the lecture hall at 9:00 a.m. the appointed day with some trepidation. Professor Townsend was a new addition to the Wharton faculty, from the London School of Economics. He wasn't physically imposing, but his voice sure was. He spoke in a clipped, precise upper-crust manner with a booming baritone timbre. Why the Federal Reserve was created way back in 1913, plus how it functioned to regulate the flow and cost of bank credit and money, was new territory for me and my classmates. We were not familiar with bank reserves or money supply, much less Federal Reserve open market operations, Reserve Bank discount rates, and reserve requirements. These were new terms for us. What did they mean? What was their significance in today's world? I could sense the classroom's collective groan as week after week Dr. Townsend plowed ahead at a rapid pace, never repeating or summarizing the material during his lectures. It proved to be difficult to keep up with him. The entire class was intimidated. No one in the hall had the nerve to raise a hand to ask a question. After an hour he would gather his notes, placing them neatly in a black leather briefcase, turn his back on the class, and exit the hall as if he'd just finished an important speech at the House of Lords. At 10:01, the hundred or so students could be seen shuffling about, heads down, fear and confusion painted all over their faces.

Townsend's lectures were so meticulously organized and practiced that they reminded me of a well-oiled machine. They were long on facts but short on description. The rumor was that Dr. Townsend had expected to be a lead lecturer in the school's master's program and would not have to stoop to teaching lowly undergraduates who didn't even know that the Federal Reserve was located in Washington. It was clear that he knew his subject well, but he didn't seem to care if the students were digesting the material or not. Fortunately the class met with an instructor twice a week for an hour in small groups to discuss the reading assignments and to review our aloof professor's lectures.

From the beginning most of the class felt lost. A common refrain was "I need help putting this all together." The instructor was a sympathetic PhD candidate whose patience was being tested by the barrage of questions fired at him by fearful students used to achieving academic excellence but who were now at sea without a compass. He would look out at the group of lost souls and deliver his favorite reply: "No one ever said this was going to be easy!"

Once the class understood why the Federal Reserve was formed, what its mandate was, and how it functioned, then slowly, slowly, the course's message became clear. While our professor was not a favorite of mine, the course material was interesting and I really started to enjoy myself. Later in the year, some lectures got my attention, such as when Dr. Townsend detailed how the Fed operated in the open market by both buying and selling US government securities. I imagined the power rush its traders had as they executed mammoth orders affecting the country's entire supply of bank credit and money supply. I would have loved to be in the trading room of the New York Fed watching and listening to their Jimbo Burns executing the game plan. There were days when I would lounge at my desk after a lecture and think of Andrews Stevens and his advice— "This is important stuff."

Years later, after I had battled turbulent markets that had been dramatically influenced by changes in Federal Reserve policy, I would think of Townsend's Money and Banking course with more respect. It sure as hell wasn't pleasurable, but it did prepare me for future hand-to-hand combat. I had come to realize that as much as students want to like a professor, such feelings were not a prerequisite for effective teaching. College professors don't have to be warm and fuzzy or outwardly entertaining, I discovered. If they can stimulate students to attack new ground vital to future understanding of a subject matter, if they can drag them through the labyrinth of a complex topic and come out of that maze on sure footing, then their charges will have earned their knowledge the hard way. So when Dr. Townsend dived back into the deep, dark waters of changes in reserve requirements, how member banks borrow from the Fed at the discount rate, and how all the monetary instruments can work together in a coordinated action to implement Fed policy, I knew I had to focus my little brain. If I had to study longer hours, read extra materials, or impose on our instructor for extra help, then I would do it because I knew it would be important to me in the future to understand "this stuff."

Driving to school for my junior year with a few other hayseeds, as the eastern privileged ones called us, my thoughts were of those I was leaving. Saying goodbye to Charlotte was never easy, but I was getting used to the drama. We would be walking along and one of us would reach out and grasp the other's hand. The physical part would be more passionate and intense. There would be less joking and longer, more serious conversations about goals and dreams that Charlotte dubbed "the forever time." New York was only an hour and a half from Philly, but at times that felt halfway across the country. On our last night together, she didn't tear up as usual when she told me, "I believe in us. This separation thing is good for us. It makes us stronger." I didn't buy into that thought! I didn't need to suffer bouts of loneliness to make me stronger. I'd been alone far too much of my life. I didn't want separation. I yearned for together.

Saying goodbye to Dad was an entirely different proposition. Now that he had accepted the fact that his son was destined to enter the big, bad world of business, we were spending our time together like the good old days—long, lazy walks, an occasional Reds game when someone interesting was pitching, Friday dinners, and wonderful wide-ranging conversations. I had no doubt that he was interested in every aspect of my life. I wanted to share it all with him, going back to my poker experiences in Kentucky, my more recent stock market adventures, and my feelings for Charlotte—but I didn't do it. I still don't know why I didn't pull the trigger. I often think about my reasons but, in truth, I don't have a satisfactory answer. Dad was pretty much an open book with me, though, as long as I didn't inquire about his social life. After all the years, his sorrow had never diminished. As I was actually packing to leave, he sat quietly in a chair beside my desk while we talked about the courses I would soon be taking. I felt a shot to my solar plexus when I watched the muscles in his face tighten as he studied the picture of my mother resting on my nightstand.

I had spent a lot of time that summer concentrating on my growing stock portfolio. Sawyer was adequate, maybe even a bit competent, but I used him only for executing orders and gathering information that I needed when I was on the trail of a new idea. Through Prescott & Prescott he had access to materials from Standard & Poor's, Value Line, and numerous brokerage firms. If Ronnie suggested I look at a stock or if I dreamed up an idea, I would contact Sawyer and he would forward me a research package. Throughout the year I kept dollar averaging into the five mutual funds we had selected. I didn't want to try to time the market. I liked the idea of buying a fixed amount of exposure every week and building up my positions over time.

The strategy was working. The market was soaring and my funds were fully participating. To me it was similar to playing poker except the numbers were grander. My investment philosophy was simple—I should win as long as I didn't lose. In the old Newport days, my risk tolerance in poker was the twenty dollars housed in my back pants pocket. If I was winning, I kept pressing ahead until I lost a few hands. Then I'd stop to reassess my position. I would either quit or bank at least half my profits and play awhile longer. I would keep playing until I either was too tired to think clearly or if I started to give back some of my winnings. I would never reach in my pocket to disturb my original bankroll or my earned profits. Sometimes I would have a gut feeling that I was too fortunate and I had made enough. I'd be hesitant to leave the party, but I had learned to respect that gut feeling and the "enough's enough" theory. I had maintained my long position in the stock market for about a year. It was working well so, much like my poker philosophy, I pressed on and continued to gradually increase my exposure. My stomach didn't dare disagree.

When I talked to Ronnie Davis during market hours that summer, I could feel the tension through the phone. He was abrupt and talking so fast that he often slurred his words. Every other sentence was punctuated by him yelling directions to subordinate traders. "Take the goddammed offer! What's offered now? If it's ten thousand or more, then take it and bid for ten thousand more!" He may have been a team player on the basketball court, but on the trading desk he reminded me of a drill sergeant directing his recruits.

I'd learned that the best time to talk with Ronnie was after the market closed on Fridays. I'd said my other goodbyes. Now it was R. D.'s turn.

"Well, I'm off to Ivy Land, big guy. Goodbye to Grammer's and Mecklenburg's."

"Good for you. I'm watching your account. By the way—congratulations."

"There's probably a lot of luck involved."

"Sawyer says you're really working at this."

"He's forgetting how helpful you've been. Any further advice before I leave for Philly for year number three?"

"Yes. Get yourself in better physical shape. You'll be better able to deal with the stress. You won't always win in this game. All you're doing is reading and studying and pining for Charlotte. Work out or play some intramural hoops or something else that physically tires you out. It'll help, and you won't look like the guy on the beach who gets sand kicked in his face."

"The Charles Atlas ads, right?"

"Bingo."

Finally exiting the Pennsylvania Turnpike early that September, we sped past Valley Forge, respectfully saluted George Washington's memory, and headed down the expressway toward the Penn campus. We soon came to my favorite Philadelphia scene, the fifteen boathouses at least a hundred years old, on the east bank of the Schuylkill River. These historic landmark buildings comprise what locals call Boathouse Row. Watching the scullers gracefully take on the currents was a surefire antidote for high blood pressure or the anxiety of final exams.

Penn was traditionally a rowing powerhouse. I can still remember at freshman orientation when the revered varsity crew coach requested that any able-bodied young man with a strong will who was at least six feet tall report to Weightman Hall for an interview. I stood in the back of the room as he described the school's crew program. I couldn't imagine committing to self-torture virtually every day, to row in a race that lasted only a few minutes.

So I was back in west Philly—two years finished, two more to go. My new room in the upper quad was sterile but surprisingly large. Unpacking and preparing for the new year, I experienced the same tightness in my gut that I did when standing on the pitching mound before a crucial game. I knew the trick was to be confident, but it wasn't always so easy. This was destined to be an important year for me. The Wharton courses I had taken so far were only warm-ups for the main event. I would be studying advanced accounting and security analysis. I needed to do well in both if I wanted to pass go and head directly to Wall Street. I also chose as an elective a political science course on the Middle East taught by a respected professor. Considering the military conflicts, the formation of OPEC, and the US dependence on foreign oil, I sensed this course could help me in the future. Classes started in a few days. I needed to meet with Dr. Whittles first.

By good chance I found the knowledgeable one sitting on his usual bench outside College Hall. He looked to be deep in thought and oblivious to the human traffic on Locust Walk. It was early September, still warm and humid, yet the professor was wearing a wool blazer and knit tie. I approached him gingerly, waiting for him to look up and acknowledge my presence.

"Ah. Good day, Mr. Stout. I trust you had a pleasant and profitable summer."

"It was a wonderful break for sure, but I did miss the drama of your class."

"Well, you certainly were an integral part of that theater. I see you're returning the suggested reading. I'll be interested to hear if it proved to be helpful. Did you, as they say, break the bank during your vacation?"

I could never tell if he was teasing me, jousting with me or being serious. When it came to Dr. Whittles, I was often confused. I could tell he had taken an interest in me. He never said anything specific, but I thought it was obvious. I couldn't help feeling honored, but I didn't know where this relationship was going. I was a young student intent on sucking the best from his prodigious brain. Was I a project for him? Did he actually enjoy my company? So I kept going.

"I read them all and learned something from each. Mackay's and De la Vega's writings in particular were enlightening," I answered. "Actually, I couldn't put *Extraordinary Popular Delusions and the Madness of Crowds* down. I read and reread it over a long weekend."

"Permit me to guess. You liked their tall tales because you think in some way they confirm the theory you are enamored with."

"It's right there in the introduction to the book—'confusions and delusions never cease to befuddle and beguile.'"

Dr. Whittles stood and we headed over to his office at College Hall. He asked if I was free and would I like to join him on his afternoon walk-about. I carefully placed the borrowed books on his desk while he removed his jacket and tie and changed into more comfortable shoes. I had no idea what to expect next.

I had to bite my lower lip when I saw him wearing a faded Phillies baseball cap. He carefully rolled up his shirtsleeves, exposing pale, thin forearms. We took the shortcut around the Houston Hall patio, filled with students socializing and relaxing before the start of the school year, then headed down Spruce Street. We soon veered to the right and entered the peaceful world of the Museum of Archaeology and Anthropology. I waited in the grand lobby while he walked upstairs to run a quick errand. I assumed that I could now claim to have visited the museum. That would please my father.

We crossed the street and approached our ultimate destination, the massive Franklin Field football stadium. It was eerily quiet inside the venerable building that once housed a Penn team viewed by many as a national champion. Old-timers still tell stories of a Franklin Field filled with over sixty thousand enthusiastic fans cheering the Red and Blue. But after the formation of the Ivy League in 1954, sports took a further back seat to academics, and the stadium's crowd count often shrank to well under ten thousand. We were here to hike the track around the football field eight times to satisfy the professor's two-mile exercise routine.

"Can't you feel the ghosts of yesteryear staring at you when you're in the stadium and it's as empty as today," Dr. Whittle mused.

"I feel more like a little boy playing in a huge sandbox. This place is cavernous!" I said, looking up at the seats rimming the top of the stadium.

"I like being here out of season when the silence almost shouts at you," he said as we began walking at a leisurely pace. Then he added, "Anything you want to say about your new friend Mackay?"

I was thinking how bizarre it was to be spending an afternoon walking in circles in a gigantic empty sports theater, discussing a provocative subject with this extraordinary man. I looked over at him, walking slightly hunched over, his arms swinging back and forth, managing to maintain a healthy pace while talking in a soft voice befitting an intimate conversation at an English men's club. I knew I was taking a risk when I told him that I was disappointed that Mackay's book only focused on manias that drove prices ever higher to absurd levels. The Mississippi scheme, the South Sea bubble, and tulip mania were all spectacular examples of human hysteria and mass irrationality. The price levels achieved in each case vaulted greed to unprecedented levels. I told him that I enjoyed reading about these bubbles and, while each was surely entertaining, I felt Mackay should have also included a chapter or two about historic panics that ultimately created great value opportunities. I also thought it would have been appropriate for him to tackle the differences between greed and fear. The euphoria about tulips in 1636 Holland was a totally different psychological phenomenon from the fright and depression felt by millions of Americans from 1929 to the mid-1930s.

I thought I saw an approving nod from Dr. Whittles as we continued to walk. He wasn't testing or playing with me. He wasn't trying to corner me or make me question myself and lose confidence. We weren't in his classroom. We were just walking side by side and enjoying a good talk on a lovely September afternoon. A few minutes went by and then he turned and looked over at me.

"You seem to be as curious about the conditions that make for fear and despair as for avarice and gluttony."

"I plead guilty." And then as we walked on, I continued to explain my thinking on the subject.

There had been many spectacular cases of stocks, bonds, or commodities that were driven to unrealistic heights. Throughout history it had been difficult for even the best investors to determine what level was too high. Was a stock selling at fifty times earnings too high? Why not go eighty times—it's probably only a bit sillier! And then there's the example of the price of gold. True goldniks fervently believe it has an intrinsic safety value. Their Four Horsemen of the Apocalypse are war, inflation, deflation, and systemic financial meltdowns. But as a commodity, gold doesn't pay a dividend nor generate free cash flow. Should it sell for more than a price set by supply and demand for its industrial uses and jewelry consumption? Yet when gold moves into high gear and one or more of the Four Horsemen materializes, then the price can soar to almost any height. These kinds of speculative gyrations create public interest. People already on the bandwagon can make big gains, while those on the sidelines are envious, so when it ends badly, there's tasty bait for the press. With the benefit of hindsight, these bubbles always look predictable. But the timing and levels attained are not predictable. It's exciting to read about incredible ups and downs where, in the end, most participants look foolish. On the other hand, when a panic sets in, everyone is drowning in the same soup. Conditions are so awful that it seems they cannot possibly improve. The negative sentiment is overwhelming and most everyone believes there is no way out. I was surprised that I could only find sparse written material about historic financial crises. I wondered if this was because speculative fantasy is rousing, while gloom and doom is depressing. I also wondered why more wasn't written about the few survivors who saw a bottom occurring and had the intellect and courage to take advantage of the opportunity.

"So yes," I told him, hoping I didn't sound irrational, "it absolutely fascinates me, and I wish I knew even more."

We had completed the first mile, and he was maintaining his steady pace. I was so revved up that I could feel my heart rate accelerating. I had to calm down if I wanted to think clearly. Had I been yakking too much? Did he think I made sense? I wanted to change the subject and ask him about his career and how he chose to specialize in the relationships between individuals and groups. Did he ever consider becoming a lawyer or doctor? Did he ever want to practice psychology and work directly with patients? Did he always want to be a college professor? I didn't have the nerve to ask him a personal question that day. Years later I would regret my timidity. I had grown to like and respect him so much that I wished he would forever be a part of my life. What a wonderful gift it would be the have the opportunity to talk with him whenever I wanted or needed to.

I could tell he wasn't going to comment on Mackay's or de la Vega's research nor on my judgmental sermon. We were halfway through the second mile of our walk and he was relaxed, apparently focused on a

Penn football player practicing punts. Two steps forward and then a booming kick that traveled almost fifty yards, sailing lazily across the autumn sky. He seemed to be locked in on the trajectory of the kicks.

I asked him for an example of an everyday situation he might pose to an incoming freshman class. "Here's one I recently thought of," he said. "Have you ever traveled on an unfamiliar country highway when it was time to stop for lunch? You were hungry and had to make a choice between restaurants. There was a cluster of four restaurants on the roadside. One was crowded and the other three were almost empty. Which one did you choose and why? I would guess that most people would choose the busy restaurant on the assumption that the other diners knew something good about the place, even though they probably would get superior service at one of the empty restaurants."

"Group influence on an uninformed mind?"

"Yes. A simple example, not as dramatic as a nation embracing the economic value of a flower over real property or a seasoned business, but one that new students will understand."

After we finished our walk, Dr. Whittles looked at his watch and excused himself. "I'm a bit late for a departmental meeting." Then, to my surprise, he shook my hand. It had been an afternoon with an extraordinary man that I would never forget.

Looking back to the time I was a senior, I can remember gabbing with Jacob Steiner one night while on a study break about our different experiences during our junior years. He had been a laser beam focused on grades and class rank. "I had to be," he said, "if I wanted to go on to a business school like Wharton directly from college." He inflicted more pressure on himself than anyone I had ever known. "I thought if I excelled academically that would obviate the need to work for three or four years before applying to graduate school. I didn't want to be a bullshit grunt at Morgan Stanley or Price Waterhouse and waste those years of my life." He knew the junior year was the important year by which graduate admissions departments would measure him. So he treated it like marine basic training at Parris Island.

When I would listen to a confident Jacob's definition of success, I thought I must be of a different breed. I knew there was a whole lot more I needed to learn, much less master, to give me a chance to execute my game plan for the future. Jacob of course believed he was ready yesterday. I was always anticipating some pernicious evil creeping up behind me. I wanted to be as prepared as possible for whatever lurked in the dark. While Jacob treated his education as medicine he had to take to survive and then move on, I actually enjoyed the learning process and found the challenge exhilarating. All that mattered to Jacob was the end result. By his definition whoever had the most chips at the end of the evening won the game. Period. But you could win at poker just by being dealt the best cards. To me that's called luck. I respected the challenge of winning with mediocre or even poor cards. That demands guile and skill and, to me, in the end, is more rewarding. At least that's what I thought back then. Yet I enjoyed these talks with the character down the hall. He was an independent thinker. He cared. He made me question myself. He was a high-energy, entertaining friend. Sitting now in my favorite chair, I close my eyes and remember it all. My junior year was going to be a doozy. I would be gorging at one hell of a smorgasbord.

I arrived a few minutes early and sat patiently in an aisle seat in Dietrich Hall's largest auditorium. I was anticipating the grand entrance of Wharton's star finance professor. A first-generation American born to Scottish immigrants, Bates MacNeer grew up on a working farm on the outskirts of Wilmington, Delaware. At the age of sixteen, he checked out of high school and signed on to the crew of a merchant marine vessel to see the world.

Five years later, a broad-shouldered, brawny adventurer, he tired of life on the water and the empty pockets that went with being a young man frequenting ports of call. A friend helped him obtain an entry-level job on Wall Street. Within a few short months, he knew he belonged in that Darwinian world. The stock market was booming, but he was a penniless clerk who seethed at his inability to participate in the orgy. When the market crashed in 1929, and then continued to crush investors in the early

1930s, he was a fortunate survivor. MacNeer had become a student of other people's mistakes. He observed traders being sold out of the market due to margin calls while others refused even to consider buying any stock at any price. Months later, as the market was approaching its ultimate bottom after all the years of tumult, he noticed that certain stocks had acquired a surprising resiliency, seemingly determined not to fall any farther. He thought there was a decent chance the stock market was finally washed out. With his modest savings intact, he summoned the courage to begin to trade. From the beginning he had the gift. The more he made, the more confident he was to accelerate his newly found aggressive investing style. It wasn't too many years before he was rumored to have the largest testicles south of Fulton Street. His success at ferreting out investable situations and riding them to the stars soon became legendary, but he knew his special talent was knowing when to signal thank you very much and bid a fond farewell.

Bates MacNeer made his fortune in a mere twenty years and then one day surprised all who knew him by declaring, "It's time for a change." He said he needed a new challenge. In his mind the thrill was proving he could succeed on his own with no family connections and virtually no formal education. The financial rewards from his investing were secondary to the rush of the big win. Richer than he ever dreamed possible, he then chose to travel a new path that included a radical U-turn when he applied to the Wharton School, located a mere thirty miles northeast of his family homestead. The admissions office is said to have argued his case late into the night, but eventually he was accepted. Five years later he graduated from the master's program with high honors. Shortly thereafter he became the school's first dollar-a-year lecturer. By 1965 he was Dr. Bates MacNeer, tenured professor of finance and voted by the students as the school's best teacher.

Professor MacNeer's lectures were typically standing-room-only affairs. Still fit in his late sixties, he presented a dignified appearance, sporting a short-cropped salt-and-pepper beard and dressed in a three-piece suit. Standing behind a lectern, he projected vigor and rugged independence. His moods were known to change radically without warning, from humor to benevolence to impatience to determined seriousness and back. It wasn't surprising that the students never tired of regaling each other with Bates MacNeer stories. Most were apocryphal or at the very least exaggerated, centering on his South Seas adventures or financial triumphs. He was respected because he beat the Wall Street boys at their own game. He was beloved because he truly cared about teaching and his students.

The hall turned apprehensive as the class sensed the MacNeer entrance. He took the steps two at a time up to the stage. His knuckles whitened as he grasped the lectern. I wouldn't have been surprised if it had crumbled into sawdust. He carefully studied his audience, slowly scanning the room from left to right, freezing the class with anticipation. When he looked my way, I felt the heat of his eyes bearing down on me, demanding my attention. He spoke with a husky voice, enunciating every syllable of every word as if each one had a special meaning.

"I requested that each of you whiz kids respond to a questionnaire before we met today. It's a little tradition of mine. I'm interested: Do you know what it means to be a security analyst? Have you ever bought or sold a stock? What do you expect to learn in this class? Are you planning a career in the investment industry? Your responses, as always, were provocative. Most of you have never traded a stock, have only a vague idea of what a security analyst actually does, eagerly look forward to learning, and expect a desk on Wall Street with a clear view of the Statue of Liberty, and here I quote, 'in a few years.' Now for a few comments from your professor. It seems that some of you didn't fill out the questionnaire. I guess I am to assume you were protesting an invasion of your privacy. Or could it be that you were just lazy or too obstinate. Well, this is how I see it. It's just bad manners. Here's some free advice from a seasoned rebel. Save your protest for something important!"

I had been looking forward to this class all summer. The lecture hall was so quiet I could almost hear myself breathe. MacNeer had spoken for no more than a few minutes, yet had already commanded the room's attention. And then, as if he were wearing a top hat, red tailcoat, and waving a baton while introducing a Ringling Bros. circus act, he began: "Ladies and gentlemen and children of all ages, welcome to Finance 100—Security Analysis."

For the next hour, Dr. MacNeer explained how the class would be taught and what would be expected of each student. He would lecture in the main hall once a week on a general topic. We would listen intently. We would then meet twice a week for classes with an assistant professor to dissect these topics, leaning heavily on Graham and Dodd's "masterpiece," the "bible of security analysis," he called it, and selected papers that he himself had delivered over the years. Early in the second semester, we would be analyzing companies on our own and presenting conclusions to the class for constructive criticism. In late spring each student would prepare a significant report on a selected company detailing thorough analysis of its income and cash-flow statements, balance sheet, footnotes, specific company dynamics, a snapshot projection of its future, and an attempt to determine the company's equity valuation. There would, of course, be midterm and final examinations.

He surveyed the blank faces staring at him. He'd seen them at the beginning of every class he taught at Wharton. It was time for his reassurance speech. "When this class is over, you will have taken a solid step forward. There will still be a long way to travel, but you will have made a good beginning. It will be important to remember what you have learned and all that you still don't know. This course will be challenging, but you will survive and, in the end, develop a measure of confidence."

Bates MacNeer was that rare speaker who could present a complex subject to a large audience while making each person in the lecture hall feel as if he was talking directly to him or her alone. He was proud to call himself a teacher, one who could inspire his students to try their best, to extend themselves because they truly wanted to learn. He told the class to close notebooks and put down pens. He wanted their attention—he wanted them to listen.

"Some of you are taking this class for credit but are planning careers in other disciplines. That's fine. Others here today believe they will eventually be active in the financial world. For them this course is a stepping-stone. This class will help all of you understand that markets are unforgiving. That competition for success is fierce. If you expect to excel, you'd better accept the reality that you'll have to spend considerable time analyzing the companies you plan to invest in. Security analysis is an important tool. Used properly it will help you deconstruct balance sheets and, for example, judge the relevance of book values, leverage, potential dilution, depreciation, amortization, and replacement cost. You'll be asked to debate if there is such a thing as intrinsic value. You will decipher income statements and research the significance of cash flow versus net income, quality of earnings, and the question of what is real continuing earnings. After you have completed this class, some of you will believe you are ready to invest. Others will be frightened of what they don't know. Remember, this is an introductory course in security analysis. We're not handing out doctorates here, nor are we awarding partnerships at prestigious Wall Street investment banks. You can progress by continuing your education—read, study, practice. Be open-minded. Even though I doubt that you'll be first-team all-Americans by June, I do believe you'll be better prepared for the future."

He stopped to drink from the glass of water resting on the lectern. When he looked back out at the students, he seemed to be even more serious. "For those of you who commit to a Wall Street career, and for those who will be investing on their own, remember to embrace this rule: you can read every word ever written on investing, you can study balance sheets and income statements until you're dizzy, you can seek advice from the best financial minds of the day, but the one element, the one crucial ingredient in the investment brew that you can't buy in any store, find in any book, or uncover under any rock is *judgment*. Some of you will be blessed with it, others will not. We at Wharton will try to help, but you will have to travel on your own discovery journey."

It was time for another sip of water. His mood changed again; it appeared to soften when he set out his closing comments.

"I've been out there in the ocean when the weather changed. I've experienced tightness in my chest and nausea in my gut. But we had the stars and we had a compass. When the waters got turbulent, when we had to be strapped to our posts, we had something to help guide us home, to protect us from the cruel unknown. Be aware that we live in a world that is dynamic and change is inevitable. Study hard, be rational, be alert, and we'll meet again next week."

I couldn't resist thinking of myself as a new übermotivated Rogers when I committed to a rigid, time-consuming routine during this first semester of my junior year. I was swimming in uncharted waters; I never before had been accused of being either organized or methodical. I thought of my father and was sure he would be questioning, "Is this my son we're talking about?" Month after month I diligently tackled Graham and Dodd and Dr. MacNeer's writings on security analysis. Sometimes the professor's lectures were meant to introduce a new subject, while in others he patiently critiqued what we had been studying, but all along it was clear that we were expected to respect these groundbreaking works and their sturdy investment philosophies. MacNeer even suggested that we read Graham and Dodd's book cover to cover during Christmas break for pure enjoyment. "It's just filled with wisdom and a better use of your time than watching football games on television," he added with a sardonic smile.

When interning at Prescott & Prescott, I had heard numerous unfamiliar terms being tossed about such as free cash flow, rate of return on investment, capex, tangible versus intangible assets, goodwill, inventory management, or takeout value. What did they all mean? Partners at the firm were too busy to answer questions from an intern like me. *But finally now*, I thought, *the clouds are lifting. Thank you very much for your clarity, Dr. Benjamin Graham. And thank you, Professor Bates MacNeer, for making me question everything, each line and footnote of a company's reported income, cash flow, and balance sheet statements.*

"Don't accept numbers at face value. Look for clues or inconsistencies. Dig into the footnotes. You may be surprised to find a hidden gold nugget. Once you've done the forensics, then sit back and think for a while: Is this a trade or an investment? If you buy shares and they decline, will you want to buy more? How confident are you of your analysis? Decide all this before you buy." It sounded like good advice to me, but later I wondered why we never discussed the other opportunity. Was it undiplomatic to inquire about selling short?

I could never remember being as busy as I was my junior year. Advanced accounting and security analysis demanded discipline and concentration, but I was a happy camper because I knew I was moving closer to my ultimate goal. I heard other students complaining about the workload or that the subject matter was dry. Not me. I had often been accused of laziness and not producing up to my potential, but I was on high alert now and laser beamed on the finish line. I could actually feel myself growing in the classroom, and to my surprise, that sense of growth also applied to the liberal arts courses I took.

Dad had suggested—or was it insisted—that I study Shakespeare. "He's the master of psychology and interpreting human strengths and frailties. Son, you have to read *King Lear* and *Coriolanus*." There was so much to learn from the great poet's insights that I soon realized that this course was just a beginning for me. Once again, Dad was right on beam. I also took a swing at History of Western Art, figuring it was time I acquired a little culture. I knew I had zero artistic talent—in fact, I could hardly draw a straight line—but I wanted to cease being an outright boob. It was time to branch out. Studying the modern history and political environment of the present-day Middle East was eye-opening to this midwestern hick. I had signed up for that course on a lark and wouldn't realize until years later how incredibly valuable that knowledge and perspective would be to me as an investor.

Most every Sunday night, I called Charlotte. I could always count on her to raise my spirits. Sometimes she was so revved up that I would forget what I had wanted to tell her. She had found her groove at Columbia and felt she was getting closer to making a decision about her future. It was good to hear her happy and confident again. Charlotte was a passionate, high-energy pistol who really had no desire to rein herself in. She refused to let either of us dwell on the separation issue. She would end every call with "we'll be together real soon. I'm counting on a happy ending to our story." When Charlotte talked like this, all I wanted to do was hop on the next express train to New York. I pictured her holding the phone while lying in bed under a quilt and wished I was there with her.

Dad called me once a week, usually on Friday night. The conversations tended to center on his questions followed by my answers. He assured me not to worry about him, but, after these calls, I always felt down because he sounded older and less lively than I remembered.

I tried to talk with Ronnie or Sawyer twice a week. I did my best to stay current with the financial markets. My portfolio was pretty fully invested and still motoring upward. "You're doing too well," Ronnie would lecture. "Don't be a greedy pig." When I asked him if that meant he was nervous about the market or if he sensed signs of an imminent retreat, he said, "No. What I see are buyers underneath the market hoping for a sell-off. They're afraid to chase. Maybe they still remember the '73 to '74 debacle." I knew by now that Ronnie was a pure trader. He would take profits as fast as he would run from losses. He probably would have sold and rebought my portfolio several times by now. He wasn't negative on the market—in fact, he was bullish—but his trader's instinct was to sell by Friday, sleep well over the weekend, and reenter on a dip early the next week. I wondered what his strategy would be if there wasn't a dip in the market and he was left on the sidelines holding Herman. As for me, I was winning at this game and still planned to sit at the table as the cards were being dealt. I couldn't realistically trade from the classroom, anyway. As it turned out, that was a sweet blessing.

There weren't a lot of breaks in my routine that year. No sexual encounters, sports conquests, trips to exotic retreats, or spiritual epiphanies. I know it all sounds boring, but I was making steady progress, and that was a good thing. I wasn't ready to take on the Wall Street legends, but I was developing the ability to deconstruct a company's financials, analyze its prospects, and better comprehend how markets work. Whether I had the gift was another question. I also learned to appreciate Shakespeare, dipped my toe in the art world waters, and became fascinated with the evolving significance of the Middle East. That was pretty much a full plate for me. To top it off, I was coining it in the stock market and on the poker tables at Penn's fraternity houses. It was shaping up to be one hell of a year.

Blessed be the fraternities on Penn's campus, for I was surely in their debt. These paragons of exclusivity were new turf for me. During my freshman year, it wasn't unusual to find a note slid under my dormitory door inviting me to coffee or a beer with brothers from the rush committee of a fraternity house. I knew all along that I wasn't a joiner but thought it might be interesting to experience the mating ritual. The closest I ever came to having a roommate was sharing the upstairs hallway and bathroom with my father. I just couldn't imagine living with forty or fifty guys who were essentially alike and who excluded everyone who didn't conform to their image. I could picture what Charlotte's response would be: "A fraternity. Are you out of your freakin' mind?"

I met with a few of these groups as a social experiment, but it didn't take even an hour for each of us to realize that there wasn't a fit. Even though I never joined a house, I still enjoyed playing poker with the brothers on weekends. It was too profitable to pass up. In moments of weakness, I almost felt guilty raking in monthly gambling winnings from the frat boys. Most of them had fat checkbooks and were playing for an amusing diversion. They violated the basic rules of Poker 101 as they were busy joking and drinking, making frivolous bets, or staying in hands too long with only mediocre cards. To them it was only a game and one that they didn't seem to care if they won or lost.

The fraternities on campus traditionally hosted the most boisterous parties of the year on the Friday night after January's semester-ending exams. The weekend was free from the pressure of exams, term papers, or class assignments and typically the winter weather was dreary and cold. In other words it was a perfect time for the collegiates to blow off some steam. I had been a hermit most of the semester, so why not let go and indulge, I thought, when I was invited to a frat party as a guest by a class-mate I had been helping get by in accounting. My friend Byron had ex-celled at Choate and thought he was coming to Penn to study architecture. But Big Daddy had other plans for his only son. He told Byron, the hell with the arts—you're going to transfer into Wharton and learn how to run a company. He demanded that his son drop architecture and study business basics like finance and management. The father was a prototyp-ical CEO bully who was used to getting his own way. I gleaned from Byron that the only reason he needed help in accounting was because he refused to study. He hated the course and desperately wanted to learn how to design buildings. Byron was a good guy caught in the vise of his father's dominance. I felt compassion for his cause. I'd also heard that his house threw great parties.

Named after the stone steeple that adorned the fraternity house, the Spire was known on campus as WASP Central. Its members had almost uniformly attended eastern boarding schools and came from wealthy families. The house was physically impressive, with rich paneling, leaded windows, large brass chandeliers, and oriental carpets that spoke of age.

The downstairs public rooms were flooded with vintage photographs of Penn's campus and oil portraits of esteemed founding members with names like Biddle and Rittenhouse. When I asked Byron if the Spire had ever admitted a brother named Goldberg or Sanchez, he visibly bristled: "Look across the street. That house is 110 percent Jewish. Do you see any Episcopalians there? Do you really think they would accept someone like me as a member?" I couldn't disagree with him, but my thoughts were already elsewhere. I was wondering if there would ever be a fraternity on campus for agnostics and if so, what would its official Greek name be?

Upstairs at the Spire, overlooking an interior courtyard, was a members-only room that was always locked, as if its mission was to protect state secrets. Only select members knew who controlled access to this mysterious place. It was wildly rumored that a variety of secret rituals were performed there on special occasions. All this voodoo, secret-society bullshit made me nauseous, so I naturally had to comment with a "What's this cult crap all about?"

A red faced Byron responded immediately. "We don't talk about that room outside the Spire. Really, Rogers, back off—please, just drop it!" These guys must have thought they were twentieth-century versions of Knights Templar. I normally would revolt against such flagrant elitism, but I was here to raise a little hell, so I kept my thoughts to myself. I was quiet but the whole situation registered with me, and I would not forget any of it.

I arrived for cocktail hour on time wearing the prerequisite tie and jacket. Even though I had put on a clean blue shirt and my favorite coat and tie combo, I looked like a poor immigrant compared to the Spire boys. Boarding school chic prevailed with the brothers, whose standard uniform was a blue-striped shirt, bold-striped tie, and conservative herringbone jacket. Socks were optional, but brown Bass Weejun loafers were de rigueur. Long hair was a must, preferably parted high and swept over from left to right. I took a deep breath as I tiptoed into a foreign land.

The party was already in progress when I entered the library room, which boasted top-to-bottom bookshelves and a corner fireplace with the Spire's insignia discreetly carved into the center of the mantelpiece. In addition to the bartender, there were waiters passing an assortment of limp hors d'oeuvres. By my count there were an equal number of frat members and girls present, and most of the latter seemed to be dressed up as female versions of a Spire brother. I knew for sure that Charlotte would have been as foreign to all this as I was, and that her unbridled surgical wit would have gotten us a lot of laughs and also into some trouble, but I sure wished she had been there with me. I was thinking of how much I missed her when Byron came up to me.

"Stout. I'm glad you came. I see you clean up well. You look very much like a brother, but what's with your hair? Don't you own a brush?"

It's true that I have an unruly mop that doesn't like to be tamed. After a shower, all I do is run my hands through the tangled mess and let it dry. Charlotte says it's another one of my endearing quirks, while Dad retorts I look like a windblown seaman. I couldn't care less what the Spire boys thought.

With an I. W. Harper on the rocks in my hand, I followed Byron over to a group of "Spirettes" who were not yet paired off with a brother. It felt like I was at a cotillion, at which I was expected to ask a girl to dance the fox-trot or, heaven forbid, a tango. I was introduced as a friend from out west who happened to be a Wharton brainiac. That was his idea, not mine. They jumped on me like a pack of wild dogs. San Francisco or LA? Where did you attend boarding school? What does your father do? My answers obviously disappointed them, but they continued to probe my background. My father would have gone bonkers at this point. I was a guest of a popular Spire brother, and that had to mean something. I could sense them thinking, *if Byron invited him, he must belong, and that means he must be one of us.* What house are you in? Where do you vacation? I was waiting for one of them to ask if I was circumcised.

Dinner was served buffet style. I sat at a table with Byron and his girlfriend Beth, who was a sister at the sorority clone of the Spire, and two damsels from Bryn Mawr College. The moment they sat down and looked us over, I sensed their hostility and knew I had to prepare for an assault. I harkened back to my youth and remembered thinking, *here come the torpedoes.* For some reason I have heightened survival instincts, like a small animal in the wild. I had learned, after experiencing too many mistakes, that if you expected to succeed on the pitching mound or at the poker table, you must be able to diagnose situations. You have to anticipate and protect yourself before disaster strikes. If you're like me and don't possess a ninety-mile-per-hour fastball or the luxury of playing poker from the strength of deep pockets, then you'd better find a way to offset those deficiencies with some special skill. I couldn't explain why, but mine was a bizarre reflex analysis that helped me know when to throw a different pitch than the one a batter anticipated or how to study the body language of a poker opponent and sense a bluff or a pat hand. It was these types of reads that told me the Bryn Mawr girls were going to be trouble.

The girls had gone to Taft with one of Byron's roommates and claimed that the experience had encouraged them to attend an all-female college. No explanatory details were offered. They made sure to tell us how special they were because they'd rejected several Ivies, including Princeton and Penn, but chose Bryn Mawr. Somewhere between tossed salad and chicken parmigiana, they felt the need to attack the idea of coed education. Erica, the apparent spokeswitch of the duo, stated their argument: "A coed environment causes campus life to be too social, and all that bullshit permeates the classroom and detracts from your ultimate education. We don't need men at Bryn Mawr. The reason our parents are shelling out thousands is to stimulate our brains, not our vaginas."

I fantasized that Masters and Johnson were dining with us. At this point they might have suggested a battery-operated friend for dear Erica. I waited for Beth to respond, but all she did was utter a muted "Whatever." Later she said that she had heard this argument so many times from girls at boarding school that it bored her. She'd been eager to graduate and move on to a coed college.

Our gracious host Byron was mum, so I assumed it was up to me to carry the ball. I initially took the high road and wished them well, but couldn't resist adding at your "cloistered, Main Line nunnery."

Erica sat up straight, adjusted her wire-rimmed glasses, and went on the offensive. "Aren't you two at Wharton?"

I was on my second I. W., feeling no pain, and ready to rumble. "Let me guess where you're going," I ventured. "Are you about to congratulate us, or are we to be treated to a trite lecture on the evils of business? I haven't heard one recently and would rather enjoy being entertained by your unique perspective."

"You really are a sarcastic asshole," she said. "So tell us, Mr. Big Shot, are you planning on changing the world by being an accountant? Money is everything to you Wharton guys. Do you really think being rich makes you a better person?"

She wasn't going to stop, and it was getting on my nerves. Byron stepped in to bring the verbal jousting to an end before I could respond. He reminded everyone that tonight was a party and the boxing gloves were supposed to be checked at the front door. I had a lot more left in the tank but nodded. "Okay."

I didn't know what to expect when I was approached by a girl who pulled me away from the dining table. "I'm Maude, your rescue committee," she announced. "Why are you arguing with those witches when we're supposed to be having fun?" The carpets had been rolled up and the furniture pushed back along the walls of the main front room. Magically, a dance floor was created. I could hear the band warming up, but I was being led upstairs to a large game room. A crowd had formed around an antique pool table donated by the class of '49. A coed doubles match was being played for five dollars a game. The room was crowded with brothers making side bets on the matches, trash-talking the players, and downing Rolling Rock from a keg in the corner. There was even an active betting market on individual shots, which usually resulted in loud booing or shouts of joy. The party had begun.

My self-appointed partner's confidence was overwhelming. I had just learned her name but still found myself throwing a five spot on the table. She had challenged the team that had handily won the last three games. When I told her that I was average at best, she smiled. "Don't worry." Growing up, I had never even held a pool cue before I met Ronnie Davis. He taught me the basics of the game, but my only talent was reading the angles and mentally calculating where I should shoot the little white ball. Beyond that I stank, because the balls didn't follow my directions. Ronnie couldn't understand why I had such a weak bridge and hands of stone. He tried to encourage me to practice, because he invariably coerced me into playing with him against his friends in bars near the Xavier campus. These adventures were expensive.

Again, I cautioned her that this wasn't my game. Rather than heed my warning, she leaned in closely and purred, "We'll play your game later." What the hell did that mean? Once the Spire brother missed a shot, she took over. She made a slow trip around the table, intently studying the position of each ball, and then whispered in my ear, "We just made five dollars."

While she was on a winning streak, a Spire brother filled me in on who this wunderkind was. For the next hour, she owned the game. I was a minor character in the play, at best every so often making a short shot. Maude Carpenter was so good there were times she almost ran the entire table. The brothers were chanting her praises as she strutted about the room holing long, powerful shots as well as making soft, deft touch shots. But the shot I wouldn't forget came late in the last game we played. The cue ball was positioned out of her reach. I was standing behind her as she hiked up her skirt and raised her leg onto the table. When she stretched far forward to attempt the shot, the muscles in her leg quivered, her skirt rose even higher, and I had a clear sighting of her all the way up. "How about that?" she said, admiring the difficult shot she had just executed. *How about that spectacular vista* was all I could think of at that moment.

"I need a celebratory kiss." She beamed while shoving our winnings into her purse. She was flying from the rush of adrenaline and alcohol. Maude Carpenter had come to Penn as a highly recruited lacrosse star. An unfortunate car accident was forcing her to sit out the year. Projected as an all-Ivy candidate, she found this situation difficult to accept. Raising hell soon became the preferred outlet for her boundless energy. Maude had the round, joyful face of a Southern California cheerleader coupled with the muscular body of a toned athlete. I had no idea why I won the lottery tonight, but I sure as hell wasn't going to question my good fortune. I kissed her warmly and added a friendly hug. She put her arms around my neck, pushed her pelvis hard against my crotch, and forced her tongue down my throat. "There," she said. "Now that was a real kiss!"

The party was going full force downstairs. The dance floor was crowded with sweaty, gyrating WASPs, while the bar was mobbed with

onlookers. The band came from Virginia and was revered on the southern college circuit. I liked the music they were playing and I loved their
name—the Hot Nuts. It was not hard to imagine every guy in the room
being turned on by their backup group's short skirts, tight red tops, and
lewd dance moves. They were appropriately called the Cherries. I was out
there with Maude doing my best. I had expected her to be a graceful
dancer, but instead she was like a wounded bird, all rapid jerky motions
and a lot of jumping around. She may have been a super athlete and pool
shark, but she was no Charlotte on the dance floor.

As the night wore on, Maude wouldn't stop drinking or dancing. She
had amazing tolerance and endurance, but she was starting to go downhill. When I returned from a bathroom break, she was dancing with a
huge brother I didn't recognize. He was plying her with drinks and aggressively grabbing and squeezing her at every opportunity. She was
clearly not in control and appeared to be disoriented. I stood next to
Byron and his girlfriend. "She's a wild one," he said, stating the obvious.

I looked at Beth and asked her what she was thinking. "This isn't
good" was all she had to say. I insisted that we had to get Maude home.

"Don't you know who she's with?" Byron said.

"I don't care. I just don't want to see her get hurt," I answered.

"That's Gordon Bryant, captain of the lacrosse team," he emphasized.

"So what?"

"He's a mean drunk and usually gets what he wants."

"I'll explain the situation to him," I said.

"You don't know Gordie," Beth chimed in. "He'll break you in half like
a piece of dry wood."

There was a life lesson at stake here. Maude had picked me out of a
crowd to be her party date. We were having a good time. I liked her. She
was a fun-loving soul who was down on her luck and needed someone to
rescue her. In her state she was vulnerable and utterly defenseless. Naturally I was scared shitless of Gordie, so I had to think my way out of this
dilemma.

If I was going to play Batman, I decided to choose Beth to be my
Robin. I couldn't rely on Byron, because he and Gordie were brothers,
bonded in a secret-laden club. I convinced Beth to maneuver Maude outside so they could talk about something private, promising Gordie that

they would soon return. I snuck out the back door with Maude's coat and scarf, avoiding at all costs a confrontation with the lacrosse ape. I had to convince her to come with me. Outside the Spire I hugged dear Maude with all the passion I could muster, took her hand, and led us up Locust Walk.

The cold air seemed to revive her. Somewhere between Thirty-Eighth and Thirty-Ninth Streets, she thanked me. "He thinks he's king shit. If I was 100 percent, I could run circles around that big oaf. That jerk has been trying to get in my pants since I was a freshman. No freakin' chance!" She was steaming mad, her face flushed, her eyes flashing anger. I was holding her hand while we walked. She spun around and, for the first time, looked me directly in the eye. Even though still buzzed, with her face showing the effects of too much scotch and beer, I thought Maude was attractive, much like an Amazon warrior. She moved in and held me so tightly I had trouble breathing. She placed my hands on her rear, high and hard as steel, pressed herself against me, and buried her face in my neck. We stood like that for a while until I felt her sobbing. "Did I make a fool of myself tonight?" she asked.

I knew how the evening would end if I chose to say the right words. I was light-headed and incredibly attracted to that taut body. I could almost hear my blood boiling. I fantasized her shooting pool naked, leaning over the table, her muscles straining and legs spread apart. I'm not a saint, and I surely ached for her body, but knew it was the wrong thing to do with her tonight. I almost changed my mind and let my pecker take over when I walked her to her door. As we said our goodbyes, she reached down and gently squeezed my unit three times.

"Once is because I like you."

"Twice to remind you of what can be."

"Three times is for good luck."

I turned down Thirty-Ninth Street and hung a left on Spruce. It was only two blocks to the main dorm entrance, but I wasn't sure I could make it. Lovers' nuts! It's definitely the wrong body part for a guy to experience severe cramps. I'd heard about the pain from frustrated high school buddies but never encountered the affliction myself. When I finally climbed the stairs to my room and lay down, tenderly holding my problem, I blamed Maude and that fabulous ass of hers.

In early May we were finally treated to warmer weather. With a touch of spring in the air, the campus felt more vibrant. The trees were flowering, and even the grass reluctantly succumbed to the sunshine by actually turning from brown to green. Maybe it was all this good feeling that helped me summon the courage to request an appointment to meet with Dr. MacNeer. I had excelled in his security analysis course, even getting an A with distinction on a major project for which I had researched the changing dynamics of the temporary employment industry. I had chosen the topic after reading in *Fortune* magazine and the *Wall Street Journal* that businesses had been hiring temps instead of full-time employees to increase flexibility and minimize the cost of severance and insurance. I then highlighted two leading companies, Kelly Services and Manpower, and provided my best Graham and Dodd analysis of each. My hope was Dr. MacNeer had noted my work and would agree to enroll me in his renowned investment seminar the next fall. The class was primarily open to graduate students, but occasionally an undergraduate was anointed. Dr. MacNeer handpicked the students only after a personal interview, which I assumed would be intimidating and gut-wrenching.

When we met, his greeting was quite formal. He rose from his desk, shook my hand, and then directed me to sit across from him. I couldn't help but be nervous. I had spent the last thirty minutes outside in the hall performing breathing exercises and upper-body isometrics to calm down. I knew how I wanted to present my case, even rehearsed in front of a mirror as I was taught in high school. But now I was in his office, subject to his penetrating dark eyes and colossal reputation. I was just a college junior, and he had accomplished so much as a South Seas adventurer, Wall Street legend, and now as a respected college professor. Probably half the finance majors in school held him in awe. I may have been considerably taller than he, but I was feeling small and fragile. He folded his arms across his chest and asked me to begin. I felt like it was a one-strike-you're-out moment and the pitch was on its way.

He wanted to know something about me, so I was encouraged to discuss my background: where I came from, why I choose Wharton, what I had done outside the classroom to enhance my knowledge of financial markets, and why I thought I was so special that I should occupy one of the prized seats at his seminar table.

I thought I was doing a reasonably good job presenting my case when he suddenly interrupted me. "You're not the only A student who has worked a bit for a Wall Street house. I need more than that!" I told him about my work experience for Andrew Stevens, and again he cut me off. "That's fine if you're interested in corporate finance, but the seminar is focused on investing in markets." I realized I had to take a chance and time was running out, so I brought up my successes going short during the market crash of '74.

Dr. MacNeer abruptly leaned forward and loudly slapped an open hand on his desk. There followed a quick back-and-forth.

"What does it meant to go short?" he inquired as if he didn't already know.

"Selling a stock you don't own and hoping to buy it back at a lower price."

"How do you sell something you don't as yet own?"

"You borrow the stock from a holder."

"How do you manage that?"

"Your brokerage house secures it from its internal pool of securities. You won't know the actual account that is lending the stock. In other words, it is impersonal."

I thought I was passing the test when he changed course again and asked me how I had learned this strategy. I told the professor that I knew you could bet against the dice in craps and that I had asked a trader at P&P if you could use the same tactic in stocks. When he said yes, I began my educational process.

We talked a bit longer. He complimented my temporary employment paper but couldn't resist criticizing my lack of emphasis on the industry's free cash flow generation. "That was a major positive you neglected to present. You should have related that to Kelly's and Manpower's valuations in the marketplace." Then he told me how much he regretted not having a place for me in his seminar.

"Is it already filled up, sir?" I asked.

"I restrict the class size to twenty and have already committed to seventeen graduate students." Then he added, "You're an impressive young man, and I wish you well. I hope you understand I must save a few openings for future contingencies."

Dr. MacNeer's body language signaled that our meeting was over, but I had already noticed the circular poker chip ensemble resting peacefully on the credenza behind him.

"Are you a poker aficionado, sir?"

"We played a lot in the merchant marine during the evenings," he answered.

"I imagine that you excelled."

"I sense you are baiting me, Mr. Stout. Where are you headed?"

"You have three places still open for next year's seminar. Allow me a chance to win one of them."

His entire body shook with laughter.

"I can't decide if you're spunky, ballsy, or just arrogant."

"Probably a little of all three, sir."

Professor MacNeer's ancient secretary, Mrs. James, slowly shuffled her way into his office carrying his appointment book. He continued to employ her way past the normal retirement age because she'd been raised in his parents' Scottish village. She still spoke with such a heavy brogue that I doubted anyone but Dr. MacNeer could understand her. "Here's your bible, Professor," she mumbled.

"I see I'm not needed until five thirty at the faculty club. That gives us an hour for you to prove your skills. I'm going to enjoy this little contest, but I really doubt I'll need half that time to school you in the friendly art of poker."

"How should we do this, young man?" he continued.

"I'm a guest in your house, sir," I answered, all the while attempting to remain calm.

"All this deference and good manners aren't going to help your cause, you know. You're going to have to beat me to win." He grinned.

The rules of the game turned out to be quite similar to my Friday night gambleathons with Dad. Here, the professor and I each started with a limited supply of chips ("You'll get no more even if you beg," he reminded me) and agreed to alternating hands of dealer's choice, with the competition ending at 5:15 sharp or when one of us lost all his stash. There was one hitch though—for me to win, the professor had to have lost at least

80 percent of his chips at game's end. He shuffled the cards and pushed the deck across the table. "Cut 'em deep and weep, cut 'em high and cry," he laughed out loud.

I had played in poker games in which the money on the green felt table really mattered to me. The pros will tell you that, at some point, you learn to live with pressure. That may be true, but I wasn't there yet. I have simultaneously been game-ready mentally and in need of a time-out physically. My constitution has never adjusted well to risk taking, whether it be pitching in tight spots or playing cards for meaningful stakes. My little brain can be on high alert while my knees shake and I taste bile in my throat when I feel challenged. This card game was one of those moments. I played cautiously at first, as if I was more afraid of losing than needing to win.

I was up a little after fifteen minutes, only because I was dealt superior cards. He started talking more and more. I couldn't tell if he was trying to distract me or just relaxing and having a good time. I didn't dare say anything other than "well played" or "I didn't see that coming." The professor reminded me that my compliments were superfluous. Then I dealt the first pivotal hand, my favorite game of seven-card stud, low hole wild, with a red-chip penalty if you requested the last card up. I was dealt a pair of threes down and a matching three up, while he showed only a mediocre hand. On the fifth card, I drew the fourth three. I bet conservatively, trying to draw him in. Fortunately he was now working on a full house and so accelerated his betting. I took the last card down, knowing that, no matter what, I had a five-of-a-kind winner. He assumed my hand wasn't that strong. He reasoned that if I had paired my down wild card, I would certainly pay the penalty and take the seventh card up. For once he misread me. He bet, I raised, and he called.

It was a big win, but I said nothing. Dr. MacNeer looked over at me and chuckled. "That was well played, son. You really sucked me in. I liked your patience. You now have my full attention."

Slowly, slowly he came back as I somehow knew he would. With only twenty minutes left, I felt the time was right to gamble and go for the gold. "Do we really have to stop in a few minutes?" I asked innocently. He nodded yes. "Well, then, I guess I'll have to go for it." I bet half my remaining chips. It was a bold move and the first time I attempted such a bluff. I didn't have a great hand, but I thought he was faltering and would fold for defensive reasons.

When he called my bet, I knew I had made a big mistake. "Nice try, son. Next time you bluff, don't talk so much—it only weakens your position," he offered as he showed me his winning hand.

I didn't have much time to recover after the setback from my wrong-headed, impetuous bluff. But the good news was I was getting a bead on his style. Neither bully nor wimp, the professor took pride in consistency and avoiding big mistakes. He was implementing a conservative approach as if he was the Benjamin Graham of poker, willing to lose a few hands but never too many chips, then snapping back and winning more than he lost. He was careful and disciplined, only making large bets when he basically knew he had the better hand. The professor was definitely formidable competition, unlike most of the drunks I took advantage of at Rory's. He seemed oblivious to pressure and my usual bag of tricks, but I didn't relent. I toiled and scratched and, with a little luck, earned my way back to near even. Suddenly the tide turned my way. I jumped on him with successive winners, and with but five minutes left I was within sight of victory.

"This may be the last hand," he reminded me. "Are you going to suffocate me or am I going to escape your grasp? Let's see how it ends . . ."

He dealt each of us five cards. He studied his hand but didn't bet. Did this portend really poor, unbettable cards or was I being suckered? I discarded and drew three new cards while he replaced only two. I was tempted to pray but I knew it wouldn't do any good. The professor instructed me to arrange my cards "provocatively" and turn them over and bet, one at a time. He increased his bets on each turn of the cards. He was too confident; it seemed that I was destined to lose one way or another. If I dropped, he would have enough chips to survive my efforts; if I called, he probably had a better hand. When I turned my last card over, I showed a pair of kings. On the board he had two eights, a queen, and a five. Before I could acknowledge defeat, Dr. MacNeer turned his cards over and folded. "Congratulations, young man. You played well and deserved to win. I trust you won't disappoint me next year."

He ushered me to the door. There was so much I needed to say, but he seemed hurried and my opportunity was slipping away. I wanted to tell him what a special person he was and that I would do my very best next year to justify his confidence in me. He shook my hand again, and that was when I told him I'd assumed he had three eights, not just queens over eights or eights over fives, and that either way I knew he was the winner. I told him my father taught me that only a true gentleman folds a winning hand in order to make his opponent feel better.

Between schoolwork, job interviews, and staying current on the financial markets, time raced by, and before I knew it, it was January of my senior year. I sat in my favorite chair thinking hard about the Christmas holiday break I had just spent back home when Jacob Steiner knocked and then came in.

"Am I interrupting your usual Sunday night psychoanalysis session?" he asked as he flopped on my bed and abused my only pillow. "Welcome back, my favorite Buckeye," my wiseass friend continued. "Guess what? Only one more semester to go before we join the real world. I'm crossing off the dates on my Jayne Mansfield calendar like a prisoner in the last six months of his sentence. By the way, how was Jesus's birthday in the land of wheat and corn?"

This was an example of what I had to endure almost every night. He was nonstop energy of the mouth. It was hard to decide what he enjoyed more, arguing or trying to bait me. One of his favorite topics was religion, but I was bored with the pros and cons of the organized religion debate and refused to respond any more to his need to understand where I stood. I reminded him that I spent the holidays with Charlotte and that she was Jewish. "That should make you happy," I added. He countered by demanding to know if I wore a yarmulke at her temple. This could have gone on and on, but I was tired of the repartee, so I kicked him out of my room.

The vacation fiasco was clear in my mind. It had all started to go downhill the very first night, when I met Dad for dinner at his club. My antenna should have been on high alert from the moment we sat down, because he was tense and surprisingly formal. He didn't even inquire about school, relate any amusing incidents, offer an update on the Reds' prospects for the upcoming season, or ask about Charlotte. Instead he showed his opinionated bulldog side by, yet again, questioning why I would want to spend my life on Wall Street just making money. I implored him to stop, but he continued to question my motives. "Are you sure . . ." he kept asking me. I loved and respected him too much to lose my composure, but I was really tired of these dogmatic interrogations. I had wanted to tell him about my recent job interviews but chose instead to change the subject, and so I gracefully redirected the dinner conversation to his practice and his career. That always worked in my favor.

The holiday season turned into a full-scale bear market when Grandma Rose died two days after I got home. This was Charlotte's first experience with loss. Everyone in the family had known it was imminent, but she refused to accept defeat. So when it happened, she crashed. I sat on a straight-backed chair in her living room quietly observing her parents' friends and family. Charlotte was dressed all in black, standing with her arm around her mother, leaning on her for support, her face swollen and her eyes lined bright red. Every few minutes she would take my hand and introduce me to someone whose name I would forget within the next thirty seconds. We stepped outside as I was leaving. As I held her, straining to think of the right words to say, I could feel her wet cheek on my neck. She kissed me softly, forced a smile, and went back inside.

The traditional mourning period for Grandma Rose lasted seven days at the Markses' house. When it was finally over, and Charlotte and I were to be alone together, she suggested we celebrate her grandmother's life at Sugar n' Spice for breakfast. "Grandma always said it was her favorite meal. She told me she loved feeling naughty when she cheated and ordered bacon." When I saw Charlotte dive into her blueberry pancakes with her customary gusto, I knew she was on the road back.

I was so happy to be with her—to be able to talk openly with someone I trusted, who knew and understood me, whom I could joke and laugh with and share life's adventures, and who was smart and had the gift of good judgment. And then there was Charlotte's boundless physical passion that jolted me like an electric shock and taught me the difference between sex and love. So when she looked up at me and said that there was something she had to do, I instantly knew I wouldn't like it.

"Doctors Without Borders? Did you say Cambodia? Holy shit, Charlotte!"

This vacation was turning out to be more stressful than final exams. The combination of Dad's actions and Charlotte's volunteering for an indeterminate time for her new humanitarian cause on the other side of the world was like a shot to the solar plexus from Smokin' Joe Frazier.

I needed to vent, so I turned to the best sounding board I knew—I reached out to Ronnie Davis to help rescue my sinking ship. He summarily disregarded my father's criticism of Wall Street: "Be happy you have a father who cares. Does it surprise you that he wants his son to mirror his career? Policemen and firemen do, so do many teachers, so why can't a doctor? Give him a break, for shit's sake." He chose his words carefully when it came to Charlotte. He knew I was gonzo for her and how much this new development unsettled me. But R. D. gave me good advice.

"If you try to hold her back, she'll ultimately resent it. For whatever reason, she needs to do this. She's in love with you. Anyone can see that, but the same way you have to go to New York and test yourself, she has to make her own mark by helping people. You have to let her do it, no matter how much you don't want to let her go. My advice is to convince her that you support her need to do her thing. Don't blow this by questioning her like a trial lawyer, and no matter what, don't argue with her. Believe me, she knows there's danger involved. She's analyzed the risks; Charlotte's plenty smart. I hope you realize you're never going to find another one like her. She's that good. Suck it up and be grateful for her."

Ronnie Davis of Over-the-Rhine, Ohio, had more common sense and good judgment than most of the Ivy League types I had met in these last three years. I knew he was right, but I still wanted to sulk and whine and complain. "I'm not going to get any sympathy, am I?" I pleaded.

"Look in the mirror! Yes, you were screwed over by life as a six-year-old. It was a tragedy; it sucks. But look where you are now. In my book you are one lucky little fucker. Add it all up, you know I'm shooting straight, so give up on the sympathy thing."

I was being selfish, but all I wanted was a little compassion, something to help me get back up off the mat. I asked Ronnie to dig in his bag of tricks and feed me an upper.

"How about this, you Ivy League pussy. Your portfolio's still ripping. Also, thank you for the great call on Kelly and Manpower—I've been trading the crap out of them. Sawyer couldn't believe how much you loaded up on those two. Good ballsy move."

"He'd better stay mum," I said. "Put these two away for a few years, Ronnie. I really believe in this industry. They're the leaders. We're probably only in the third inning of the game."

"Hey, you know me, I'm a trader. I hear you, but I'll make more trading them back and forth than salting them away."

Before I left, Ronnie mentioned Sawyer's call to me on a turn in the housing industry.

"He said he sent you some good research reports. All I know is I see big-time buying from two of the smartest institutions we trade with. Whenever the stocks soften, these gorillas are there with a basket. You should get serious here. I would concentrate on the Sunbelt, especially Florida and Arizona."

I knew he was trying to be helpful, but I had already refocused my thoughts away from the stock market and back to a very special Columbia student who was going to be putting her life at risk to help victims of war and natural disasters in some fucked-up, dangerous faraway lands.

A few days after returning to school, I lay in bed in the middle of the night sweating profusely while squeezing a pillow between my knees, the seriousness of Charlotte's new commitment pressing heavily on my chest. I was awake, I wasn't dreaming—she really had made a decision to go. She'd been introduced to DWB by her father, who admired the group's innovative approach to dealing with emergency assistance for refugees. Her French professor provided a glowing recommendation to a participating doctor he knew from Paris. Charlotte took the reins from there. The organization was still in its infancy, and volunteers like Charlotte were openly embraced.

I was confused by my own thoughts. My master plan had included her as a forever companion. Other than my father, she was the only person I had ever truly relied on. Would the whole arc of my life change if something happened to her? I obsessed about the physical risk she would be taking.

Cambodia in 1977 was a war zone that had been devastated by the Khmer Rouge's revolutionary transformation program. This resulted in an epic refugee crisis during which thousands of starved and tortured people roamed the countryside seeking sanctuary. While the Red Cross offered assistance, it wasn't nearly enough to turn the tide. Doctors Without Borders may have been the only medical response group willing and able to field doctors and nurses on the Cambodia–Thailand border to administer aid to the refugees. This new organization was staffed primarily by volunteers who were willing to take risks and bend local rules to achieve the ultimate goal of saving lives. Their courage and dedication to provide medical assistance to anyone who needed help inspired Charlotte. She had become addicted to the evening news. The chaos and brutality that was besieging Cambodia played out on American television networks every night. She had been searching for a cause worthy of her commitment, and Doctors Without Borders qualified. She signed on to report for a training session in France in late June, a few days after graduation.

In the darkness of my room, I came close to praying for her. My fear of danger for Charlotte was spinning out of control. I knew very little about Doctors Without Borders, but I was plenty aware of the brutality of wartime soldiers and the health risks inherent in surgery, triage medicine, and close contact with diseased patients. I had become emotionally conflicted. At one level I was angry with Charlotte for putting herself in such a dangerous position. Why not volunteer in some impoverished area of the US or after a tornado in the Midwest or a hurricane on the Gulf Coast? *Life is so fleeting*, I thought. *She is driving too damn fast.* Yet I couldn't help but admire her enormous capacity to care about others, her fearlessness, and the fact that she wasn't willing to be just another pontificating armchair participant.

As the night wore on, I accepted the fact that I should have seen something like this coming. But the truth was that I was too involved in my own pending career. There were so many questions I needed to ask, but the most important ones couldn't be answered. From the first night I spent with Charlotte at the New Year's Eve party, I was attracted to her vitality, her hunger for life. Even then she made clear that she wanted to do something important that would help people in need; she didn't want

to be just another woman who lunched with friends and collected jewelry. I had to try my best to support her in her new mission, even if I knew
I would worry about her every hour of every freaking day until she returned.

I jumped on the first available train to New York as soon as I had completed my January exams. All month I had been in a deep funk, worrying
about Charlotte. Could she have chosen a worse address to perform humanitarian aid? I had been having trouble generating energy and found
myself staring at my watch every fifteen minutes the way I used to in
high school Latin class. I didn't need written notes to remind me of the
questions I had to ask her: What exactly is DWB? What will you be qualified to do for this organization? Why do you think you'll be safe on the
Thailand side of the border? Do you know anyone who had been there
who can verify that the refugee camps are safe? What is your commitment? For how long? Will you be in direct contact with the refugees?
And—even though I had to be careful when asking this—*do you really
have to do this?*

   That first evening we shared a long dinner at a local campus dive that
was one of Charlotte's favorite retreats. She looked tired from all the
studying and stress, but her mood was upbeat. She read me like an open
book. "Let's get the Q&A over so we can enjoy being together." She proceeded to describe the conditions that led to the formation of DWB, why
it started in France, how it had a difficult infancy but had grown since its
mission in Lebanon the last year, what its ideals and goals were, and why
they were now focusing resources on the Cambodian tragedy. I knew she
was well organized but was nevertheless surprised when she handed me
a large manila folder stuffed with materials on the organization. "Read
these. I think most of your questions about DWB will be answered."

   As I was about to ask Charlotte to tell me about her role, where the hell
she would be located, and, most of all, to address the safety issues, she
motioned to the waiter and ordered a brownie à la mode with two spoons.
She smiled. "We need a sugar high before I hold your hand." When she
then leaned across the table and laid the softest, sweetest kiss in modern

history on me, I was sure this was pure manipulation. I took both her hands in mine, lowered my voice to a whisper, and told her I understood the gravity of the plight of the refugees. I also realized they had little hope of relief unless international organizations came to their rescue. I agreed that the United Nations and the Red Cross probably would be of limited assistance, and therefore a group like DWB was needed to step forward and shoulder a large share of the burden. I made sure Charlotte knew that, yes, I got it, and I wasn't going to argue against aiding these refugees. I told her I believed this was a worthy cause, a noble cause. I just wanted to hear what I needed to hear from her.

We finished our dessert in silence. She slowly stirred her chamomile tea. It was time for her to tackle the risk issue.

"Rogers Stout, I remember every detail of our first so-called date. I had only known you as Dr. Charles Stout's son—a cocky, aloof, distant, tall, lanky, first-class prick. That night you were wearing a blue shirt and a stretched-out-of-shape, well-worn navy-blue Shetland sweater. Your shoes were brown and in need of a good shine. Your hair was all over the place—I wondered if you had driven to my house in a convertible with the top down. You stood up straight when you met my parents, looked my father directly in the eye, and exhibited surprisingly formal manners. You were quite a good listener, truly paying attention to what I was saying, and even gracious when absorbing my initial venomous attack. I didn't want to like you, but you were so interesting and I was surprised by your vulnerability and honesty. I soon realized that you really weren't conceited, it was the effects of living all those years alone with that brain of yours. To my utter shock, you were witty, fun to be with, and you made me light on my feet. When you kissed me goodnight on that fateful eve, I felt a shudder all the way down to my knees. Back in my room that evening, I looked in the mirror and asked myself, 'What the hell just happened?' Over time I learned how driven you could be toward goals that you defined as important. You called it 'the independence thing.' I'd never been with anyone so focused and sure of himself. I liked that side of your character but was envious of your self-confidence. I know you value independent thinking and are strong-willed once you make a decision. That's why I'm counting on you, of all people, to understand why I have to do my thing now."

She looked directly at me, eyes brilliant but 100 percent composed, concentrating on delivering her message exactly as she had planned.

"These doctors have wives and children and obligations like everyone else. They want to return to their families. They're traveling to far-off places where people are in danger because they believe they have to. If they don't go to help, who will? They're trained to do a job and that's it! They want to avoid conflict, deliver medical aid and get the hell out of there. Look at me, Rogers. I'm not a Navy SEAL. I'm not impervious to danger; I get afraid just like anyone else. I can't lie to you—this thing I'm volunteering for is not without risk, but I'll just be doing nonclinical support. I'm obviously not a doctor or a nurse positioned on the front line. I believe I'll be helping needy people, and that's important to me, just as your mission is vital to you. I know you grasp that. Please look at me and promise you're with me."

That was it. The cards had been dealt; there was nothing else to be said. The wonderful times we had spent together over the years flashed through my memory bank in a blur. The truth was I couldn't resist her. I paid the check and we walked hand in hand back to her room.

It took the class most of the first semester that year to catch on to what Dr. MacNeer expected from us and to get into the rhythm of his investment seminar. Each day we were to read the *London Financial Times*, the *New York Times*, the *Wall Street Journal*, and the *Philadelphia Inquirer*. We also read magazines and periodicals such as *Businessweek*, *Forbes*, *Fortune*, and *Barron's*. When I noticed the *Economist* protruding from the professor's briefcase, I added it to my weekly must-study list, which turned out to be helpful because of its Europe-based perspectives on politics, economics, and finance. There were nineteen MBA candidates and one disheveled undergraduate from Ohio in this class. Bates MacNeer would close the door, place his carefully written notes on a lectern, and begin walking back and forth until the room was absolutely silent. At this point, I could usually feel my nerve endings vibrate waiting for him to pose a question. The class was unique for Wharton. We would be his research department, and he was the senior portfolio manager.

"Anything new happening out there?" he might begin. Or he would look at an analyst and ask, "What about the article in the *Journal*? Is that important? Does it alter your investment thesis?" It was always up to the student to know which article and company he was referring to. Sometimes he might begin the seminar with "I could swear I heard somewhere that there was an attempted coup in a Middle Eastern country. Anyone know what I'm talking about? If it's true, what impact would that have on oil prices and companies that we have been recently discussing?"

There was no dozing off in this seminar; if you weren't excited by his class, you probably should have considered a career change. The professor assumed that all twenty of us had a solid grasp of accounting and security analysis. He refused to spend any time hand-holding. We worked for him, and he wanted new ideas and research support for his portfolio. If you had the courage to offer a market opinion, you'd better have something concrete to say. Dr. MacNeer had zero tolerance for premonitions, feelings, or "sense" of the market. If one of your recommendations was up or down a lot, he would typically ask a simple "Why?" It only took a few confrontations with him to know that you'd better not try to bullshit. If you didn't know why a particular stock was dancing or plunging, you were better off stating the truth: "I'm not sure why. It could just be the market, but I'll dig around and try to find a reason."

Each week the senior portfolio manager would assign projects to either an individual analyst—"I'm interested in XYZ, look into it for me"—or to the group at large, such as, "How will the pending congressional tax bill affect my holdings?" These reports were then subject to class debate and professorial analysis. His probing questions and follow-up comments demanded my full attention. I came to believe that Dr. MacNeer's compulsive pacing was his way of working off excess energy. It wasn't unusual to find him suddenly standing next to you when asking a specific question of one of his analysts. I couldn't help being seduced by the way he spoke. He would speak clipped Wall Street jargon when communicating as if we were operating in real time during market hours at a no-nonsense money management firm, yet when he lectured the class or offered his opinion on a subject, he returned to his formal style. Then, after one of his analysts made a presentation on a stock or industry, the senior portfolio manager would methodically scan the room asking for "constructive criticism from the floor." We all knew that his opinion of our worth was influenced by our performance during these interchanges.

I learned very quickly that the other students visualized a target painted on my chest, and an even bigger one on my back. I was on my own, swimming in the deep end with the big boys. What they would never know was that I liked it that way. They were afraid of being upstaged by a lowly undergraduate. Their weakness was their overly aggressive desire to put me down. The more one of these classmates-analysts tried to trap me or attack my recommendations, the more I came to class prepared and sure of myself. I had played enough poker to know that, sooner or later, I would be dealt a winning hand and I would be able to suck them into a pot where they didn't belong. I would be patient and cautious, but when I had it right, I would relish delivering a knockout punch smack into their collective MBA guts.

When we returned in late January from the semester break, Dr. MacNeer had already graded our exams. He had surprised the class earlier by introducing a real-time case study issue as a take-home exam. We had two weeks to research and prepare an analysis of the well-publicized proposed acquisition of West Pecos Pipeline by Gulf Oil. Why would a major oil company be willing to pay a substantial premium for this pipeline? Was this a good purchase for Gulf's shareholders? If you were a Pecos director, would you embrace Gulf's bid? Discuss the positives and negatives of this transaction from both the buyer's and the seller's perspective.

The senior portfolio manager instructed his analysts that they were permitted to utilize a variety of resources beyond annual reports and Form 10-Ks. He also reminded us we were on our honor not to discuss this project with classmates. As I left the classroom, annual reports and SEC Form 10-Ks in hand, I felt Dr. MacNeer studying me as if he were preparing to challenge me to a duel. A few members of the class approached him to lobby for clarifications, but he refused to respond. "It's clear what I'm asking for. Stop acting like teenagers—you're supposed to be MBA candidates. This is an exam. I expect quality work from my analysts."

Back in my apartment, I spent all day on a Saturday reading, rereading, and then rereading again the Gulf and Pecos annual reports, their SEC filings, and the merger proposal documents. I couldn't suppress believing that good ol' Dr. MacNeer was baiting his class. Of course this merger was a win-win—in fact, it was so obvious that I was suspicious our cunning professor had a trick card hidden up his shirtsleeve. Why did he choose this particular transaction to test our analytical competence and judgment skills? What was the wily Scot up to?

I became convinced that there had to be a clue somewhere that exposed a chink in this deal's armor. Pecos's shareholders were getting a huge premium for their regulated, undercapitalized, slow-growing company, and they would end up owning stock in a much larger, growing enterprise that paid a substantial dividend. Based on Pecos's record and limited resources to accelerate its growth rate or pay a higher dividend, it was difficult to imagine its stock reaching Gulf's bid price in even five years. Was it possible there were valuable assets hidden in Pecos's financial statements beyond their Permian Basin landholdings and pipeline system? I put on my Sherlock Holmes deerstalker but couldn't uncover any gems. After hours of digging, I decided to accept the fact that this was a great deal for Pecos's shareholders and that the directors would be ecstatic with Gulf's bid.

It required more research to understand why Gulf Oil coveted this particular acquisition target, but it was already early evening, my brain was fried, and all this concentration had made me famished. I popped down the hall and knocked on Jacob's door. He was polishing off a paper, but I knew his evening would be free because his social life was almost as abysmal as mine, so we agreed to pasta up later in south Philly. I was listening to the news when I heard him enter my room and bellow, "Before we leave, three out of five for a dollar. Cash money!" Jacob Steiner did not know how to accept defeat. The competition had started when he once saw me throw an old pair of socks in a waste can across the room.

"I bet you can't do that again," he baited me.

"Of course I can."

"Show me, Mr. Hot Dog."

"What's the bet?"

"One dollar that you won't make that shot seven out of ten times."

"Screw you. I'll take the bet at five out of ten."

"You remind me of a Turkish carpet dealer. Let's see your stuff at six out of ten for one dollar."

After I made six out of eight successful throws, I missed the next two on purpose.

I had conveniently forgotten to tell Jacob that I practiced those shots virtually every day. Five matches later and five dollars more in my pocket, he finally moved on to a contest he thought he could win—Jacob believed he was a master of three-card monte. He'd learned to play on the streets of New York. After losing umpteen times and practicing for hours in his room, he finally became a consistent winner. He bragged that he was eventually banned from the street corners of the Upper West Side and, soon thereafter, his friends at school refused to play against him as well. He assumed that his midwestern hick friend didn't know the game and would be easy pickings. He was right.

So, with no planning or intent, we soon had committed to a healthy competition: socks in a waste can versus three-card monte, one dollar per game. He volunteered to keep score, insisting that debts were to be settled on Sunday afternoons. We played so often that all one of us had to say was "ready" and the games would begin. After a few months, he had improved his throwing skills and I had caught on to many of his card tricks. He claimed that his winnings were stretching his jeans pockets, but I had been maintaining my own detailed account and knew otherwise. It didn't matter—it was a good diversion from the books, and it sure as hell was fun.

That Saturday, Jacob refused to quit when he was down twelve dollars. He only relented when I offered to contribute my evening's winnings to help pay for the parking tickets he had accumulated. I wasn't being compassionate. I was just that hungry!

Sunday morning I treated myself to a gargantuan breakfast at a diner down the road on Walnut Street: scrambled eggs diced with red peppers and bacon, a large glass of grapefruit juice, strong coffee, and, of course, rye toast swamped with my beloved peanut butter and strawberry jam. I wanted to fill the tank because I knew what lay ahead. Saving the newspapers for later, I let myself fantasize that I was Bates MacNeer, a beloved but demanding college professor concocting an exam for his signature investment seminar. I would want my students to prove to me and to themselves that they were ready to think like security analysts/portfolio managers. How to do it? I would have them study a publicly announced merger proposal: analyze the buyer and seller's motivations, determine if the consolidated company was better or worse off due to the transaction, and opine from the shareholders' perspectives. But that would be too much of an up-the-middle pitch. I would have to challenge these cocky future MBAs with an issue that required intensive foraging and focused thinking to uncover. I wouldn't go so far as to professionally hide the tidbit, but I would want to reward only those students who discovered there was a valid question with this merger through their own hard work and perceptive judgments. Okay. Now that I had set the table, where do I bury the mysterious clue?

Back in my room, I imagined sitting around a conference table along with Gulf Oil's senior management discussing West Pecos Pipeline. Why was this an acquisition we have to make, the CEO might begin. For competitive reasons we haven't trumpeted our recent exploration successes in the Delaware Basin of the Permian. We've made the required public announcements but downplayed their significance. We have sizable Permian landholdings and have learned as we explore north and northeast in the Delaware that the productivity of our wells improves substantially. Pecos owns in fee over forty thousand acres in the Delaware Basin, much of which is adjacent to our northerly holdings. They aren't an exploration company so haven't as yet realized the worth of these properties that were acquired decades ago to protect Pecos's right-of-way passage for future pipeline development. Sooner or later savvy rivals will learn of the potential in the basin and approach Pecos to buy exploration leasehold rights. We should secure these properties now for future exploration. This could be a major development project for Gulf lasting years and years. The voices around the table responded with an emphatic aye.

"What about the pipeline itself?" an independent director might ask. A report would be produced by outside consultants that specialize on the pipeline industry, which concluded that the line was generally in good shape, notwithstanding a tendency toward deferred maintenance. "Why do we need to own a pipeline?" the director might continue.

The CEO would confidently respond that, assuming current exploration success rates continued, Gulf would have a lot of oil for sale and controlling the distribution of the product would provide the company with an important competitive advantage. "We will be putting thousands of new barrels of oil on the market a few years from now. We'll want to sell it to someone. If we own Pecos, we'll have the ability to hook up with other existing pipelines and ship our product either west to the Pacific Coast or east to the Gulf refineries, wherever demand is the greatest and prices are the highest."

The CEO would then defer to the chief financial officer to discuss the financial ramifications of the merger. He could predict that by "just plucking low-hanging fruit," Gulf could take out over $40 million in expense savings. The combined company would not require two financial departments and duplicate land managers, purchasing and marketing employees, legal departments, and so on. Furthermore, he could say Pecos was an "old, bloated company riddled with inefficiencies." He might end his presentation by predicting that once we get Pecos to adopt Gulf's operational culture, he was confident more savings would be apparent and therefore Gulf's acquisition costs would be considerably less than what appeared on the surface.

So there it was, I thought, three solid reasons for Gulf to buy Pecos: vast landholdings to drill and develop that were contiguous to the company's emerging Delaware Basin play, an established pipeline that would provide access to markets both east and west for Gulf's production, and the positive impact of significant cost savings. It wasn't too difficult to see why this all added up to a sweetheart transaction. At first glance the offer price might seem too rich, but after some basic restructuring, cost savings, and improved efficiencies, the deal would actually enhance Gulf's financial performance after only one year.

I walked away from my desk and started pacing back and forth. This deal was way too pat. Why would MacNeer be soft on his graduate students? It just wasn't in his MO! I moved a waste can across the room and started heaving sock fastballs. I felt like I was being lured into inviting ocean waters, where underneath the calm surface lurked a dangerous undertow.

Before I could write my exam paper, I had to suffocate my paranoia, so I positioned myself in a comfortable chair and reread the Gulf–Pecos materials one last time. Maybe I was a pathetic version of Hansel and Gretel, but I thought I saw a bread crumb on the forest floor when I tackled Pecos's footnote number five. How could I have missed this cautionary clue? Buried in the Legal Issues footnote, along with numerous nuisance lawsuits, was a "possible environmental issue" involving pipeline leakage near the Pecos River. I literally jumped out of my chair to grab an accounting book and began frantically turning the pages to a chapter entitled "Liability Exposure." My immediate reaction was that I just hit a line-drive single that could split the outfielders and turn into an extra base hit and, with some good, old-fashioned luck, maybe even an inside-the-park home run.

Bingo. There it was in the opening paragraph of the chapter—the three categories of potential liability. If the liability were remote, then no journal entry or footnote was required. If it were possible but not probable nor estimable, then disclosure was mandatory and a footnote to the financial statements would suffice. If the liability were labeled a contingent liability, that meant it was both probable and reasonably estimable. In that case the liability had to be clearly evident on the balance sheet and labeled as a reserve for future exposure. Our dear professor was testing us after all. The liability would have been easy to see if it were right there, clear as day, on Pecos's balance sheet, but because it was only deemed to be possible, and not probable or estimable, his students had to decide on their own the significance of this environmental exposure. Should I assume that Gulf Oil and its bevy of high-priced advisers knew of this leakage risk? How could I possibly evaluate this situation? I could just mention footnote number five and carry on with my assessment of the deal, but that would make me out to be a wussy and Professor MacNeer would be disappointed in me. It was time to take a break and think this out.

Jacob was napping under an afghan that must have been knitted by his grandmother sixty years ago. It was incongruous to see him so peacefully wrapped up in red and blue flowers, but I didn't hesitate. "I need your help." After the anticipated banter, he swung his legs around, appearing to be reasonably alert. I explained my conundrum, emphasizing that I only had a week or so to come to a conclusion and finish off my take-home exam. "How do I get solid information that sheds light on the scope of this issue?" I asked.

"Do you know where in the basin the leak might have taken place?" Jacob responded.

"The footnote states, 'near the town of Banksville.'"

"There should be articles in the local newspaper about something like this!"

"Good idea, but what do I say to a reporter if I can get him on the phone?"

"Be straight. Tell him you've seen the notice in Pecos's financials. Ask him if the town is concerned. Is it a leak into the groundwater? Could it possibly have polluted the river? Don't talk down to him. And be sympathetic."

"Would it be wrong to ask him to send me any articles that were written in his paper on the situation?"

"Ask for the articles plus any other sources he can think of. Promise to update him on any findings you might discover."

I literally ran down the hallway to my room, tore the phone off the wall, and called information. "Banksville, Texas, please, ma'am," I begged.

I laid the charm on as best I could. After a few false starts, the Texas operator located the telephone number of the *Banksville Star*. It was Sunday afternoon and the only employee on duty was one Chip Ryan, who told me he was a high school junior whose father happened to own the newspaper. I didn't rush it. We talked baseball for a while. He told me how he thought the Big Red Machine was "awesome, really big-time awesome." His favorite player on the Reds was Johnny Bench. "I'm the catcher on our high school team, and man, I know what a difficult position it is. That guy Bench has a gun for an arm." I kept him lubricated. I related a few of my pitching experiences and stressed how important my catcher was to my performance.

When I sensed an opening, I didn't hesitate. A half hour later, Chip promised to send me newspaper articles for the last six months on the "river situation," as he called it. I asked him to airmail them and I would pay the postage, but he acted insulted. "We're not bankrupt down here, you know," he reminded me. When I told him I was just trying to be East Coast courteous, he burst into laughter. "What's that?" he chuckled.

I thanked him profusely and was ready to hang up when Chip told me I should read the town council's motion authorizing the mayor to hire an engineering firm to study if the pipeline had leaked oil into the Pecos River. My pulse rate instantly doubled. "Did you say there is a study underway on this?" I gulped. I had underestimated Chip Ryan. He told me to call tomorrow afternoon and speak to his father, Chip Sr. He would brief him on our conversation. Chip Jr. was my newest best friend.

It was a short jaunt down Locust Walk to the library, where I studied maps detailing the Permian as a whole and the Delaware Basin in particular. I couldn't resist smiling when I located the Pecos River weaving its way through the basin, and there, nestled along its southern shore, was the country town of Banksville. Back in the stacks, I found a book titled *Texas Rural Life: Farming, Ranching, and Wildcatting.* Why was it in a university library? Maybe it was source material for a course taught in the sociology department, or maybe R. Stout was just on a lucky run. In truth, Banksville's history was rather uninteresting. No famous residents. No Jesse James or Billy the Kid. No gold or silver discoveries. It was the home of ranchers, farmers, and, I would bet, a lot of good people. There was one fact, though, that rang my inner bell: every five to seven years, the Pecos River rose over its banks and flooded the lower elevations of Banksville. I made a mental note to ask Chip Ryan Sr. when it last flooded his hometown.

I had so much nervous energy to burn off Monday waiting to call my favorite reporter in Texas that I agreed to meet Jacob at the gym at three. Once he laced on his running shoes, Jacob morphed into a workout fanatic. His idea of exercise was to run to exhaustion, then push himself farther until he reached an intolerable threshold of pain. Naturally he belittled my regimen, which consisted of a few laps around the gym, some sit-ups, push-ups, and light dumbbell sequences. After running three or four miles and racing through what he called aerobic weightlifting, Jacob would stand shirtless in front of a mirror and admire himself. Teasing this madman had zero effect on his chronic narcissism. While Jacob was pushing himself, I would drift off to the steam room, where I relished sweating out the poisons of the day in silence, surrounded by the privacy of steam clouds.

My hands were tight as I dialed the *Banksville Star* later that afternoon. Chip Ryan Sr. had a rich voice and spoke slowly, with the assurance of someone who was used to giving orders and demanding respect from his subordinates. It didn't take him long to communicate his love for his town and indignation at the hubris of a large company like West Pecos Pipeline. He was fond of saying that he had worked for the *Star* since the beginning of time. Chip Sr. told me how he started at the paper as a cub reporter and rose to be its owner. He had been appointed senior editor of the *Star* by the local banks that were lugging worthless bonds during its bankruptcy days in the '40s. He had graduated from Rice University only five years earlier. With borrowed money and a pair of brass balls, he assumed control of the paper "during the Kennedy days." Over the next decade, he bought out the other shareholders and took full control of his baby.

Chip Sr. spent an hour educating me on pipeline construction, welding techniques, proper pipeline maintenance, and, above all, the safety precautions that should be enforced when laying pipe underneath a river. Ever since a few farmers had noticed oil drops bubbling to the surface of their fields in the valley beside the river, his newspaper was on the case. He couldn't prove that the pipeline had leaked oil into the river itself, but he was worried enough that he started a crusade to demand that the town hire independent engineers to research the issue. A few months later, cattle ranchers downriver saw oil slicks in an eddy and on a dead bird's carcass. The *Star* arrived, took pictures, and interviewed the ranchers. When Chip Sr. called Pecos Pipeline for a confirmation or rebuttal, the company's spokesman only said, "No comment." Chip Sr. exploded shortly thereafter when he heard from a good source that the ranchers had somehow found the funds to pay off their mortgages.

I began to think I was in over my head. I had only been trying to determine if the "possible environmental issue" footnote in Pecos's financials was a significant enough risk that it should make Gulf rethink their merger proposal. I wasn't an investigative reporter, but I had to dig further to answer Dr. MacNeer's question—"Was this acquisition a good deal for Gulf's shareholders?" The articles from the *Star* were not sufficiently convincing. I thought the locals who were interviewed were clearly biased and the reporters relied too much on hearsay. I needed to confirm that Banksville's mayor had hired an independent engineering firm. I called Chip Sr. to see if he could arrange for me to talk to the mayor's office or, better still, have a short chat with a representative of the engineering company.

"If you want that, you'll have to haul your Ivy League ass down here," an agitated Chip answered. "Son, I told you that the firm had been engaged. I gave you my word—what more do you need!"

Bates MacNeer stood erect, welcoming back his flock from their brief vacation. Our exams rested in neat piles in the middle of his desk. As usual he paced about, waiting for everyone to be seated and for the room to be in a hushed state.

"In general I was pleased with your performance," he addressed the class. "We had unanimous agreement that Pecos's board and shareholders should be content with the purchase offer. The bid price was generous and had the added benefit of being a tax-free exchange. No one tried to make the case that the company was an interesting stand-alone investment with an underappreciated future and, therefore, shareholders would be better off holding stock in an independent Pecos Pipeline." He stopped to sip water from a glass on his desk. "The class also agreed that Gulf had solid strategic reasons for making its offer for Pecos. Everyone understood that the primary advantages to Gulf were the flexibility of moving product to different markets from Pecos's pipeline infrastructure and the exploration potential from its landholdings in the Delaware Basin of the Permian. Accepting that it was difficult, if not unrealistic, to claim the ability to assess the value of these landholdings from afar, the class opted to accept Gulf's knowledge of the basin's geology. A few of you did some interesting matrix work where you suggested how much oil Gulf would have to find and bring to market in the next five years at various costs and selling prices per barrel to justify the land values inherent in the acquisition price. Recognizing that predicting finding and development costs, oil and natural gas prices, and levels of productivity five years in the future is an extremely speculative endeavor at best, nevertheless your attempts to bring economics into this equation were worthwhile."

The professor appeared to be deep in thought while his attention jumped across the room from student to student. We had learned that meant criticism was on its way.

"I was disappointed that too many of you overlooked the significance of Gulf's ability to effect cost savings. You should have related the potential for cost savings to affect the ultimate price Gulf was prepared to pay for Pecos. With a little more effort, you could have specified overlapping expenses, duplicate senior employees, and entire departments that could be rationalized as well as showed that Pecos's operating expense ratios were quite high versus comparable pipeline companies. A few of you, however, did grasp this key point and made a strong case that costs could be significantly cut, and then the Pecos acquisition would be accretive to Gulf in the second year."

Our desks had been rearranged into a large circle. Dr. MacNeer was holding court and walking about addressing the class from a variety of odd angles. He might stand in front of one student and state a fact or introduce a new theory, and then cross the floor to ask another student his opinion on that subject. He could also surprise the group by posing a provocative question, then spin around and point to someone expecting them to provide the required answer. He would cajole, praise, lacerate, encourage, and obliterate all in the same response to a student's or the class's answer to one of his questions. The beloved professor was at his best when he was probing, confronting us, forcing us to state our position without bullshit equivocations. I could feel the electricity in the room— all the ass kissers trying to impress him, while other students sat frozen, afraid to offer an opinion.

He wanted an open, far-reaching discussion of the exam. He asked if anyone wished to question the proposed merger from Pecos's point of view. The class responded with a resounding nay. He tried to stir up some debate, but no one took the bait. He then posed the same question from Gulf's side of the transaction. Hands were confidently thrust upward. One after another my classmates stated their reasons why Gulf was making a sensible, if not intelligent, long-term move. I waited patiently to see if anyone was going to address footnote number five in Pecos's financial statements.

I was particularly pleased to then witness the class "I know more than all of you put together" guy build the case that Gulf was getting a steal. *Go, baby, go*, I thought to myself. *Let's see how far you will go to ultimately embarrass yourself.* Derrick (I forgot his last name already) was one of those super-high-IQ brats who test off the charts, have an impeccable memory, and get straight As in any course based on regurgitation. The way he tried to lord it over his classmates took pomposity to a new level. On three different occasions he had publicly reminded me that I was only a lowly undergraduate. The more I listened to him pontificate, the more I came to believe that he had a one-way brain that was lacking the vital ingredient of balanced judgment. I was beginning to enjoy myself as Derrick proceeded to explain to everyone the geological history of the Permian. "This is something you all should learn," he said with a haughty grin. He produced a map showing that numerous companies were expanding their exploration efforts in the direction of the northern Delaware Basin. He confidently predicted that Pecos's land values would soar and, with additional oil supplies available from successful drilling, the pipeline's capacity would take on a scarcity value. "It's all there right in front of you," the jerk-off concluded.

Dr. MacNeer scanned the room for questions or rebuttal, but there were none.

Our professor was standing in the middle of the circle, tie neatly knotted, resting on a dark-blue checked shirt, sports coat formally buttoned, looking more like a country gentleman than a college professor. He rubbed his hands together while informing the class that only one of the twenty students in the class raised an issue with the Gulf-Pecos merger. The mood of the room immediately changed, paranoid eyes darting right and left, wanting to know the traitor's identity and the reason for this heresy.

In shock, Derrick shouted an arrogant challenge. "They're wrong! Whoever it is, stand up and state your case. You're about to be shot down."

The room was quiet until I heard a soft voice from across the circle. "It's footnote number five, isn't it?" In unison the class turned and stared at the most stunning woman ever to grace the halls of the Wharton School. Tall, willowy, and elegant, Elsbeth Aylesworth looked more like a *Vogue* model than a J. P. Morgan banker. It was pure comic relief watching every guy not suffering from impaired vision syndrome attempt to approach or impress her. She looked directly at me. I could read her lips. "It had to be you. Am I right?"

I remained silent, sensing what was coming and trying my best to remain calm. It would soon be my turn at bat. I knew that I had a golden opportunity to break from the pack of wolves and distinguish myself if I handled this challenge with distinction. I was ready when Dr. MacNeer acknowledged that I was the one dissenter. "Well, Mr. Stout, the floor is all yours."

They came after me in full force as if I were blocking their path to the only watering hole in the desert. I kept my artillery at bay by choosing not to mention that Banksville's town council had empowered the mayor to hire an engineering firm to determine the extent of any pipeline leakage. Derrick and his followers bared their teeth and attacked the significance of the word *possible*. I relished the opportunity to ask them, in the presence of Dr. MacNeer, to explain their understanding of footnote number five in Pecos's financials. They stuttered and babbled in a vain attempt to camouflage their ignorance. I graciously offered to help them along.

"Okay, if the risk is only possible but not probable or estimable, what's the big deal?" one of them implored.

I had to do it! I questioned sweet Derrick, "Do you agree with that statement?"

"Of course I do. I don't get why you're making a federal case out of this."

It helped that I was well prepared. I had been waiting for months to plug this mob, and my chance was *now*. I was careful not to paint myself into a corner by stating that I knew as a fact that the pipeline was leaking oil. I instead said the issue needed to be highlighted because, if the pipeline had been leaking oil into the groundwater and the Pecos River, the potential financial ramifications were significant enough that they could change the economics of the merger. I added that just because the liability was not currently estimable didn't necessarily mean it couldn't be enormous.

They were desperate, panicking because this was all happening in front of the entire class and its professor, so they bored in once again.

"Explain why you think you know something that all Gulf's high-priced lawyers and investment bankers don't?" they argued.

It was time. I brought down the hammer when I told them that Banksville had recently contracted engineering specialists to research the extent of the environmental problem. I finished by opening my final secret envelope—where I informed them that the local newspapers were on the case in a major way and had already produced damning evidence of leakage. I looked around the room and stated that those were the reasons I took issue with the merger, because Gulf Oil needed to properly evaluate the risk of this "possible" environmental problem to determine if they should go through with the Pecos Pipeline acquisition as planned.

I looked out at the circle of angry faces, my presentation completed, and then to Dr. MacNeer, who offered me a complimentary nod. The class was utterly mute until Elsbeth Aylesworth spoke out in my defense. "Let's all admit that we missed this one and he got it right." Dr. MacNeer distributed our graded exams with little fanfare; attached to mine was a handwritten note requesting a brief meeting at his office later that afternoon.

She was waiting for me in the hallway, leaning against the wall in her camel-hair overcoat.

"Congratulations. That was quite a performance in there. When I saw that damn footnote, I was suspicious but didn't follow the trail. Shame on me. I wanted you to know I liked the way you held your ground against that jerk Derrick. I was surprised he so easily took the bait you cast out. I'm glad you stuck it to that bozo. He deserved it."

I almost didn't know what to say. I had never seen Elsbeth talk to anyone. She was all business in the classroom—succinct, self-assured, smart, eager to speak out on issues or defend her stated positions. Beyond the academic environment, she was aloof and distant. She usually left the seminar room alone, in her own private world. As a keen observer of attractive women, especially those exuding primo sexuality, my bet was at least four to one there wasn't another one like her in all of west Philly. She took a step closer, flashed a killer smile, and wished me goodbye. I couldn't think of anything to say except a meek thank-you. I thought I had outgrown the pathetic teenage pervert stage, but the stirring between my legs said I was wrong once again. I was left standing alone in an empty hallway nursing my fantasy of a naked Elsbeth Aylesworth.

I wasn't sure why Professor MacNeer had asked me to stop by his office, but I assumed poker wasn't on the agenda. I entered his private sanctuary to a resounding, "Well done, young man. You exhibited good instincts, perseverance, detective skills, and appreciation of the vagaries of the accounting profession. Please tell me how you solved the puzzle. I'm interested in each step, how it evolved, and how you came to your conclusion." I took my time and told him my story in detail.

I said that I was suspicious from the very beginning. It was too obvious, too pat. I admitted glossing over footnote number five the first few times I read the financial statements but, when the light finally went on in my brain, I went into action. I told him which accounting reference book I used to pinpoint the proper definitions of possible and probable, how I studied the maps of the Permian and Delaware Basins in the library while also charting the path of the Pecos River, and my luck in finding an obscure book in which I learned about the history of Banksville and its environs.

"That's fine," he said, "but how did you uncover all that juicy information about the engineering firm and the local newspaper's coverage?"

"A Texas operator gave me the area code for Banksville, then I hit the jackpot when I made contact with a cub reporter at the area's only local newspaper. It was on a quiet Sunday; he was bored and happy to take my call. He couldn't answer most of my questions but agreed to send me the newspaper's articles on the river situation after we talked baseball and I told him stories about his hero, Cincinnati's catcher Johnny Bench. A few days later, the paper's owner and managing editor took me by the hand and led me through the labyrinth."

"Is there anything else I should know?" the professor then added.

I felt it was prudent to be careful with my answer. I had studied all the newspaper articles and listened to Chip Sr.'s impassioned sermons. He had told me about the engineering study that was underway, but I never could confirm it. I hardly knew him, we'd never had a face-to-face discussion, but I couldn't help putting trust in him. Was I being naive? Was Chip too much of a zealot or was he a passionate reporter willing to risk his credibility to help correct a major environmental screwup? *Son, I gave you my word . . .* still rang in my ear. Would Chip Ryan Sr. want me to share his insights with a college professor he didn't know?

My teacher could read me like an open book. I was spent. It was the ninth inning, and I had nothing left in the tank. He complimented me once again and apologized for the persistence of his questions.

"I'm just trying to understand you a little better. You're an intriguing young man, and I'm glad you bluffed your way into my seminar class. You remind me of someone I knew long ago."

As I reached for my coat and scarf, he stood and told me he wanted to recommend me to an investment bank in New York led by a friend of his.

Before I could thank him, he said, "I wouldn't call him if you didn't deserve the opportunity. Just remember when you're on the Street, don't try to draw to an inside straight." He leaned back with a hearty laugh, patted me hard on the back, and away I went, skipping down the stairs like a ten-year-old who just caught a foul ball in the stands at Crosley Field.

I was looking forward to the March meeting with the senior partners of Burr, Addington, and Merritt at their New York office. My first interview a month earlier in Philadelphia had gone well. Dr. MacNeer had prepped me on what to expect and why he thought this firm was a good fit for me. "High-quality people, grand corporate finance and money-gathering relationships, excellent research department. Frankly, they're a little weak in money management and trading. The kind of place you could make an impact on if you mature into a bona fide moneymaker."

His longstanding friendship with Ambrose Burr was a plus. They had been trading amigos for years before MacNeer turned to academia and Burr joined a white-shoe firm noted for its close relationships with old East Coast money. Ambrose Burr had earned his stripes by helping to transform the company. He'd rejuvenated their corporate finance efforts, built a first-rate research department, and attracted assets to be internally managed. His vision was to leverage the firm's pristine reputation and blue-blood connections to create a well-diversified investment bank, short on risk taking and long on fee-generated income. The firm's aged, stodgy founders were pleased to accept the buyout offer he put together with two younger superstars, Barrett Addington and Hollis Merritt. BAM, as it was soon to be affectionately called on the Street, was born.

Ambrose didn't want the headache of opening regional offices so, a few years later, he purchased two large clearing firms and began marketing BAM's research and money-management skills nationwide to local brokerage companies that maintained high profiles in their own markets but couldn't afford to support research or investment-management departments. The financial arrangements he proposed worked well for both sides. By the early 1970s, BAM's brand was present in most of the US's important cities. Throughout this building process, Ambrose relied on Bates MacNeer to be his trusted sounding board and chief consulting rabbi-priest.

I spent most of that New York day being grilled by the major department heads and the director of research at BAM during a long lunch in their office. He was the super-serious type, interested in my technical skills, wary of my lack of experience. I couldn't imagine this cold fish ever telling a thigh-slapping joke. A few partners, including Hollis Merritt, interrupted the interrogation by popping in to introduce themselves and shake my hand. As the clock struck two, I was escorted to Ambrose Burr's office. I learned at lunch that I was only the third student Dr. MacNeer had recommended to BAM. The first became a partner in corporate finance, while the other moved on to law school.

I was expecting to meet an elegant silver-haired gentleman with old-world manners, formal, with a deep baritone voice and dressed like the duke of Windsor. His first question might be to inquire where my ancestors were from and when did they immigrate to the New World. Instead I was greeted by a short, wiry Yalie, a tightly wound Ivy League welterweight boxing champion circa 1932. Ambrose Burr had grown up on Park Avenue, with servants, trust funds, and a giant chip on his shoulder. When other boys at St. Bernard's were practicing squash or the piano, he opted for boxing lessons on his twelfth birthday. His father was tall and had rowed crew at Yale, but his only son never breached five eight. Ambrose took out his frustrations in the ring, where he became known as a fierce fighter willing to take a punch if he could deliver at least one of his own. He reluctantly agreed to attend Mother Yale only after his grandfather bribed him with season tickets to the Yankees. Ambrose always had been an independent cuss, intent on making his own way in life. When he turned his back on the family business, a century-old insurance company based in Lower Manhattan that had been run by a Burr from its inception, his disappointed father pleaded with him to reconsider. His son held firm and went on his own way, probably thinking, *Why would I want to spend my life watching grass grow?*

I can clearly remember that first meeting with Ambrose Burr—a brief, warm greeting coupled with a bone-crushing handshake, then off to the races getting down to business. He wasn't the type to waste time.

"So you want to be a security analyst, graduate to managing portfolios, and then retire before you're forty having made a whole bunch of money. Your financial future secure, it would be a good time to take a year off to see the world before settling down to devote yourself to curing world hunger. Is that an accurate summary?"

I certainly wasn't ready for that preamble, but I had to say something. All I could come up with was a weak "Is that scenario a job requirement?" He let loose a boisterous laugh and slapped his knee.

"Not bad! I'm told you have spent the day learning about us. Tell me about Rogers Stout and why we should hire a twenty-one-year-old neophyte."

Even though his name was on the door, and he had a larger-than-life personality, I felt comfortable talking with him. He listened intently to everything I said without interruption, asking questions only after I had completed my thoughts. After thirty minutes I thought we were finished, but then came a question from far left field.

"I understand from that old codger MacNeer that you're an expert on the Gulf-Pecos merger. Tell me why you think Gulf might be making a mistake."

I didn't need a doctorate from MIT to know my response to this request might decide if I would ever have a future at Burr, Addington, and Merritt. We talked briefly about the two companies, why the deal was a good one for Pecos, and the reasons why Gulf coveted these assets. Then his questioning began. I was trying to project knowledge and maturity while he made it clear that he wanted crisp, succinct answers. No rambling, no BS! I told him why the local newspaper was deeply concerned about potential pipeline leakage into both the groundwater and the river itself. I mentioned their interviews with local farmers and ranchers plus the pictures documenting some oil spillage in and around the river. I reminded him that the Pecos River connected with other bodies of water in the basin.

Ambrose Burr leaned back and massaged his forehead. Then came the question: If I were advising Gulf on this matter, what would I recommend to their management and board of directors? I said that if I could definitively confirm that Banksville had commissioned an engineering study to determine if there was oil leakage, I would postpone the merger until the study was completed, because at this stage it was not possible to properly evaluate the environmental risk. I reasoned that the findings might be minor and inconsequential to the overall transaction, but it was possible that the pipeline had been leaking for years and had caused significant damage. If that were the case, then the financial exposure to Gulf needed to be evaluated before a merger was consummated.

He didn't say a word. I felt young and awkward. I tried my best to remain calm and composed while he sat still, his eyes studying me until he slowly uncrossed his legs, stood and asked me his final question.

"Bates thinks you could become an unconventional but superior money manager. That's a hell of a compliment from a man like him. You should know he was a real star in his day, one of the very best. He suggested I ask you this: What would you do if you had stock positions in Gulf and Pecos?"

I wasn't going to allow myself to be afraid of this question. I reasoned that if Dr. MacNeer suggested it, then he believed it would be an opportunity for me to shine. I wouldn't disappoint him; I would answer like a seasoned pro.

"I'm not a student of the oil industry, so I have no particular opinion on Gulf's stock. I wouldn't own Pecos. First of all, the upside is limited to about 1.5 percent based on the terms of the deal. I realize that the closing is supposed to be in about two months, so the annualized return would be 9 percent plus one dividend of 1 percent. That's a fine total return, but in my opinion, it doesn't compensate for the downside risk. Remember, Pecos's stock was trading at forty before there were rumors of this deal. Now it's almost seventy. If Gulf extends the closing date, the stock will decline, perhaps materially, due to the uncertainty. If the merger is called off based on a material adverse change, the stock will plummet."

"How low would it go?"

"I think it could go below forty, because that would mean the costs of an environmental cleanup would be Pecos's responsibility. Their balance sheet isn't all that strong. It's quite conceivable they would need additional funding. The magnitude of the downside would depend on how serious this issue actually becomes."

"That's a pretty difficult investment proposition," he mused.

"Sir, I should tell you what I have already done in my own little portfolio. I sold Pecos short after I wrote my report for Professor MacNeer. I liked the risk/reward of maybe a one- to two-dollar loss versus a thirty-dollar gain."

This time the interview really was over. He crunched my hand again.

"I wish you good luck, young man," he concluded. "I guess I owe my friend Bates a thank-you."

I was anxious to call Ronnie. He had questioned earlier whether BAM was the right place for a bumpkin like me, and I wanted to hear his reasons.

"You look the part, you're an Ivy League guy, and your last name doesn't end in a vowel. That's a good beginning, but you're an outsider and not like them in a whole lot of ways."

"What the hell does that mean? In what kind of ways am I so different?"

"Are you so in the clouds that you didn't notice the characters walking around there? It's the WASP version of the caste system. They come from similar backgrounds, attend the same schools and churches, dress and act the same, probably even beat off with the same hand. I'll bet half of them belonged to some bullshit Yale secret society or Princeton eating club. How many of them do you think actually earned their way into that fancy firm? I've seen too many of those types here at Prescott with their superior attitudes and sense of entitlement. A big difference between us and them is that we will work hard, strive to do our very best, perform, and hope to be rewarded. These guys don't hope—they expect to become partners based on connections and lineage."

I'd heard that sermon from Ronnie too many times. When we first met in the P&P cafeteria, he accused me of being a "silver spooner," which was one of the favorite descriptive phrases for spoiled kids on the Over-the-Rhine streets. I had to convince him otherwise before we could even begin a friendship. His was a reverse snobbism, not unlike my initial views of the Spire brothers at Penn. I should have known he would have a bias against Burr, Addington, and Merritt, because he was incapable of trusting anyone he believed had inherited their position in life.

Ronnie continued, "You could become a real racehorse for them, but you won't be accepted at their clubs or be allowed to date their daughters.

That's reserved for the insiders. They may pay you well, but you won't be anointed a 'blessed one' and be offered a seat at the senior management table."

"Honestly, that wasn't the impression I got there," I said. "The head of the firm was a real guy. He was a boxer in college—his nose told the story that he wasn't afraid to mix it up. Also, the research director looked more like an astrophysicist nerd than a Waspy dilettante. They never probed my family's background, religion, or status in society. They were interested in my business studies, how well I was trained at Wharton, and about my near- and longer-term goals on Wall Street. They asked if I was prepared to commit to long hours in a pressure-packed business environment."

"They didn't zone in on anything personal?" he asked.

"One of the stereotypes you have been referring to wondered how I could turn down Yale, as if I were rejecting being crowned by the royal family. That was ludicrous, I admit," I answered.

"Besides a starting job at a below-market salary, presumably because they are the one and only BAM, what did they offer you?"

"A comprehensive training program, two years in the research department, and then a level playing field where my advancement would be based on my own performance. Mr. Burr himself promised me there was no ceiling at BAM when it came to rewarding accomplishment."

I could hear Ronnie grinding his teeth through the phone. "You're really set on this New York thing, aren't you?"

"Yes, I am," I answered, recognizing that it disappointed my special friend.

"I guess if it doesn't work out, you could always come back home and the Prescotts would kiss your highfalutin, big-city, eastern ass."

Ronnie Davis wasn't going to change his mind—it wasn't in his DNA. He had been schooled on the streets and in public playgrounds where your last name didn't carry any weight. His respect was reserved for the underdog, someone who could will himself up from the old neighborhood into a position of authority. I could tell we had gone far enough.

"Hey, big man. If I returned home, I could spend my afternoons watching an older, slower Xavier star waddle down the court and make an occasional shot or two. That could be worth the move."

I pictured R. D. sitting in his apartment wearing a gray athletic T-shirt (Property of Xavier Basketball) smiling and simultaneously flashing me the finger.

I heard the music blasting from down the hallway. It was Jacob's way of listening to southern gospel. "You don't just hear it, Rogers, you've got to feel it. Picture yourself sitting in a pew at an old wooden-frame church, the building shaking from the sounds and the people stomping their feet." He was waving his arms and jumping around like he had hot coals in his underpants. He took turns singing with the chorus and directing the organist. His parents would have gone nuts had they seen their beloved son sweating to music that wasn't composed by Brahms or Mozart. Jacob had tried his best to convert me to gospel—"check out the passion, the rhythm, and the fabulous harmonies"—but I was more of a folk-rock guy. "Gibberish. No soul. Too damn sweet" was his retort. When I asked how he felt about gospel's message, he cut me off with, "There's nothing wrong with good spiritual stuff—you don't have to believe it, just buy in for a few minutes and enjoy that sensation of faith and hope." I tried, I really did, but as much as the music itself was uplifting, I kept hearing the words and I knew what they meant.

The school calendar that final year only provided for an abbreviated spring break. My two amigos had made their plans; Jacob was off to New York to accept a coveted job offer at McKinsey and to search for an apartment, while Charlotte was trekking down to the homeland for a last visit before leaving in early June for France and then the Far East. She postponed her trip to Cincinnati a few days so we could spend "a proper farewell together" (those were her words) at her place near Columbia's campus. "I'll be back next April before the Reds take the field for opening day. Don't forget to mark that date on your calendar!" she reminded me.

"Do you have room for me in your Bentley tomorrow?" I asked, watching Jacob pack. It was quite entertaining observing the neatnik he had become, with shoes packed in individual cloth bags, shirts folded meticulously as if by an experienced butler. "I haven't seen you all week and I wanted to tell you I was formally hired by BAM. They sent their proposal by registered mail; I'm to report for duty the first Tuesday after Labor Day. It's hard to digest the fact that this is really going to happen."

"Well, m'boy, we really are sitting pretty. First choices both. A management consultant and a Wall Street dude. Not bad for an Upper West Side Jew and a midwestern hick! We'll pay our dues, and then a few years from now I'll be running a major company and you'll be managing zillions."

That evening we went to our favorite hole-in-the-wall bar downtown on Pine Street for a celebratory "we're on our way" burger and a few beers. Munching on his fries and then stealing mine, Jacob suggested we room together for the first few years if we could find the right apartment. "I think it could work well for us," he suggested. "We both will be working odd hours, want privacy, and have limited funds. I should be able to find an adequate two-bedroom separated by a living room and eat-in kitchen that fits our budgets. I'll even make sure it has enough shelf space for your freaking peanut butter." I knew he was serious when he promised to swallow hard and ask his mother for help. "She's a killer, Rogers. She'll pull it off." I told him that my needs were quite simple—my priorities were my own bathroom, a natural-light environment, and easy access to where I would be working. We shook hands and agreed to check out a few places together after Charlotte left the city.

My New York adventure was set to begin in only four months. I was excited, nervous, confident, unsure of myself, happy to be in a major city, afraid of New York, and a convoluted combination of every other conceivable significant emotion.

It was the right time to ask Jacob what he thought of my newest idea. I would usually whip through the *Philadelphia Inquirer* primarily for daily updates on sports and weather, but the paper's obsessive coverage of New Jersey's gaming referendum had caught my attention. After much debate and failed attempts, legalized casino gambling in Atlantic City was approved in late 1976 by the state authorities. A small company called Resorts International had jumped ahead of potential competitors when it secured options on a large tract of prime real estate on Atlantic City's fabled boardwalk and then also purchased a company that owned a huge, ancient hotel that they planned to convert to a casino with restaurants, shops, and a Las Vegas–style theater. Their goal was to open for business during the spring of 1978, at least one year before any newly built casino could offer competition. I knew Resorts' stock was a real speculation with questionable management, marginal balance sheet, plenty of opposition from all sorts of interested groups, big-time execution risk, and unproven economics. It was definitely not a Graham and Dodd special, but it was the ultimate juicy dream stock. It would be the only legal casino easily accessible by car or bus to the largest population concentration in the US. Until there were bona fide competitors, Resorts would be operating a monopoly, the near-perfect business model. I could almost taste the potential rewards.

I wanted Jacob to ride down to Atlantic City with me; he could educate me along the way on this part of New Jersey. He also had a knack for making virtual strangers feel comfortable when talking with him. I thought that those conversations could help me determine how this venture was progressing.

Nursing my Rolling Rock while my future roommate inhaled a hot fudge sundae, we discussed Resorts' Atlantic City opportunity. I set the table—the initial failed referendum attempts, my understanding of the political dynamics, Resorts management's backgrounds, how they optioned the land on the boardwalk, the reasoning for their purchase of the Chalfonte-Haddon Hall hotel, and how they could own Atlantic City for at least one year.

"Are we talking about a play in the stock, or are we thinking of this as an investment—in other words, as a real company?" he asked. Good old Jacob knew the difference between trading and investing. "I like the concept," he offered, "but how do you know these are the guys to manage such a complex, multifaceted project?" I told him that's why we should go down there together. We could probe and ask questions, meet with some locals, talk with the guys on the building site.

"It might be a wasted day or it might be intriguing—either way, it's only a day. Let's go! It'll be my treat. If the stock idea doesn't pan out, we could walk the boardwalk, breathe in the salt air, and gobble a few Nathan's Famous Hot Dogs. If we strike out, you can shit on me all the way back to New York." I studied him as he finished his sundae and could tell that I already had him safely on board.

I was flying high, like a big-game hunter must feel when preparing to track elusive prey in the wild. In a rare magnanimous gesture, I sought out the waiter to settle the bill, when I saw Elsbeth Aylesworth approaching our table.

"Holy shit," I heard Jacob mutter, "it's the ice goddess herself that I've seen lighting up the halls at Dietrich all these months. She must be the loveliest but most untouchable piece of ass in greater Philadelphia."

She glided over to us, designer boots barely touching the bar's tile floor, sure of herself, knowing that every male in the joint was looking at her. She helped herself to a chair, greeted Jacob as if she already knew him, and rested a vodka martini on our table.

"Welcome to my neighborhood haunt. Do you mind if we join in your celebration?" she asked as she waved at an overdressed gentleman to come over. "I understand you both really scored on the job front. News like that travels fast at Wharton, especially with the pirate types who would gladly knife you in the back for such quality offers. McKinsey and BAM. Wow! Really well done."

We were greeted by her older brother, who clearly had no desire to spend time with two young, overly energized sarcastic types. He was formal and uptight, looking over at his younger sister wondering why he had to pretend interest in our conversation. She clearly wasn't intimidated.

"Geoffrey came all the way down to Philadelphia to convince me to attend law school and then join Daddy's firm. Everyone else in the family is a lawyer, so why not little Elsbeth? Banking is such a dirty business, you know—numbers, trading, and all that money-grubbing stuff. I wasn't bred for that way of life—it's really not what an Aylesworth should stoop to for a career. If I was a lawyer at Daddy's firm, I would be a proud partner before I was thirty-five. Now, wouldn't that be dignified? I could hold my head high when advising clients and never get my own lily-white hands dirty. Isn't that right, brother?"

He was seething. "Let's discuss this in private. I wouldn't want to bother your Wharton friends with family business."

"Oh, we don't mind," Jacob volunteered, relishing the chance to stir up mischief and all the while staring at Elsbeth with a lustful animal hunger.

She turned to face me. "What do you think, Rogers? You're level-headed under pressure."

I didn't hesitate. "I think you've earned the right to make your own decision. Were you planning on returning to the J. P. Morgan private bank?"

Elsbeth replied, "I spent two years in London learning the business from the management side. They're offering me the chance to work with the investment team in New York. I think it's an exciting opportunity."

At that moment she seemed vulnerable, a proud individual being bullied by an older brother, but I had seen enough of Elsbeth Aylesworth in action to know that she was strong willed and would survive this battle.

"Sorry, Geoffrey," I said. "I think your sister is going to chart her own course."

I lifted my Rolling Rock and clicked her martini glass with a flourish. Jacob joined in. She smiled warmly and thanked us for the support. I was beginning to think that she was a real person after all. The three of us came from very different backgrounds, but we shared the desire to prove ourselves on the big stage against all comers. We were willing to face the challenge on our own, because the juice from the victory goblet was intoxicating.

Driving with Jacob on the New Jersey Turnpike was like standing next to Judah Ben-Hur during a chariot race at the Roman Colosseum. He would dart in and out, cursing at drivers who didn't know you're supposed to drive twenty miles per hour over the posted speed limit. The only thing he was missing was a whip to encourage his car to go even faster. I was exhausted but relieved when he delivered me to Charlotte's apartment. She ran outside and jumped on me, then attacked Jacob with a hug. He was outwardly embarrassed by her wild enthusiasm but loved it all nonetheless. Her cheeks were glowing, her eyes sparkled, her smile so genuinely exhilarating. She pulled me inside. "We have so much to talk about."

Three days together was not enough. Charlotte had bought a book featuring interesting neighborhood walks and proceeded to fill our time with sightseeing and ethnic food. I knew her master plan was to keep us so busy that we wouldn't dwell on the loneliness of the upcoming months, but the packed bags resting in the corner of her bedroom told a revealing story. Charlotte said that whenever she was stressed out and needed a break from school, she would hop on a subway and head downtown. She believed there was a certain integrity in the old districts of New York, especially those south of Fourteenth Street. As if I was her young son, she explained to me the concept of cultural pockets and then encouraged a lively debate on the pros and cons of living in a homogenous environment.

On successive days I was introduced to moo goo gai pan in China-town and shrimp scampi in Little Italy; I couldn't pronounce the former and couldn't get enough of the latter. After avoiding the hawkers on Or-chard Street, Charlotte insisted it was time to eat lunch with "Grandma Rose's people." She laughed uncontrollably watching me navigate my way through Katz's Delicatessen. "Remember," she said, "no cheese with the corned beef and definitely no mayonnaise." Lunch at Katz's brought back memories of Sugar n' Spice and made me nostalgic for the good times we shared there.

The more we walked, the more natural it felt wandering about with her, holding hands and talking like a couple who belonged together. This was all so new to me that I couldn't help wondering if I deserved to be so serene. I didn't want her to go to Boston or Washington, much less Paris or Southeast Asia. My master plan was in motion, and I needed to know that she was with me. She listened carefully as I laid out my near-term goals in New York and then questioned me unmercifully. "Tell me again why this money success thing is so important," and then, "How can you expect to achieve all this in so few years?" She didn't care a whit about business, markets, or money, but she cared about me. Her challenging logic helped me think through decisions. She didn't know squat about Wall Street or Burr, Addington, and Merritt, but she knew what ques-tions to ask to provoke me to think with clarity. If she disagreed with me, she didn't hesitate to speak up; when she thought I was on beam she would clap her hands in enthusiastic agreement. She was Charlotte!

Cruising along the side streets of the Lower East Side, I analyzed the most recent Rogers Stout scorecard. In truth I was ahead of plan—except for the monumental risk of Charlotte's future adventures. I knew by now that the Cambodian tragedy would be only one of the many causes she would undertake. I admired her, wanted her to have self-respect, knew her causes would be worthwhile, and surely believed in her. All that was fine, except her commitment scared the crap out of me beyond any limits I had ever known. The fact was that my brokerage account at Prescott & Prescott now had an extra zero attached to its total, but this financial success wouldn't offset my sorrow if anything ever happened to this high-energy life force.

We were both talked out and emotionally drained. We shared a pizza and finished off a bottle of cheap red in her room. There was no need to speculate anymore about the future. We ate quietly and watched an old Katharine Hepburn movie (Charlotte's favorite). That last night, spooning in bed as if we had been together for decades, not years, I was surprised to feel my eyes welling up. I held her extra tight. "Is something wrong?" she asked.

"Of course not, I just want to remember this until you come back," I answered.

As usual, Jacob was on time, waiting in his car outside Charlotte's apartment, ready for the ride to the Jersey Shore. He handed her a clumsily wrapped going-away present.

"Let me guess, it's something to protect our meek little Charlotte?" she laughed as she unwrapped a pair of chopsticks he had lifted from a local restaurant.

"Kiddo, you are so far from meek," he joshed.

"I promise to think of you when I use these guys feasting in the field." She smiled, genuinely touched.

"Jacob," she said, suddenly serious, "take care of my wonder boy. Can I count on that?" Before he could respond, she turned and whapped me on the rear as I was getting in the car.

I looked back at her standing on the sidewalk, smiling bravely and waving goodbye simultaneously. As our car pulled away, she blew me a kiss that I swear I could taste all the way to Atlantic City.

I had bought Charlotte a present in Philadelphia from a jewelry store near Rittenhouse Square. I chose a silver butterfly necklace, because I had read that butterflies symbolize freedom and joy, rebirth and new beginnings. I left it on her pillow on top of a card with a poem I wrote for her.

Jacob and I drove in silence over the George Washington Bridge. I was pensive, digesting the fact that I wouldn't be seeing Charlotte for a very long time. Staring down at the Hudson River, its power and beauty didn't register with me. One year, she had said. At that moment I thought a year would feel like an eternity.

Jacob spoke up. "I hope you realize you're one lucky Cornhusker! Every time I'm with her, I feel better. I know you're frightened of the unknown here, but listen to me. She's smart and she won't take unnecessary risks. For some unfathomable reason, she loves you, so she will find a resiliency within herself to will her way back to New York. Why she wants to return to be with a louse like you is another story. Having lived down the hall from you for eight months, I probably should have told her that she'll be making a huge mistake."

"Thanks for the support," I responded. "You have a unique way of raising my spirits. By the way, not everyone from the Midwest lives next to a cornfield, and, to be precise, the term *Cornhusker* applies only to people from Nebraska."

"Really? I always thought everything west of the Hudson River was the Great Plains."

Looking out the window driving south, I saw nothing visually appealing nor particularly interesting that would attract the attention of a tourist on the way to Atlantic City. I told Jacob of my concern, but he was in a reminiscing mood.

"Years ago the beaches at AC were pristine and the boardwalk was alive with all sorts of fun activities, like a country fair. There were jugglers, mimes, and tricksters of all types. There were games for the children and artists drawing charcoal and pastel portraits for a few dollars each. There was ice cream, cotton candy, hot dogs, and all types of ethnic goodies. It was a bona fide vacation destination easily accessible from New York, Philadelphia, Wilmington, and all of New Jersey. And, of course, there was the ocean itself."

The closer we got to Atlantic City, the more run-down the surroundings appeared. It all reminded me of the sad slums and weary, neglected neighborhoods I had seen many times in northern Kentucky towns like Newport and Covington.

We parked near the boardwalk, making sure to lock everything that moved in the trunk. Two young boys ran over and offered to watch our car for five dollars. Jacob gave them each a dollar and made them promise to protect his chariot with their lives. I volunteered to double their fee if they were successful. I also succumbed to the apparent leader when he asked for an additional buck if they washed our windows. Walking over to the boardwalk, Jacob told me I was the worst negotiator he had ever met.

I can still remember my initial sense of doom standing in front of Chalfonte-Haddon Hall that morning. In poker vernacular, Resorts had made an all-in bet when it purchased Leeds & Lippincott, the owner of this thousand-room monstrosity. The complex was originally built in the early 1900s as separate hotels and was later joined by a skyway, thus creating the largest hotel in Atlantic City at the time. Like most of the buildings we saw on the boardwalk, it was in a state of unloved disrepair. It reminded me of a gigantic haunted house occupied by the Addams Family. Resorts had been actively involved financially and was lobbying politically to encourage a positive result from the Atlantic City gaming referendum. The company completed the purchase of Leeds & Lippincott four months before the referendum was successfully passed in late 1976.

"This conversion is going to cost a fortune," I mumbled. "It was too big a gamble," I said to Jacob, "unless Resorts management had special insights into the results of the pending referendum."

"It's New Jersey," Jacob came back quickly. "How naive can you be? Of course the results are known in advance of the vote."

Resorts was planning to close the older Chalfonte and to pour $50 million into the renovation of Haddon Hall. The goal was to open for business by Memorial Day 1978, which would give the company a monopoly on the East Coast for almost one and a half years. Four months or so into the renovation, the site looked like a poor survivor of a Kansas tornado. "Dresden, 1945," Jacob muttered as he scanned the construction workers tearing out the guts of the old hall. I had already reviewed Resorts' balance sheet and concluded that the Grim Reaper would be blowing taps at the company's funeral if this project failed.

The construction site was barricaded and security guards were posted strategically. Jacob approached a small group of workers on a coffee break and tried his friendly "I'm a nice guy who was hoping you could help me out for a second" routine. They looked at him like he was from Mars; one workman enjoying a Bud with his doughnut pointed to a mobile home parked on a side street—"That's the office of the project manager. Ask him your questions." We went on our way, but before we knocked on the office door, Jacob implored me to loosen up.

"This is going to be a tough crowd. Your formal, aloof shit isn't going to work here. Remember, these guys don't owe you anything; they'll think they're doing you a favor by giving you the time of day."

"I'm with you, Coach. I'll be quiet and follow your lead."

A large woman sporting a Philadelphia Flyers jersey and matching sweatpants greeted us with a grunt. She was seated behind a gray metallic desk and seemed to be functioning as receptionist, secretary, and bookkeeper wrapped up in one oversize package.

"What's up, fellas," she barked in her New Jersey best.

Jacob oozed charm. "I can see you're the workhorse around here. Sorry to bother you, but we were hoping to greet the boss man."

"Mr. Vega's over at the Haddon. Have a seat, he'll be back in a few. Now I've got work to do," she said, leaning over her calculator and pounding away.

"Are you excited about the casino opening here?" Jacob asked in his most flirtatious voice.

"Sure, why not?" she answered while rearranging some incoming invoices.

I had decided to let Jacob carry the ball until I noticed a model of the renovated Haddon Hall in a corner of an adjacent room. Ms. Personality agreed to let us take a peek as long as we didn't touch anything. There wasn't much to see. The building's exterior looked basically unchanged; the hotel's rooms were displayed as empty rectangular cubes. As I pivoted to leave the room, I saw a pot of gold at the end of the rainbow. Displayed on a huge piece of plywood was a replica of the new casino floor layout. Cardboard gaming tables and stand-ups representing slot machines were strategically positioned, filling the room's space.

As I stared in wonder at the future gambling extravaganza, a booming voice shook the room. "What the fuck are you two doing here?"

Carl Vega was going to be a difficult man to con. We soon found out that his reputation as an attack dog was well earned. He would scream at suppliers, threaten subcontractors, and berate workers all day and then repeat this performance week after week. He hadn't risen to project manager by being Mr. Nice Guy, and he never even considered playing that role. He knew that Resorts management wouldn't accept any excuses if their project wasn't completed on time and on budget. He even had to deal with the president of Resorts constantly demanding detailed updates. What a pain in the ass Mr. James Crosby turned out to be.

"Who let you baby-face pussies in my space?" he demanded.

Per usual Jacob was unflappable, but even my cocky friend knew that Mr. Carl Vega—wasn't a man to argue with unless you were armed with a bazooka. Blessed with Popeye forearms, meaty hands that could palm a basketball with ease or crush a grown man's bones, scars on his face that showed his experience and an ultra-quick fuse, I had the feeling he would cause us severe pain at the slightest hint of aggravation. When Jacob attempted to explain that we were just two students down from Philly to experience the excitement of what was being built on the boardwalk, he issued an order: "Don't be here when I get back!" Then he turned to the trembling hockey fan, glued to her chair by weight and fear. "I'll return for that meeting with Stephan Witten at two thirty. Make sure these faggots are gone!"

"Is he always like this?" I asked her after he left.

"Only when he's in a good mood," she answered with a sardonic smirk.

Jacob let out a brief guffaw. "You know, you're okay. What's your name, by the way?"

"People call me Deedee. That's not my real name, but I like it."

"Deedee," Jacob continued, "we're sorry if we got you in any trouble. All we wanted to do today was see what was going on with the Haddon. We love shooting craps and can't wait for the casino to open."

I could tell that my boy's charm was melting the Flyers devotee, so I asked the dealer for two cards to fill out a pathetic attempt at a flush.

"Deedee. Who is Stephan?"

"Oh, he's the architect on the project."

"When do you think he'll get here?"

"He'll probably show up around one to look around, check out the progress, and then meet with Mr. Vega. You can't miss him. He's a giant. Played hoops for Rutgers years ago."

I stepped outside the trailer a little lighter on my feet. We hiked down the boardwalk and entered Mom's, a hopping little joint on a side street that Deedee recommended for lunch. It was filled with workmen and locals. It had been an interesting morning, but I didn't believe we had made much progress on our mission. Jacob reminded me that lunch was to be my treat, so he ordered half the menu. "One day your metabolism is going to change and you'll be looking to Deedee for a relationship," I told him.

"Eat your peanut butter and be happy," he joked back.

After lunch we had some time to kill before the architectural messiah was due to arrive. It would be the first time Rogers Stout had ever experienced an ocean. I had never seen, touched, or even skipped a stone on ocean waters. I felt like a six-year-old rushing down the stairs, across the wide, sandy beach, and splashing the Atlantic waters while laughing out loud. When I told Jacob that this was a first for me, expecting to be unmercifully teased (such as "you really are a rube"), he instead spoke eloquently about the psychological powers of the ocean and why it justified our reverence. I still remember that moment and the private promise I made to spend ocean time alone with Charlotte when she returned.

You couldn't miss Stephan Witten even from a distance—he was that tall, wearing a tan army jacket, floppy hat, work boots, and a flamboyant red scarf. He still looked to be in good shape. He was quietly confident, whistling to himself while he walked along, shaking his head alternatively up and down and side to side as he observed the workmen's progress. While inspecting the building, he would ask questions, write notes to himself, and draw adjustments on a legal pad attached to his clipboard. He was one of those people who seemed relaxed and intense at the same time. I wondered, was he too pleasant to interact with the volatile Carl Vega?

We had no choice but to push our remaining chips into the middle of the table. Jacob gave me a supportive high five and we approached the Haddon's newest architect. He was our only realistic chance to gain insights into the building's progress. We asked for a few minutes of his time, and I ended up learning yet another life lesson: you can't live on this planet without sooner or later encountering unpredictable ironies. You meet a Carl Vega, treat him with respect, and get eviscerated anyway; you present yourself to an architect named Stephan and he graciously tells you far more than you ever expected to learn.

"So far we're actually three and a half days ahead of schedule. The weather gods have blessed us this winter. There's a long way to go, and I'm sure something will go wrong, but when Resorts set up a special incentive pool for the workers if they finish this project on time, I could feel a positive energy on the site. My sense is that it's already helping."

"Are the workers unionized?" Jacob inquired.

"Yes."

"Isn't that a big deal?"

"I was worried about that, but the project manager is like a lion tamer with a big bad whip."

"The workers respond to that?"

"I think everyone on this site is frightened of him."

"How about Resorts management—are they heavily involved?" Jacob asked.

"Are you kidding? They know this is their big chance. My phone is ringing day, night, and weekends."

Why not try, I thought. *He seems like a talker.* "They're thinking big numbers when this opens, aren't they?" I prodded the architect, not really expecting an answer.

So when he said, "The financial guys believe they're going to shoot the lights out," I felt a lucky shot of adrenaline.

"Have you heard any numbers bandied about?" Jacob chimed in. Stephan said the he wouldn't know anything about that, but I thought his smile told another story. We had gone far enough. We weren't going to learn any more at this early stage, so we thanked him for his time and wished him success.

"I hope you win a bonus along with the guys," I added.

My gut was screaming at me to buy some Resorts stock, but my analytical side cautioned patience. I was seduced when Stephan showed us the drawings of his vision for the converted Haddon Hotel. I knew nothing about architectural design, but it just looked right to me. It shouted out to come on in, have a jolly good time, try out your luck and skill at a game of chance.

As soon as Jacob dropped me off at Penn Station, I began to play with Resorts' financial statements. On the train back to Philadelphia, I tried to justify a fundamental basis for placing a bet. I was enamored with the idea of owning the only legal gambling facility east of Nevada, but the company's overleveraged balance sheet, punk cash flow, and questionable management gave me pause. Was the company's executive team capable of quarterbacking this project? What about the political uncertainties?

Jacob had warned me on the ride back, "Remember, this is New Jersey—funny things happen here." If the hotel's conversion was completed late or over budget or their casino's legal approvals were not forthcoming on time, financial peril could be around the corner for Resorts. As I agonized over all these issues, I forced myself to look in the mirror and question if my love for gambling was overly influencing my decision making.

The more I tried, the more I realized that this situation was not analyzable. How could you possibly estimate the revenue from gaming tables and slot machines in a new casino? Would they be in demand all day and night or only be in limited use? How could an outside investor guess at the expense of running this enterprise? My conviction kept vacillating. On the one hand, I felt it was going to work, the upside was enormous, and if I was lucky, this score could raise my portfolio to a whole new level. On the other hand, I feared this really could fail and the stock would then plunge into oblivion. As I argued with myself, new possibilities and imponderables emerged, one of which captivated my imagination. If Resorts' future was unpredictable, and its stock therefore difficult to value with any degree of precision, could that conundrum actually be a positive? If there were no conventional metrics to analyze, then the fundamental inputs investors study would be useless. Maybe then the stock's price action itself could become the focus of interest. If the stock appreciated, then Wall Street types might assume, possibly even believe, it was confirming a bright future for Resorts. That would be a Dr. Whittles classic—the stock taking on a life of its own. In that case, the higher the stock went, the more investors and traders would want to own, and they would pile in and pay up regardless of valuation.

As the train pulled into Philadelphia, I must have been struck by a thunderbolt delivered directly from the beloved gambling gods. The message was clear—reread *Extraordinary Popular Delusions and the Madness of Crowds* by good ol' MacKay! I immediately knew *I had to buy this stock*. It could go up, down, or nowhere at all, but if it ignited, Resorts stock could become the tulip mania of the twentieth century.

I was so excited that I sprinted down the corridor to a pay phone at 30th Street Station. I had to talk to Ronnie Davis.

"Did you get a chance to look at Resorts?"

"Hello to you, too," he responded in a sarcastic tone. "Yes, I'm well, and so are my sisters. Thanks for being so concerned."

"Sorry, Ronnie, but I saw what they're doing in Atlantic City yesterday, and my heart's pounding."

"I get the message, but listen to me—just slow down and take a deep breath. Now, here's the deal. No one I've talked to follows Resorts or even cares about it. I asked a player I know, a young honcho on the desk of a go-go firm who usually hears the grass grow, and he said it was dog shit."

"He'll be drooling over it when the casino is set to open. By then the stock could be anywhere."

"Look. I know you want me to like this stock, but I have to tell you the truth. I'm afraid of it. I've been watching the trading, and it swings like crazy on no news, we can't find any positive research reports on it, and the management has a bad reputation. It's the kind of stock that might not open one day because the legal beagles jumped down their throat. I will say this, though, ever since you asked me to follow this turkey, it's been choppy, but definitely working higher and on gradually increasing volume. I have to say that's a good sign."

"Here's what I'm thinking. I've been fortunate. Luck or skill, who cares. I'm way ahead, and if I take a chance and lose some of my profits, it's not the end of the world."

"I took a good look at your account over the weekend," Ronnie said. "You're right, you're in great shape. Kelly and Manpower have been big winners, and I think this temporary employment story still has legs. Also the housing stocks you bought are working higher. The short on Pecos was a stunning score—thank you, Gulf Oil, for walking away from the deal. The only things that aren't currently doing that well are your mutual funds."

"Ronnie, I've decided: let's go for it. Tell Sawyer to write up the tickets to sell half of all my mutual funds and buy me a 10 percent position in Resorts. I know you think I'm nuts, but I plan on watching this like a hawk. Let's bank the extra cash from the fund sales for now."

"You're sure you want to do this? It's not that you're already missing Charlotte and need to go on a thrill-seeking trip?"

With only a few months of college left and a signed job contract from Burr, Addington, and Merritt in hand, I returned to classes feeling pretty loosey-goosey. The formality of signing all the papers in BAM's New York office made me feel like I had already graduated to some form of adulthood. While many of my Wharton classmates soon would be off on grand European tours or adventure trips to places like Argentina and Alaska, I had already decided to spend the summer months at home with Dad, Ronnie, old friends from high school, and, of course, Mecklenburg's. I'd get a short-term job somewhere, help Dad at his office, hitch up with some baseball pals to play a few games, and consider getting into better physical shape per Ronnie's persistent suggestion. I also expected to work the hell out of my stock portfolio, either hanging out with Saul and his cronies at Merrill Lynch, or, if they'd let me, taking a spare desk at Prescott & Prescott. I especially wanted to pal up with Dad as much as possible on long drives, lazy walks, a few old-fashioned gambleathons, and for sure a couple of Reds home games. I wasn't the slightest bit envious of the fat cats whose fathers heaped riches on them for actually graduating from the famed school. To me it all smelled like a payoff. Let them cruise the Mediterranean for a month or go shooting grouse in Scotland. That would be fun, but would such a boondoggle help advance me to my ultimate goal?

I could sense Dad's enthusiasm for my summer plans. Ronnie, on the other hand, delivered his usual wise-guy mockery: "I wouldn't fuck around with the portfolio if I were you. You do better when you're hiding in Philly, but I'll look forward to watching you get pounded when you attempt to throw that meatball knuckler of yours."

Spring came late to the East Coast that year, but when it finally arrived, the Penn campus also awakened from its winter doldrums. The flowering trees and bushes coming to life on Locust Walk and the grass in the quads actually boasting a color other than brown helped bring the masses out of their cold-weather cocoons. With the skies a brilliant blue and the temperature breaking sixty on an uptick, heavy winter apparel and glum determination was replaced by grand smiles on the faces of the students and faculty alike. I was never a raving nature boy, never even considered joining the Boy Scouts, and as a little guy I never dreamed of being an explorer or a forest ranger, but when I left my room and stepped out into the warm sunshine, I too felt a sense of joy and optimism.

I stopped to say hello to Dr. Whittles on my way to class as I always did if I saw him sitting on his favorite bench or walking about the campus greens deep in thought. He never said it out loud, but I knew he was disappointed that I was headed straight to Wall Street after graduation. He would have advised me to exercise my brain—one of his favorite sayings—by studying other worlds at the university for a few years before I committed to a career in finance (i.e., making money). I could almost hear him thinking, *Don't be afraid to dream. Take your time and search the horizon.* Dr. Whittles meant well, but my mission was to reach that horizon as soon as possible before taking a deep breath and considering what lay beyond.

I still had a few spare minutes, so I told the good professor about my excursion to Atlantic City. I explained how uncertain the new venture would be and the questions associated with the quality of Resorts management. I also said that the upside of a successful casino monopoly on the East Coast was impossible to measure. His smile told me he immediately grasped that I was testing my concept of group sentiment on a speculative stock.

"I applaud your effort and willingness to take a risk. I'll follow this situation and see how it develops. In any case, thanks for sharing your thoughts with me and, of course, good luck to you."

As I left I continued to admire the clever Dr. Whittles, who provoked my thinking but never imposed his own opinions on me. I had come to believe, no matter the probing and questioning, that I could count on him, that he was on my side.

I nodded at Big Ben, walked past College Hall, and climbed the stairs of the Music Department. I had one last course credit to fulfill this semester and surprised everyone at school who knew me when I signed up for Opera Appreciation. "You know less about classical music than you do about hieroglyphics," Jacob reminded me. To this day I never told him why I had to learn about opera. He wouldn't understand the depth of feeling I had for the mother I hardly knew. Some of the memories I had of her were her sweet smell of spring and the way she hugged me when singing softly to me at night in my room. The rest came primarily from studying old pictures and the stories Dad told me. In truth he wasn't very good at talking about her, even to his only son.

But I also clearly remembered the sounds of opera coming from the old RCA Victrola in our living room. The music was so loud that the candlesticks on the mantel would shake and Dad would have to step outside to read his newspapers. By the middle of the third act, my mother would be standing, singing along in a sweet voice, and, as the opera's tragedies were building to crescendo, she would then engulf her young son in her arms, spinning him around until the hero or heroine met a sad end. What I remember most was when the opera was over, she would continue spinning about while kissing me on the cheek and neck, over and over.

With only two weeks left before finals, Dr. MacNeer sprang a new assignment on his class of hungry vultures. We were to describe a fantasy Wall Street job to the class in a fifteen-minute oral presentation.

"Tell us the optimal job you aspire to. You're free to use your imagination, but it must result in a practical solution. You can bounce your ideas off anyone you wish, including your classmates, but, in the end, it's your idea that I'll be evaluating. Have fun, my dreamers!"

He turned and, with his patented jaunty step, left the room.

I already knew my dream job by the time I reached the sidewalk. I had been weighing it since an interview I had with a money-management firm earlier in the year. I had thought it could be a good alternative for me if BAM didn't work out as hoped.

"What do you think the old boy has in mind now?" I heard a soft feminine voice behind me ask. I turned and faced the beautiful one as she closed in on me.

"I've heard it's the last game he plays on his seminar class each year," I answered.

"I've already got the job I prayed for," she purred while running her hands through her hair and taking another step closer. "Why don't we have a coffee at the new place on Sansom Street and work on something Dr. MacNeer might approve?"

Like a well-trained golden retriever, I followed Ms. Aylesworth up Thirty-Fourth Street, turning west on Sansom and into a quiet café where twosomes were huddled in private conversations. She ordered a cappuccino while I stuck with my favorite mint tea. It was the first time we would be having an uninterrupted, one-on-one chat. She came prepared with questions.

"You're an odd bird. Did anyone ever tell you that?" she began.

"Other than everyone I know, I guess not."

"Do you realize that most everyone in that class is secretly jealous of you or otherwise just hates your guts for being so young and for showing them up?"

"My pet goldfish Spunky loves me. Isn't that a good offset?"

"Do you always talk in riddles or wise-guy answers to people who hardly know you?"

"I try to protect myself, it takes me a long time to trust anyone."

"Have I ever done anything to make you not trust me?"

"No."

"Let's start over! Hi, I'm Elsbeth. I'm in your finance class. I'm the one who stood up for you on the Gulf-Pecos controversy. I don't hate your guts and I'm not envious of you. I think you are the star of the seminar. I have a few good ideas, too, so I thought it might be helpful if we worked together on MacNeer's newest provocative question. Let's please him, graduate, and get on with our lives."

I had never met anyone quite like her. She was a potent combination of smarts, drive, confidence, determination, and killer good looks. Before I could respond to her, my brain was racing for an answer to the "why me" question. Was her interest in me as innocent as, we're both good at this stuff, so why not join forces and make for an easy, graceful exit to the school year? Or was she a seductive siren, bent on crashing my boat on the rocks of her enticing shoreline? I decided to play it safe, act as if I was just sitting down at a poker table, where I would be cautious and see how my cards were playing out. I only like to take risks when I'm already winning.

We talked into the late afternoon. I was enjoying myself, yet it was unnerving the way she leaned across the table while emphasizing a point or asking an insightful question, becoming so intimate that I could feel her breath on my face. I was keenly aware that Elsbeth had two years of practical work experience at J. P. Morgan under her belt, while my Wall Street experience was only a two-month corporate finance internship at P&P. My bet was she would be a lifer, destined to manage an investment department from the top down, focused on raising assets and charging fees, building a solid business where she would be respected by the industry. For a brief second, I imagined the slobbering reporters she would easily tool when being interviewed as she promoted herself to the financial press. They wouldn't stand a chance.

As for me, my goal was straightforward and simple. It hadn't changed since high school. I wanted to answer only to Rogers Stout. My dream was to buy and sell stocks, become financially independent in my thirties, then somehow or someway clear my little brain, whether it be mediating in the desert or atop a Himalayan peak, and think out my future. Elsbeth and I shared some ideas and agreed to talk again in a few days after we both had time to think over the professor's assignment. I did not mention the idea I had already been pondering.

Back in my room munching on yesterday's pizza, I reread the offering memorandum of Crawford Partners. Earlier in the year, I was interviewed on campus by the founding partner, who told me I would need a few years of practical experience before he would consider making me an offer. He barked, "We're not a training ground, and I won't have time to hold your hand. We come in every day to make money." He was an entertaining character who might have placed first in a speed-talking contest. I could barely understand him when he explained at warp speed his fund's mission and how it went about achieving success. I thought he was convincing and scary at the same time as he rolled out his victory formula with ease: "Speculative techniques for conservative ends; yes, we trade a lot, but we also are long-term investors; we don't worry about the market because we're both long and short at all times; it's all about stock selection; I'll take care of everything else, and best of all, we don't live off fees—we get paid 20 percent of the profits."

I listened carefully to his pitch. It sounded too pat, too much like stealing candy from a kindergartner. I knew by then that projecting confidence was part of the Wall Street game, but it seemed to me that Ike Crawford actually believed his own BS. I was happy with the BAM opportunity; it suited me well and was, after all, endorsed by Bates MacNeer, one of my heroes. Nevertheless, you could bet that I would surely remember Crawford Partners' compensation incentive. When I offered up the firm's model to the seminar class, there were a number of blank faces looking back at me and very few follow-on questions. I couldn't tell if they were bored or just didn't get it. I thought I did okay, but my heart wasn't in the project. I was ready to move on.

I found myself starting to like Elsbeth Aylesworth. Once I got past her personal aura of beauty and aloof privilege, I saw a hard worker who stood up for her beliefs. It probably wasn't easy dealing with her overbearing father and brothers, but she had the backbone to succeed. Standing in front of the class describing her dream job, she was poised and assured, as if she had just been dealt a royal flush. In a polished presentation, she envisioned running a subsector of a major bank's money-management operation. Her idea was to pattern the business after a private Swiss bank which would be particularly attractive to high net worth individuals, foundations and family offices. Having worked at J. P. Morgan, she could explain the degree of regulation that would be imposed on the entity and how aggressive the bank could be with its fee structure. She stressed flexibility and limited competition from similar institutions in the US as being important advantages of this structure. It seemed that her performance impressed Dr. MacNeer, while every guy in the class, including me, was drooling over her personal merits. Predictably the girls wore their envious frowns as she returned to her chair like a graceful, lithe feline.

Traditionally the last seminar class with Dr. MacNeer was held at six thirty in a private room at Bookbinder's, the historic Philadelphia restaurant. A heavy oak table supported large bowls of shrimp and unshelled lobster, a selection of aged cheese, unsalted almonds, and the restaurant's sine qua non crab cakes. Waiters passed nonalcoholic drinks in tall glasses then quietly exited, leaving the professor in charge of his handpicked students. Elsbeth was standing by herself sipping a Pellegrino, seemingly unapproachable, until I waved and ambled over. The house monkeys looked on in disbelief.

"I've never seen you wearing anything other than a blue shirt and maybe a worn-out Shetland sweater. You look reasonably spiffy in your blazer and tie," she greeted me after looking me over from top to bottom.

"I thought it was time to acknowledge I'll soon be living in the real world."

"I'm going to miss this class. I really enjoy the challenging banter."

"I'm going to miss him! He's the real deal."

"I meant to tell you I like that 20 percent of the profits proposition."

"It's a hell of a way to leverage off someone else's money. I'm attracted to the concept also, but remember it's a knife that cuts both ways—20 percent of nothing is nothing."

"I would have thought you would only be focused on the success aspect."

Our conversation was interrupted when the host clinked his glass to address the group.

"Welcome, everyone. I'm glad you all could be here tonight. We're going to sit down in five minutes, so fill your plates and choose a chair. If you don't try the crab cakes, I'll be forced to question your judgment."

I overdosed on lobster and crab cakes, then sat next to Elsbeth. I thought it quite telling that the only vacant seat in the room was on the other side of Ms. Aylesworth, though I doubt she noticed or cared.

Dr. MacNeer proceeded to analyze the class's performance for the year. In general he was pleased, but he didn't hesitate to mention our mistakes. He was careful not to attach names to shortcomings, but, on the other hand, he forcefully reminded us that sloppy errors would not be tolerated by our future employers. He asked his students to share any suggestions they might have to improve the usefulness of the seminar. A few brave souls raised hands while most of us chose not to venture into those waters. I, for one, was appreciative just being in the class and therefore content to sit still and not rock the boat. About an hour later, my last official class at college had concluded. In unison the students stood and, in the best of Penn's traditions, gave Dr. MacNeer a rousing applause tribute send-off. The professor took the time to make eye contact with each student, clearly pleased and in a quite jolly mood, and then returned the applause, adding a hearty "well done!"

I stayed until the end. This man had come to understand from whence I came. There was a strong bond between us that only years later would I be insightful enough to fully grasp.

"You didn't disappoint," he said as we shook hands at the door.

"Sir, if I disappointed you, I would despise myself forever." And then I couldn't hold back, "You have been a major influence on me, and I am most grateful. I will do my best to make you proud that you once folded a winning hand a year ago."

"I had you, didn't I?" he said with a laugh so genuine, so uncontrollably robust that it even spread to his eyes, which sparkled like those of a good Scotsman telling a joke in his favorite pub. "For a while there, I really thought I was cooked," he confessed.

"I'm glad I lost," I said. "It makes the opportunity you gave me all the more precious."

Before I left Dr. MacNeer patted me on the shoulder and whispered parting advice. "I know you're in a hurry, but don't rush those first years at Burr, Addington, and Merritt. You still have much to learn. You'll have plenty of time to scale the mountains on the horizon."

The group dispersed, leaving Elsbeth and me alone on the street.

"Are you hungry?" she asked.

"I'm stuffed. I think I decimated the East Coast shellfish population all by myself."

"Feel like something stronger than iced tea?"

"Absolutely." I jumped at the thought.

She took charge, hailed a cab with a loud whistle, and a few minutes later we were welcomed like family at her neighborhood haunt. "Hi, Frankie." She smiled at a waiter while pointing to a quiet corner table.

"We've been saving it just for you, first lady," he answered.

"I do like the feel of this place," I said, sitting across from her.

"It's my home base. They watch out for me here."

Soon we were sipping a pinot noir and talking easily about Bates Mac-Neer and our future conquests. School was over for both of us, and it was time for some lighthearted fun, to get recharged and take the next step.

"I liked the way you handled my brother a while back. He's a poor imitation of my father, the real 'it has to be my way or else I'll find a way to crush you' kind of emperor. What about you, any brothers and sisters or just that pet goldfish of yours?"

"Just me."

"Rogers, you already warned me about your privacy walls, so if you'd rather confine our conversation to Wharton and Wall Street, that's okay, but I thought this would be a good time to get to know each other."

"I don't mind, it's just that I'm not very good at talking about myself."

"Great. Now I know something that boy genius isn't good at! How about your parents? I'm guessing your dad is a midwestern mogul and your mother is a teacher, maybe a college professor. Are my predictions right, because if you haven't already figured it out, I'm an amateur psychic."

I led her on. "I hope this isn't an example of your future stock-picking ability or you'll run Daddy's net worth down the drain pretty damn fast. Try again. Stick with my father, if you don't mind."

"My crystal ball now says you're so mysterious because your dad is a CIA operative, all brains and analytical skills, much like Le Carré's George Smiley."

"Strike two!"

"My last-chance guess. He is a famous psychiatrist. That's it. I'm sure of it," she boasted confidently.

"Close," I said. "My father is a doctor whose specialty is diagnostic medicine and, by the way, he is also my best friend."

"Your best friend. You mean that, don't you? That's a feeling I can't even imagine. My family's so cold and distant that friendship would be a very far-out concept."

"Well, for both of us, it's going to be difficult when I move to New York. We're almost like an old married couple."

She was beginning to study me too closely—her curiosity was mounting, and I could sense where this was headed. There would be questions I didn't want to answer, but she would be offended if I cut her off, so I reversed course and went on the offensive: "Okay, ma'am, it's my turn now. Why Wall Street? There are a lot of career paths you could have taken if you didn't want to be a lawyer like Daddy or your big bad brother."

Her face hardened and her eyes turned dark as she sat back away from the table. It all seemed to come out in a rush, as if she had been wanting to verbalize her thoughts for some time. She didn't want her success to be based on lineage, trust funds, or because her father pressured a client to do him a favor. When she looked in the mirror, she wanted to see something besides a pretty face. By the time she graduated college, she was tired of the scorched-earth land war with her brother ("the Informant") and her father ("the Intimidator"). She'd leaped at J. P. Morgan's offer because it made her a free person and, if she gave it her all and was worthy of advancement, it would be due to her accomplishments alone.

We both tired of the Q&A at the same time. She was emotionally spent after painting the depressing picture of her family dynamics, and I wasn't prepared to talk much more about my own history. It was a short walk back to her apartment. To me it had been a confusing evening, oddly full of both warmth and distance. I was wondering how it would end and what we both would be thinking in the morning when she suddenly stopped and stepped in front of me.

"How come you've never made a move on me?" she asked. "I'm the one who's supposed to play hard to get."

I stood there dumbfounded, a mute version of myself. We turned the corner, and a half block later we were at her apartment.

"Let's have a fond-farewell-to-Wharton nightcap," she suggested. "Sambuca with three beans for good luck, that'll do it."

Her living room was contemporary, all grays and tans and stainless steel. As she poured the drinks, I noticed an intricate sterling-silver picture frame sitting prominently on a side table. An elderly woman was resting comfortably, looking up from a book, a heartfelt smile gracing her face.

"That's my grandmother Elsbeth. Isn't she beautiful? She's my only family ally. Grandmother has always been there for me whenever I needed support, advice, or to be comforted. She's a real character and the one person who can put her son, my father, in his rightful place. I bet she was a hellion in her twenties."

She sat in a chair directly across from me. When she bent forward to click our glasses in a "we made it" toast, I noticed she had unbuttoned her blouse down a notch (or was it two?) to the exact level where I could admire the swelling of her breasts, but no more. I was on the cusp of losing all control when the phone rang.

Elsbeth apologized, "I forgot that I promised a girlfriend from college she could borrow my couch for the night. She'll be here shortly."

My blood pressure crashed after the call, but then exploded to a new high when she leaned back and slowly crossed and uncrossed her never-ending legs, providing me with a perfect vista up her skirt. She knew exactly what she was doing. She must have practiced the move in front of a mirror. I lifted her out of the chair, pulled her in close, and kissed her with abandon.

"That's a little more like it"—she smiled—"but you really do have to go."

At the door she handed me a card with her New York address and telephone number. She put her arms around my neck and breathed into my ear, "Until September." I had two long months to reflect on what that meant.

ON THE
ROAD TO
INDEPENDENCE

IT ALL HAPPENED SO FAST. SUMMER WENT BY IN A BLUR, and soon I was unpacking my meager belongings in New York. Jacob's mother helped situate us only three blocks from Grand Central Terminal in the Murray Hill section of the city. The prewar building, the Giles, was primarily a modest hotel, with the top four floors rented as apartments, mostly to residents who were quite old and had lived there for decades. Kudos to Mrs. Steiner, because the apartment and its location fulfilled all of my requirements: it was a short walk to the subway, offered a smorgasbord of neighborhood haunts for the locals, and the area was filled with retail shops of all kinds that met my every need. The Giles even had what I came to believe was my own Irish lounge, on the building's ground floor. In its quiet way, Murray Hill was distinctive, a gracious neighborhood there to serve its residents, not flashy but representing home to the families who lived there.

Our apartment had an airy living room facing a quiet Thirty-Ninth Street, twin bedrooms with private baths on either side, and a railroad kitchen wide enough for one thin person to cook while standing sideways. Jacob complained that the rooms were furnished like a 1950s retirement home, but as long as the furniture was comfortable, the utilities and appliances worked, the toilets flushed, and I had privacy, I was pleased. Yes, the building was in need of more loving care, but there was a warm feeling about the place because most of the tenants and employees felt fortunate to be there. It didn't take too long before I was on a first-name basis with the doormen, the hotel manager, and of course, the barmaids.

A few days before Jacob and I were due to begin our illustrious careers, we drove down to Atlantic City to observe the progress of my investment.

Resorts' stock was on a tear, so my heart was pounding with anticipation as we approached the boardwalk. The contractor's trailer was locked, and with no Deedee to guide us, we went on high alert to avoid the menacing Carl Vega. It was also unfortunate that our newest, best architect friend, Stephan, was not on the premises. We were on our own.

Jacob cautiously approached a few crew members on break and asked if the project was still progressing on schedule for a Memorial Day opening. He assumed his cajoling act: "You guys are really plowing ahead. We were out here last spring, and you've made a hell of a lot of progress since then. If the weather holds up, do you think you can make the magic date?"

"We'll see then," one of the hard hats muttered.

"The architect guy, I think his name is Stephan, said everyone gets a fat bonus if you make it."

"He talks too much," the hat responded, keeping communication to a minimum.

"Mind if we look around?" Jacob asked, realizing that this conversation was going nowhere.

"You're on your own," came the caustic reply.

We walked around the Haddon, stealing looks inside whenever possible. If they were making significant progress, it wasn't obvious to either of us. I observed workmen everywhere, lots of noise and movement, but how was I to measure where we were in the renovation process? Jacob looked equally lost.

"This isn't getting us anywhere," I said. "We probably should have trekked down here later in the year."

"I'm impressed with all the activity," Jacob volunteered. "For all that's going on here, it looks surprisingly well coordinated. But I agree that we're wasting our time trying to sort out this chaos."

I couldn't help feeling dejected as we left the building. Resorts stock may have been talking, but I had no incremental information to help me assess the probability of success for this behemoth venture. All that was to change when we saw a well-dressed young woman approaching the site, carrying a leather portfolio case.

"The casino's not open yet," Jacob said, smiling.

She kept her distance and sarcastically replied, "Oh, really? I couldn't tell from here."

"Would you like a tour?" he persisted.

"I can take care of myself. Thanks anyway," she said, rejecting his pathetic attempt to engage her in conversation.

I would have been embarrassed by now, but Jacob, the bulldog, wasn't fazed by her lack of interest. Undaunted, he pushed forward.

"Let me guess," he continued, "you're a reporter here to write an update on the casino."

We were there on a lark with plenty of time to spare; it was clear that she was there for a business meeting and beginning to evidence real annoyance. Jacob's charm wasn't working, so I stepped forward. I explained that as students we were interested in the project and had been following the progress of transforming the Haddon into a hotel and casino. Her face softened up a bit, so I played the humble card. Pointing to her professional-looking satchel, and hoping it included pictures of the refurbished building, I pleaded, "Is it possible you could share with two aspiring entrepreneurs a peek at what the new facility will look like when it's completed?"

The positive karma of my Resorts investment continued to improve. It turned out that young Laurie was an associate at an advertising agency hired to promote the grand opening of the first casino east of the Mississippi. Her leather case was stuffed with newly drawn color images of the hotel-casino, which she reluctantly offered to share with us if we promised to skedaddle out of there within the hour. I didn't need to know whom she was meeting with. I just wanted to see if the images of the building and its interiors coming to life were in sync with the stock's vertical rise. And I got the look I needed.

In the car driving back to New York, Jacob was frazzled. I knew he was second-guessing his decision not to buy Resorts stock the past spring. It was higher now, what should he do? If he chased and the company faltered, he'd want to commit hara-kari; if he didn't buy and the stock continued to rise, he'd feel like a stubborn idiot. I was thankful he didn't ask my opinion.

I slept miserably that night, with my brain and stomach engaged in mortal combat. I went to bed feeling good about the size of my position in

Resorts, but somewhere in the middle of the night, my emotions took over and demanded that I double my holdings. It was all about my visceral reaction to the interior drawings. Even though I knew that my design and decorating skills were nonexistent, that it would be idiotic for me to invest real money based upon my own sense of taste, I couldn't resist being seduced by what I had seen that afternoon. The space looked both inviting and exciting; I had to believe it would draw huge crowds and, at the very least, be an initial success. It sure as hell wasn't a free bet, but it was a good sign that my balls were gyrating like Mexican jumping beans. Maybe this was one of those times I should press my bet and go for the gold.

After a long morning shower, two open-faced PB&Js, and a cup of coffee, I settled down and began to think more rationally. The stock market had been sloppy all year, and I didn't feel it was the time to increase my exposure. After all, being agnostic on the markets isn't the same as being bullish. If I decided to buy more Resorts, then I should probably reduce positions elsewhere. I was still confident holding my temporary-help stocks, Kelly and Manpower, and my Florida housing plays. Those stocks were working well for me, and I viewed them as longer-term investments with plenty of upside potential. My mutual funds were going nowhere fast in '77, and I thought they were just market proxies anyway, so to make room for more Resorts, I thought I would liquidate those positions. I decided to walk around the block a few times and, if I still felt the same way, to call Ronnie Davis and execute my game plan.

Later that morning Ronnie was free to chat. I was all business as I explained the changes I wanted to make in my portfolio. His reaction was instantaneous.

"You're telling me you want to load up even more on this marginal piece of shit based on some pretty pictures you saw. Since when did you get soft in the head? What I'm hearing is, 'Gee, Ronnie the casino looks so nice, and I love the beautiful colors in the lobby, and the crapper even has powder-blue toilet paper.' What the hell are you thinking? This will be the largest position you've taken by a mile. In this spec?"

"Are you finished?" I responded coolly.

"For the time being, yes."

"I'm redeeming more mutual funds than I'm buying Resorts by two to one. I don't have any edge or particular confidence in the funds. If the market goes up, I'm willing to bet that Resorts will significantly outperform them based on sex appeal alone. If the market goes down, Resorts will probably decline worse, but will it go down double those funds? Maybe, but remember we'll still be in a news vacuum, so I think the real risk in Resorts won't be apparent until the spring of next year, when the casino is due to open."

R. D. responded, "Haven't you learned that buying up is not a good recipe for success? This stock has about doubled since you bought it. You're going to be breaking one of the golden rules."

"I agree with you on that, but I also have to be flexible," I said. Then I reminded him, "By the way, how many times have you told me you reversed positions for some reason or another? Tell me, how does the stock feel to you as of right now?"

"Jesus, you are bullheaded! The stock's strong, okay," he conceded, "but have you noticed that the higher it goes, the more the short sellers pounce on it, betting it will plunge sooner or later? Maybe they know something that you don't."

"Why is that such a bad sign?" I asked.

"Because it shows their conviction—they're losing money but still willing to increase the bet. Short sellers tend to be pretty damn professional. You'll be bucking a savvy crowd."

"I'm thinking all that can be a positive! They've been wrong and they won't throw the towel in. They're the ones who are bullheaded. If the shorts had covered and everyone bullish had already bought, then who would be left to buy the stock? Ronnie, I like the controversy. Look, I'm aware there are plenty of potential negatives, but, on the other hand, if this project opens on time, functions well, and gamblers from all over flock to the action, then the company will be in a unique position and the stock could go anywhere, because it will be impossible to value. The hell with Graham and Dodd on this one, think about monopolies, manias, and Dutch tulips!"

"Okay, pal, you've been warned. I'll have Sawyer call you back with the execution reports, and I'll make sure my sisters pray for you Sunday."

Even though I had just made a big decision, I was oddly calm. I borrowed Jacob's bicycle, and headed south down Lexington Avenue. I needed to get outside and exercise something beyond my head. I circled around Gramercy Park, continued south on Irving Place past the venerable Pete's Tavern, crossed Fourteenth Street, and headed down to Washington Square. The first time I witnessed the scene at the park was when Charlotte guided me on our grand tour of Lower Manhattan. She loved the history and energy of the place, and made sure I understood that this square was a democratic mecca for neighborhood regulars, NYUers, and tourists from near and far. I couldn't cruise these few blocks and not remember her earnest lectures followed by hours of sitting on a secluded bench, my arm around her shoulders, talking easily about our future together. I looked up at the clear skies. It felt good to generate honest sweat and not have to worry about my next term paper or final exam. In a few days, the next chapter of my quest would begin.

There were two messages on my answering machine back at the Giles, one from Sawyer confirming my portfolio adjustments, and the other from Ronnie requesting a call back. I immediately noted his concerned tone.

"Enough with Resorts and the other crap. I've been worried about your dad since we talked last week. How's he doing?"

"He'll be fine. I've been assured that it was only a scare."

"What was wrong?"

"They're saying he was just overtired, but I think it was the stress from work. He's been going at it full throttle recently. He gets this way sometimes when he allows himself to get too involved in a case. I've seen him go without sleep for days when a particular patient is fighting to stay alive. He won't give up. He'll keep searching for a solution until the very end. He won't worry about himself until it's all over."

Ronnie still wanted more. "Was it still the blood issue with that young woman you told me about from downtown?"

"Yes. He can't seem to solve it."

"I know how you worry about him. I'll join the girls on Sunday for this one."

When I hung up with Ronnie, I couldn't block out the thought that the young woman's case sounded horribly familiar.

Like the other daily commuters on the early a.m. subways to Wall Street, I had to learn the acrobatics of reading the *Journal* while standing with one hand gripping a metal pole for support and the other turning the pages of a folded newspaper. It was the most athletic move I would accomplish all day. Riding a subway, surrounded by folks of all types, was a whole new experience for a kid from the southwest corner of the Buckeye State. I did my best to avoid staring at other passengers, but some were so intriguing that I couldn't resist speculation on their personal lives. I would wonder if the man next to me was a hotshot trader, a security analyst, or a stuffy investment banker. And the fellow standing in the corner with the oversize cuff links—was he a promoter, a stock jockey, or just a plain ol' pigeon? I looked down at the short, meticulously dressed gentleman sitting near me, his shiny bald head buried in his work papers. I asked myself if he was an insurance executive, an accountant, or a securities lawyer. While I didn't relish being underground and breathing stale air for twenty minutes, the trip to work was in its own way quite entertaining. I was still in the stage at which everything about life below Maiden Lane was new and exciting.

I was anxious for the games to begin, but before I was permitted to sit at the table, I had to complete Burr, Addington, and Merritt's required training program. The firm's chief compliance officer, Harold Brauer, escorted me through the four-month regimen. From day one I knew he resented me, a young buck eager to make his mark in the securities jungle, while he was a lawyer who couldn't survive at a Darwinian downtown law firm. Brauer was resigned to his days toiling away in the constipated world of compliance, spending his life sitting in a car hiding behind a cluster of evergreen trees trying to catch a speeder or someone jumping a stop sign. I was to spend a few weeks in each of BAM's departments learning the basics, most of which proved to be rather tedious. I wanted to get my hands dirty with real work and not just sit and observe. I didn't really care how the back office functioned, I just wanted to learn how to research new ideas that would help turbocharge my portfolio.

A few days before Christmas, Brauer invited me to lunch at the Bankers Club atop 120 Broadway. We sat at *his* table and were served by *his* waiter while he ordered *his* lunch for both of us. He never inquired whether I also wanted a half-and-half cocktail of clam and tomato juice, grilled salmon, and rum raisin ice cream. I watched him sip his cocktail with eyes closed, emitting a discernible sigh as if his drink was a nectar concocted by the bartending gods. His performance made me believe *his* waiter knew how to discreetly add vodka to ol' Harold's brew. I wanted to double my bet when he ordered a second.

It was clear that Mr. Brauer had no interest in learning more about me, that he viewed this lunch as a menial task, and that all he really wanted to do was enjoy his drinks, eat his favorite lunch charged to BAM's house account, and get back to his private office, where he could close the door and watch the clock tick down to five o'clock. He ordered coffee and then addressed the purpose of our luncheon. He delivered his message to me with a solemnity usually reserved for decisions handed down by the Supreme Court.

"Young man, I hope you realize how fortunate you are to be hired by Ambrose Burr. He must see potential in you that has so far been concealed from me. As your training is about to be completed, I want you to know that adherence to compliance is taken most seriously at Burr, Addington, and Merritt. It is my job to protect the firm against any, and I do mean any, violation of our standards. I sense you are an aggressive type, so we will be watching you accordingly. You've had ample time to study the compliance manual, so do you have any questions?"

I wanted to ask if it were a violation of the code for an officer of the firm to act like a pompous asshole. Instead I asked if I was allowed to do any trading at another brokerage firm as long as duplicate confirmations and statements were forwarded to his office. His beady eyes enlarged when he answered with an emphatic no. I told him I understood and thanked him for lunch. I never wanted to see him again.

For the next two years, I was a junior security analyst working for the firm's special situation group, headed by Ezra Carter. Like the other senior analysts, his office faced downtown and was blessed with a clear but distant view of the convergence of the Hudson and East Rivers. I quickly learned not to interrupt him when his desk chair was spun around and he was looking south, at one with the rivers and deep in thought. I sat directly outside his door in a large nondescript room surrounded by secretaries and the other junior analysts. Whenever Ezra wanted me, he would fire a paperclip from a rubber band at the glass wall between his office and my space. If the ping didn't jolt my attention, he would call out, "Stout. Now!"

Ezra Carter was one of a kind, a character you'd expect to encounter in a novel or a movie created by an artist's fertile imagination, not a real, live human being working for an investment bank. He was an unsolvable puzzle because the pieces of the whole didn't fit together. At least twice a year, the partners debated easing him out of the firm, only to be drowned out by the research director's vote of confidence and the strong endorsement from Ambrose Burr. Ezra was impatient with most everyone and unwilling to play games. In a firm that emphasized teamwork and collegiality, he was staunchly individualistic and brutally demanding of others. BAM's research director said it best: "Ezra's not warm and fuzzy, but he's too damn smart and too damn good to let go. He's a pain in the ass, but he's worth it."

Each day I came in early to read the Dow Jones wire service for premarket news and updates on what was happening around the world. I'd finish the *Wall Street Journal*, quickly knock off the *New York Times* and then call George O'Leary, my favorite BAM trader, for his take on the markets that morning. I had gravitated toward O'Leary during my training regimen, when I sat in the trading room learning how stock trades were consummated. The other traders were loud and hyperactive, while George was composed and private, seemingly impervious to the noise and activity of the room. He appeared to be working in his own world, studying the ticker tape as it crossed the wall high above the trading floor, simultaneously punching the keys of his Quotron and responding to the flashing lights of incoming calls. He had been at BAM since he graduated from high school in Queens forty years earlier. He had worked his way up from wire-room operator to position trader until the firm experienced horrendous losses in the bear market of 1969 to 1970. The situation was so upsetting to senior management that risk exposures were reduced to negligible levels. George was one of a few traders who navigated the decline and even managed to squeeze out a few dollars of profit, but nevertheless, he suffered when management purged the department of trading capital. By the time I met him, O'Leary was executing orders only for institutional customers and a few select partners who understood that this was a man of integrity and talent who had been screwed by circumstances beyond his control.

I was immediately attracted to this quiet, introspective man sitting off by himself, dressed always in a starched white shirt buttoned at the wrists and neck, tie knotted precisely, displaying Irish green and decorated with shamrocks. I liked the way he was under control while the other traders were screaming at each other and wildly waving their hands as if trying to shoo away attacking hornets. I approached him gingerly and asked if I could sit next to him, that I was a new trainee and here to learn. He looked me over as if he were a rancher considering a livestock purchase and asked for my last name. After a few questions, we established the fact that I was not related to any BAM partners and my family hadn't arrived on the *Mayflower.*

"I'm sorry if you are disappointed," I said with a note of sarcasm.

"On the contrary," he answered. "We'll try it out until you stub your toe."

I watched O'Leary perform his tasks every minute of every day for three weeks. He worked each order with care, as if he were an obstetrician delivering a firstborn. Depending on the circumstances, he was patient or aggressive, or sometimes just flowing with the prevailing market trend when executing his strategies.

I wasn't ready to move on when the next training location beckoned— there was so much more to learn from him. I knew it sounded awkward, but I couldn't just get up and leave.

"Thanks for all the time you spent with me. I hope I wasn't too much trouble."

"As long as you showed interest and progressed, it was okay by me," he replied matter-of-factly.

Here sat a prideful man poised at his station every day executing orders for others when his dream was to trade capital for the firm, take measured risk and share in the rewards of his efforts. He had proved his worth in a difficult market environment but was sabotaged by the losses of others. The markets were much better now and he should have been offered another chance, but he accepted his fate with a dignity that I knew would elude Rogers Stout.

"Could I check in with you every once in a while, maybe even toss out an idea occasionally?" I asked my last day as a trainee in the trading department.

He looked up from his desk and answered, "I'm in by eight o'clock every morning having a coffee. Same place. Same chair."

I was ecstatic the first day I started working in the research department. At last I was no longer a trainee. As a research associate, I was expected to be productive. It was time for me to earn my salary. Once my little brain had processed each day's current events, the business news and George O'Leary's view of the markets, I would gulp down a coffee and the PB&J I brown-bagged from the apartment and begin my job duties at Burr, Addington, and Merritt. Jackie, the secretary I shared with Ezra Carter, had already stacked the wires I was supposed to respond to on my desk, along with newly published research materials from BAM analysts. I would immediately search through the piles until I located the other compulsory read of my morning—the one-page technical analysis memo penned by the firm's mercurial soothsayer, Paal Van Horne. Since I had been at BAM, his batting average was in the stratosphere. Of course I had wanted to meet him, but was emphatically denied access to his office by Harold Brauer, aka Mr. Obnoxious. After trying to understand the logic behind Van Horne's market commentaries, then speed-reading the other BAM research, I was ready to greet Ezra and learn what he had planned for me that day.

Most mornings I would spend researching and responding to wire requests from our sales force and the correspondent firms that cleared trades through BAM. If we hadn't published or answered a recent request, I would follow the firm's policy of writing a brief synopsis of the subject company's business, financials, and outlook based on information found in annual and quarterly reports as well as Standard & Poor's research sheets. The firm's library was incredibly well organized and the librarians were helpful. My charge was to provide a broad summary on a company's fundamentals. "Remember," Ezra warned, "these wires are supposed to contain only general knowledge—they're not intended to be detailed research reports." I learned to churn these requests out with minimal effort because I wanted to spend my time digging deeper into the companies that the firm had not yet reported on. I found the trolling for new ideas part of my job interesting, and, if I was lucky, maybe I could uncover a hidden jewel.

I was typically famished by noon but only had time to reward myself with a tasteless lunch in the BAM cafeteria, usually with a few of the other junior analysts. We'd chat up sports and market-moving news of the day. When the conversation inevitably turned to office gossip, I would find a reason to excuse myself. I wasn't well versed in the nuances of family names, clubs, and exclusive vacation destinations. I didn't care where someone was from, whom they were related to, or if they had a humongous trust fund. I had already become a believer in George O'Leary's theorem: "There's only one reason to go south of Fulton Street, and that's to make money!" So after my brief lunch break, I would head back to my desk to finish up any remaining wire work, arrange it in coherent order, leave it on Ezra's desk for review and approval, and wait for the master to return.

One afternoon in early March, I was deep into reading an article in the *Economist* when I simultaneously heard the ping and a loud "Stout, come in here now!"

"These wire responses are fine," Ezra barked, "but you didn't rate the stocks like you're supposed to. Did you forget or are you just lazy today?"

"I didn't forget," I protested, "and actually I'm quite alert today. I just don't know how I can sign my name to these wires when we use these nonsensical ratings. It's really embarrassing."

"What's your problem with the ratings?"

"They're gibberish. For example, 'Appropriate for Widows and Orphans,' or 'Businessman Risk Accounts.' Who will take those labels seriously? What do all those words really mean? What's appropriate for a widow who is in her forties may be a lot different than one who is in her seventies, not to mention if she is destitute versus filthy rich. And then the businessman label, is he successful or a loser? Where is he in his career? Does he have mucho debt or a fat savings account? I don't know who thought up these ratings, but can't we do better?"

"Good for you, kiddo," Ezra interrupted. "You're right, the ratings are bullshit, but guess what, that's what management wants, so why not give it to them? Is that really such a big deal?"

"Are you asking me or telling me that's what I should do?" I replied.

"Well, well," he said, putting his pen down and sitting up straight at his desk. "They finally found someone for me with brains and balls. No wonder you're an outsider without a fancy last name. Maybe you'll be the first junior I'll be able to work with in years. Most of your predecessors begged for transfers after a month or two. Go back to your desk and rate the stocks, send the wires out, and we'll live to fight a more important battle. Let's talk some more later this afternoon—and by the way, feel good about yourself. You're doing okay."

I had come to believe that most everyone at BAM was thoroughly intimidated by Ezra Carter. His disheveled outward appearance was out of sync with his analytical mind and almost encyclopedic knowledge of military, economic, and political history. From our late-afternoon talks, I had learned that he had grown up just outside the city limits of Waterville, Maine, the son of a doting mother of Iranian descent and a stern Yankee father who was the head of the History Department at Colby College. While his classmates were hunting anything they could shoot and playing seasonal sports, Ezra was absorbed by the mesmerizing life of his hero, Alexander Hamilton. The more questions he asked his father, the more books he was given to read. Ezra attended Colby because it was free to faculty children and graduated summa cum laude in only three years. He then worked for two years in Boston before sucking it up and attending Harvard Business School. He was determined to make enough in short order to permit him to research and write "the definitive biography of Alexander Hamilton and his influence on the trajectory of American financial history." Ezra found it monumentally difficult to reconcile that he was still at Burr, Addington, and Merritt decades later, toiling away in financial land when he should have been a published scholar admired for his insightful analysis of one of America's greatest Founding Fathers.

Ezra's prodigious research prowess was well recognized throughout BAM, making me assume that his contentious personality was the primary reason he was denied partnership status. As I sat outside his office, waiting for him to call me in later that afternoon, I wondered if the firm was so myopic that Ezra's physical image was the primary reason he was still only a senior security analyst. He was a somewhat odd-looking fish, of medium height with the bent-over posture of a much older man, undeniably pear shaped and soft from lack of physical exercise, and with curly, unkempt hair. I feared most of all that the reason he never was promoted to general partner was the prominent nose and almond Middle Eastern skin he had inherited from his mother.

The market had been closed for an hour, and most of the analysts and secretaries had already left, yet Ezra was still in his office, head down, buried in a pile of papers, leaving me time to reread Charlotte's latest letter. She had been in the field over six months. Doctors Without Borders had moved their camp into Thailand as a further security precaution. She told me not to worry because it all felt "pretty darn safe." She had learned a lot, seen a lot, and couldn't wait to tell me how exhilarating it was to be involved in helping people in dire need. My stomach was in knots as she continued, "Soon we'll be together and be even stronger. You'll see I'm right, and maybe by then I'll have learned to cook a genuine Thai dinner for us." I was so immersed in memories of Charlotte that I didn't sense Ezra standing next to me.

"Is everything copacetic?" he asked, clearly noticing my state of tension.

"Yes, sorry. I was lost there for a minute."

"Come on in," he said, returning to his office and closing the door even though the research room was almost empty.

We sat across from each other for a few minutes, talking about nothing in particular. I knew by now that this wasn't typical Ezra, so I waited for the real purpose of our chat. It didn't take too long before he abruptly changed the subject.

"You should be aware that I am required to monitor your personal trading account. I don't like playing policeman—it's not in my genes, but it is my responsibility."

"I haven't been trading."

"I know that. It isn't your activity, it's simply the question that if you didn't inherit a boatload of money, how the hell did you build a portfolio of this size? I've looked at your current holdings. Tell me what made you own Kelly and the home builders, and where the hell did the huge position in Resorts International come from?"

Thankfully Ezra's humanity surfaced. He knew me well enough by now to understand that I was a private person and would feel as if I was being interrogated by the CIA. He almost looked benevolent as he continued.

"Look, you're not in any trouble. It's just me needing to understand who I have working with me. Frankly, I've never seen a kid who's been able to acquire this much money by the age of twenty-two. I wish I had done it."

I wasn't comfortable, but I did feel less threatened, so I told him to fire away and ask me anything he wanted to. He took his time and patiently asked me to start at the beginning. I told him how I learned to play poker in my gambleathons with Dad, how my local friends were easy picking, and how I graduated to Rory's across the Ohio River. I could tell he loved my Newport adventure sagas, even though I left the Shani story out of the discussion.

It was dark outside when we finished. Ezra looked at his watch, excused himself, and called his wife to tell her he'd be home for dinner soon. I then told him how I multiplied my winnings from the fat cats at Penn whose fathers' wealth was the source of their bold bets. He knew I had been following the temporary-help industry intently and my horse was Kelly. He liked the story, immediately understood the dynamics of the business, and surprised me when he promised to read my Wharton report. He even said if the report was "good stuff," he would consider letting me update and improve it for possible release by BAM. Then he warned me about the Florida housing stocks, citing rising interest rates as a major negative headwind for new home purchases. "I'd watch out here if I were you," he tutored. I could see his jaw drop when I told him about reading an article in the *Philadelphia Inquirer* as the genesis of the Resorts idea, how I visited Atlantic City and interviewed the architect and construction workers, how I then applied my untested concept of group thinking, as influenced by MacKay's writings on the tulip mania.

"We've got to talk more about this one. You own this stock in the mid–single digits? You've already more than tripled your money. What are you waiting for?"

I answered quickly, "They haven't even opened the casino yet. In fact, they won't be applying for the appropriate permits until sometime in April. As long as they're on schedule, I'm going to let it ride. I plan on deciding my exit strategy after I see the casino open, hopefully by Memorial Day."

"You do realize how much you've already made? This is a dangerous speculation. Why not bank it?"

"I have no idea what it's worth or where the stock could go, but neither does anyone else. It's a unique monopoly."

"All the more reason to sell," he said.

"I beg to disagree, sir. I think it's all the more reason to dream."

I had started eating Thai food because it helped me feel closer to Charlotte. At first I would sit at the counter and watch the cooks perform, but I soon tired of being alone in a restaurant that was filled with large families or friendly foursomes. At least twice a week, I would bring home dinner from a small Thai place around the corner from the Giles and entertain myself with television and a cold beer. After that afternoon enduring Ezra's probing questions about my account and polishing off my favorite chicken dish for dinner, I turned the volume down and called Ronnie Davis. I wanted to hear his interpretation of my session with Ezra. He was in an expansive mood, because Xavier had just trounced their dreaded rival Ohio University, and he was finally long a boatload of Resorts for the firm's account.

"When will it stop?" he asked.

"I've got no idea," I said. "It's now in the hands of the speculation gods."

Ronnie came back with, "If they get the permit and the stock doesn't make new highs, I think we should sell. Don't forget the old saying to buy on the rumor and sell on the news."

I countered, "I'm willing to play it out if it looks like they'll make the Memorial Day opening. Then we should reassess."

"I hope you're not going bonkers on me. What have you been snorting up there in New York? Remember, a stock is only a piece of paper!"

I respected Ronnie's judgments, but he was a trader to the core. I also found it quite interesting that no one I talked with, including R. D. and Jacob, actually believed in the Resorts story. The only reason they owned the stock was because it was going up. And then there was Ezra's consummate skepticism, which probably fairly represented what any seasoned Wall Streeter would believe. So I couldn't help thinking, maybe the higher Resorts went, the more they all would be convinced that this casino play was for real.

Ronnie wasn't surprised that compliance at BAM included monitoring the account of a new junior analyst who apparently was burying jump shots from beyond the arc. He even thought it could work in my favor if it made them realize I had potential beyond writing reports for others to use as moneymaking tools. He advised me to be forthright and not attempt to camouflage what I was doing.

"Don't worry about this—they're only doing their job." As I got ready for bed, I couldn't help reflecting on how well-grounded R. D. was and how much I wished he'd move to New York.

Ezra was out of the office the next two days on a marketing trip he had been trying to avoid for weeks. I knew he'd be in a vile mood traveling through Hartford and Boston with a salesman who would be shit-faced drunk after his luncheon martinis. It was virtually impossible for Ezra to accept that a blabbering buffoon who sold other people's ideas could be making double his income. Early Friday morning I was surprised when he called me from his hotel.

"I'm onto a new subject. Aren't you almost from Kentucky? You must know something about bourbon. Right? I'm getting interested in Brown-Forman. Don't talk to anyone, have Jackie get you my file and read up on the company this weekend. Focus on Jack Daniel's—why it's so special, growing so fast, and still on allocation. Are you with me?"

"I'm here. By the way, you should know there's a real difference between Kentucky bourbon and Tennessee sour mash whiskey. When you're bored in Boston, why not do a blind taste test?"

Ezra could rant with the best of them. I imagined he would have been a formidable debater. He continued, "You really are from way down there in Okieland. In Maine whisky means Canadian Club or VO, not some crap made of corn mash and whatever else they throw in there. You drink it straight or on the rocks, not mixed like the dickhead I'm with here who ordered a Jack and ginger the other night and embarrassed the hell out of me."

I thanked Ezra for the opportunity and told him I'd be ready to talk on Monday.

Despite my best efforts, I had succumbed and Elsbeth was now part of my life. Most Friday nights I reserved for her, although sometimes she was partial to Sunday mornings at her place. This was going to be one of those Sundays. I was so wired after a quick read of the Brown-Forman file Friday night that I spent all day Saturday locked in my room consuming every word and number in their public reports and filings. It was my first opportunity to view the way Ezra wrote notes to himself, which he customarily scribbled in the margins, with question marks and arrows pointing every which way. He had drawn lines connecting numbers in the balance sheets and income statements, labeling each with bold plus or minus signs. By evening I was mentally exhausted but physically energized. I made a few calls but couldn't connect with anyone, and Jacob was busy with a family event at Juilliard, so I went for a quickie workout at the gym, showered, grabbed a couple slices of pizza next door, and headed downtown to a Spencer Tracy film festival in the West Village.

I was an hour early when I knocked on Elsbeth's door at ten o'clock on Sunday morning, much like the teenage Rogers who wanted to devour the nurses in his father's office, dreaming of ripping off starched uniforms and then slowly undoing bras and peeling off underwear with the dexterity of a brain surgeon. Elsbeth opened the door with the security chain still on. She peeked out and wondered, "Aren't you early?"

I sheepishly smiled and whispered, "I can't wait any longer."

She was wearing a sheer off-white nightgown. I could see the outline of her breasts and the shadow between her legs. I had tried to resist seeing her when I returned to New York. I succeeded for less than a month before we hooked up after meeting for a drink in early October. I could hardly walk the next day—even Jackie noticed that I was limping like an old man. After the first few weeks of almost constant carnal acrobatics, we settled down and met for a weekly rendezvous at her apartment. It was as if we needed this release, or at least the semblance of some type of relationship we could count on with each other. I'm pretty sure the word *love* was never uttered, even in moments of passion. Neither Elsbeth nor I knew where this was headed; for now it was all about physical gymnastics, and that was fine with both of us.

One night as we lay side by side after a particularly glorious tryst, I blurted out the question that I had wanted to ask her ever since we got together—*why me?* "Do you really need to know?" she responded. "Sorry, but you're going to have to figure that out on your own. Where's that famous Rogers self-confidence?" she added. Her mood abruptly changed and she became serious. Elsbeth turned and looked at me and made me promise to take to my grave what she was about to tell me.

"I'm not unaware that my looks make men stare at me. It can be an irritating curse. I don't like them fantasizing that they're touching me, much less having sex with me. Sometimes I can actually hear them breathing faster and muttering to themselves. It's revolting! Do you have women push up against you in elevators or accidentally on purpose brush across your body in a pathetic attempt to cop a feel? How many times has a flirtatious broad told you she'd like to make a man out of you, just give her a chance and you'll see how good she can be? Do you understand that this type of creepy bravado happens to me all the time?"

I could only joke back, "Well, last week Mrs. Bettman, the librarian at BAM, told me that I was a nice young man. Does that count?"

"Only if she grabbed your rear when you passed by. Seriously, do you get where I'm going here?"

"I think so."

"Remember, I have two older brothers. I grew up hearing them boast of where they got with their dates that night or how they would bag her for sure the next Saturday. I knew from them that guys in school would brag to their mates of their so-called conquests. I had too much self-respect to be anyone's score, so I shut them all out. Let those jerks call me a bitch tease or an ice goddess. I said to hell with them and their macho crap!"

I almost couldn't believe it. "All the way through college? What about J. P. Morgan and grad school?"

"I never gave in at either place."

"Okay. You've set me up perfectly. I'm ready to hear the big, bad secret."

"By my senior year at high school, I couldn't take it any longer. I wanted to experience a climax. I had consumed all the relevant books in the library and knew I needed some help, so on my eighteenth birthday, I took a train to New York and bought myself a dildo as a present. I rushed home, holding my purse tightly under my arm. I locked the bathroom door and read the instructions. I was nervous and excited at the same time. I waited for my parents to go to bed, raided the liquor cabinet, and poured some vodka into a juice glass and barricaded my bedroom door. I got myself in the right mood with those expert hands of mine, turned on the vibrator, and rubbed it over my body. I didn't need Vaseline; I was already wet and ready to fly. I followed the directions like a good little girl, but it hurt like hell. I tried it a few more times but was never successful. One night I threw it out in a garbage bin behind a Walgreens. You'll like this—before I put it in the can, I wiped my fingerprints off."

I was enthralled but trying hard to be calm. "Keep going, I'm all ears."

"The men in our family all attend Yale, therefore I was expected to go to Vassar, its sister school at the time. It was a wonderful four years educationally. Great inspirational teaching, small classes, and fellow students from around the world who helped to broaden my experience. But the social life was nonexistent. There was no way I was going to be a piece of meat for a Yalie boy's one-night stand. It was time for Elsbeth to break out."

I interrupted with, "How the hell could you accomplish that in Poughkeepsie, New York?"

"There was pretty good train service to Manhattan. That was destined to be my coming-of-age salvation. What I wanted was a safe place to meet married men who didn't know me, who understood it would be sex in their hotel room, thank you and goodbye forever. No names, no trading telephone numbers, just adios."

"I'm not sure where you're going with this."

"I'd sit at a table alone in the barroom of a fine hotel like the Waldorf or the Plaza and wait until I found a suitable candidate. He'd have to be married, from out of town and in New York on business, and pleasant to be with, and he had to showcase some physical traits that appealed to me. It wasn't difficult to find willing candidates. I was disciplined. I'd shoo the slobbering masses away but encourage the chosen few."

"This is how you discovered your passion for sex?"

"Actually no, most of these types were more like uncoordinated athletes who bumble and fumble their way about. It turned out to be most disappointing."

I encouraged her to continue. "You probably intimidated the hell out of those Kansas City salesmen."

"My eureka moment came the summer of my sophomore year. My father was so pleased that his darling daughter was awarded high honors at Vassar that he treated her to a summer tour of Europe. When I was tired of the gory crucifixions in the Uffizi and had seen enough annunciations for a day, I broke off from the tour group and wandered about Florence. In the late afternoon, I was looking at silks in a store near the Arno when a man approached from behind me and laid a Pucci scarf over my shoulder. He said the scarf was only an accent to my beauty, but it was intended for me. Before I could decline his generous offer, it was being tenderly wrapped around my neck and he was guiding me out of the store. He took me up in the hills to see the city at dusk and then for a glass of wine at his villa. I couldn't resist his charm. It was the first time I wasn't in charge. He wasn't like the others in New York. Every touch, every caress was meant to heighten the experience. When I finally climaxed, I thought I would explode. His chauffeur drove me back to the hotel. I never saw him again."

"That just can't be topped."

"Well, why don't you try? I told you my story—let's hear about your first time."

I wasn't prepared to cough up the embarrassing truth to Elsbeth that my first experience was with a prostitute, so I started off relating one of my favorite teenage fantasies. I got on a roll and couldn't stop.

"One Saturday a few months after I got my driver's license, my father was home with the flu. He needed a file from his office, and he volunteered me to be his messenger. As usual the office was quiet after lunch on Saturday. The receptionist was preparing to leave but agreed to guide me to the file room before she helped close up for the weekend. I was sitting on a chair looking for the correct file when Nurse Betsy Bernstein knocked on the door and entered. She said that everyone had already left, but before she locked the front door was there anything I needed from her. I thanked her and said I would only be there a few more minutes, that I thought I had already located the file my father requested. She took another step closer to me and asked if I was sure, that she was willing to stay if I needed her. I looked up at her, unsure of what she meant. She was maybe thirty-five years old and, with her elongated neck, resembled a slightly overweight version of a Modigliani sculpture. Her breasts were firm and sat high on her chest, pressing hard against her white uniform as if begging for freedom. She came even closer and told me that she was recently divorced and would be moving to Cleveland at month's end."

"Rogers, what the hell were you waiting for? Did she have to completely undress for you to realize what you were being offered?"

"I was young, inexperienced, and terribly naive. Also, my father had warned me never to even say anything inappropriate to a nurse in his office."

"So what happened? I'm rooting that you didn't blow this opportunity."

"She didn't take off her clothes and wasn't even wearing a bra. She hiked her skirt up and pulled her underwear down. She almost tore my pants off and mounted me while I was still sitting on the chair. She kept moaning, 'Yes, yes, yes,' but I couldn't understand why because I had already come within thirty seconds after we had started."

"Wow, that's some story," Elsbeth said. "Did you ever see her again?"

It was time to tell her the truth. Elsbeth had exposed herself to me, and I had grown to trust her. When I fessed up that my story was only a teenage fantasy, she was disappointed, but my stock rallied when I told her the truth, described the entire Newport saga and then hoped she would understand why I'd never forget Shani as my first.

Elsbeth concluded, "The Betsy the nurse story is a good one to tell around a campfire. The Kentucky extravaganza is more a complete coming-of-age experience. It's heartfelt, so I like it better. You're forgiven."

Elsbeth never answered the "why me?" question, but rather repeated that I was smart enough to figure it out on my own. Then she flashed a devilish grin and with no warning rolled on top of me and whispered that all these remembrances inspired her.

"What did Shani do that was so special for you?"

"She used muscles I never knew even existed."

"How did she use them?"

"She squeezed and pulled me from deep inside. I thought I was being consumed."

Elsbeth put her hands on my shoulders for support, rose up, and then pushed her hips down on me. She tightened herself and began to move up and down.

"Like that?" she asked.

"Please don't stop," I moaned.

I could hear Jacob's gospel session blaring from our hallway at the Giles. He greeted me from the floor of the apartment, where he was performing the salute to the sun. My roommate had recently added yoga to his exercise routine.

"Look who's back from his Sunday morning bagel and back bender. It still boggles my mind that every guy I knew at Wharton was auditioning for the Elsbeth derby, but the one who didn't even seem to notice her came away with the prize. I can't believe it to this day. What an injustice!"

"Apparently she has a midwestern hick fetish," I laughed in return.

"Well, stay healthy, my friend. I'm worried that she's sapping all your energy. I'm afraid that too much of that woman might affect your judgment."

I came back with, "On the other hand, it could be a release from all the tensions of my job and be beneficial to my performance."

"Yeah. Sure. And if the queen had balls, she'd be the king. How about an early dinner at your favorite Thai place? We have a lot to talk about."

"Let me guess the topic—what should we do with Resorts?"

In my room, while organizing my Brown-Forman notes in preparation for meeting with Ezra the next day, I thought about how interesting it was that a super-self-confident Jacob could be so nervous and unsure of himself when it came to taking financial risk with a stock investment. I had witnessed him in action many times before. He wasn't the type to shy away from taking charge or being assertive and employing an aggressive response to a question or difficult situation. He projected a certain aura of conceit, that he knew more than anyone in the room and that his solution to an issue was the only correct one. Yet when it came to trading in Resorts stock, Jacob wavered indecisively. He initially passed when I bought the stock—"It's way too early and who the hell knows if it ever will succeed"—chased it higher after it already was a rocket shot—"I can't take it, this freaking stock is driving me nuts"— and now that he had just about doubled his money, he was mortally fearful that his investment was at grave risk and his savings would evaporate. His position was "Promise me that you'll make me sell if you sell!"

Jacob's way of sharing food at dinner was to finish what was on his plate as fast as possible and keep moving on for more. I once told him it was a shame there wasn't an Olympic event for speed eating, because he would have been a good candidate for a medal. Finally satisfied after consuming a preposterous quantity of Thai delicacies, he leaned back and asked me what my pecker was up to.

"What's going on here? I thought it was to be Charlotte forever. You told me when she was leaving for Cambodia that there would never be another one like her in this cosmos. Now you're hooked on Elsbeth like a heroin addict."

I was slow with my reply. "Charlotte's not returning for quite a while, according to her last couple of letters. She loves what she is doing and believes she's making a difference."

"So that's it? That's your answer?"

"I didn't say that."

"What are you saying?"

I had held my feelings in check for almost a year, but at that moment I couldn't stop them from pouring out.

"When she got on that plane for Doctors Without Borders, I felt like part of me was leaving. Knowing that I couldn't just hop on a train and be with her, hold her tightly, smell her hair, and talk with her about everything dear to me was devastating. I ache for her, I really do, and I worry about her safety every day, but I can't just sit in my room whining like a lost cocker spaniel. That was me during the last summer. I was home alone with my dad, the Reds, and the stock market as my companions. That wasn't enough."

"Is it just physical, or is there more?"

"Stop thinking of her as just a pretty face. She's smart as hell and fun to be with."

I had to take this conversation down a different path, because I was starting to choke up thinking about Charlotte. Jacob was a true friend, but he didn't understand that even though I needed Elsbeth for now, that didn't diminish my feelings for Charlotte. I ordered tea and changed the subject.

"Our friends at Resorts should soon be applying for a permit to open our casino if they still expect to be operative by Memorial Day. It's crucial that they don't screw up."

"Shouldn't we just run for the exit? The stock is way up, and if management stumbles, even in the slightest way, it will get trashed."

"So far I believe they're still on schedule. If the application leads to a permit, the stock can continue to soar as it discounts a Memorial Day opening."

"Hasn't it gone far enough?"

"Maybe, I don't know, but neither does anyone else, including the CEO, Mr. James Crosby himself."

I spent most of the evening arguing with myself about my relationship with Ms. Aylesworth until I finally tired of playing the dual roles of prosecutor and defense attorney. I was asking too many questions and had trouble answering most of them. It was time to ready myself for the upcoming meeting with Ezra to discuss the pros and cons of recommending Brown-Forman. I needed to be alert.

Ezra was all business. Today there would be no "hello, how was your weekend," no witticisms or arcane references to some obscure literary work he read years ago. I had become accustomed to his recounting historical vignettes in minute detail to illustrate a particular point of view, or his fulminating about someone at the firm who he felt was unworthy because they didn't possess a broad perspective or were lazy or intellectually dishonest. I was beginning to understand why he had the reputation of being so difficult, because these tirades could almost go on ad infinitum. I had worked for him for only a few months but already knew the penalty for disagreeing with Mr. Carter unless I was holding a virtual pat hand.

Yet today Ezra was on surprisingly good behavior, focused and raring to go. I sat across from him tingling with anticipation. This was where I wanted to be: I was ready to be introduced to how a research idea progressed from an analyst's initial brainstorm to being approved as a full-fledged buy or sell for BAM's sales force.

Ezra announced that he expected me to work until we finished up with Brown-Forman. He handed me a rough draft of a report he wrote over the weekend and suggested we reconvene later that afternoon. He reminded me to remain radio silent as if I were protecting the location of D-Day's landing site in June '44.

"Read this over and give me your thoughts. I plan to put my stock picker's approval star on this puppy. You're welcome to sit in when I present the idea to Edwin tomorrow. Our beloved research director always gets first crack at critiquing a new recommendation."

I must have really surprised Ezra when I thanked him for including me in the process, because he looked at me with a quizzical expression and responded, "What did you think I would do, leave my pirate standing out there on a wobbly plank staring down at a bunch of hungry sharks?"

My first thought after reading Ezra's report on Brown-Forman was *I HAVE TO BUY THIS STOCK*. My next thought was, how did he write such an elegant but comprehensive piece in only a few hours over a weekend? It was all there in just seven pages, the tale of a conservative family-controlled company generating free cash flow that was evolving into a bona fide consumer growth stock due to the dynamism of a branded cult product.

Later that day we sat in Ezra's office reviewing the Brown-Forman report, paragraph by paragraph. The big room was emptying out, but his door remained shut. His office was airless and hot. We worked with our ties loosened and our shirtsleeves rolled up, guzzling peanuts from a jar, and drinking lukewarm tea. I felt like I was living an all-hands-on-deck kind of moment. There was an urgency in the room, because Ezra believed the stock was "pregnant and ready to deliver." He asked me to attack the five major premises of his recommendation:

The spirits industry is slow growing but profitable and throws off lots of cash. It's like watching grass grow, but by the end of the day you get paid for it.

Brown-Forman is an established leader whose operating numbers are best in class. The company has a solid balance sheet, rising returns on equity, and is projected to have an accelerating growth rate.

The company's most important product has been in short supply, but with a new capacity addition in place, its sales and earnings are set to explode.

Jack Daniel's is undoubtedly a unique franchise with a cultlike following. Demand still exceeds supply and is growing year after year, while foreign sales are still in their infancy and offer further upside potential. The product remains on allocation with distributors, which enhances the company's ability to raise prices with only negligible customer resistance. There is no apparent top for J. D. in sight.

The stock is not yet appreciated by Wall Street analysts, is underowned by institutions, and is currently selling at a significant discount to the overall stock market and other consumer products companies.

"Well, hot stuff," he said, "what do you think? Give me a yes or no but not a maybe."

"I know I sound like an ass kisser, but I truly love the idea. I'm not all that experienced yet, but I think your reasons for liking the stock are solid. Actually, from where I sit, they're compelling. If you are close to being right about the next two years' earnings, the stock could rise 50 percent just to put it on par with peers and the overall market." I paused for a second and then asked, "Am I permitted to make two suggestions?"

"I'm listening . . . they better be insightful!" he said with agitation.

"I think we should deal more thoroughly with the Brown family influence. They control the company through the class-A stock. Isn't that a negative? Yes, they've been good managers, but still, the shareholders should have equal rights."

"That's fair. I mentioned that early in the report but can expand on that later. Next!"

"The juice to the recommendation is Jack Daniel's, but there's nothing in the report describing why it has become so dominant, so coveted by loyal customers. I think we should add a paragraph on the specialness of the whiskey itself and why consumers are willing to pay more for their beloved J. D."

"You really love that Tennessee hooch, don't you?" he interjected.

"It's an acquired taste. It's not bourbon. If you like it, there's no substitute. Where I come from, people don't want to like it, because it competes with our own Kentucky hooch."

"But they drink it anyway."

"The advertising is seductive. I think you spell that out quite well in your report."

"Well, thank you very much, great seer. I think I'll start bringing you along on marketing trips as my cheerleader."

"There's a problem with that, sir. I can't jump or execute the necessary gymnastics moves."

Ezra actually flashed a smile, then told me to compose a short paragraph on the J. D. legend and technically how it's made and why it's different from other whiskeys. I handed him the write-up I had already done. At first his eyes darkened, but after a quick read he nodded and gave me a thumbs-up. Coming from Ezra, that was like getting an A-plus on a physics exam.

It was past seven o'clock when we went down the elevator together. He guided us down Broad Street then veered east over to Hanover Square. I could hear the chatter from the bar a block away. When Ezra opened the door, the noise was deafening.

"This is where the parasites hang out," Ezra barked in disgust. "Look at these guys! All they do is sit on their butts and trade on other people's ideas. Are they even necessary? I can't fathom why they get paid so well."

We walked to the far end of the bar. Ezra told the bartender to line up three shot glasses in front of each of us. He covered my eyes and had me down a swig of Canadian Club, an I. W. Harper bourbon, and lastly a Jack Daniel's. "Name them," he insisted. I pissed him off when I immediately identified all three. He blindfolded himself with a handkerchief. I first gave him the bourbon. He sipped it slowly then declared it was deer piss. When he finished the C. C., he sighed and said it reminded him of cold nights in Maine. As he worked the J. D. in his mouth like a sommelier tasting a great burgundy, I held my breath in anticipation.

"I get it. It certainly is different. I'm not sure I like it, but I don't dislike it like that bourbon crap I tried. To me it's good that it's not as sweet as bourbon, but I have to say it doesn't have the wonderful clean bite of C. C."

Then I chipped in, "Now you can tell the BAM sales force that you thoroughly researched the Brown-Forman idea."

"I'm sure that will impress them," he said, and then, looking at his watch, added, "We should go home now, Rogers."

I was keenly aware that was the first time Ezra had addressed me by my given name. I skipped dinner and went directly to bed. I slept that night as if someone had slipped me a Newport version of a Mickey Finn.

Edwin Henderson was so thin, I wouldn't have been surprised if a good wind could blow him off course. Sucking on his pipe and blinking too often behind oversize horn-rimmed glasses, he reminded me of a detective character I had seen in an old Dick Tracy cartoon. The lure of a Wall Street salary to support his growing family short-circuited Henderson's master plan to become a tenured finance professor. He was steady and cerebral, well liked by most everyone at BAM, but constitutionally allergic to risk taking. In short he possessed the perfect DNA for being the head of a research department. Of course I knew that someone had to direct BAM's research effort, but I wondered why anyone would want to just sit back and monitor other people's efforts rather than lace up their spikes and get in the game.

Ezra sat in front of Henderson, who was on a leather chair, with his back resting against a needlepoint pillow that read "Good Old Dad." My role was that of a guest, a student placed in the corner to observe and learn. I sat there thinking about what an odd triumvirate we were—a frustrated intellectual security analyst, an understated gentleman professor, and an overly zealous postpubescent stock junkie—all working in a world of famished carnivores and here to opine on a stock recommendation. It didn't take Ezra long to articulate his new research idea. It wasn't all that complicated. He described Brown-Forman as a quite good company flying under Wall Street's radar screens that was about to become an even better one, a fairly priced stock that would soon be recognized as an undervalued growth stock.

Edwin tinkered with his pipe, a ritual he indulged in when deep in thought. He closed his eyes, dropped his head to his chest with his hands clutched together so tightly that I even noticed his knuckles turned white. Looking up from the floor, he asked Ezra, "What can go wrong?" Even though it was clear they respected each other, it didn't stop them from jousting back and forth until the research director was satisfied.

Ezra began, "Their base business is stable. Even in recessions the company tends to display sales increases. They have a few growth engines besides the superstar status of Jack Daniel's, such as Canadian Mist and an expanding presence in table wines. Management's acquisition strategy has been conservative but nevertheless incrementally accretive to earnings. If I'm wrong, to use your distasteful pejorative, it would probably be caused by an earnings shortfall relative to my estimates that I don't presently anticipate or an acquisition that backfires."

"How about an operational screwup?"

"They've been making this crap for decades. Why would they screw up now?"

"And the balance sheet—accounting, other assets, et cetera?"

"I haven't counted the cases in the warehouse, but it all seems fine."

"Your footnotes indicate revisions to inventory and goodwill valuations. Explain, please."

"Both are clearly highlighted in my report and both are immaterial to the story. Actually, in fiscal '78 they almost offset each other dollar for dollar."

Henderson then moved on. "They have heavy advertising expenditures. Are they playing around there?"

"Their advertising campaigns, especially with Jack Daniel's, have been an important positive to the growth of the company. Management has no plans to cut back. In fact they increased expenditures by 20 percent in fiscal '78 and will increase them an additional 22 percent in fiscal '79. I think it's a positive."

"What about management? I don't favor family-controlled public entities."

"I'm with you on that one, but the new Mr. Brown Jr. looks to be a real winner."

I thought the meeting was going exceptionally well for Ezra until Edwin posed a question that clearly pissed him off.

"Any chance of some corporate finance business for the home team? Did you explore that possibility with Brown-Forman's senior management?"

Unfortunately Ezra exploded. I'd seen him act this way before when it was suggested he play in a sandbox for suck-ups, but I was surprised he couldn't control himself under these circumstances as he answered his boss, "I'm a research analyst, not a freaking peddler with an organ grinder and a performing monkey tethered to a leash!"

That outburst brought the meeting to a close.

Later that night, after Jacob had thoroughly punished his body to the point of exhaustion and I had taken his bicycle for a relaxing ride through Central Park, we settled down at home to share some warmed-up pasta primavera. Without mentioning Brown-Forman by name, I related my experience with Ezra and the firm's research director.

"He just doesn't get it, does he?" Jacob stated.

"No, he's up there in the clouds."

"It's curious," he continued. "I'm all for business and getting ahead at almost any cost, but I do respect Ezra for standing firm with his own principles."

"You mean, 'This above all—to thine own self be true,'" I said.

"Easy, show-off, you're not the only Shakespeare scholar in the room!"

"That may have been the most profound nine words he ever wrote," I couldn't help adding.

Jacob pushed on, "But do you agree with Ezra's stance? I think it's important that you consider this, because pretty soon you'll probably be faced with a similar quandary."

"I know my father never bends when it comes to value judgments, so he would side with Ezra. That has occasionally put him on the hot seat at the hospital, but he has always stood unwavering with his positions. I'd like to think I'm on the same page as those two, but in this specific case I think Mr. Henderson's request was reasonable. He only inquired if Ezra would tell the company that BAM has a first-rate corporate finance department that is quite active and would like to compete for some of their business. I really don't see any ethical dilemma there. He wouldn't be begging, it's only—give us a chance. What wrong with that?"

"Well, your boss sure responded emotionally," Jacob reasoned.

"He believes he loses self-respect whenever he markets. He likes to say he didn't go to business school to become a door-to-door salesman of cosmetics and cleaning products."

"He would fail miserably at McKinsey with that attitude," Jacob acknowledged. "We're the ones who have to whore for new accounts. It's the lifeblood of the consulting industry."

The next day as Ezra was proofreading the Brown-Forman report in preparation for distribution, he looked up at me and asked my reaction to the meeting with Edwin Henderson.

"I imagined we were sitting in on a strategy session with Ohio State's longtime football coach, Woody Hayes," I answered.

"How many more Ohioisms have you got in that grab bag of yours, and why the hell would you be thinking about that fat bully?" Ezra questioned.

"Because his offensive strategy was limited to 'three yards and a cloud of dust.'"

"What in heaven's name does that have to do with our recommending Brown-Forman?"

"Ol' Woody's philosophy preaches a willingness to grind out a win yard by yard, even though his team could be blessed with all sorts of talented offensive weapons. He'd rather run up the middle for a few yards than attempt a pass downfield. I thought you wanted to go on the offensive when recommending Brown-Forman stock, but our research director surprised me when the focus of yesterday's discussion was primarily on risks rather than wondering about the upside potential."

"That's just Edwin," Ezra said. "He's very careful and always wants to know where the exit door is located, but once he approves a stock's buy rating, he'll be an avid supporter. You'll see."

"When do we go public with the recommendation?" I asked.

"After the investment committee approves it, we'll enlighten the sales force."

"Could the investment committee be a problem?"

"Never with one of my ideas, and it won't happen with this one!"

Absent from our conversation was any mention of yesterday's outburst.

That was fortunate, because that whole episode made me uncomfortable.

Burr, Addington, and Merritt's sales force and senior members of the investment management team filled the conference room awaiting Ezra Carter. The room was in the southwestern corner of our building between the partners' private dining room and the corporate finance department. I cherished the view from the vast windows, because it encompassed all of lower Wall Street, Trinity Church and its ancient graveyards, as well as Battery Park and the waters beyond. The meeting was scheduled for two hours in advance of the market's opening bell. Coffee and copies of the Brown-Forman report were available at a rear table. I stood by myself in the far corner, eager to witness my bosses' performance. I stood even more formally when I noticed Ambrose Burr in the front row, intently studying the report.

Ezra arrived and closed the door behind him as if to signify the meeting was private and latecomers were not welcome. He sat behind a library table with his notes spread out in front of him. He clapped his hands together in a vain attempt to quiet the room, yet every present living organism snapped to attention at the mere sight of Ambrose Burr rising from his chair to command order. For the next twenty minutes or so, Ezra articulated the reasons for his Brown-Forman recommendation, sounding more like a college professor than a brokerage firm security analyst. I was rooting for him like I would for the Reds needing a run or two in the bottom of the ninth, but when listening to his presentation, I found it too easy to recognize why he had the reputation of being an overly cerebral elitist. It wasn't what he said but rather how he delivered his message, communicating the idea as if he was doing the room a favor by condescending to share his thoughts.

I was wishing there was a magic pill I could have slipped into Ezra's tea that morning to make him understand the impression he was projecting. The Brown-Forman idea was destined to be a winner, but it wouldn't butter Ezra's bread if the sales force spent their time debating the recent Rangers hockey loss rather than making marketing calls to their customers.

During the Q&A, thankfully, Ezra rallied like a racehorse coming down the stretch at Churchill Downs. He was more relaxed and surprisingly responsive when handling questions, and even on occasion appeared to warm up when explaining his theory about why the financial community would reward Brown-Forman stock with a substantially higher valuation when the company demonstrated an improving growth rate and return on equity.

The room was emptying out and Ezra was still gathering up his papers when I heard a cryptic voice mumble, "These yahoos wouldn't know a good idea if it were gift wrapped in a little blue Tiffany box." I looked to my right and there, standing next to me, was the market-meister Paal Van Horne. I had been warned many times to avoid contact with this hot-tempered, scowling Dutchman. His impatience with humanity was legendary at BAM. Alone in his office, bent over his desk in deep concentration while updating his precious charts, he made bold predictions based on his readings and interpretations of technical factors that he believed ultimately influenced stock prices. I had yet to meet anyone who actually understood his methodology, and no one dared to ask him to explain his black magic, but his recent calls had been unerringly accurate, so most everyone in the firm assumed he must have a special talent. His early-morning market letters were talked about throughout the office as if they had come directly from the heavens and were transmitted to special clients by salesmen in hushed tones: "Paal now thinks this" or, "Paal believes this stock just had a reversal and therefore . . ." or, "Check into your bomb shelter, buddy, because Paal says we're really breaking down here." What amazed me was the volume of orders that poured into

BAM's trading desk based on one man's opinions. I knew my Wharton professors would be dismissive of Paal Van Horne's technical approach, and I couldn't even comprehend the specialized language he employed, but if his voodoo would help get me to the Promised Land, I needed to learn more about it.

My knees buckled when he continued, "Aren't you the wunderkind who is long all that Resorts stock?" I suddenly felt the glare of a bright, hot lamp on my face. I was unprepared for this encounter. I didn't know what to say or how to act.

"I doubt this crew realizes you should peel a banana before eating it," he continued, pointing to the sales force. "Did you know that even most chimpanzees take their time and carefully peel away the skin before indulging in their favorite meal?" he said out loud, I assumed directed to me.

"I've never actually dined with a chimp before" was all I could think to answer.

Paal Van Horne was overweight, of average height with curly white hair and piercing blue eyes. His thin wrists, elongated fingers, and finely sculpted hands were out of place with the rest of his ruddy features, as if they were modeled after a sixteenth-century Mannerist painting. He spoke with a slight accent in a deep, serious voice with an air of self-confidence befitting someone who had recently discovered a cure for cancer. I wondered if he ever smiled or suffered self-doubt.

"What made you get involved with Resorts back in '77? Weren't you still in college?" he asked as we were walking back to our offices. He looked at his watch and went on, "The market's getting ready to open. Come on back around two and fill me in on Atlantic City. I'm interested."

I summoned up the courage to ask him if he would then show me how to read the technicals on Brown-Forman. Van Horne managed to nod a yes.

Ezra was in a good mood because the orders were piling up to buy what the traders had already christened "Captain Jack." He was positively expansive when I entered his office while dodging a paper airplane heading straight for my crotch. "I almost got you," he laughed. The rest of the day he would be out of the office on dreaded marketing duty with our New York institutional clients, drumming up even more enthusiasm for Brown-Forman. I was told to finish up with our research wire responsibilities and then continue to dress up my temporary-help industry report so he could judge if it were a worthwhile project for us to push forward. When I mentioned encountering Paal Van Horne, he closed his briefcase, clenched his teeth, and warned me not to be influenced by "that man."

"Rogers, people who think they are demigods are dangerous" were his parting words as he left for the day.

At two o'clock sharp, I sheepishly knocked on Van Horne's door. His shirtsleeves were rolled up, but I refused to stare at the peculiarity of his feminine hands as they carefully turned the pages of a chart book. He wasn't as gruff as I expected. He was most interested in the chronology of Resorts' new venture. Whenever I mentioned a relevant date, he marked an X on an axis of the chart he was maintaining on the stock. He didn't inquire about Resorts' revenue potential or earnings estimates—fundamentals apparently didn't matter to him, he just wanted to know the presumed dates for permit application and the ultimate time the casino would eventually be approved to open for business.

"You're still holding on?" he asked.

"Yes, sir," I answered too confidently.

"That takes a lot of grit! Do you think the permit application date matters?"

"Yes, because it will confirm that the process is moving along."

"What are the chances of them opening by Memorial Day as planned?"

"They will if my prayers hold any sway with you know who."

"Do you have a price target for the stock?" he asked.

I answered carefully, "None that I feel confident in repeating."

Van Horne then went on, "I've been charting this stock since the beginning of the year. It can go anywhere. Analysts will model all sorts of cashflow estimates, but in truth they're all nonsense. The stock is flying solo on its own technicals. This is the ultimate high-risk/high-reward stock."

"Is that a bad thing?" I timidly inquired.

"All that matters is for the stock to maintain its relative momentum. Also, monitor the short position. If it continues to increase, that's a positive; if it decreases, that means the shorts are covering and responsible for the stock's rise. I wouldn't like that if I were you. It's phony strength."

"I drive down to Atlantic City every few weeks to check on their progress. If you're interested, I could relay what I'm seeing and hearing from a few of the workmen I've gotten to know," I then told him.

The barking dog Paal emerged when he snarled, "I don't care what they think. I'll listen to the stock. Its action will speak volumes."

Talking one on one with Paal Van Horne in his stuffy, overcrowded office was thoroughly intimidating. I couldn't imagine sharing a bag of peanuts and a few beers at a baseball game with this tightly strung egotist. He was the kind of man my father would characterize as believing that even when he's wrong, he's right. My hands were sweating, and I could sense the onset of a mild headache. It was time to leave. At the door he handed me a Xeroxed copy of a chart he'd constructed on Brown-Forman and said, "This stock has a solid base in the low twenties. It shouldn't violate twenty-one and a half. It's a buy on a twenty-four breakout if the trading volume also increases."

When I thanked him for his time he added, "You're on your own now."

The market was meandering about while Brown-Forman continued to creep higher, crossing twenty-three for the first time in a few months. I was anxious to buy some stock for my own portfolio but had to wait three days for compliance clearance. Each morning I continued to stop by George O'Leary's desk to gab about the market. I handed him an approved buy order for Brown-Forman and asked his advice for timing my purchase. He promised to watch it carefully and treat the execution like he would be buying a stock for the Vatican.

Only one day later, the market buckled when the Consumer Price Index was reported to have risen precipitously. Georgie O. told me to hold tight. Late the next morning came the call: "Get down here fast!" The Federal Reserve had surprised the pundits by announcing it was raising the discount rate in an effort to curtail inflation. A flood of sellers hit the market. Captain Jack was fading fast along with the general market, and a large seller on BAM's trading desk wanted a bid for their block of stock. "It's time to dive into the pool," Mr. O'Leary said as he looked at me with urgent eyes.

I borrowed a nearby phone and called Ronnie Davis. He shouted at me, "I only have a second. It's busy as hell here. This better be a life-or-death call."

I quickly told him the situation. I had already sold my Florida housing stocks on Ezra's warning, so I had a lot of cash in the account. All I owned of significance was my temporary-help stocks and a crazy, outsize position in Resorts, because it had more than tripled. Ronnie's opinion was that the market would be choppy for a while, but he didn't foresee a significant sell-off. Then in typical Ronnie fashion he added, "If you like the stock as an investment and you've done all your work, then step up there and take the shot. If this were a basketball game, you'd probably throw up an air ball, but this is your game and you're good at it, so go for it, because it could be a swish."

I knew that this wouldn't qualify as an important life lesson moment, but it surely was going to be a trade I would remember a year or so later. I told Mr. O'Leary to double the size of my order, reasoning that the block would come at a nice discount and I could decide later if I should trade out of some of the position or hold it all for the longer term.

"Are you sure you want to go so large?" he asked. "I'm not a math whiz, but the way I do the numbers, that adds up to 20 percent of your account."

I had learned to rely on this man's common sense and impeccable instincts. I thought that in his own way, he was an older version of Ronnie Davis, and that was a high compliment to bestow on anyone. I told him, "I'm not sure of anything but, I'm only twenty-two. No wife. No kids. No pets, not even a turtle. I like the stock, and the price seems right. I think it's a good time to shoot for the moon."

By the end of the day, I had convinced both R. D. and Jacob to take a flier on Brown-Forman. I had never been responsible for an investment recommendation to a friend before, except for Resorts, which was really more a crapshoot than a well-researched idea. I found the risk of a screwup to be positively exhilarating, almost like turning over the last card in a high-stakes poker game.

Ronnie was easy—"I'll play on the block cleanup, and then see how it goes. I'll leave the long term to you. All I want to do is trade the hell out of it."

Jacob took his usual paranoid approach—"How can they maintain the Jack Daniel's mystique and charge such a premium for it? What happens to this company in a consumer-led recession?" And lastly, the objection that made me laugh so hard I had stomach cramps: "Who the hell names their kid W. L. Lyons Brown Jr.? You can bet that the president of this company wasn't bar mitzvahed!"

As usual the BAM research offices were a virtual ghost town late Friday afternoon. I had bought my Brown-Forman on the big trade at twenty-one and three-quarters. Ezra was credited with generating the buy orders to accomplish the cross. The firm's block traders were pleased, because they booked sizable commissions on both sides of the trade, and I was fortunate that O'Leary squeezed me in line to participate at the last minute. The stock bucked the market and closed higher at twenty-two and a half. I sat alone at my desk, writing my weekly letter to Charlotte, drained by the emotions of the day but nevertheless flying high.

I wrote to her about the characters I was working with, a unique mixture of capitalists trying to navigate their way to the rainbow's end, where a pot of gold presumably awaited. I did my best to describe the talented and unpredictable Paal Van Horne; Edwin Henderson, the firm's resident nervous Nelly; unctuous Harold Brauer, the SS officer; my brilliant educator Ezra Carter; and the very special, ageless leprechaun Mr. O'Leary. I told her about Resorts, Brown-Forman, and how I was spending my days learning the investment business at BAM. I tried to help her visualize my apartment at the Giles and what it was like living with my hyperenergetic roommate. I brought her up-to-date about Ronnie and my father. I told her how much I looked forward to her letters, that they told a story of a young woman who was committed to living a purposeful life and that I was proud of her. I told her when I closed my eyes I could picture her smile, smell her hair, and hear her soothing voice. I told her how much I missed her.

After a first-quarter hiccup, the stock market snapped back with some vigor in April and then moved a bit higher in May. I was sitting in Ezra's office for one of our afternoon talks. He was in an effusive mood primarily because of the praise he was receiving for his Brown-Forman report and the bold prediction he had made to the firm's investment committee that interest rates were going to march appreciably higher. "My recommendations should be significantly impacting their normally abysmal performance," he boasted with his usual air of contempt for the group's investment acumen. I learned to savor these conversations when Ezra was open and upbeat, because there also were days when it seemed he was living on an alien planet, unapproachable as he growled to himself and slammed the phone down in disgust. These symptoms of unmitigated aggravation were easy to read, so in those cases I avoided his office, as if breathing the air within those four walls would cause me to contract leprosy.

"Do you believe that psychology plays much of a role in how a stock acts?" I asked my boss.

"In the short term, I suppose it can, but eventually fundamentals always win out. Where are you going with this?" he queried.

"Our sales force and their supposedly sophisticated customers initially embraced your Brown-Forman idea. Then the market started to tank. The institutions abruptly canceled their buy orders and the salesmen went AWOL. The lower the stock went, the more nervous they all became. At one point after the big block traded at twenty-one and three-quarters, we didn't have a single buy order in Brown-Forman on the desk. After a few days, the market then settled down, apparently taking the Fed's actions in stride. Captain Jack found some friends and started to bounce. Two of the buyers on the big trade chose to reverse themselves and run for the hills, afraid of a further sell-off and content to have made a few pennies. So much for investing! When the stock busted through twenty-four, Paal Van Horne jumped on it with a technical breakout recommendation. Guess what? The morbid salesmen and their follow-the-leader clients decided to love the stock even though it was less undervalued than just a few weeks before. If that's not psychology, then please explain their actions to your dimwitted assistant."

"I don't dispute the conclusions of your rampage, but your time frame is quite short term. In the longer term, none of that crap matters," Ezra concluded.

I wasn't going to argue with his experience and intellect, but the lessons I had learned from Professor Whittles still resonated vividly in my consciousness, and I had just observed psychology at work in real time: I watched Brown-Forman weaken and buyers take a hike; the stock then strengthened and they jumped back on the train at higher price levels.

Yes, this took place in only a matter of a few weeks, and yes, that hardly qualifies as a long-term horizon but, for the few brave souls who took advantage of that window of opportunity, there sure were sweet profits to be banked. Is it sacrilegious to make a 10 percent return in less than a month? Am I wanting too much to be a piglet at the trough stuffing myself with profits in both the short and long term? Is it realistic for a Wall Streeter to be capable of executing that dual strategy? Should I even try?

Ezra was off and running on inflationary risks and where interest rates were headed. He was a rigid fundamentalist and essentially wary of the impact of psychology on markets. He implored me to pay close attention to his concerns. "If interest rates keep rising, there will be hell to pay in stocks. The ice gets pretty damn thin when banks increase the prime rate due to the Fed's reaction to pressure from inflation. A year ago the prime rate was in the low sixes; now it's 8 percent. I think we're headed into double-digit land in the autumn. Write that prediction down and don't forget who made it!"

The sermon on the mount was rudely interrupted when a salesman bypassed Jackie and knocked on Ezra's door. I recognized him as Billy Bennett, the son-in-law of an important corporate finance partner whose institutional accounts were heavily skewed to the super aggressive. I had heard Ezra typecast him as one of the empty-suit pretty boys occupying a chair on the sales floor.

"Good afternoon, Ezra," the suit said, not even acknowledging me.

"His name is Rogers," Ezra answered, pointing at me. "What's up, Einstein?" he continued with his best sarcastic grin.

"I need you later today to tout Captain Jack to a couple of hot hedge fund accounts uptown. We'll be done by six."

"Sorry, but I can't make it."

"What? You know these guys really shake and bake and generate big commissions. This is important!" he implored.

"No can do," Ezra repeated. Then, to my utter surprise, he volunteered his young, untested assistant. "You can handle this, Rogers. Just stick to the fundamentals. Walk them through my report and don't get entangled in any arguments. Billy boy here will do the rest. Be confident. You know the story and they don't. Remember that. Stay calm and don't let them manipulate you."

On the cab ride uptown, I remembered a ball game against Roger Bacon when I was relaxing on the bench thinking about Dad's newest receptionist's spectacular wahooies, envisioning how she would look sitting topless answering the phone, when the momentum of the game radically changed. Coach called me over and told me to quickly warm up and go out there to preserve the win. I was too lost in lust and not mentally prepared to pitch. I wasn't ready for competition then and I didn't feel ready in the back seat of the cab now. Was Billy Bennett to be my catcher signaling for a fastball that would be crushed for the opponent's come-from-behind victory? I had been the ignominious goat back then. I looked out the window at the tall buildings and gathered myself to stand upright and deliver a better pitch to the uptown honchos.

The first session went well. We sat with the fund's consumer products analyst, who was already familiar with the spirits industry and its various players. All he wanted from me was to justify why Jack Daniel's had staying power and pricing leverage. B. B., as he liked to be called, was pleased with the way I handled his questions but warned me that the next meeting would be difficult and probably stressful. I guessed there wouldn't be much time to enjoy the good feeling I had from holding my own with an experienced analyst and maybe even taking a small step forward in my career.

I hadn't seen Ike Crawford since he interviewed me for a job over a year ago in the career-placement offices at Penn. His office didn't disappoint, sitting high on the thirty-fifth floor with a splendid view looking south at the United Nations and the East River. The space must have been decorated by an Anglophile whose mission was to make it feel as if it belonged to a merchant bank that had been trading and investing around the world for over a century. The furniture and oriental carpets were expensive reproductions posing as genuine antiques. The only authentic wall decoration was an absurd portrait of the magnificent one, Mr. Crawford himself, standing stiffly, a shotgun resting on his shoulder, flanked by a pair of English setters and dressed in full hunting regalia. He recognized me.

"Didn't I reject you last year?" he laughed. "Why should I back one of your ideas now?"

"It's good to see you, too," I replied, doing my best to avoid any confrontation.

Billy Bennett formally introduced me to Ike and a member of his team who had quietly entered the room, then apologized for Ezra's lack of availability. His voice trailed off as he looked down at his shoes and began to crack his knuckles nervously. I felt sorry for the poor guy, because he was clearly uncomfortable and sinking fast. Ike Crawford smelled his vulnerability. He pointed to a six-foot stuffed grizzly standing in the corner and addressed Billy.

"Don't be rude, B. B. Why don't you shake hands and give a warm greeting to Bart over there? He's part of our investment committee, you know."

"Come on, Ike, not this again," Billy pleaded, emitting a genuinely pained sigh.

But with Ike staring at him and saying nothing, Billy Bennett actually walked over to the bear and shook an outstretched paw. Ike and his flunky started to giggle and smirk like a pair of teenagers. Then, producing a space command from his desk, Ike pointed the handheld at the bear. When the tape recorder hidden in Bart's midsection clicked on and the giant grizzly grunted—"Buy 'em, sell 'em, buy 'em, sell 'em"—they broke out in uproarious laughter. B. B. was left standing, red faced and humiliated.

"You're not amused?" Ike asked me. I didn't respond but wished I had a pin to prick this prick's inflated balloon-like ego.

The Crawford team wasn't interested in Brown-Forman's fundamentals. They didn't ask a single question about the company's balance sheet or income statement, why Jack Daniel's was still on allocation, or why Ezra's earnings estimates were so much higher than those of his competitors. All they wanted to know was did we think B.-F. was a takeover candidate. Ike pressed me to repeat any juicy rumors I might have heard around our shop: "Has anyone accumulated a large block? Have you heard if a rival company is sniffing around? Is the stock on your banker's restricted list?"

I was beginning to taste a nasty bile in my throat. I had heard about jerks like this from Ronnie Davis, but this was my first direct experience. I looked over at Billy Bennett for support. Even he knew that these guys had crossed the line. Finding strength from a newly discovered backbone, he stood, bravely shook Ike's hand, and said that the meeting was now over.

"I need a drink," B. B. was saying in the lobby. "Make that a double. Please join me—it's quiet next door and we can talk."

I nursed a cold beer while Billy hit the Chivas Regal real hard. Somewhere into the second scotch, his pained expression was replaced by a glassy-eyed look that reminded me of the frat brothers on a Friday night back at Penn.

"Those guys are always looking for an edge," B. B. said while trying to charm the waitress into treating us to some pretzels from the bar.

"I would say it's worse than that," I stated coldly.

"Look, I know Crawford is a snake, but he trades 'em up real big, and the commissions on his account help pay my mortgage."

"Is he really that successful?" I questioned.

"I've never seen his numbers, but he claims to manage over a hundred big ones at 20 percent of the profits."

It's staggering, I thought to myself. Ezra worked fifty-hour weeks, generated all his own ideas, spent weeks researching and validating them, then had to market himself to self-important Ike Crawfords who shamelessly sat on their butts and traded on other people's creativity and hard work. These money masters then have the balls to tout their investment acumen while raising more money to manage, when in fact most of them are just bottom feeders. No wonder Ezra despised a Wall Street that rewarded these guys with earnings ten times greater than he had averaged over the last five years. I didn't have the nerve to ask my boss why he still was a security analyst after all these years and not running a fund of his own.

Billy Bennett wanted to ask a favor. I knew that was the reason we were having drinks together and chatting up. He was hurting, so why not make it easy for him. Before he pleaded for omertà, I promised not to discuss the Bart episode with anyone at the office. I told him I had already forgotten the entire incident. I thanked him for the beer and headed home.

Much to Ezra's delight, the New York banks increased the prime rate twice during May, thus confirming his prediction. The stock market fluttered somewhat, but Resorts continued to confound the skeptics by moving even higher. The company had filed its permit application on schedule, and the New Jersey newspapers were awash with hope that the casino would open by Memorial Day. Jacob and I continued to make our monthly pilgrimage to the boardwalk. We watched the workers install massive lighting fixtures, tasteless furniture befitting a Miami Beach hotel lobby, industrial carpeting by the mile, as well as the all-important eighty-four gaming tables (which I counted with my very own nervous eyes) and 893 slot machines (I took a delivery man's word on that number). At the end of the day, we looked at each other and nodded yes, this crazy project might indeed open as planned.

When New Jersey's governor Brendan Byrne cut the ceremonial ribbon at 10:00 a.m. on May 26, legalized gambling was officially open for business on the East Coast of the United States. A loud cheer erupted from the crowd that had waited outside for hours to enter the casino. Meanwhile, on the southern tip of Manhattan, the floor of the stock exchange was in turmoil. Buy orders were flooding the system and the orderly market dikes were about to break down. An hour before the markets were due to open, the Resorts specialist on the floor notified the exchange governors that he couldn't open the stock without a delay and a substantially higher price. Traders and investors alike seemed to be assuming that this opening-day phenomenon was predictive of the future success of Resorts' fantasy project.

I was sitting next to George O'Leary when the call came from Atlantic City that sent my nervous system into orbit. It was Mr. O's idea to persuade his nephew from Trenton to be our sleuth that historic morning. He told nephew Mikey Doyle that he owed him a favor and to get his little Irish ass down there by 8:00 a.m. and be his eyes and ears.

"Mikey's a good boy but can't hold on to a job, because he's always thinking about the horses. He always thought he'd be a jockey or a trainer, but it hasn't worked out for him yet. Too heavy or just not that talented, I guess. The kid lives at the track, hanging on, trying somehow to fit in. He'll do this for his uncle, though, and call us at nine o'clock to report on the situation at the casino. To be extra sure, I gave him a twenty to lose."

Mikey called from a phone booth on the boardwalk, looking back at a mass of people willing to stand in line for most of the morning to try their luck at the slots or table games. Where else could they go on a day trip to experience big-time gambling in an attractive public setting? He told us it felt like he was waiting for the gates to open at Yankee Stadium for a World Series game—the chaos, the buzz level, the utter rush of excitement in the air. Uncle George told him to call us back after he was inside the casino itself and to focus on whether the throngs were placing bets or just standing around observing the scene. The trader in Mr. O'Leary took over when he declared out loud, "This stock is going to bury the shorts!"

Every Monday, Wednesday, and Friday during May and June, Mikey Doyle called Uncle George at 9:00 a.m. using the phone booth across the boardwalk from the Resorts complex and at 3:00 p.m. from a phone in the grand hallway. The crowds weren't diminishing no matter the weather, and they seemed to be enthusiastic about their overall experience. He reported constant action on the slot machines and people packed in at least three deep for a chance to participate at one of the game tables. He passed on rumors he was hearing from employees that the casino wins were way above budget. The stock's price seemed to confirm his observations, as it kept moving inexorably higher. Mikey kept the twenty warm in his pocket until late June, when he secured a seat at a two-dollar blackjack table by patiently weaving his way through the scrummage of avid gamblers. Uncle George wasn't surprised when his nephew dropped his stash in less than twenty minutes.

The huge dollar exposure I had in Resorts stock was now dominating my life. I wasn't sleeping well and had developed a nasty rash across my back and underneath my left shoulder. I'd wake up in the middle of the night scratching myself like a mad dog, debating the size of my Resorts holding. I had trouble thinking about anything else. Every day I strategized with my trading confidants Ronnie Davis and Georgie O, consumed every written word by the New Jersey press on the future of gambling in their fair state, and argued with the internal twin demons of fear and greed. On my usual Sunday evening call to my father, the best doctor I knew offered a diagnosis of my condition: "What's going on up there, son? It seems you've got a bad case of nervous agitation."

Even I knew he was right on, so I begged him for a wonder pill to lift my confidence. Instead Dad made me feel like a ten-year-old again by suggesting I come home for a while where he could look after me and we could go to a few Reds games and together talk through whatever issues were bothering me. Whenever we finished these conversations, I always realized how vulnerable I would be if anything ever happened to take him from me. Advice came free from Ronnie, that it's never wrong to take profits and sit on the sidelines. A trader to the core, he believed I could always step back up to the plate and reenter the game. When I queried George O'Leary, he suggested I sell a bit each day until I felt comfortable, wait awhile, and then if I was still tense, sell some more. He said I'd know when I sold enough if I starting looking at the skirts walking by on Madison Avenue. I knew by now the importance of having access to quality people I could trust. I also knew that I alone had to make the ultimate decisions.

It's true that sometimes the way my mind works puzzles even me. I can be concentrating on an important issue or even just daydreaming about a particular subject when suddenly my brain races forward like an out-of-control locomotive. I will end up reaching conclusions without knowing how I got there and wondering if I was, in fact, the conductor of that train. There were times in school when I would whiz through a test, be praised for my efforts by my teacher, but not be able to remember any of the questions I had just answered. Even though this condition was unnerving, I hoped it would rear its quirky head and lead me to decide when to unwind my position in Resorts stock.

All this introspection got me to wondering how I made decisions in the first place. Did I try to carefully analyze all the variables and methodically weigh these inputs before reaching a well-thought-out conclusion? Was I really that scientific in my approach, or did I just absorb these informational inputs, allow them to swirl about in my consciousness, and in the end yield to my emotional self to spit out a course of action for me to follow? I could feel the onset of an unhealthy self-doubt creeping into my system as I questioned why my batting average had been so grand and whether I had really been that good—or had my successes been mainly due to nothing more than fortuitous luck?

In late July Elsbeth agreed it was time for the princess to experience Atlantic City and all its manifold charms. On a steamy Saturday morning, we drove south two hours in a rented green Chevrolet that Ms. Aylesworth said reminded her of being transported by an army hearse. I urged her to dress down, as if she were a housewife with four screaming kids and a large husband with a farmer's tan. She tried her best but failed miserably—it was summer, after all, and next to impossible to camouflage that provocative body. I insisted she try a Nathan's hot dog before we waited in line to enter the holy shrine of New Jersey on the Atlantic.

I felt a huge surge of hope as soon as I scanned the casino floor mobbed with excited patrons. Even though it was a sunny summer afternoon, every table was crowded and every slot machine was in use. I could almost hear the profits being raked in by the dealers and croupiers. Elsbeth digested the scene, then admitted, "I can't believe I didn't listen to you. What a gold mine, and I don't own one share of this stock." We checked out the public rooms, restaurants, entertainment facilities, and even the bathrooms. They all looked fine to me, but what was really impressive was the pulsating energy in the casino. Elsbeth's take was that it didn't compare to Monte Carlo but would be attractive enough to satisfy the local marketplace, an unnecessarily snobbish comment, I later recalled.

"Let's try the dice," she said.

"It's not my game. Why don't you play for us?" I suggested.

We each contributed a few twenties to the partnership as I watched her spirit come to life.

"It's all in the way you caress the dice," she said. "Treat them with genuine affection and they'll work hard for you."

"I didn't know you were a student of gambling."

"I'm not. I think a friend of my father's might have said that."

An hour or so later, the dice were resting in her finely manicured hands.

She was the star of the craps table, swamped with encouragement from the salivating men who were admiring her cleavage when she leaned over to roll the dice while wearing a loose tank top. I found myself studying her. Elsbeth was clearly out of her element in Atlantic City, uncomfortable with the masses at the casino and self-conscious about her totally different background. When her turn with the dice was over, our partnership was 50 percent in the hole. Her new friends continued to cheer for her, but I knew she wanted to be rescued and to leave for a more familiar environment.

"Don't you want to try the dice or play some twenty-one? Maybe you can get us back to even," she said as I guided her through the phalanx of gamblers.

"No. It's okay."

"I can stand behind you and be your good-luck charm."

I told her I never liked the idea of tossing two cubes down a table, relying on inanimate objects to determine if I won or lost. Neither did I enjoy playing blackjack, which was too robotic, with the dealer obliged to take another card at sixteen or fewer but not if his total count was seventeen or greater. I thought I could teach an eight-year-old the knack of knowing when to draw again or when to stay pat and force the dealer to play on. I reminded her that my game of choice was poker, that I liked reading and psyching out the other players and the challenge of analyzing betting motivations in real time as each card was dealt. I explained that in craps and twenty-one, your opponent owns the casino; on the other hand with poker, your opponent encompasses all of the other participants around the table. Elsbeth listened attentively, then looked at me and shook her head as if to say, "Where the hell did you come from?"

We stood outside in the fresh air watching the waves roll in. Having grown up in New England, Elsbeth took the mysteries of the sea for granted, while my experience with running water was an Ohio River badly in need of a doctor's appointment. I was lost in thought, mesmerized by the ocean's majesty and unconquerable independence, when I felt her poking me on the shoulder.

"Where are you? What are you thinking about?"

"Could you ever imagine yourself as a Magellan or Balboa?" I asked.

"Not even for a minute."

"Think about it, taking off from Europe around the beginning of the sixteenth century without communication systems, navigating by reading the stars, totally dependent on the winds and not really knowing if the world is round or if the ocean ends with a perilous drop-off into a dark oblivion."

"That's what you're pondering?" she questioned.

"Imagine having the courage to begin that journey to a new world where you have no idea what's really out there."

"Sometimes I worry that you're from another planet. Why are you staring at the horizon and now fixated on explorers from hundreds of years ago?"

"I was just thinking that all I'm worried about is deciding when to sell a stock where I'm sitting on a humongous profit and how trivial that is compared to the risks those guys took over 450 years ago."

"You seem to be making the right decisions so far."

We walked down the boardwalk until we were standing directly in front of Resorts' future competition. I was confronted by a large, ominous sign announcing that Caesars World was planning to begin construction of their casino complex later that autumn. I approached a hard hat mending a fence, hoping to learn some kernel of information about the Caesars project. He was old and bent over, but that didn't stop his lecherous eyes from scanning Elsbeth up and down, then back again. I introduced her as my sister LouAnn, then asked if he knew when Caesars expected to open to the public. Looking directly at LouAnn's chest, he answered, "By July 4 next year." I tried a few more leading questions, but he only groaned ignorance.

On the way to the parking lot Elsbeth couldn't wait. "LouAnn. That's the name you chose for me! Why not something elegant like Samantha or Veronica? And did you notice how that foul man was leering at me? I told you that's the way it is for me, and you wonder why I'm so defensive."

She was probably going overboard, but I didn't care because I was concentrating on the significance of the Caesars casino opening. It had been announced months ago, and Caesars stock had responded by blasting ahead. Resorts' price action had so far been impervious to the upcoming competition, but I assumed that would change. The $64,000 question was *when*.

"There you go again," she said as we strolled on the boardwalk. "It's eerie when you get distant like this. It's as if you encircle yourself with an invisible shield and block everything out, including me, and I'm standing right here next to you. For the record, it's really unnerving."

Elsbeth had been surrounded by wealth her entire life. She grew up in a grand house, coddled by servants with every advantage that money could grant. When she graduated from college, her grandmother took her to lunch at La Côte Basque and told her that she had established a trust fund for her favorite namesake that vested on her thirtieth birthday. She kissed both her hands and whispered to her granddaughter that she would never have financial worries during her lifetime.

I knew she wouldn't understand my journey, how motivated I was to achieve my goals and how much joy I experienced when succeeding in the stock market or even pulling off a small coup at a poker table in Kentucky. Of course, the bigger the pot, the better, but that wasn't always the point. I loved winning at any game in which thinking was involved. Elsbeth was highly intelligent and wore her independence proudly, but still she didn't want to risk being proven wrong. Unfortunately for her there was a scorecard for those who played the game on Wall Street, and you couldn't argue with it because the numbers spoke out loud, clear and true.

"Have you ever been afraid of losing a significant part of your wealth?" I asked her as we continued our walk.

"I remember back in 1973–74 that my advisers were flush with excuses when the market was in such bad shape."

"What did they say?"

"They regretted losing so much of my money, but my account was down less than the S&P averages, so they claimed to be proud of their overall performance."

"What did you think?"

"I was happy that I still had so much left."

"You didn't want to hang them from a tree? What would you do now if it happened again?"

"I'd cast a spell on you to make you love me, then I'd latch on to your wave, sleep like a baby, and live happily ever after," she answered with a curious expression. "And how about you, dauntless? What gives you the shakes in the middle of the night?"

I answered honestly. "That I'll wake up and all my gains these last few years will turn out to have been a mirage. That I'm standing alone in the middle of the desert searching for my supply of water. Remember that

this money thing is all new for me. I never had any savings to lose before."
That response seemed to end the conversation.

A few minutes later, we gathered in our car and set off for Manhattan.
I was listening to the radio, cruising along on Artic Avenue toward the
Garden State Parkway when Elsbeth suddenly pointed at a billboard.

"Quick! Turn off here," she said, almost vaulting out of her seat.

"We don't need any gas," I told her.

"Look across the street. It's the Love Nest Motel. I've heard about
places like this—we've got to check it out."

The motel's rooms wrapped around an open courtyard with a decay-
ing fountain centerpiece depicting centaurs ravishing spoils of war in a
variety of erotic positions. We were greeted by a middle-aged woman with
a huge goiter and teeth that reminded me of tree bark. At the desk Elsbeth
chose a room that was supposed to resemble a tent because she never before had had sex in the desert. We rented the place for two hours at a cost
of twenty-five dollars, which included a bonus of an ample supply of
quarters for the vibrating, heart-shaped bed.

"This is great," said the Vassar graduate. "It's just like I would have
imagined. The raspberry shag carpet is perfect, and the blackout curtains
add a touch of intrigue. The ceiling mirror will be a first for me."

We slowly undressed each other while being serenaded by the sultry
music of Johnny Mathis. At first we both were into the humor of our surroundings, but five quarters and an hour later, I lay exhausted. Sex with
Elsbeth was like competing in an Olympic event—spirited, inventive, even
athletic, but the passion of the moment was always under control and I
could tell she was suppressing her innermost feelings. The truth was that
we each had secrets we didn't want to share. Elsbeth returned from the
bathroom and stood naked in front of me, posing like a Parisian model on
the runway. "What do you think, is the Love Nest inspirational?" she said,
spinning around 360 degrees to showcase all she had to offer.

As it turned out, that was the last time we slept together. I would miss
her but knew that there was an emotional bridge neither of us was willing
to cross. The next week she was off to Europe to help solidify J. P. Morgan's relationship with a legendary private Swiss bank. She ended up
staying in Geneva for a month, working closely with Claude Beaumont,
who just happened to be the founder's grandson.

When Elsbeth returned to New York, she suggested dinner at an obscure café near her apartment. As soon as she greeted me with a phony European air kiss, I knew change was in the air. After the waiter cleared our plates, she sat subdued, nervously stirring her tea.

"You don't have to explain anything to me," I said, breaking the ice. "I'm sure it all will work out wonderfully for you."

"It just happened, Rogers. I wasn't looking for romance. He just swept me away."

"That's the way it's supposed to happen," I told her.

"Will you still remember me once you're a zillionaire?"

"As long as you don't morph into the receptionist at the Love Nest."

As I hugged her goodbye at the entrance to her apartment building, she whispered in my ear, "I don't know who she is, but she sure is one lucky girl. Awfully tough competitor, I might add."

Walking back to my place, I wondered how Elsbeth knew about Charlotte. Was her sixth sense that good, or was I really that obvious?

It was apparently time for another Ezra Carter American history symposium, today focusing on George Washington and the Constitutional Convention that culminated with his being elected president in 1789. He wanted to know if I was familiar with the controversy concerning whether George Washington was offered the title of king and that our beloved country could therefore have been a monarchy rather than a democracy had he accepted. My father challenged me once on this very topic when I was studying American history in high school. Dad might not have been a historian, but he sure knew how to motivate his lazy teenage son. To please him I researched the subject and learned that the suggestion that Washington become America's king was the idea of the army officer, Colonel Lewis Nicola, and not one popular with our Founding Fathers. I didn't relish the idea of debating Ezra on this or any facet of American history, so I sat back and just listened to him lecture. It was easier that way—also, I knew Ezra enjoyed teaching his young assistant.

After expounding on the vital differences between monarchies and democracies and why Washington was "really, truly a great, great man,"

Ezra shifted over to dissect the "pathetic" quality of leadership we had
been forced to endure in recent years. He wasn't criticizing just our political leaders; he also couldn't picture the egomaniacs on Wall Street or the
narcissistic titans of American industry ever turning down the chance to
be anointed as king. Ezra admired Washington's liberal and republican
values but even more the fact that he willingly left office, enabling the
new country to move seamlessly forward. As he was emphasizing how
different the course of American history might have been if Washington
had followed the lead of Caesar or Napoléon and stayed in power until
death or defeat, Jackie sheepishly interrupted to tell me that someone
named George had called and wanted me to know that Resorts was trading in the stratosphere at eighty and a half. I was shocked at the price.

Ezra looked at me as if he had just seen a ghost. He leaned forward on
his desk and shook his head. "What the hell are you waiting for? You
must know that you proved your point long ago that this stock can trade
at almost any price, but you're now gambling in fantasyland."

I wanted to remain calm and rational, but that was asking too much.
I excused myself and raced to the nearest Quotron to check the current
prices of the other casino stocks. It wasn't just Resorts soaring. So were its
future competitors like Caesars, Bally's, and Golden Nugget.

In a nanosecond I mentally calculated my net worth with Resorts at
eighty dollars. The number astonished me, even though I had been evaluating my portfolio at least twice every day.

I had no idea where Resorts' stock would peak, but competition was
on the horizon. Caesars World was due to open the next summer, and the
Atlantic City success story had already attracted the interest of other le-
gitimate operators. The stock's price told me that a major psychological
change had abruptly taken place, one from skepticism to belief and greed.
The time had come for me to ring the cash register. There was no reason
to call Ronnie, because I knew he already had sold out the week before, as
had Jacob, who told me he had "gone to the mattresses, Mafia-style, like
the Corleone family in *The Godfather*."

"Have you ever seen anything like this?" I asked George as we watched
the stock pass by at 82.25 in the trading room.

"Honestly, only a few times," he answered. "During the blow off in
1962, there were a few crazies. I can't even remember their names, be-

cause most aren't with us anymore. Also when the invention of television was on the horizon. That one was ballistic. A few survived, like RCA; the others bade sad farewells."

"I'm going to start selling Resorts, but I can't decide how much."

"Here's some free advice from a weary trader. Make the decision on your own and then don't look back. If the stock trades lower, don't punish yourself for not selling more; if it trades higher, don't regret the sales you made."

I told him I'd be right back. I went into the men's room and closed the door of a toilet stall. I found a quarter in my front pocket and flipped it high in the air—heads I sell 10 percent of my position, tails I sell 20 percent. That's the truth. That's how I made the first of many fateful decisions.

New York suffered a late heat wave that August, but it didn't impede the advance of the gambling stocks in the marketplace. Like a puppy listening to his master, I continued to sell Resorts stock a little every other day, so when the company reported surprisingly strong profits at month's end, my position had already been reduced by a third. I was positively giddy at the stock's reaction and elated when I made a sale at $100 per share. After the close Ronnie called.

"There's a rumor that a fund is in deep trouble because they're short a ton of Resorts. I'm hearing they clear their trades through Neuberger & Berman. If they choke and start throwing in the towel, other traders will run in front, buy shares, and try to force them into an outright capitulation."

"Do you believe this? I don't know anything about that kind of stuff."

"Have your guy watch Neuberger & Berman's floor broker. Anything could happen, but I'll bet you a burger and beer at Mecklenburg's that a surrender by that fund would mark a near-term top in the stock."

As the rumor of a short squeeze spread, Resorts stock vaulted higher. George O'Leary couldn't confirm its authenticity, so I kept selling even more aggressively. At $125 a share, I was 60 percent gone, and almost naked when Neuberger & Berman paid as high as $190 on September 4 to complete covering their client's short. I sold my last few shares the next day and went to bed early, drunk with happiness and well on my way to being worth half a million dollars.

Once a month the research department convened at 8:00 a.m. in the firm's cafeteria. For me it was one of the highlights of working at Burr, Addington, and Merritt. Each senior analyst presented a brief review of the current fundamentals of the industries they followed, updates on their specific recommendations, how they viewed the overall landscape, and what changes in the environment would be necessary for them to alter their ratings. Like the other associate analysts, I sat behind my boss in listen-only mode. The meetings were normally quite lively, with new ideas generating the most spirited controversy. Sitting on the sidelines gave me the opportunity to enjoy the theater and broaden my horizons. At times I felt like I was in a Wharton classroom listening to a lecture and absorbing new information.

This month's meeting was unfortunately a dud. The room was almost uniformly cautious, worried about creeping inflation and paranoid about the rise in interest rates. The only emphatic recommendation came from the bank analyst, who raised his estimates on virtually every stock in his group based on widening net interest margins. He was attacked by his peers, claiming he was only making a macro call and not really focusing on the specifics of each bank. Edwin Henderson probed, "Are there any other reasons to change our targets on these stocks besides potentially higher interest rates?"

The analyst was timid. "Not that I can think of right now."

The room turned quiet until Edwin concluded, "Well, maybe that's all we need. After all, we have to be positive on something."

"This morning went nowhere fast. What a waste of time," Ezra said back in his office.

"There was no energy in the room," I agreed.

"Good ol' Edwin tried his best to stir the pot, but no one took the research director's bait. That's a bad sign for the market. There's no enthusiasm, because everyone's afraid to fight the Fed."

"We need something fresh to work on. Don't you think there are stocks outside the mainstream that can succeed?"

"If interest rates continue to climb, the investment waters will become polluted. It's hard for stocks to rise if price-earnings ratios are contracting."

"By the way, I noticed that Paal Van Horne wasn't present today," I said.

"He's no longer invited to the research meetings," Ezra volunteered. "It seems Paal is too confrontational for this crew."

It had become increasingly difficult to find new ideas within our universe of stocks. If higher interest rates were the bogeyman, then I had to find an investment that benefited from that condition and treat it like a rare jewel. I knew it wouldn't be easy. I had a relaxing weekend to look forward to, so I decided to worry about all the uncertainties on Monday.

Since I no longer was involved with the Connecticut temptress, my Friday evenings were wide-open. I met Jacob downstairs at our table in the Lounge after his biweekly run around Central Park. He entered with a flourish, still flushed from his jaunt, waving hello to the bartender. This had become our home kitchen, and Nellie was our favorite waitress. She sauntered over and sat in a spare chair, greeting us as always with a clever quip or new nickname.

"Cheers to the Katzenjammer twins, Hans and Fritz."

"Who are they?" we asked in unison.

"Are you two such snobs that you don't read the comic strips? I thought you fellows were well educated."

"We'll work on it, Nellie. In the meantime, would you be kind enough to bring us two Harps on draft and a cheese plate?" Jacob asked with a warm smile.

We both liked Nellie and hoped her luck would improve. She was five months pregnant when her husband was shipped out to Vietnam in '66. He returned in a box wrapped in a flag with a love letter addressed to his wife and newborn son pinned to his uniform. She was forced to move in with her parents, still juggling two jobs, motherhood, and a disappointing social life while always praying to somehow win a lifesaving lottery.

Nellie was one of those characters you meet in life whom you don't know well but nevertheless truly care about. She returned to our table and sat down as if she belonged.

"What's with you guys tonight? You seem so solemn. And how come neither of you have commented on how lovely I look in our new uniforms with plunging necklines?" She leaned forward and smiled. "Look! You get a free shot down my top and gain the pleasure of viewing most of my lovely pink Irish titties. Do you think this will help business here?"

"Indeed, they are spectacular," Jacob offered. "I would duel half the Irish infantry for the chance to cherish them for life."

"And Mr. Wall Street, now that your rich model has fled New York and left you alone with your millions, where does sweet Nellie stand?"

I kissed her swollen, overworked hands. "The mirror on the wall doesn't lie—you are the fairest of them all!"

"Okay. Now that we've settled that, what'll you two have for dinner tonight?" She took our order then walked back to the kitchen shaking her round, plump ass, knowing full well that we were admiring her act.

It was time now, however, to focus on Federal Reserve policy and interest rates. Jacob didn't want to be specific but mentioned that the word was spreading within McKinsey to be wary of rising rates and how that could diminish a client's cash flows. He discussed a study that was circulated internally showing the effects of various levels of rising rates on consumer disposable income. It wasn't a pretty picture. The conclusion was that housing, autos, and overall retail sales were the most negatively impacted.

"You're talking about over 60 percent of GDP," I reminded him.

"That's why consultants are advising companies to be proactive."

"What can they do?"

"Maintain lean inventories, aggressively manage receivables, rigorously study the worth of any proposed projects, hedge commodity needs to protect against unusual price volatility, and most importantly, lock in current interest rates on debt."

As usual, Nellie had tuned in to our conversations and had no hesitation chiming in.

"And forty-year-old mothers, who's going to counsel them?"

Jacob was sympathetic. "It's going to be pretty damn difficult for most families. There's not too much they can do, because almost all their income is used for necessities."

"What should I tell my parents to do with their mortgage? I think it comes due next December."

"They probably should extend it now before rates go any higher," I advised.

Then Nellie became philosophical. "You know, I grew up believing this was the land of opportunity: if I studied at school, gave 100 percent effort at my job, went to church every Sunday, and saved my cherry for the right guy, my future would be bright and my children's future would be even brighter. I don't know why, but I sure have been screwed."

The restaurant was thinning out. I brought three more Harp lagers to our table while Nellie was recovering from her somber state.

"There you go again, plying me with drinks. It's not going to help you, because I'm saving myself for a good Catholic man."

"Rogers is not the one, then," Jacob laughed. "Have patience, Nellie. You can do a lot better than this guy."

Leaving our table, Nellie ran her hand slowly through my mop of hair. "You're okay, but I think you should visit a barber before your next confession."

Back in our apartment, the conversation returned to the future course of interest rates. After I methodically repeated the reasoning behind Ezra's case for appreciably higher rates over the next year or two, Jacob's face indicated worry.

"Other than trading your recommendations, my entire savings is invested in bonds. I thought bonds were a safe investment, a good place to hide out while I make my mark at McKinsey. I knew I wouldn't get rich buying them, but I didn't think I could lose big. If your boss is right on his interest rate forecast, then bonds have to come crashing down."

It was at that very moment that I had my next thematic investment idea. It was as if I'd been struck by a lightning bolt of knowledge and foresight. I was so exhilarated that I literally jumped out of my chair. "We're going to take the other side of that trade! We're going to make a killing shorting bonds!"

As a young boy at Cincinnati's version of Coney Island, I was terrified of the giant roller coasters. My father would patiently stand in line holding my hand, assuring his little guy that when our turn came to board the Shooting Star, I would enjoy the ride and learn to conquer my fear of heights and speed. This was one of the few times when Dad was absolutely wrong. To this day I still tighten up when driving over bridges or speeding around tight corners. But as I went to work the next morning, preparing to embark on my newest speculative adventure, I wasn't concerned about tacho- or acrophobia. I was wondering, on the other hand, if I was in danger of becoming a financial-risk junkie. I knew I was playing with fire betting big on Resorts International and, at times, I was plenty nervous and filled with self-doubt, but the game itself was flush with excitement and the thrill of winning was intoxicating. When I sold my last shares in Resorts, I initially felt liberated, but it didn't take long for me to feel a little lost, as if something of consequence was missing in my life. I had to be sure of my level of conviction before I shorted even one dollar's worth of bonds. I had to be sure I was doing this for the right reasons.

"Can't you keep Big Ed in your pants?" George O'Leary said, shaking his head when I told him of my newest investment idea. "You've just stuffed your pockets with some big bills, why not be a good boy and sit back to enjoy the rest of the year?"

"I'm having a swell time, thank you. Wouldn't you rather play this game than volleyball or Frisbee in the park?"

"But sometimes you have to recuperate, regroup, and ready yourself for the next contest," George advised.

"I already did that this weekend. I had a few good meals, saw a John Wayne Western, and biked the north end of Central Park," I answered (although later that day I regretted sounding like a wise guy).

"You know I'm not a bond specialist, but I'll try to help. What do you want me to do?"

"I need to know the best way to wager on higher interest rates."

"Leave it with me, but promise to keep your fly zipped until tomorrow," he said, spinning around to answer an incoming call with an infectious grin.

I had already reached out to R. D. for creative strategies for shorting the bond market. I left Ezra's inputs for last, leaving adequate time for one of his in-depth tutorials. My knowledge of the bond market couldn't even fill half a glass, but the timing of this bet felt right to me. I'd experienced plenty of dispiriting ice-cold runs on the tables in Kentucky and on the ball field at school, where my confidence would be shot and all I really wanted to do was go home and take a shower. But I was clearly on a roll now: Would Reds manager Sparky Anderson bench Pete Rose if he was on a twenty-game hitting streak?

Ezra was organizing the papers on his desk and loading his briefcase for the night. I asked if he could spare a few minutes and quickly spun out my bond idea. He came back just as quickly.

"Don't you think you might be too hungry for risk? What the hell do you know about bonds, anyway?"

"I know if interest rates increase, then bond prices will tank. The math here isn't that difficult. The Federal Reserve has been vocal about the dangers of our country's rising inflation. The question is does the Fed mean what they say—will they follow through and vigorously act to fight inflation? If they do, and persistently hike the Fed funds rate, then the whole interest rate complex should follow along as predictably, as night follows day.

"Rogers, selling short is a dangerous game. I don't know anyone who has been consistently accurate at calling tops. Why not just dump your stocks, sit on the sidelines, and wait out what could be a difficult period?"

"Because there could be a lot of money to be made."

Ezra's impatience was evident. As he was leaving, he reminded me that you can't learn to swim from reading a book. "Good luck in the pool" were his parting words.

Ronnie Davis and George O'Leary must have consulted the same honcho, who suggested I could get maximum leverage by trading US government bonds at a major New York bank. I chose a more conservative strategy influenced by a debate I recalled in a Bates MacNeer seminar focusing on the pros and cons of closed-end funds: Why should a mutual fund ever trade at a premium to its net asset value? Of the six such bond funds trading on the New York Stock Exchange, I found two that were selling at roughly 10 percent above the value of their holdings. Both exclusively owned debt of the US government and publicly traded bonds of American companies. Because I shorted them in a margin account, I could bet double the dollars on this position. Two-to-one leverage was enough juice for me.

"I like your thinking here," Mr. O'Leary said after completing my order. "If you're right, you'll capture the bond's downer and maybe the fund's premium will also shrink or even go to a discount when shareholders realize they're no longer moored in a safe harbor. Then you'd really make a score."

"I can't understand why these funds are so overvalued. I hope I'm not missing some obvious explanation," I said, questioning myself out loud.

"I see you're betting real large again. Do you mind if I follow along?"

"Just keep wearing that good-luck leprechaun tie for both of us."

In early November when Dad called me at work for the first time, I knew I had to brace myself for serious home-front news. He told me that Charlotte was suffering from an acute case of mononucleosis and was being sent home from Thailand. Dr. Marks had consulted the senior physician on-site at DWB, who agreed it was prudent for her to recuperate in the States as a precaution against more difficult complications. Dad promised to visit her as soon as possible and to let me know when I could hop a plane home. Charlotte and I had not seen each other for over a year and a half, which seemed like an eternity to me. Our weekly letters were informative, filled with warmth and understanding, but we had been apart far too long.

The next week I was jumpy and out of sorts, waiting for Dad's call. I didn't feel relieved until he finally told me that she had turned the corner, the fever had passed, her spleen and throat were approaching normal, and her overall aches and pains had diminished. She was still experiencing the exhaustion and nausea that would probably linger for a few more months, but Dad was confident she would be 100 percent before springtime. Then he lifted my spirits, telling me, "She's still Charlotte. She's still that very special young woman you always needed. She managed a smile when asking about her guy. She wanted reassurance that her Samson hadn't cut his hair and was still the same Rogers she loved before he became rich and famous. Those are quotes, by the way—you know I couldn't have made that up."

Edwin and Ezra approved my absence for a few days the next week. I bought a ticket to return home.

The day I entered Charlotte's room, she blew me a kiss. She sat wrapped in a quilt as if protecting her body from a winter storm. Her once glorious hair had been cut short by a nurse who must have used antique garden shears, but her eyes still sparkled, refusing to give in to exhaustion and high fever. She was thin and pale, but bravely disguised her obvious fatigue and discomfort. She was next to me now, and I so wanted to hug her tightly and feel her breathing. Her first words were pure Charlotte: "Don't act so worried—I won't look like Lady Dracula in a few more weeks."

"My dad said you're one tough cookie, but you have to be a good patient or this thing will drag on and on."

"Aye, aye, Captain," she whispered with a weak smile.

Once a month for the next four months, I caught the evening flight on Thursday heading home for an extended weekend. I had been such a determined workaholic that I still had plenty of vacation days left in the bank. With New York in the rearview mirror, I eased into a routine of spending my days with Charlotte at her house, and evenings with Dad or Ronnie.

Charlotte's mono lingered, but as the weeks rolled by, I could tell she was making progress. At first I would sit next to her bed, where she rested, head supported by large pillows and blankets piled high under her chin. Her inner light occasionally returned when she graduated to positioning herself on the living room couch, but she would soon tire and excuse herself to nap. I would read a book or busy myself with Wall Street trivia waiting for her to wake up. One afternoon I heard crying in her bedroom. When I knocked and went in, she pulled the bedspread over her head to hide her tears.

"It's the horror of it all. When I close my eyes, the vision of the children returns. They didn't have a chance, trekking for weeks through hostile countryside to reach safety. Almost no food, no clean water. By the time they arrived at the refugee camp, they were so terribly emaciated. You can't imagine . . . The doctors were amazing, dealing with these victims of unmentionable abuse and torture, sick from starvation, disease, and mental suffering beyond anything I've ever read about. They were forced to leave their homes, lost everything they owned, and were without hope. Their bravery and will to survive will stay with me, no matter where I live."

I reached out to hold her hands. I didn't know what else to do. She buried her head into my shoulder. "This will haunt me forever if I don't find a way to help these people."

Charlotte's parting words stayed with me on the plane back to New York. After carefully retying my scarf and warning me to be aware of the icy road conditions, she told me that soon she would be able to use her experience in a positive way.

"I'm glad I went over there, even though it was difficult. I had to do it, you know. This will help me grow and become the person I want to be."

BAM's policy was to award bonuses in December after each employee had the opportunity to participate in an evaluation. Edwin and Ezra were pleased with the quality of my work and complimented my initiative and work ethic. When the research director suggested that I could be more supportive of the other associates and that it wouldn't hurt my cause if I would be more outgoing, I noticed Ezra shaking his head *no!* Ezra's only criticism was the time I spent fretting over my personal trading account. BAM must have had a record year, since my bonus equaled half my salary. I would have been grateful no matter the size of my bonus—I was happy just being there. I thanked them both for the firm's generosity, for giving me the chance to belong, and then promised to deliver my best in the next year. Together they smiled and told me, "Get the hell out of here!"

Burr, Addington, and Merritt's year-end holiday party was traditionally held a week before Christmas at an uptown club whose members included many of New York's most prominent families. The club was a hallmark of understated elegance, the kind of place Spire members would hope to join. I felt awkward entering a grand room crowded with people I didn't know well, but was relieved when I saw Ezra sitting by himself at a corner table munching on a plate of appetizers. I moved over to him like he was my security blanket. Between bites he mumbled that cocktail parties were utter bullshit, that he couldn't remember ever learning anything meaningful at one, and that his wife was under strict orders never to accept an invitation to any such event unless Brigitte Bardot would be present. We gabbed for a short while, until he finished his drink and quietly disappeared through a side door, leaving me to survive the ordeal on my own.

I was standing alone like a misplaced obelisk when I noticed a familiar face sipping a drink at the bar while observing the scene. He motioned for me to join him.

"It's good to see you," my old Wharton mentor greeted me. "I hear your head is still above water."

"Well, I probably would have drowned by now if you hadn't been my swimming coach," I said, shaking Bates MacNeer's hand, still powerful from years of honest labor.

"How do you like working for the most sarcastic man in the building?"

"I'm learning a lot, and that's a good thing," I answered.

"I do my best to attend this event each year. Ambrose likes me to make an appearance, and I don't want to let him down. We go far back, you know, all the way to the beginnings of our careers."

"I was wondering how they got you away from your family only a few days before Christmas," I said.

MacNeer continued on a different tangent. "I'm told you're off to a roaring start. I suggest you enjoy the moment, because you'll surely experience your share of confusion and difficulties along the way."

"I'll try not to disappoint."

"Good. Remember that financial markets have a nasty way of humiliating all of us. Stay modest—it will serve you well in the long term."

I knew I would have His Sageness to myself for only a few more minutes, but I was bold enough to ask his opinion of my negative bet on the bond market. His cheerful holiday demeanor abruptly changed. Professor MacNeer believed that inflation was an insidious disease that robbed hardworking people of the opportunity to improve the quality of their lives. He felt the Federal Reserve would be forced to aggressively raise interest rates to tame inflationary expectations, that we couldn't wait too much longer to take our medicine. He said he was hopeful that the president would appoint a strong leader as the new chairman of the Fed, because he would need an iron will to do the job. He thought the whole process would be painful but necessary, much like a dentist performing root canal surgery, and that there would be howls from Congress every time the rates notched higher. The more he talked, the more he sounded like Ezra Carter, but with a sensitive social conscience. Then he added a warning that would prove to be prescient: "Watch the Middle East, especially what is going on in Iran. It's fragile and could easily become combustible."

All I knew was Iran's location on a map, that it was an important player in the OPEC oil cartel, and its leader was an ex-general who called himself the shah. Dr. MacNeer clearly wasn't impressed with the limited nature of my knowledge. He went on to tell me that he believed change within Iran was inevitable. The shah had already caused Muslim opposition leaders to be arrested, and the past September had imposed military rule, which resulted in widespread strikes and disorder. When Iran's oil production precipitously declined, the other OPEC members took advantage of the situation and enforced a 15 percent increase in world oil prices. Professor MacNeer thought these actions would surely influence the Fed's future policy. Even I knew that higher energy prices would be unwelcome tinder feeding America's inflationary fires.

"So, no more poker in your life," he jested with a grin. "Just the boring world of financial statements and interest rates, now embellished by your interest in the dynamics of international affairs."

I had to ask him another question while I had the chance. "What should have more impact on interest rates, rising energy prices flushing through the system or the choice of a new Fed chairman prepared to make an Alamo-like stand against inflation?"

"Broaden your scope, Mr. Stout," he answered formally, as if he were standing behind a lectern in Dietrich Hall. "Inflation, oil prices, and the central bank's policies are all interrelated. It's your challenge to decide if we are at a point in the economic cycle where a meaningful increase in oil prices would affect inflation rates and, if we are, then how boldly the Federal Reserve would institute polices to reverse that trend."

I was concentrating so intently on every word he uttered that I stood speechless. I admired him and wanted even more education at this cocktail party.

"The *Wall Street Journal* is speculating that the president is going to choose a Princeton professor as the next Fed chairman," I managed to say.

"Paul Volcker would be an excellent choice."

"You know him?"

"We've served on a number of committees and panels together over the years. He's a good man, strong and resilient. He'd get the job done. We share a passion for fly-fishing—I've seen him in action. He'd be patient when he had to be, but forceful in the end."

"You can tell that by fishing together?"

"You can learn a lot about someone standing side by side in a river for hours, waiting for trout to rise," Dr. MacNeer said before turning to recognize the approach of a BAM partner.

I realized I only had a week left before heading home for the New Year's break, with volumes still to learn about Iran, OPEC, energy markets, and how they together could affect US inflation and bond prices. All this was complex as hell and way out of my comfort zone. For instance, if Iran continued to smolder, would OPEC keep jacking up oil prices? Did oil prices have to increase for the stocks to be good stand-alone investments? With energy prices possibly headed higher, would the new head of the Fed press much harder against the inflation winds, making bonds an even better short?

I commandeered Jackie into service. She went through the library's files and gathered relevant research reports and articles in business magazines written within the last six months. It was a daunting task to consume the pile of materials staring up at me from my desk. *Well*, I said to myself, *you claim to love research that results in investment decisions, so say goodbye to your plans for the weekend.*

Early Sunday evening I sat downstairs at the Lounge drinking tall glasses of iced tea, reading about the origins of the OPEC cartel. I had given this new project my best all weekend but couldn't reach an actionable conclusion. Plowing through the material was time-consuming and frustrating but nevertheless a challenge worth pursuing, much like training for an athletic contest you couldn't ultimately win. The pieces of the puzzle would all fit nicely together if Iran imploded, but, without having the benefit of a crystal ball, all I could do was wait and watch developments unfold in the Middle East.

"You look as tired as a prune on a stick," Nellie offered, standing over me, refilling my glass.

"Just concentrating on a difficult issue I'm working on," I volunteered.

"Will the world be a better place once you solve the problem?"

"There will be peace and serenity for all." I smiled at her attempt to raise my spirits.

"Is all the money worth it, with the crazy stress and pressure and competitors trying to knife you in the back? I see them in here Friday nights arguing about money like hyenas fighting over a carcass. When I find my Lancelot, I'll make him so happy he'll want to stay home just to be with me and our swarm of little guys. And as for you, laddie boy, I want to see a Jolly Rogers, even if his pockets aren't filled with big bills yet."

"It's great coming in here on Sunday for the barley soup–soda bread special and getting a free session with the resident psychoanalyst," I said, even though I appreciated her concern.

"It should have been my career—Dr. Nellie, you could call me. I'd be real good at it!" She looked down at her chest and then up at me. "You know, in Galway they say big boobs indicate a big heart. I bet I have a first-class ticker."

One of the junior analysts I related to was Boyer Stubbs, who was responsible for the oil service stocks within the energy group headed by long-standing BAM fixture Toby Gaines. I latched on to him for an early lunch that Monday. Boyer grew up in Big D (that's Dallas, he informed me the first time we met) and majored in geology at UT (that's the University of Texas at Austin, he added). He worked summers as a low-level roustabout, drank beer by the gallon, and traded punches to prove his manhood with the roughnecks who despised college grads. A broken jaw and a few teeth later, he graduated from college with his dignity intact and a job in the exploration division of Texaco. After three years the lure of Wall Street grabbed him by the balls and wouldn't let go. Boyer stood out in BAM's research department as someone who had lived within his industry, not just read about it in business school textbooks.

Oil company managements could sense that Boyer Stubbs was the real deal. When they checked off the attribute boxes—Big D, UT, blue-collar work on the rigs, geologist, and, maybe most of all, a few scars in the right places that showed he could be tough when he had to—he was their kind of guy, a young man they would want to do business with. Boyer knew how to work these relationships, which helped him become an informed analyst and eventually a trusted investment banker. As maybe the only juniors in the research department whose family connections didn't connote profitable business for Burr, Addington, and Merritt, we were open to giving each other a chance at friendship. Without mentioning his name, I told Boyer about Bates MacNeer's concern that an unstable Iran could empower OPEC to dramatically raise oil prices. I said when it came to projecting OPEC's desires and influence on oil prices, I was starting in the basement and he was on a floor well aboveground. I asked if he would take a few minutes to educate me.

"Toby isn't all that worried," Boyer told me. "Also, the December price increase you referenced is supposed to be implemented gradually over four quarters. He's not so sure they have the oomph to pull it off."

"What would happen if the shah is forced out, imprisoned, or even assassinated?" I asked. "The country's bonkers now—can you imagine the chaos if the military leader leaves or is ousted? And wouldn't OPEC then attempt to stick it to the West?"

"You'd have to assume if Iran's oil production took a further hit that OPEC will go for the jugular, but I can't predict what's going to happen with the shah and Iran."

"Boyer, what would you do if you knew that world oil prices were going to fifteen or twenty dollars a barrel?"

"I don't want to be flippant. I'd obviously do some buying, but let me think this over. We can chow down on the usual cafeteria mush tomorrow and hash it over. You're thinking about making a play here, I assume. I take it that you really respect your source."

"He's very good at reading the tea leaves. He's the best I've met. No one knows for sure what's going to happen, but we should be prepared if Iran detonates. We should have a plan of action."

"Rogers, you're the most aggressive midwesterner I've ever met! I always thought you boys sat on the porch, shucking corn and watching the sun go down."

All I could come back with was, "I don't rumble with guys on oil rigs, but I love the challenge of the markets."

When I returned to the apartment, I found Jacob entertaining a Dolly Parton look-alike. I knew he was expecting to score, because the gospel music that he alone viewed as seductive was turned down to a level normal human beings could tolerate. He was supposed to post me on any scuttlebutt within McKinsey concerning the triumvirate of Iran, OPEC, and oil pricing. I guessed that would have to wait. As I was on the way to my room, lover boy called out, "I checked around but learned nothing of substance. You're on your own with the sheikhs. Enjoy the holidays. Best to Charlotte."

I ate my microwaved Thai dinner alone while watching the Knicks lose to the Celtics but thinking about Dr. MacNeer.

The day after Christmas, the office was more than half-empty. Ezra was on vacation, leaving me alone to daydream or plot my next financial adventure. Boyer stopped by in the midmorning.

"Toby's pretty confident that oil will trade in a narrow range. Supply and demand are well balanced unless there is a major disruption somewhere. He's been around a long time and discounts all the rumors from that neck of the woods. He says the shah is a mean dude who won't cut and run. Toby guesses he will use the military to crush the opposition leader, Ayatollah Khomeini. He doesn't anticipate Iran becoming a radical Muslim state."

"What does Big D think?" I asked.

"I don't like all the demonstrations. Doesn't it look like the shah is panicking when he institutes military rule? I sure as hell wouldn't visit there for a golfing vacation. I'll think some more on this and we can talk when you return."

George O'Leary was playing liar's poker with a few of the other old-timers as the quiet afternoon was coming to a close. He introduced me to the cast of characters and insisted I sit in on the game. I lost eight out of ten hands before realizing I was in way over my head. George giggled like a little boy while saying, "Those George Washingtons will warm up my pocket on the cold trip home tonight."

Soon after the market closed, George cleared his desk and spread out the forms I would have to sign to open a commodities account, allowing me to trade in the oil market. I liked the idea of making a direct bet on oil itself, rather than relying on BAM's research to choose stocks that should benefit from an oil price rise. Boyer agreed: "If you're gambling on higher oil prices, why buy stocks in companies that are also refiners, own gas stations, make chemicals, or drill for natural gas? If you own the commodity, then you're assured to win if the price increases. But listen to me, buddy. You could be in for one wild, bucking bronco ride when trading commodity futures!"

I signed all the necessary papers and thanked Mr. O'Leary for his help. He wanted me to understand that this was a serious step I had just taken. "If you must do this, start small. None of that bold stuff like with Brown-Forman or sleepy old Treasuries. This is very different. You can stay with it if the trend is going your way, but always limit your losses. Remember, you have to be alive to play tomorrow. I've seen too many so-called smart guys get wiped out trading commodities because they neglected to follow their disciplines."

During the flight home, I weighed the downside risk of owning oil. For the next three hours, I alternated between reading and arguing with myself. Were the mythical seductresses of the Mediterranean luring my financial boat into a destructive crash? The political unrest in Iran had been well-known for over a year; nevertheless, the price of oil had only risen 10 percent, to $9.50 a barrel. Why wasn't it a lot higher? Saudi Arabia carried the biggest bat in the OPEC cartel and was itching to press prices upward. Why weren't they more successful? Should I sit at a poker table where I didn't even know the rules of the game? Yet if the good professor's warning became a reality, I knew enough about supply/demand dynamics to dream of a significant upside from oil's four years' narrow trading channel.

By the time the plane landed, I'd decided that a small bet would force me to treat the oil market with respect, that I should slide a few chips into the pot to see the next card. I didn't want to sit this hand out, so I called Georgie O from the airport to buy a few oil contracts when the market was set to reopen.

I was surprised to see a smiling doctor at the airport welcoming gate. Dad rarely left work early unless the Reds were playing in a pivotal game. We stopped at his office on the way home, so the nurses had the opportunity to squeeze and poke at me. How many times did I have to hear, "Goodness gracious, you really are grown-up. I remember when you were a skinny little bag of bones…you were a quiet, pensive boy who dreamed of pitching at Crosley Field…you were a raging pervert trying to sneak a peek up my dress or down my blouse."

Dr. Stout defended, "But look at him now. I couldn't be more proud." That was vintage Dad, I thought, always championing his son whenever anyone sought to criticize him in public.

Dad suggested a quick bite near his office so we could be home in time for the NBC movie of the week. "Are you ready?" he asked after dinner, meaning I was going to be tested by one of his favorite mind games. Dad wouldn't care that Brown-Forman was closing the year over thirty, up 40 percent in less than twelve months from Ezra's and—to a much lesser extent—my recommendation, nor that Kelly and Manpower were performing well or how I saved a bundle selling my housing stocks before the upturn in interest rates. He probably didn't know what the Federal Reserve was all about, nor the meaning of the Fed funds rate. But Dad would have savored the game I was about to play on the international playing field of energy markets, because he admired deductive thinking, and to him the OPEC bet would be an interesting risk based on reasoned thought processes.

"What do you think we'll be seeing tonight?" Dad asked, leaning forward and folding his napkin neatly. "As usual, you've got to choose the theme and name the movie correctly. Let's see if all those Wall Street numbers have slowed you down." He looked at this watch. "The game clock has started."

He was in a jolly mood, just the two of us entertaining each other like we did in the old days. For as long as I could remember, Dad had peppered me with mentally demanding games, puzzles I had to decipher, history and geography questions, or other challenges from deep inside his bag of what-if tricks. I had been so busy, so focused on piling up chips to reach my goal of financial independence, that I had forgotten how much I enjoyed these times together.

"What's taking you so long? You used to be good at this game. Has my son been polluted by osmosis from all those New York muckety-mucks? Do I have to give you a hint already?" He cackled as if he was holding a winning hand I couldn't have anticipated.

I told him my first guess was a sports movie, presumably featuring America's pastime, such as *It Happens Every Spring*. Dad interrupted me with a hearty no and started to laugh and clap his hands in victory.

"Okay," I said. "I'm going with an Ingrid Bergman flick, maybe *Casablanca* or *For Whom the Bell Tolls*," knowing that she had Dad's vote for the most mysteriously beautiful woman in film.

"Wrong again," he said slapping his thigh with pleasure, then looking at his watch. "You only have eighty seconds left."

I was back to being his young son determined to beat his father in a contest. "A Western, a John Ford Western about the men who opened the great frontiers," I blurted enthusiastically.

"Name the movie! You've got thirty seconds to go till defeat."

"I'll do better than that." I smiled confidently as I proceeded to whistle the theme song from *She Wore a Yellow Ribbon*.

"I never knew you could whistle," he conceded.

We knocked on the Markses' door on a bitterly cold New Year's evening, Dad loaded down with a plate of assorted cheeses and his son with enough wine to make the room merry. We were greeted by the Five Satins on the stereo, an effusive Dr. Marks, and Charlotte's mother waving hello from the kitchen, bedecked in a bizarre apron featuring dancing bears. "I didn't know you were a '50s rock aficionado," Dad teased his longtime partner.

I heard a familiar voice from down the hall: "Don't touch the controls—those are my guys at their best. It's my dressing-up music."

Dad looked over at me. "I'm guessing her recovery is ahead of schedule."

I felt the anxiety of a groom on his wedding day needing to see the woman he loves before her grand entrance. She sauntered into the room with her chestnut hair tied back in a colorful scarf and a smile that could stop a speeding truck on a dime. I couldn't contain my excitement, but before I could say a word, she was in my arms. "I've almost returned," she exclaimed.

"Better than ever," I whispered in her ear. When she stepped back to wish my father happy holidays, I literally gasped at how she looked in a dress that seemed molded to her body.

Charlotte could feel me visually devouring every inch of her. "Do you approve?" she teased.

From across the room, Dad bellowed, "Remember, I was the one who told you to call her."

During dinner Charlotte and I tolerated hearing embarrassing stories of our childhoods while gorging on her mother's famous brisket and potato pancakes. Our parents clearly enjoyed themselves at our expense, playing the game of I Can Top That as the disc jockey continue to whisk through her repertoire, making sure her audience understood the relevance of each performer. She was a child of the '60s and '70s but loved the simplicity and harmonies of 1950s music. The conversation inevitably turned more serious, ranging from new breakthroughs in treating cardiovascular disorders to the disheartening state of affairs in Cambodia and, predictability, to the Reds' pennant prospects in the upcoming season. After knocking off Mrs. Marks's dessert of delectable apple cobbler, her daughter suggested that all those at the table under fifty and either recently back from the Far East or currently living in Manhattan wrap themselves in their winter warmest and head to Eden Park for the New

Year's Eve fireworks. She sweet-talked both docs—"I'm fine. I took a lengthy nap. I'll be a good girl. I promise"—and we were on our way to our favorite hometown lookout.

We parked facing the river below us. Looking out at the Ohio and the party boat lights, Charlotte leaned into me. Her kisses made me light-hearted and slightly dizzy; my brain almost went numb. How wonderful it was to be with her, to blank out New York and plotting to profit in the financial markets. It was as if all those months we'd spent separated by continents and oceans had never happened.

Charlotte was already outside when the fireworks started, holding our blankets, encouraging me to hurry so we wouldn't miss any of the show. Without difficulty we found an empty bench with a good view, because only Siberian huskies would have been able to tolerate the night's wind-chill factor. We lasted a short while before I urged the recovering patient to take her enthusiastic cheers back to the warmth of our car. It was good to see Charlotte's energy level returning and that all those months witnessing unfathomable horrors had not purged her joy for the simple pleasures of life. Ten minutes later she was sound asleep, stretched out with her head in my lap. I looked down at my dynamo resting peacefully, monumentally grateful for her safe return.

I recalled when I first saw her on that fateful evening five years ago, confidently bounding down the hill to my car. She was one special package. Years later when I asked if she was disappointed that I was just slugging it out on Wall Street, she told me that the full story of my life's work wasn't written yet and that she believed I would successfully chart my own path, which might involve more than just making money.

I sat in the car gently stroking Charlotte's hair, watching the night skies explode in bright flashes of color with a grin spreading across my face. How could it be that a singular whimsical decision would forever alter my future? If my father hadn't pressured me to call his partner's daughter and offer to drive us to a high school New Year's party, we might never have given each other a chance at friendship, much less love. I wouldn't have experienced her wit and intelligence, the feeling I had watching her attack life, her outrageous laugh, the enjoyment I got just being with her and the excitement of her physical passion. I was lost in thought when she woke up to remind me that tonight was our not-so-technical fifth anniversary. She pulled me down and kissed me so softly that it felt like a sweet-tasting feather had just touched my lips.

Back in the office, I barely had time to warm my seat before I was jolted by a new reality. Only a few days after my return, the shah left Iran for a family vacation, notwithstanding his country's civil strife. Sensing potential drama, I immediately purchased additional oil contracts. Shortly thereafter, I doubled my short bet against bonds, with a nod to Professor MacNeer's view that if Paul Volcker were appointed chairman of the Federal Reserve, he would be a man who would bravely attack the country's inflation woes. I promised myself I would reduce my short position in bonds if the president didn't replace the sitting chairman with Volcker in the relatively near future. I was feeling pretty feisty until Ezra summoned me into his office with his bellicose "Stout, get in here now!" He was incredulous.

"Here you go again, playing financial Russian roulette. I go away for one lousy week and my assistant thinks he is a Middle East maestro, an oil market maven, and Fed policy seer, all wrapped up in a package labeled HUBRIS in bold capital letters. Holy shit! What's up with you, do you have a congenital gambling problem that I should know about? Shorting bonds and buying oil futures? What's next, and what makes you think you know diddly-squat about this stuff? You make a few lucky moves and now you're a master of the universe. Be serious, for Christ's sake! Tell me, do you intend to spend any of your precious time on projects for yours truly that would benefit the firm that employs you?"

I knew by then to avoid Ezra when he went on the warpath. I knew it would be suicide to argue with him, that he would rant on that I was supposed to be training to be a security analyst and not a wild pirate focusing on my own account. When he was through venting his wrath, I returned to my desk without saying a word in my defense. It wasn't easy to turn mute and walk away, but I didn't want to risk losing access to the research department's treasure trove of valuable information. I needed to listen to the analysts present their industry's current fundamentals and the reasons for specific buy-and-sell recommendations. Best of all was the stimulating repartee between these players as they agreed or voted thumbs-down on their peer's ideas. All these open discussions helped me to gauge sentiment and each analyst's commitment to their views. From there on I knew I was on my own.

Oil's price volatility began to move into high gear when Saudi Arabia announced a large cut in its first-quarter production and an estimated one million Iranians marched in Tehran to show support for the exiled Ayatollah Khomeini. In a private corner of the library, Boyer confided that his boss was shocked at the rapid turn of events and was in the process of reassessing his stance on the energy markets. He then showed me a memo penned by the "I'm never wrong" Paal Van Horne positing a failed rally in the commodity to be followed by a downward correction. "I'm not sure where Toby's going, but I don't like betting against that prick Dutchman," Boyer added.

Van Horne's door was slightly ajar, so I peeked in and summoned up the courage to ask for a minute of his time. "Not now," he barked, not looking up. "Bother me after the market closes." I wondered what Paal Van Horne was like growing up, how he treated his wife and the little Van Hornes and if his brusque style was all act or if he was just a flat-out snarling SOB all the time.

I came back an hour later to grovel for his opinion on the oil market.

"It's bumping the upper band of a trading range. This will be a failed rally; soon it will fall back asleep. It probably won't awake for a long time."

That was his call. There was absolutely zero equivocation. His unstated message was also clear: *Now close the door and leave me alone!* I couldn't help but question how he had such positive faith in lines drawn on graph paper to create his sacred charts. It all seemed so arbitrary to me, too subject to abrupt changes if future price movements were to violate his precious trading boundaries.

By now I was addicted to the British journal the *Economist*, primarily because I relied on its insights on all things Middle Eastern. I was reading an article detailing the basic differences between the Sunni and Shiite branches of Islam and how this all had spilled over into a history of conflict when Boyer tapped me on the shoulder.

"You goin' eurotrash on me?" he joked, looking down at the magazine.

So I quipped back, "Well, the *Post*'s sports page isn't going to help us understand OPEC's strategy."

"What do our effete British friends think?" he asked.

"They're hedging, but the tone of this piece implies that the Saudis and Iranians can't agree on anything."

"If those dudes decide to put the squeeze on, I can't imagine where new supplies will come from in the near term."

"Gee, do you think that might cause oil prices to go higher?" I said with maximum sarcasm.

"Easy, wiseass," he cautioned. "You haven't made jack shit yet in your big trade. I've interrupted you for a reason—why don't you join me tonight for a Barton Energy dinner? Toby can't make it, so you can fill in. These guys are on the front line, and maybe they'll shed some light on what's really happening in the desert."

One of Ezra's doctrines, made clear to me early on, was that company managements were touts at heart, so he stressed relying on information gleaned from suppliers, customers, and competitors, as well as trade magazines and a company's publicly filed documents, rather than "canned, sugar-coated glorified pabulum" concocted by well-oiled public relations departments. Remember, he once told me, most CEOs are just egomaniacal hawkers that rose to the top of their organizations, often by sheer chance alone. Ezra's skepticism included company-sponsored dinners at fancy restaurants, which he believed were essentially promotional hogwash and an utter waste of time. He would rant, "I'd rather watch *I Love Lucy* reruns than sit for two hours with a bunch of nitwits listening to an arrogant CEO push his stock."

I kept this all to myself as I headed uptown with Boyer. Barton Energy was an oil and gas exploration company that also operated a fleet of drilling rigs and provided a variety of other energy services. They were in town to raise funds for a pending acquisition. Boyer thought the meeting could prove valuable to us because the company would be discussing the current landscape of the industry, including the outlook for oil and natural gas prices. He told me to seek out a lady named Bonita Curtis.

"She'll surprise you. Bonita isn't like the other women who work for Buck. She's no bimbo—in fact, she's one hell of a classy lady. Her father was a big-time troubleshooter for Royal Dutch. Have her tell you how she grew up bouncing around from one country to another. Two years in Kuwait, a couple in Argentina, back to Lebanon for a few more, then eventually to boarding school in Scotland, where her father finally settled down to help manage RD's efforts in the North Sea. Bonita's in charge of Barton's drilling division, but she spends every spare hour studying worldwide supply-and-demand forces for oil. Buck relies on her for this input. Make sure you sit at her table. Work her real slow. Treat her with respect, and you'll learn a ton."

Barton Energy was led by its founder, Big Buck Barton, a renowned wildcatter, a larger-than-life character you'd expect to see on the cover of *Outdoor Life* magazine with his size-fourteen boot resting on the neck of a recently shot one-ton water buffalo. He was rumored to have been christened Leslie Barton at birth, but no one can remember a living soul having the nerve to call him anything but Big Buck since he grew to six four and 230 pounds of chiseled muscle late in high school. He was a Texas version of a Renaissance man, excelling at middle linebacker at A&M, guzzling copious quantities of tequila, utilizing his rugged good looks to full advantage bagging any attractive coed within reach, and working summers for A&M alumni who went elephant hunting for oil. By the time we entered a private suite at the St. Regis, I was bursting with anticipation to meet this legend and his ace in the hole, Bonita Curtis.

A waiter handed us longnecks as we approached our host.

"Heh, boys, how they hangin'?" the CEO greeted us. "I see Stubbsy hasn't graduated yet to the hard stuff. You know, I used to do a case of the long guys after a big game just to keep my weight up, but then I found tequila and I've been in love ever since."

"It's good to see you in high spirits, Buck," Boyer said with his best exaggerated drawl.

"Business is good. I'm farting through silk." Buck smiled. Later that evening I had to ask Boyer what the hell that meant. It was just Texas talk, he informed me.

Buck stood taller and broader than anyone in the room, confident that they all knew his history and his credentials as a self-made member of the $100 million club who consumed life on his own terms. As his presentation was about to begin, he noticed a late arrival, a young lovely scanning the room for an empty seat. A nanosecond later Big Buck was leading her by the arm to the head table, displacing the surprised occupant of the chair next to him, and seating his naive target with a gentlemanly flourish and a beaming, lecherous smile.

Buck Barton sure knew how to seduce his audience, endearing them with sincerity, pouring on the southwestern charm and selling the dream of making record-breaking oil discoveries that would vault his company into the big leagues. His was the best show I'd seen so far, better even then the barkers I'd watch perform at rural carnivals across the Ohio in the valleys of Kentucky. He reminded the group of Barton's recent successes in the Gulf of Mexico and the North Sea and its superior financial performance versus industry peers. He talked confidently about his company's future even in the current ten-dollars-a-barrel oil environment. He said Barton was generating free cash flow and in a comfortable position to fund development of its portfolio. He professed frustration that his stock was selling at a discount to the sleepy old majors and even to some exploration and development companies who weren't growing in the same league as his baby.

He was just warming up. Big Buck went into a higher gear when he removed his suit jacket for emphasis and assumed the role of a fervent evangelist. *This is going to be a good show*, I thought.

"Listen up. I want all you to remember what you're about to hear. I'm gonna share with you a secret: the sweetest play in the future sits way over there in a country called Australia. In a few months, we'll be closing on a deal making Barton Energy the biggest landowner in the biggest potential oil play since the North Slope. We've studied the seismic surveys delineating some real pretty structures. The geology is as clear as a Texas prairie night. The down-hole pressures should be there, and we don't have to drill all the way to China to locate the mother lode. Ladies and gentlemen, this sucker is goin' to be one helluva honeymoon hard-on!"

I had made sure that I was seated next to Bonita Curtis. She sat composed, listening closely to Buck's speech. I couldn't resist whispering to her, "Is he always like this?"

"From the time the man wakes up each and every morning," she answered.

"How can he be so positive on Australia when it's all so unproven?"

"Don't ever sell Buck short! He can puff out full of bluster, and maybe he's a cocky dreamer, but the big guy does his homework and has hired first-rate geologists who are motivated to take risks. He doesn't mind traveling solo to places where other companies have shied away."

"He sure was right on the North Sea," I conceded.

"He's a big man with big appetites who happens to be blessed with an acutely sensitive nose. He trusts his gut, and he's not afraid to back it up with his company's balance sheet."

When the meeting ended, Boyer left with Big Buck, a few other analysts, and of course the attractive redhead, to meet downtown at Molly's Tavern to raise some hell. Later, I was told they closed the place after the bartender claimed to have run out of Buck's favorite tequila and that no one was surprised when the redhead left with Buck in his limo. I stayed on at the St. Regis with Bonita, who had promised to share her views on oil prices if I accompanied her to the parlor for a cup of her favorite tea.

We sat in oversize upholstered chairs separated by a small antique circular table. Bonita Curtis was so short that her Manolos barely touched the carpet. She presented an interesting paradox, a diminutive, soft-spoken exterior disguising a tightly strung, competitive nature. She had suffered a riding accident while a young girl in Argentina, requiring her now to walk with the help of a cane which her father had purchased at a Moroccan street market. She proudly demonstrated for me how it converted to a sword when the outer shell was removed. "My husband taught me how to use this for self-defense," she said, waving it wildly above her head. I immediately liked Bonita's spunky personality and thought her husband was probably one lucky guy. She slowly stirred honey into her tea and told me to fire away.

"Before we attack the world of oil economics, I have to ask how you acquired such a wonderful given name."

"My family vacationed in the Bahamas, where my father would unwind from the pressures of his job. His favorite pastime was fishing, and he relished the challenge of boating a bonita on light tackle."

"I've heard from a college friend who fished the Florida Keys that they're real fighting fish."

"You bet they are," she said, pointing her index finger at me.

"He said that those boys really didn't want to be caught," I added.

"Neither do the females"—she smiled—"and that's why my father named his daughter Bonita."

She carefully removed a folder from a briefcase that turned out to contain her detailed oil production estimates for countries representing over 95 percent of worldwide supply. She was willing to accept the demand projections generated by a variety of think tanks because they rarely varied by more than a couple hundred thousand barrels and tended to be reasonably accurate. The supply numbers that she held close to her chest were her own.

"How can you verify these supply-side numbers?" I inquired.

"Some people dig for gold, others dig for truffles, I dig for information. I've put a lot of effort into this project, and I trust my conclusions."

"How do you feel about the oil market now?" I pushed on.

"Demand is stable, growing a bit each year, and supply is sufficient to keep the market in balance. But it's a precarious balance in which any supply hiccup could cause a meaningful near-term price spike."

"Where does OPEC fit in this puzzle?"

"OPEC is still a new phenomenon," she answered, "a prepubescent learning how to flex their muscle. If the members were to coordinate and play their cards right, they could function as the swing producer."

"What does that mean?"

"Managing their output to push prices higher, but not so high as to encourage other countries to spend more to find and produce more."

"I don't know if those guys are holding hands under the table, but it sure seems like they're doing their best to disrupt the supply side of your equation."

Bonita's face stiffened. "These are the facts: the non-OPEC producers have very little spare capacity. Iran's oil output has been declining; the country is facing a leadership vacuum and possibly serious civil strife. Saudi Arabia initially increased its production but then abruptly reversed course and announced a significant cut. Iraq is not now in a position to replace lost supply, and while the other OPEC members might increase production, their efforts can't fill the gap."

"So if your supply numbers are close to accurate, then all hell might break loose if Iran goes ballistic."

"My numbers are good" was all she said.

"Bonita, you've lived in that neighborhood. How serious is the Sunni-Shiite conflict?"

"It makes Ireland's schism look like a sweet sixteen party!" came her immediate reply.

"And Iran. What are the chances of the shah returning and successfully righting his country's ship?"

"That's not a bet I would like to make," she answered.

Sitting in the parlor of the St. Regis that night, I couldn't help but think that Bonita Curtis was the real deal and that I owed Big D a huge thank-you. She gathered her precious briefcase and Moroccan sword-cane, then rose to return to her room before posing a final question.

"Why didn't you join your friend at the downtown bacchanal? Buck's a hell of an entertainer when there's tequila and young vixens around."

Before I could think of a witty response, she went off to the elevator.

I was definitely hooked on the business I was in. The big surprise was that I had gone from being a lazy coaster to a committed workaholic, and I loved it. It was hard for me to believe that only a few years ago I would blow off school and home responsibilities without any concern for the consequences, and now I was focused and dedicated week after week. What had I morphed into? I'd hop out of bed most mornings, eager to get downtown to battle the ticker tape at 11 Wall Street. I'd wolf down my PB&J on the way to the subway headed for Burr, Addington, and Merritt. After reading the papers, sharing an a.m. coffee with George O'Leary, and whizzing through any reports penned by BAM analysts, I would call Ronnie Davis. We'd gab about Xavier's basketball team, hometown updates, and, of course, the all-important financial markets. Then I would prepare myself for Ezra's entrance. He would usually saunter in, disheveled and grumpy, minutes before the opening, grunt a hello to Jackie, slap my desk, and without looking at me say, "Do something smart today!"

I knew that buying more oil would not be considered smart by my boss, but I was hungry for a bigger position in the black stuff. Before I could talk with Ezra, Boyer called to moan he was major-league hungover and not coming to work.

"I have a pounding headache and my body feels like I came in last in a bull-riding contest. The only person who left Molly's in one piece was Buck, and I'll bet that big bastard scored with the redhead."

"I thought you used to go toe to toe with the roughnecks," I gibed.

"I did, but freakin' Buck's in a whole other league. He drinks tequila like it's lemonade."

"Did you learn anything I should know while you were still standing?"

"Buck says he has good contacts on the ground in Iran who believe the shah is bye-bye. They're expecting Ayatollah Khomeini to return."

"What would that mean?"

"Probably an attempt to pull off a fundamentalist Muslim takeover."

"If that happened did Buck's sources say if it would affect their oil production?"

"Do you really think you need them to tell you that?" he groaned. I heard no more, so I assumed Boyer had crawled back to bed.

I was prepared to be verbally eviscerated, but I owed it to Ezra to explain my rationale for betting on higher oil prices. He listened carefully, interrupting only a few times to ask a question, and then sat eerily quiet. When I was finished, he reached for his favorite toy, an old wooden slide rule he used in high school, and appeared to be distracted as he played with the logarithmic scales. Only then did he respond.

"So, what it boils down to is your belief that Iran's oil production is on the verge of declining because the country's political system is about to pull a Vesuvius-type eruption."

I did my best to answer Ezra's challenge and not sound overly defensive, but I already knew he wouldn't agree with my position anyway.

"I know I'm not a Middle Eastern seer, nor am I predicting anything such as an Iranian holocaust. What I am suggesting is that the markets aren't discounting the very real possibility of chaos erupting over there. If the ayatollah rides into Tehran on a white horse, don't you think oil prices could skyrocket based on uncertainty alone?"

I still remember the look on Ezra's face that day, as if he were a cold stone sculpture carved up there high in the hills like the four greats at Mt. Rushmore.

"Where does this all come from, this sprint to achieve some magical personal net worth number, this willingness to take such unconventional positions?" he asked.

And I answered, "Isn't that what we're supposed to be doing? Isn't that why we're here?"

During the following weeks, both interest rates and oil prices drifted higher.

My playbook was apparently working, and that made me one happy camper. I had already maxed out my positions in short bonds and long oil, so I sat back and assumed the role of rabid cheerleader. The positive price action I was enjoying reminded me of occasional sweet runs I would have on the tables at Rory's or the rich-boy frat houses at Penn. I had no idea how long this good fortune would last, but as a budding contrarian, I was encouraged by the prevailing investor sentiment that OPEC was but a paper tiger and the current Fed chairman would continue to be reluctant to fight inflation by substantially raising interest rates. We would soon find out who was on the right track. The ayatollah had returned to Iran and was revving up the masses and demanding radical change, while the shah's status remained unclear. How would OPEC respond if one of its most important members' production dropped farther due to internal disorder? Back in DC uncertainty was also in the air. The Fed chairman was starting to talk tough but had yet to act forcefully. Would we have to wait for someone like Professor MacNeer's fishing buddy to be appointed chairman for the Fed to drop the hammer down on the bond market?

All of this drama didn't go unnoticed at Burr, Addington, and Merritt. The early March research meeting turned into a Wall Street version of a Hatfield/McCoy standoff. Ezra got the donnybrook rolling by attacking any stock recommendation that would be negatively impacted by higher interest rates. "I warned you all months ago that inflation would be a problem leading to higher rates. This is going to be a real issue. It's not too late to listen to me," he boasted, pissing off at least half the room with his usual dose of egotism.

The tone of the meeting was alternating between fuzzy collegiality and abject vitriol until late in the morning, when the potential higher energy cost question was raised and the discussion took on sustained heat. Head of Research Edwin Henderson set the table. "There's little reason to believe we're going to face another '73 to '74 with the attendant oil shortages and long lines at gas stations, but the lack of clarity in the Middle East is starting to keep me up at night. Remember how our consumer-related stocks got decimated back then—everything from retailers, restaurants, airlines—you name it! I think we have to start factoring in the energy cost risk with our recommendations."

"How are we supposed to know where oil prices are going?" the senior retail analyst lamented. "Does the firm have an official view on this that we have to follow? You know if we pull back on our buy-rated stocks and oil is flat to down, we'll look like a horse's ass, the stocks will go higher, and we'll be left holding Herman."

"Toby, you're awfully quiet over there. Where does our resident energy guru stand on all this?" the transportation group head questioned.

I stole a look over at Boyer, who seemed to be especially tense, knuckles white and teeth locked as if preparing to pounce. As Toby Gaines rose to speak, Ezra turned around to warn me, "If I were you, I'd stay mute. We can talk about this later. Keep your 'oil going to the moon' theory to yourself!"

I had decided months ago that Toby Gaines was the kind of person who would have questioned the Big Guy himself if presented with the Ten Commandments on Mount Sinai. I could picture him looking up at the heavens while asking a litany of hows and what-ifs: "Did you really dream up this ten stuff all by yourself? Do you realize if these commandments aren't the real deal, I could look foolish recommending them to my clients? Is it okay with you if I just say I'm more than 50 percent sure that we had this little chat?"

Toby rambled on for a full ten minutes, doing his best to impress his peers with the breadth of his knowledge about all things related to energy prices. It was clear to me that the intended goal of his speechifying was to justify his noncommittal, neutral ratings on his group.

Edwin couldn't let him off the hook because the future course of oil prices affected the outlook for inflation, interest rates, and countless stocks. In the most nonconfrontational, diplomatic voice he could muster, he asked, "There's a lot riding on this, Toby. We need your best guess."

"But I'm not really sure," he answered weakly.

"For Christ's sake, Toby, isn't it clear the risk is to the upside!" someone interrupted angrily. Then, against all precedent, the voice asked Toby's assistant for his opinion. "Boyer, what are you thinking?"

Boyer rose from his chair. "For the first time in years, I'm hearing the tom-toms beat for the oil service companies I follow," he responded. "The new orders aren't there yet, but there's a helluva lot of quoting goin' on. That's usually a precursor to an industry turn. We've been in the doghouse too long; if oil prices rise any more, I think the dogs are going to come out barking. I've upgraded my group to overweight, because they're cheap and poised to turn."

I wanted to stand and applaud my friend's ballsy, virtuoso performance. I guessed he would have to deal with Toby's pride later, and in private.

"And oil prices?" the voice pressed on.

Boyer was careful. "I'm not going to disagree with Toby. Look, it's hard to read, but it's likely we're now hostage to OPEC until new supplies can be generated elsewhere. That'll take time and big money. How do you feel about our economic destiny being in the hands of those nice fellows in the Persian Gulf?"

The next day I followed Boyer's lead. My thinking was simple. If a sophisticated group such as the BAM analysts were collectively worried about higher oil prices but had yet to act, then even a subtle change in Middle Eastern dynamics could cause the energy stocks to fly. I liked the bet, so I banked most of my profits in Brown-Forman and Kelly Services and bought a package of offshore drilling contractors.

Burned into my memory was the thirty-minute tutorial I had received from Bonita Curtis when I asked about her competitors. She'd told me, "You'll want to invest with the best operators owning the newest equipment. The shipyards haven't expanded in years, so there's little likelihood of major new capacity coming on soon. If the premise is right, and oil prices rise, then exploration should pick up and drilling day rates will have to go higher. It's simple supply-and-demand economics. If this were to play out, the earnings leverage could be dramatic, because the revenue increase is all price and would drop directly to the pretax income line."

"Are there any stocks you would suggest I buy?" I had asked quite timidly.

"You're on your own, cowboy" was her only answer.

I debated telling her the truth—that I could never be a cowboy because I was afraid of horses—but I chose to keep that embarrassing fact to myself.

My father believed country clubs were so socially exclusionary that they should be abolished. He also couldn't comprehend why anyone with a functioning brain would want to waste four hours chasing a little white ball up and down hills or across manicured lawns. Therefore it wasn't surprising that his son never learned to play golf. I did, however, regularly devour the local sports pages and had read with interest how a golfer could occasionally feel his hands enter a "divine state" and positively know that every putt he stroked would find its way into the center of the cup. For the next months, I too had that glorious feeling as my investment putting was unwaveringly accurate. I might not have been wearing a funny-looking floppy hat or elitist club logo on my chest, but my hands were scorching hot. What followed was a news environment that wasn't positive for all financial assets but was a veritable orgy of good news for my net worth.

US inflation was already increasing at a menacing rate when OPEC added fuel to the fire by announcing they would be enforcing their full 14.5 percent price increase as of April 1. Less than a week later, the ayatollah declared Iran an Islamic state after receiving an overwhelming majority vote on a referendum to replace the existing monarchy. Boyer stopped by that morning to tell me he thought Toby was getting ready to crack. With Iran's political stability in disarray and the OPEC cartel appearing more coherent and influential than ever, Toby sensed oil prices had to head higher. I watched him pacing back and forth in his office like a caged prisoner confined to his cell, verbally berating himself as he gathered up the will to publicly change his view on oil equities. "It ain't easy to admit you're wrong when you're supposed to be the authority," Boyer said with genuine sympathy for his boss.

The bullish scenario for oil was clearly building momentum. Prices climbed continuously over the next few months, further exacerbating our country's inflationary trends. In April, a reactive Federal Reserve began raising the funds rate and continued to do so into the summer. Then, Paul Volcker assumed the leadership of the Fed in early August. Dr. MacNeer's prescience proved to be correct as the new chairman immediately let the markets know that he intended to battle inflation with every arrow in his quiver. It was now time for the bond market to experience a nasty bear market.

It turned out that oil prices and US interest rates were just leaving the starting gate. Between January and October, US crude prices rose 50 percent, the Fed funds rate went from 10 percent to 15.5 percent and the borrowing cost for prime US customers increased from 11.75 percent to 15 percent. During this period my portfolio's value went ballistic, blowing through the million dollar mark like a Kansas windstorm. I couldn't believe my good fortune. Each day my emotions alternated between giddiness, greed, and full-on fear that these posted prices couldn't possibly be true and I should immediately liquidate my holdings and bury my winnings on some distant island.

I was tallying up my portfolio in late August when George O'Leary called to inform me it was time we share a celebratory dinner at a restaurant managed by an old friend of his.

"I know we'll be breaking new ground by doing this, but you've made me a pot full of money. I've paid off my mortgage and I'm sitting pretty for the first time in my life."

"Please, George," I said, "you don't have to do this. You're the one who has been helpful."

"You're not listening to me, I want to do this. Besides, it's about time you put down a few pints and loosen up. I'm worried the pressure of all that weight in your Brooks Brothers pockets is beginning to affect your well-being."

"You don't think I've been too much of a pain in the ass?" I asked.

"Son, I'm enjoying work for the first time in years, and it's mainly because of you. I feel rejuvenated by your enthusiasm. I'm back in the game I love, and that makes this old geezer light on his feet."

"I'll come if we play dollar poker for the bill," I challenged.

"No! Because I know you'll lose even if you try to win," he said while making little effort to suppress his laughter.

George was sitting at the bar when I arrived that evening, sipping a Jameson, sharing a joke with the bartender. A Harp lager was waiting patiently for me. For the next ten minutes, I was introduced around the restaurant as "the young lad I've been telling you about." I had never seen George like this, smiling and expansive, the center of attention, commanding the room. We sat at a table isolated from the Friday crowd. It was soon apparent that he had an agenda in mind.

"When we first met, I could tell you were different from the other stuffed shirts," he started.

"And I thought back then you were so mysterious, sequestered at a desk off by yourself whispering orders into a phone, as if you were planning a hostile bid on a target company."

"You asked too many questions!" he said.

"But I did listen carefully to your answers."

"That's true. And then you asked more and more until you started to get on my nerves and I wanted to find your off button."

"I wanted to learn," I said earnestly.

He clicked our glasses together in a formal toast and looked at me with a sweet sincerity as if he were my grandfather. "And learn you did," he said, "and then even more . . ."

The waiter placed a large wooden platter between us, piled high with lamb chops and hash browns. Georgie O shifted over to a black and tan while I joined in with another Harp. I had thought we would be talking about the market and how stocks were reacting to higher interest rates, but he was here on a mission to warn me to watch my backside.

"You should know that your success isn't going unnoticed. It's appreciated by some, but others are envious. I'm concerned you are too naive to know how vindictive these people can be! Competing on the Street isn't like playing a team sport. If the other guy makes the big shot, it doesn't help your career even if you passed him the ball at the right place and at the right time. In this business an assist isn't rewarded like a score. All that matters are the numbers in the firm's bank account at the end of the day. Don't think for a second that Paal, Toby, and, yes, maybe even Ezra aren't embarrassed by your recent wins. What I'm trying to tell you is important. These people will work behind closed doors to hurt your chances to advance, to become a partner and run a department. The first time you stumble, they will move in to sabotage your career."

All the way home that night, I thought about George's prophecy. The implications of his message were both serious and disconcerting. As I closed my bedroom door that evening, I was already dialing Ronnie Davis's number.

"Did I wake you?"

"No," R. D. answered. "I'm watching the Reds get punched out by the Phillies. I swear your chickenshit fastball is livelier than our new reliever's. We're down by five with only an inning left."

"Sorry, but I need to ask you something."

"Fire away."

When I repeated George O'Leary's warning, Ronnie said he was probably right.

"I don't know the inner workings of your shop, but I do know it's Darwin's law out there in Wall Street land. No one's going to like a kid just starting his career blowing past them like they're standing still."

"But I don't brag or tell anyone what I'm doing!"

"You don't have to. News travels fast when someone on the floor is slam-dunking in the market."

I pulled myself together to answer, "I don't want to manage anyone or run a department here. I don't want to sit by a window looking out. All I want is to sit in the middle of the action where ideas are being vetted and the markets are percolating."

"The Reds just lost, and I'm going to bed. If you're too wired to sleep, call your love muffin and bother her," Ronnie said as he hung up on me.

One afternoon after Labor Day, I was working up the cash-flow statements on a new company Ezra was preparing to recommend when Jackie approached. She asked if I would fill in as a guide to show a potential client around the firm as a favor to Hollis Merritt. The lady was apparently a superrich heiress in search of investment advice. I was to give her the grand tour and drop her off at his office at five o'clock. I freshened up, retied my tie, and ran damp hands through my unruly mop to calm it down somewhat. I buttoned up my suit jacket and walked out to reception to greet Ms. Olivia Whitney. Her back was turned to me as she stood leafing through a book on the history of Burr, Addington, and Merritt. I forced myself to resist taking in the full measure of her slender legs and perfect ass. Her hair was pinned up, and she was dressed in an exquisite gray outfit. When I told Ms. Whitney that I was here to show her around before her meeting with Mr. Merritt, she turned and ran into my arms. "I told you I would soon be coming to New York," she said.

I looked over at the receptionist, who was laughing so hard she had tears running down her cheeks.

"Perfect! Absolutely well done, you really got him! I can't wait to tell Jackie and the other girls!"

"He thinks he's so smart, but I know which buttons to push," Charlotte announced triumphantly.

There she stood, dear Charlotte, bursting with her special version of contagious energy. Her patented exuberant smile made my heart rate soar like I had just won the jackpot in Vegas. There was no doubt that Charlotte was back in full force, loaded with her special spunk and eager to move forward with the dream of doing something important in life. She planned to bunk with an old Columbia girlfriend in the West Seventies while interviewing for a position at the United Nations. In addition, she had an appointment to meet later that month with the Red Cross at their headquarters in DC. She was hoping to land a job at either institution, where she could become an active manager of relief missions for people in distressed regions of the world. Her résumé was highlighted by the time she'd spent in the field with Doctors Without Borders.

Charlotte was also in hush-hush discussions with the *New York Times* editorial board on an article she had proposed detailing the Khmer Rouge atrocities taking place in Cambodia. They were especially intrigued by her idea of an open letter to be penned by a young girl who had witnessed the tragic loss of her family and the utter devastation of her beloved country. At first the *Times* was concerned the piece was too raw for its readership, but Charlotte convinced them otherwise after she passionately laid out the true extent of the KR's brutality toward its own people. She later told me that the *Times* only agreed to move forward after seeing the photographs she had taken of the refugees at the DWB field hospital. The managing editor was apparently visibly moved by the images of horror and declared to the board that no one with a conscience could deny that this story had to be told.

We both were überbusy during the weekdays that month but were together most every evening and weekends. I had never been so happy as when we spent our time reading, lounging, wandering the city's neighborhoods, and speculating about our futures.

"Don't you have any work to do?" Charlotte asked one typical Saturday afternoon as I lay on the bed practicing my favorite contest of tossing a baseball up toward the ceiling. She herself was trying to finish rewriting her *Times* piece.

"My job is to read and think and then occasionally make a bold decision. This is the way I work—it helps to focus my thought process."

"You're not working, you're staring at me planning some type of clandestine sexual attack. How am I supposed to be productive with you drooling over me like I'm a dog in heat?"

"I haven't said a word," I defended myself. "The rules state I'm permitted to look as long as I don't beg for physical attention."

"I'm serious. I'm on a deadline here. This final draft is due at the paper by 9:00 a.m. tomorrow, and I don't intend to disappoint. By the way, I never agreed to your rules, so be a good little boy and maybe we can play catch later. All I need is another hour or so. It's a shame that Jacob is still in Denver toiling away for McKinsey, because you guys could ride your bikes up to the park and shoot marbles or fly kites with the other youngsters while I tighten this up and give it a final proofread," she said, leaning back and giggling before waving me out of the room.

When she was writing, Charlotte was all business, striving to deliver her very best effort. She had transformed herself into the character of Soky, an orphaned six-year-old Cambodian refugee beloved by the doctors for her spirit and compassion for others. The young girl's cry for help painted a vivid picture of the inhumanity taking place in her homeland. Charlotte had witnessed the results of the Khmer Rouge's purge firsthand. In her dreams she pictured countless children wandering about the refugee camps lost and alone, wounded mentally and physically. She hoped the *Times* readership would understand that Soky's letter was telling the truth. The dire circumstances weren't exaggerated. They were the conditions these people were forced to endure.

As I watched Charlotte, sitting at my desk wearing one of my ancient, faded Reds T-shirts, leaning over the typewriter fiddling with her hair, eyes fixed in deep concentration, I couldn't imagine ever being without her. We were only in our twenties, but I was sure, absolutely positive like I had never been about anything else, that we were supposed to be together.

I threw a windbreaker on and took off, headed for the neighborhood deli. With an hour to waste, I walked down Madison to a peaceful park in the Twenties where Charlotte had told me of her ultimate plan to introduce DWB to the United States. I admired the brashness of her idea. Here was a young woman committed to helping educate our country about the good work being done by volunteer doctors treating people trapped in perilous situations with little hope of medical care. I remembered her telling me she had now found her calling. When I reminded her that this would be quite a mountain to climb, her answer was simply, "Yes, but a worthy challenge for sure."

Walking home from the deli, I questioned the worthiness of my goal of financial independence. What would I do if I actually succeeded in scaling that peak? Did I have an ultimate plan that I could be proud of?

When I returned to the apartment, Charlotte was dancing to one of Jacob's gospel albums. "It's finished! I think I got it right," she said while spinning and jumping about like a graceful athlete on steroids. She pointed to four neatly typed pages on the coffee table.

"Give it a good read to see if you agree. I can handle constructive criticism, but leave the grammar and punctuation to me. This isn't a stock report written by a Wharton boy," she added with a dig.

"If this all doesn't work out, maybe you could dance with the Rockettes over at Radio City. I understand they favor Columbia grads," I teased as I watched her shake and shimmy.

"Finish reading my piece, wise guy, so we can demolish those sandwiches and enjoy this beautiful weather."

"When will the world be introduced to Soky?"

"Next Saturday if all goes well," she said as a magnificent smile spread across her face.

I should have known there was another life lesson lurking in my future. In retrospect, it was obvious that everything was just too rosy for young Rogers Stout. I had been spending my weeks levitating in a blissful zone while enjoying work, managing my portfolio, and waiting for Charlotte to return to New York. I was about to be ambushed but wasn't sharp enough to see the dark clouds on the horizon.

The holidays were approaching and I was actually looking forward to my year-end review as I sat across a conference table from Ezra and Edwin Henderson. I had always thought the research director's office looked more like a musty library than a place where coldhearted decisions were commonly made. I would soon find out I was wrong about that observation.

Ezra was eerily quiet, hands folded in his lap, dark eyes projecting a sad aura that I later realized foretold his gloomy assessment of my future at BAM. Edwin sat rigid, in control but clearly uncomfortable. The research director was very much a gentle soul who tried to avoid conflict. His management style was to encourage and support his analysts by maintaining a collegial office environment. After a wordy, wandering preamble where he lauded my talent and work efforts, he paused, ominously looked up at the heavens, and delivered a blow straight to my gonads: I wasn't a team player. I didn't interact well with the other analysts. I was a loner. In short, I had become a disruptive influence within the department. I was stunned!

Ezra's silence filled the room. I waited for him to say something, but he just stared at me. I sat still, determined to make him speak first. He didn't budge until Edwin asked if he had anything to add. I knew our relationship had deteriorated, nevertheless, the tone of his response surprised me.

"You are the best junior I've ever had. I admire your energy level, the quality of your research analytics, your desire to learn and improve and grow. I don't care about your interpersonal skills or whether other people here like you or not. But I want all of you. I object to your spending so much time on your personal account. It's a distraction that you've taken too far."

I could tell the research director expected me to respond to their criticisms, but I didn't want to say anything until I knew exactly where this was going. I didn't have to wait too long.

"We plan on releasing you from the research department. Technically you're not being fired. After giving the other areas of the firm a chance to make you an offer, we'll decide how to proceed further. I'm sorry it turned out like this. I'm sure you'll succeed on your own in the future, but here at Burr, Addington, and Merritt, we work together for a common goal."

I hid my shock and disappointment as if I were an injured athlete not wanting his opponent to know the extent of his pain. George O'Leary was right: I had been stabbed in the back by malicious envy; I was being sabotaged by the success of my personal investing. Ronnie Davis was also right when he reminded me I would always be different from the hierarchy at BAM. I hadn't seen that clearly enough until I was told the reasons for my dismissal. By then I had heard everything I needed to hear.

I tried my best to maintain an outward calm as I raced through my alternatives. I couldn't remember ever reading the cards this badly. I had hoped for congratulations on my investing coups. Maybe even a hearty "well done." I expected compliments on my Kelly call and comprehensive report on the temporary-help industry. I thought they would recognize my everyday contributions responding to salesmen's requests and the background work I did for Ezra on his various research projects. But instead of raising my salary and awarding me a handsome bonus, there was an awkward, deafening pause. Where was the praise? How about the "let's get 'em even better next year" mantra?

Ezra turned away to look out at the river. Only then did I accept the reality of the bad news. Henderson again said how sorry he was, but I didn't fit in with the other analysts, and he felt it would be better for everyone if I transitioned out of the department.

I harked back to the steady hand of my father. He would have told me to look in the mirror and accept the fact that I'd made an egregious judgmental error. "Now move on," he would advise. "Control your emotions and learn from this experience. It won't serve any purpose to whine or second-guess yourself. Be rational. Ask good questions and solve the puzzle." Good ol' Dad, the clearest thinker I've ever known.

Deep in my memory bank was the Saturday I stole a moment in a confessional at a church near home. I was curious about how it would feel sitting there, telling a stranger all my secrets and asking forgiveness for my evil thoughts and deeds. I remembered the dark, almost claustrophobic quarters, the smell of burning candles, and the fear that I was doing something horribly irreverent. When I heard a priest entering the other side of the booth, I chickened out and made haste to get to the street. Dad had once told me I needed to know the difference between asking and begging for help. I decided to ask Edwin and Ezra for an explanation, but I wouldn't beg for a second chance. Why should I when I hadn't done anything to justify being let go?

Henderson repeated his complimentary appraisal of my analytical skills. He even acknowledged the sales force viewed me as an asset that should be paid a significant bonus. But then he added it was his job to look at the bigger picture. I had to suppress the urge to inquire what the hell that meant, because to me that was only business school hogwash. He pressed on that my peers thought I was aloof, distant, and excessively private. I wondered how that mattered in a performance business—after all, I wasn't trying to join a country club or become a Spire brother. At last he addressed the heart of the matter: "Everyone knows that you have made a small fortune in just two years. The guys are trying to figure out how you did it, and that is distracting them from their jobs here at BAM. I need them to focus all of their energies on their industry responsibilities."

So there it was. The cards had been dealt and my winning hand turned out to be a career loser. Bend over, Rogers, and give the research director a better target for a kick in the ass out the door. Before I could leave his office in utter disgust, Edwin offered me a chance to voice my take on the situation. I didn't dare tell him what I really was thinking. I didn't have the nerve to question why he chose to coach from the sidelines rather than to play on the field. Did I need to remind him that this game's scorecard was in dollars, that we weren't playing Candy Land or tiddlywinks? Would it help my cause if I told him that my goal wasn't a career at an eleemosynary institution, that I thought I was working on Wall Street, not for the United Way?

I kept all this to myself as I thanked them both for the wonderful experience I had enjoyed in BAM's research department over the last two years.

I returned from my end-of-the year holiday homecoming knowing I soon would have to make some serious decisions on my future. I knew my situation required action, but I had never been big on change. My stint at BAM had gone well, so why not stay with the winning formula? I had learned how to utilize the firm's resources. I knew the other analysts, whom to treat with high regard and whom to avoid, the traders whose opinions mattered and even when to be influenced by random individuals such as Paal Van Horne. I especially coveted George O'Leary's market acumen and his gentle hands helping me execute my game plan. I didn't want to learn how to navigate waters elsewhere, but I couldn't just sit by myself, sequestered in a closet, trying to duplicate my investment results. I felt confident relying on my judgments, but I needed a variety of inputs to weigh and analyze. All vacation I replayed the lecture I'd received in Edwin Henderson's office in a vain attempt to answer some questions. Why did I have to leave my seat at the party? Was there any way to salvage the game in the bottom of the ninth inning? Before leaving home I had confided my predicament to the big three.

Dr. Charles Stout: "If you're determined to adhere to your own principles, then you have to be willing to differ with the crowd. I respect that. Stand tall and do what you think is right. Accept the consequences of being your own man and move on, but be sure that you're moving forward."

Ms. Charlotte Marks: "I don't understand how they could do this. Is that the way big business works? Look, you're already a real life version of Richie Rich, so if you're unhappy, why not just move on and gain satisfaction by helping others in need?"

Mr. Ronald Davis: "Those WASPs are such dilettantes they can't even recognize a winning ticket when it's right in their hand. You're too good for them. Get the hell outta there. Fuck 'em!"

Back in New York, I cornered Jacob in the apartment before he left on a date with another of his Hollywood look-alikes and gave him the quick version of my being ambushed. He was short on sympathy.

"Come on now! Ever since we met in Philly, I've thought you were blessed with some kind of preposterous gift of luck. After all, you were the one who porked Elsbeth Aylesworth. You were the one who landed a prized job that was handed to you on a silver platter. I've seen your skills on the Atlantic City tables and watched in awe as you multiplied your net worth on the Street. I've seen you gamble as if you had ice in your veins. You're probably smarter than anyone I've met, but at times you can't even tie your own shoes. For Christ's sake, get off the damn floor! I'm dealing right now with people who have real problems. Next week I'm going to have to fire 135 employees for a client company in Minnesota. These are real people with kids and mortgages and probably zero savings. What do their futures look like? On the other hand, you could put yourself out there on the market and get ten Wall Street offers in a week. I'm sorry to sound hard-ass, but I'm the one who should be depressed. Consulting companies that require restructuring is a lot uglier than I ever dreamed. I get nauseous thinking about facing those people and delivering the sad news."

"That's it?" I asked. "That's your pep talk? That's your advice?"

"Yep. Now I'm off to get laid," he answered. "Good night, dear roomie."

On my first day back at the office, Jackie was waiting for me with a message from our eminent chief Ambrose Burr. She motioned for me to join her in the library. "I'm guessing this is very important," she whispered with concern spreading across her face. I was being summoned to lunch with Burr at one o'clock in conference room one.

"Do you know why?" I asked, endeavoring to remain calm.

"No, but it's just the two of you, and his secretary said he's in a foul mood," she answered. I'd always believed Jackie was on my team, and she proved it once again when she stepped back to look me over. "I suggest you get a shoe shine and do something with that mess on top of your head before lunch."

"Anything else?" I asked.

"Yes, go buy a new tie. Pick one out that says you're here to stay."

It was a bitter cold that greeted me that morning as I walked down Broadway toward Battery Park. I needed to clear my head from the pressure about my uncertain future before I met with the boss man. I was so desperate for answers that I considered the peace of Trinity Church as a retreat where I might absorb some clarity of thought. Being inherently superstitious, I resisted the temptation to enter, because I feared a bolt of lightning from the heavens as retribution for my persistent heresy. Praying for the first time wouldn't solve my problem anyway, so I continued past the church to the island's end. I looked out at the waters that delivered millions of brave immigrants seeking a new life. They were willing to take risks to fulfill their dream of a new beginning. I felt a sudden rush of energy. It was time for me to stop feeling sorry for myself and stiffen up.

Twenty minutes before lunch, I sat in a bathroom stall repeating isometric and breathing exercises that my father had taught me to help counteract the tension I always felt before pitching assignments. Dad's playbook might have worked for me then, but I was facing a big-boy conundrum now. Was this lunch destined to be a gentleman's farewell, a trite "sorry we have to let you go, even though you're a fine young lad with a bright future"? Would a man of Ambrose Burr's stature really stoop to such a disingenuous performance? What should my position be if the senior partner of Burr, Addington, and Merritt actually blessed me with an alternative offer? I knew he was a wise old fox and I had to be alert to any surprise he might have hidden up his sleeve. All these thoughts rushed through my mind as I knocked and entered conference room one.

The waiter was a retired boxer who had trained Mr. Burr as a young upstart. He might have been years beyond his prime, but the muscles in his arms were still imposing. I half expected his starched white jacket to erupt in defiance as he moved about the room. A. B. greeted me.

"Max taught me the difference between boxing and fighting before I knew what stocks and bonds were. In his best days, he could drop a heavyweight with one right cross. His hands were that good, but his footwork never matched his punching power. He's been with me all these years. I don't have to worry what's behind me when Max is around.

"Well, young man, let's get down to business," he continued. "The word around the firm is rather unanimous. It seems the research department may have treated you unjustly. I'd like to hear your view."

I responded as best I could. "I see it as being disturbingly simple. I've been told that my investing success has created a problem for the research director. Some in the department are envious and want to try to duplicate my performance. Others think this money thing has made me an outcast prima donna and would like to see me taken down. Either way, Edwin believes I'm a disruptive influence."

"And?"

"I don't understand how I'm disruptive. I've been productive and my research ideas have worked out. I get high marks as an analyst from Ezra, Edwin, and the sales force. I'm serious about research, but I'm also market sensitive. I think that's a positive for the firm. Would you rather I write hundred-page tomes that are impressive in depth but don't produce moneymaking ideas?"

"And?"

I probably had said too much already, so I only added, "Can I borrow Max for an hour or so?"

The senior partner roared with laughter while telling me that BAM's insurance wouldn't be sufficient to satisfy the claims from Max's handiwork. I then swore I heard him say, "Maybe you belong in investment management rather than the research department." Had I heard that correctly? I carefully studied my cards. Had my puny pair of deuces just morphed into an aces-over full house? Was it possible that I'd been dealt a winning hand at lunch? I felt a jolt of optimism lift my spirits. Suddenly I sat taller and more alert to the nuances of each word he spoke.

"I'd like to know how it all started. Did you inherit wealth, win the lottery, or print dollars in your basement, because when you came here you already had a nice nest egg."

I answered without hesitation. "I made a bit over the years filling in at my father's office when he needed help. I'd book appointments, work the files, answer phones. Occasionally he'd remember to pay me. Sometimes we'd play poker as an incentive for me to learn to respect the value of a dollar. I multiplied my meager stash in games with friends. These social games were easy pickings. When I turned seventeen, I graduated to playing in less-than-legal games across the river in Kentucky. I learned the hard way how to minimize my losses. Later on I learned the power of momentum and how to capitalize on winning streaks."

"Where were your parents in all of this?" he asked.

As usual I left that question only half-answered. "My father works long hours at the hospital. We'd talk about other things when together. If he had asked me where I had been, I would have told the truth." Then I added, "I'm proud to say that I never deceived him except when we played liar's poker."

"Isn't northern Kentucky pretty rough? How did you get out of there in one piece with all their money?"

"I never boasted or taunted the other players. In fact, I could go on for hours and not utter a simple sound. I'd hide my winnings in my coat pocket, make sure to lose an eventful final hand, and leave with my head down."

"This was your initiation into the world of risk management?" he questioned incredulously.

"To me it wasn't gambling. I treated it as if I was going to work like most everyone else. My job was Friday nights at Rory's Tavern."

"I assume you continued on this path at Penn. Speaking of sweet pickings, I can only imagine how you scalped the pigeons there!"

"It wasn't particularly challenging."

"So then you multiplied your winnings with the Resorts bonanza, followed by your trading here at BAM?" he asked, seeking confirmation.

I nodded yes.

Max cleared the table and served coffee. I was caught staring at his mammoth hands.

"Can you imagine one of those babies delivering a haymaker to your jaw?" Ambrose mused while shaking his head.

"Those mitts look like they should belong to André the Giant," I answered.

"They would be unwieldy for a wrestler like him but forces of doom to a prizefighter," he corrected while nodding at Max for approval.

The preliminaries were coming to an end. We both knew that I couldn't remain in the research department, but could I stay at BAM in some other capacity? If that wasn't a viable alternative, where could I envision myself working? Should I explore the possibility of joining an established investment firm? Maybe I could land a job at a hedge fund and participate in their juicy performance-fee structure. Would A. B. instruct Max to throw me out the window if I suggested that BAM start an internally managed hedge fund? I had been fantasizing about such an opportunity ever since my meeting with Ezra and the research director. What would A. B. say if I nominated the Cincinnati Kid as its senior portfolio manager?

Ambrose Burr chose his words carefully. "I'd like you to stay. I see a future for you here. We've been too complacent in the investment management division. We need a spark, a new energy. Does that interest you?"

I decided to take the plunge. "Yes, but they don't have the flexibility you need to truly excel. You complimented my performance over the last year or so. My stocks did fine, but I also really scored by shorting bonds and owning oil. There will be times when owning equities isn't all that interesting and the opportunities for profit will be on the short side or elsewhere."

A. B. was quick to interject, "What are you suggesting? You know our clients don't hire us to play in that sandbox."

He'd given me the opening I was hoping for, so I kept going. "We manage money for only a 1 percent fee. Hedge funds charge that plus 20 percent of the profits. Every month a new fund hangs its shingle out for business. Why don't we round up a select group of our clients and start a new profit center for the firm?"

"And let a green kid with a two-year track record run it?"

"We'll start out the same way I played poker in Kentucky. We'll limit our losses and be ultraconservative until we're playing with house money. Then slowly, slowly we'll get more aggressive as long as we're up on the year."

"But you know it's not as simple as that," the senior partner insisted.

"It'll be challenging, but it's the future of investing, and there's no reason why we can't be at the forefront. The firm already has all the resources in place to back a first-class effort," I assured him.

"Bates MacNeer predicted this outcome."

"That you would start a hedge fund?"

"That I wouldn't regret hiring you. I think his exact words were, 'He's a real fireball. He'll attack the cobwebs,'" Ambrose concluded.

Ambrose Burr championed his new idea to the partnership as a modest risk with substantial upside potential. He told me what had transpired at the partners' meeting when he proposed the firm incubate an experimental pool of capital to be run similarly to the new vehicles commonly called hedge funds. He suggested that BAM initially seed the fund with capital and compensate the manager based on performance. The fund would have the ability to invest both long and short across a broad spectrum of assets. An oversight committee would be established to ensure the fund's mandate was observed. If the fund did poorly, it could quietly be put to bed; if it excelled the firm would raise outside capital and charge investors 20 percent of the profits. The partners apparently looked favorably on this novel adventure—until Ambrose named the fund's manager. The arrows assaulted the senior partner's torso as if he were Saint Sebastian on the cross.

"Rogers Stout! You mean that gangly kid in research, the one who hangs out with old O'Leary the trader?"

"Yes."

"I hear he crapped all over Paal Van Horne," another partner added.

"He disagreed with him on oil prices, and it turned out he was right."

"Hasn't Edwin labeled him a troublemaker?"

"It seems the other analysts are envious of his successes. He's a private young man. He's not a troublemaker."

"Why him, of all people? Why not a star from investment management?"

"Let's be honest here, we don't have any stars in IM."

The tirade of questions continued until Hollis Merritt spoke. Known for his integrity and clear sense of vision he asked Ambrose, "I know you think highly of young Stout, that you're impressed with his unusual set of skills. You've said he has exceeded all expectations so far and that his personal account's success speaks volumes. Do you think, though, that this is asking too much from him? Is he ready to accept such responsibility?"

"Our world is changing," A. B. responded. "More than ever performance is the name of the game. Of course I'm somewhat nervous about this venture, but maybe that's a good sign. We'll monitor the fund closely and see how it goes."

I chose a quiet office adjacent to the research department. I breathed a sigh of relief when Ezra graciously let Jackie join my fledgling operation. The communications department provided me with direct lines to George O'Leary, the bond desk, and a special connection to Ronnie Davis in a far-off place called Cincinnati. In addition, a Dow Jones news terminal was installed next to Jackie's desk and the latest Quotron machine next to mine. With a newly designed accounting system in place, all I needed to begin was clearance from the legal department.

When I told my roommate that we would soon be launching a new hedge fund, he suggested we pick a catchy name for the venture. "It's Marketing 101. It will help create an aura, a mystique surrounding the fund. It's the kind of thing we advise at McKinsey." All weekend we called friends, searching for the right name. By Sunday evening we'd decided that the incoming ideas were wanting, so we might as well pick three out of a hat, choose one, and the hell with Jacob's marketing idea. An hour later he came running into my room.

"I've got it! It's perfect!"

"I'm all ears," I said.

"It's right here in the entertainment section of the *Times*. Check out the features at the Bijou Theater." He grinned, handing me the newspaper.

"I don't see anything appropriate."

"Look again. Open your eyes."

"This must be a real Forty-Second Street skin house. All I see are ads for *Cheerleaders in Heat* and *Olga*."

"Read the caption under *Olga*."

"Holy shit," I almost screamed out loud. *She Goes Both Ways*! Just like a hedge fund, right?"

"Do you agree? Both ways, long and short. It's a classic."

That Monday I bounced the Olga idea off Boyer Stubbs. He immediately wanted to bet me tequila shots until one of us dropped I wasn't man enough to even suggest that name to the partners. I didn't mention any of this to R. D. or George O'Leary, because I was afraid they might think I was losing my mind.

As liftoff was approaching, my level of self-doubt increased exponentially. I spent hours hiding out in my office to avoid the inevitable sneers of criticism. I tried to be positive, to not be overly intimidated by the task at hand, but I had never dealt with such large numbers before. I kept wondering if I was too inexperienced to run a portfolio of this size. Did I need the security blanket of an Ezra Carter as a supportive mentor? I was already at a tipping point where fear of losing could overwhelm the dream of winning. I knew failure meant years of exile in a Siberia for Wall Street losers, and there were plenty of warm bodies walking about the firm that would love a chance to deliver a serious sucker punch. When I told R. D. that I hadn't slept well in weeks, he responded with authority.

"Now you're going to find out what it's like to be the one who's expected to make the crucial shots late in the game. It's tough to keep your nerves in check."

"What can I do to help conquer this?" I asked.

"It's not going to be easy. I know because I've been there. Maybe you should pray. It works well for me," came the reply.

"Thanks for the dose of compassion, Father Davis."

"I can still remember standing on the foul line my sophomore year at Xavier having to make two shots to send a game into overtime. Suddenly my throat went dry, and I was crazy thirsty. Almost simultaneously my legs turned weak and my arms felt heavy. The hometown fans were enthusiastically screaming my name. Somehow the first shot was successful. Seconds before the next one, I knew in my heart I was going to throw up a real clunker. I did and we lost. I was so pissed off that I practiced one hundred foul shots every day thereafter until my confidence returned."

"So the moral is after I screw up, I should reread Ben Graham's *Security Analysis* every night and then I'll be able to turn my performance around?"

"You have to do something to reverse the negative juice before it becomes a permanent part of your psyche," Ronnie continued.

"I've never felt this way before," I confided. "I'd rather face Babe Ruth with the bases loaded than dig a hole with this fund. In my dreams I hear people laughing at my failure, and I haven't even started yet."

"You have to search within yourself to find a way to turn the pressure to your advantage. When I played in hostile environments, I learned to enjoy hearing the insults, it inspired me to do my best to stick it up their butts."

"Tell me the truth. What are you thinking right now?"

"I'm not surprised your pecker's all shriveled up. You're going to be playing in a big-time game. Just don't let the markets play you. If you stay true to yourself, then everything will work out just fine," R. D. reasoned.

"Am I supposed to believe that I have *the gift*?"

"You know you have it!"

FIVE YEARS LATER

WHEN WE MOVED INTO A LARGE APARTMENT ON THE TOP floor of the Giles, we looked at each other and started laughing. "Do we deserve all this?" Charlotte questioned, waving her hands at the size of our new place and the view of Manhattan pulsating beneath us. She pointed east toward the United Nations. "Look over there at my daytime home. Doesn't it look proud, as if it's standing tall for a purpose?" I was studying the river, mesmerized by the boat traffic when she broke my concentration. "Hey, space cadet. I'm talking about a special institution that's doing some good humanitarian stuff and you're probably betting with yourself which boat will reach the bridge first."

She was right, of course, but I also was reminded of a bedtime story my father would tell his young son about a small tugboat that could outperform newer, larger boats based on sheer grit and determination. One night I asked him if that's all it took to win. As Dad turned off the light, he answered, "No, but you'll never do your best unless you try your best."

For five years I managed the fund and tried my very best. I worked long hours, read everything that crossed my desk and more, attended countless research meetings and company presentations, argued market timing with Ronnie and George and fundamentals with the analysts I respected, questioned myself back and forth on every decision I made, and studied my portfolio's structure and performance at least twice a day. The result of all this was too many fitful nights and a litany of stress-induced physical aggravations. But, holy shit, I did it! The fund (formally named BAM Capital Partners, but secretly called Olga by the cognoscenti) grew to a sweet nine figures and performed like a champ. Between incentive compensation and appreciation on my own invested capital, I could earn millions in a good year. By the spring of '85, a few months before my thirtieth birthday, I had already more than achieved my financial goal.

When I saw the results on my brokerage statements staring back at me, I would shake my head in disbelief.

Charlotte was wearing her most serious expression when she turned the music down to a whisper. She wanted to understand why I wasn't ecstatic on this beautiful Saturday afternoon. With no preamble, she dove right in.

"Isn't it time to step back and take a deep breath? You've done it. No one can deny that. We don't need any more money, and this whole thing has taken its toll on you. I see you gazing out in space thinking about beating markets and making financial scores instead of enjoying what we already have. Sleeping next to you is like sharing a bed with an orangutan with a nervous tic."

"Am I that bad?"

"Not yet, but I worry about you dealing with all the pressure. And for what? We already have gazillions. What are we going to do with all of it? Are you doing this to give it to a worthwhile cause or just to pile chips all the way up to the ceiling?"

"I don't know. I've spent all of my energy getting here, I'm not sure what to do now."

"Let's go back to the beginning of all this. How did you get here in the first place?"

"There's no simple answer. At first it was the independence thing. Then I saw how good I was at it, and I liked feeling positive about myself. Work wasn't a chore then—it was exciting and I couldn't wait to come in. With Olga I realized a window of opportunity had been presented. It was an enormous challenge on a very big stage, and I wanted to prove I could excel. I felt like I was playing in the World Series every day and I was winning. Why wouldn't I love it? Somewhere along this journey, it all became a job. The highs weren't as high and the lows were lower."

"That's sad. Why are you stuck in this position now?"

"Because I can't perform much better, and I sure can do a lot worse. On the upside, all I can do is repeat past successes and extend the length of my performance record. If I continue to do well, the partners will cheer 'Bravo' and our net worth will increase beyond what we rationally will ever need."

"What happens if you stumble?"

"The partners will wonder if I was just lucky in the first place. My record will be blemished, and I'll feel lousy. I'd probably never forget that I messed up."

"Are you listening to yourself? You're acting as if you're on a treadmill you can't get off."

Charlotte sat on the couch waiting for me to respond. I told her that I was confused. I couldn't help wondering if my dream of financial independence was a worthy goal. I knew how difficult it was to win at the game I had been playing, and if I didn't manage the fund with maximum effort, my performance would suffer. Maybe it was time for me to cash in my chips and take a breather, but I was afraid that I would miss the challenge, the drama, and the excitement of a score. After all, just minutes ago, there I was, handicapping the boats heading for the Queensboro Bridge like a compulsive gambler that I feared I was becoming. I needed a reason beyond more money to keep putting myself at risk. I missed having a goal to work toward, when all of the monetary success meant so much to me. If I had already climbed to the top of a mountain, did I have to find a higher, more treacherous one to scale to prove myself?

Charlotte eased herself into my lap and placed my hand on her stomach. She kissed my neck and cheeks while holding my hand in place. Her eyes glowed with an intensity that never ceased to move me.

"Do you know what she's thinking?" she asked.

"She's wondering what my next challenge will be. Tell her I'm going to gamble on myself, that I'm working on an interesting new idea. It's not all about money. It's innovative and something I care about. I think she'll really like it."

"She knows there's more to her father than just making money. She believes in you, just like her mother believes in you."

"Ask her what my future looks like."

"She's absolutely unqualifiedly bullish! And so am I."

AUTHOR'S NOTE

WHEN ROGERS STOUT PLACED A LONG-DISTANCE CALL THAT rang simultaneously in my heart and brain, I refused to believe his message. But he persisted, and repeatedly dialed my number day after day. A few months thereafter, the calls also started to come in the middle of the night. I had to sleep with a pen, legal pad, and flashlight on my nightstand to jot down refinements to his thoughts. Even when I tried, I couldn't get Rogers's journey out of my mind. I eventually succumbed to his wishes and agreed to tell his story.

A year and a half later I showed my manuscript to a few friends I respect and asked for constructive criticism. They were, of course, stunned that an investor-type would attempt to accomplish anything creative, much less to write a novel. I learned especially to rely on Peter Lattman, Paul Roth, Judy Hilsinger, and Michelle Picker for their keen observations. Thanks guys for continuing to answer my phone calls and for offering your remarkable patience to this first-time novelist. I'm most sincerely grateful to all of these friends for their thoughtful suggestions.

I was told to reach for the stars and, just maybe, Marc Jaffe would gamble on the gambler and agree to edit *Make Me Even* . . . It's not often that you meet someone in a professional context and that person becomes a genuine friend. As Marc pushed, prodded, and encouraged me—often all in the same conversation—I came to understand why he is revered as an eminent editor of the written word. I also came to comprehend the level of dedication I would need to create a coherent story out of three hundred plus pages of plain white paper. When the book was completed, and Marc had moved on to other projects, I still made sure to save time to enjoy this witty, cultured, and absolutely wonderful man.

While all the characters in the novel and the journey they experience are fictional, the dates and facts that accompanied Rogers along his adventure were researched and verified thanks to the diligence of Sara Brady. I learned the hard way not to argue with copyeditors.

For help in a whole variety of ways, I am indebted to Sandi Mendelson. She proved to be an enthusiastic advocate of the book early on and her team at Hilsinger-Mendelson encouraged me onward with positive, energetic support. Both Sandi and Deborah Jensen were always there for me, providing professional guidance and good cheer. Thank you all.

Now that I've finished relating Rogers's story I need to apologize to my four children and their families for poor attendance at athletic events and school plays. Don't fret, I'm still a bombastic cheerleader for anything involving our family members.

Lastly, to my One-of-a-Kind: You made a difficult task much easier. Thanks for sharing this wild ride with me.

ABOUT THE AUTHOR

JERROLD FINE graduated from the Wharton School of the University of Pennsylvania and has served multiple terms on its undergraduate executive board and the Board of Overseers. At twenty-four years old, he founded a hedge fund and worked as a managing partner. Fine lives in Connecticut with his artist wife and a ridiculously spoiled Portuguese water dog.

OPEN ROAD

INTEGRATED MEDIA

Find a full list of our authors and titles at www.openroadmedia.com

FOLLOW US

@OpenRoadMedia

EARLY BIRD BOOKS

FRESH DEALS, DELIVERED DAILY

Love to read?
Love great sales?

Get fantastic deals on bestselling ebooks delivered to your inbox every day!

Sign up today at
earlybirdbooks.com/book

www.ingramcontent.com/pod-product-compliance
Lightning Source LLC
Chambersburg PA
CBHW020427030726
47495CB00006B/1701